Gabi heard the door open and turned, assuming it was one of the staff to clear the remnants of the wedding away.

Instead it was Alim.

'I was just…' Gabi started. Just what? *Thinking about you.*

She was one burning blush as he walked across the room, and she didn't know where to go or what to do with herself as he approached the old gramophone.

And then she shivered.

Not because it was cold, for the air was perfectly warm. Instead she shivered in silent delight as she heard the slight scratch of the needle hitting the vinyl. The sounds of old were given life again and etched for ever on her heart as he turned around and walked towards her.

Without a word, he offered her this dance. And, without a word, she accepted.

'Listen…' He spoke into her ear and his low voice offered a delicious warning. 'I am trouble.'

'I know that.'

'If you like me, then I am doubly so.'

'I know all of that,' Gabi said.

The trouble w ns— Gabi didn't ca her face to his.

Billionaires & One-Night Heirs

Secret babies they are determined to claim!

Raul, Alim and Bastiano—
three billionaires renowned the world over
for their charisma and commanding ways.

Lydia, Gabi and Sophie—three innocents
who cannot resist their seductive appeal.

And when sizzling nights lead to nine-month
consequences there is no other option—
these billionaires *will* claim their heirs!

The Innocent's Secret Baby

Bound by the Sultan's Baby

Available now

Sicilian's Baby of Shame

Coming soon!

You won't want to miss this addictive new trilogy
from Carol Marinelli!

BOUND BY THE SULTAN'S BABY

BY
CAROL MARINELLI

MILLS & BOON

First Published in Great Britain 2017
By Mills & Boon, an imprint of HarperCollins*Publishers*
1 London Bridge Street, London, SE1 9GF

© 2017 Carol Marinelli

ISBN: 978-0-263-92521-0

Printed and bound in Spain
by CPI, Barcelona

Carol Marinelli recently filled in a form asking for her job title. Thrilled to be able to put down her answer, she put 'writer'. Then it asked what Carol did for relaxation and she put down the truth—'writing'. The third question asked for her hobbies. Well, not wanting to look obsessed, she crossed her fingers and answered 'swimming'—but, given that the chlorine in the pool does terrible things to her highlights, I'm sure you can guess the real answer!

Visit the Author Profile page
at millsandboon.co.uk for more titles.

CHAPTER ONE

GABI DERAMO HAD never been a bridesmaid, let alone a bride.

However, weddings were her life and she thought about them during most of the minutes of her day.

From way back she had lived and breathed weddings.

Gabi was a dreamer.

As a little girl, her dolls would regularly be lined up in a bridal procession. Once, to her mother's fury, Gabi had poured two whole bags of sugar and one of flour over them to create a winter wedding effect.

'Essere nerre nuvole,' her mother, Carmel, had scolded, telling her that she lived in the clouds.

What Gabi didn't tell her was that at each wedding she made with her dolls, she pretended it was her mother. As if somehow she could conjure her father's presence and make it so that he had not left a pregnant Carmel to struggle alone.

And while Gabi had never been so much as kissed, as an assistant wedding planner she had played her part in many a romantic escape.

She dreamt of the same most nights.

And she dreamt of Alim.

Now Gabi sat, flicking through the to-do list on her tablet and curling her long black hair around her finger, trying to work out how on earth she could possibly organise, from scratch, an extremely rushed but very exclusive winter wedding in Rome.

Mona, the bride-to-be, stepped out of the changing area on her third attempt at trying on a gown not of Gabi's choice.

It didn't suit Mona in the least—the antique lace made her olive skin look sallow and the heavy fabric did nothing to accentuate her delicate frame.

'What do you think?' Mona asked Gabi as she turned around to look in the mirror and examined herself from behind.

Gabi knew from experience how to deal with a bride who stood in completely the wrong choice of gown. 'What do *you* think, Mona?'

'I don't know,' Mona sighed. 'I quite like it.'

'Then it isn't the gown for you,' Gabi said. 'Because you have to *love* it.'

Mona had resisted the boutique owner's guidance and had completely dismissed Gabi's suggestion for a bright, white, column gown with subtle embroidery. In fact, Mona hadn't even tried it on.

Gabi's suggestions were dismissed rather a lot.

She was curvy and dressed in the severe, shapeless dark suit that her boss, Bernadetta, insisted she wear, so brides-to-be tended to assume that Gabi had no clue where fashion was concerned.

Oh, but she did.

Not for herself, of course, but Gabi could pick out the right wedding gown for a bride at fifty paces.

And they needed this to be sorted today!

Bernadetta was on leave and so it had fallen to Gabi to sort.

It always did.

The bigger the budget, the trickier the brief, the more likely it was to have been put into the 'Too Hard' basket and left for Gabi to pick up.

They were in the lull between Christmas and New Year. The wedding boutique was, in fact, closed today, but Gabi had many contacts and had called in a favour from Rosa, the owner, who had opened up just for them.

Rosa would not push them out, but they had to meet Marianna, the functions co-ordinator, at the Grande Lucia at four.

'Why don't you try Gabi's suggestion?' Fleur, the mother of the groom, said.

It was a little odd.

Usually this trip would be taken with the mother of the bride or her sister or friends, but it would seem that it was Fleur who had first and last say in things.

Fleur was also English, which meant that, in order to be polite, Gabi and Mona did not speak in Italian.

Yes, it was proving to be a long, tiring day.

And they would be back tomorrow with the bridesmaids!

Reluctantly, *very* reluctantly, Mona agreed to try on Gabi's suggestion and then disappeared with the dresser.

As Rosa hung up the failed gown she saw that Gabi was looking at another dress.

Silver-grey, it was elegant and simple and in a larger size, and when Gabi held it up she saw the luxurious fall of the fabric. Rosa was a talented seamstress indeed.

'It would fit you,' Rosa said.

'I doubt it.' Gabi sighed wistfully. 'It's beautiful, though.'

'The order was cancelled,' Rosa said. 'Why don't you go and try it on? It would look stunning, I am sure.'

'Not while I'm working.' Gabi shook her head. 'Anyway, even if it did fit, when would I get a chance to wear it?' Her question went unanswered as the curtains parted and a smiling Mona walked out.

'Oh, Mona!' Gabi breathed.

The dress was perfect.

It showed off Mona's slender figure, and the bright white was indeed the perfect shade against her olive skin.

'If only she had listened to you in the first place,' Fleur muttered. 'We are going to be late for the hotel.'

'It's all taken care of,' Gabi assured her, checking her list on her tablet. 'We're right on schedule.'

Ahead of it, in fact, because now that the dress had been chosen, everything else, Gabi knew, would fall more easily into place.

Measurements had already been taken but fitting dates could not yet be made. Gabi assured Rosa she would call her just as soon as they had finalised the wedding date.

They climbed back into the car and were driven through the wet streets of Rome towards the Grande Lucia but, again, Mona wasn't happy. 'I went to a wedding at the Grande Lucia a few years ago and it was so...' Mona faltered for a moment as she struggled with a word to describe it. 'Tired-looking.'

'Not now it isn't.' Gabi shook her head. 'It's under new management, well, Alim has been...' It was Gabi who now faltered but she quickly recovered. 'Alim has been the owner for a couple of years and there have been considerable renovations; the hotel is looking magnificent.'

Even saying his name made her stumble a little and blush.

Gabi saw Alim only occasionally but she thought about him a lot.

Their paths rarely crossed but if Gabi was organising a wedding at the Grande Lucia and Alim happened to be in residence at the time then her heart would get a rare treat, and she was secretly hoping for one today.

'Let's just see how you feel once you've actually seen the Grande Lucia for yourself,' Gabi suggested. 'Remember, though, that it's terribly hard to get a booking there, especially at such short notice.'

'Fleur doesn't seem to think it will be a problem,' Mona said with a distinct edge to her voice, and Gabi watched as she shot a look towards the mother of the groom. From all Gabi had gleaned, Fleur had agreed to finance the wedding on the condition that it was held there.

'It won't be,' Fleur responded.

Gabi wasn't so sure.

Marianna, the co-ordinator, was rather inflexible at the best of times and they wanted this wedding to be held in just over two weeks!

They made good time as the streets were comparatively empty. The rush of Christmas was over and even the Colosseum was closed to visitors.

Gabi stifled a yawn, wishing that she could put up her own *Do not disturb* sign to the world for a while.

She had hoped to spend the Christmas break going over the plans for starting her own business. Instead, she had again been called in to work through her leave. She was tired.

Almost too tired to keep alive the dream of one day owning her own business.

She had started working for Matrimoni di Bernadetta when she was eighteen and had hoped that it would provide the experience she needed to one day go it alone.

Six years later, at the age of twenty-four, that prospect seemed no brighter.

Bernadetta had made very sure of that—there was barely time to think, let alone act on her own dreams.

Still, she truly loved her job.

Gabi looked up as the gorgeous old building came into view and they soon pulled up at the entrance.

The car door was opened for them by the doorman, Ronaldo.

'Ben tornato,' Ronaldo said, and Gabi realised that it was Fleur and not she he was welcoming back.

Fleur must be a guest. And a favoured one too from the attention that Ronaldo gave her.

As Gabi got out there was a flutter of excitement at the thought that she might soon see Alim.

He was always polite, even if he was somewhat aloof. She didn't take it personally. Alim was the same with everyone and maintained a certain distance. There was just an air of mystery to him that had Gabi entranced. An entire floor of the Grande Lucia served as Alim's residence when he was in Rome, and so, through the hotel industry grapevine, Gabi knew more than a little of his reputation. He loved beautiful women and dated as many of them as he could—though one night with him was all they would ever get.

Breakfast was definitely not included in this particular package. In fact, according to Sophie, a friend of Gabi's and a maid at the Grande Lucia, cold and callous were the most frequent words used to describe him by his lovers after they had been discarded.

That didn't seem right to Gabi for she always felt warm in his gaze, and when it came to business, his professionalism was never in doubt.

Still, Sophie had told her, for all the tears there were perks for, rumour had it the reward for time spent in Alim's arms came in the shape of a diamond.

It sounded crass.

Until you saw Alim.

He was completely out of her league, of course, and that was not her being self-effacing. He veered towards slender blondes of the supermodel kind, and women who definitely knew the ropes in the bedroom.

Apparently he had no inclination to teach.

Gabi didn't mind in the least that Alim was utterly unattainable, for it made it safe for her to dream of him.

There was no sign that he was there when she walked through the brass revolving doors and into the magnificent foyer of the Grande Lucia.

It was *almost* perfection.

Stunning crimson carpet and silk walls were elegant—even sensual, perhaps—and worked well against the dark wooden furnishings. The space was vast and the ceilings high, yet there was an intimate feel from the moment you walked in, alongside the lovely buzz of a busy hotel.

As a centrepiece, there was a huge, crimson floral display.

Yes, *almost* perfect.

Gabi had an eye for detail and this arrangement irked her. It never varied, or moved with the times. Instead, there was a perpetual display of deep red roses and carnations and it had become a slight bone of contention when Gabi had negotiated on behalf of her brides.

Marianna came to greet them and took the trio for coffee at one of several intimate lounges just off the foyer.

There they went through a few details and though Marianna was delighted to announce that there was an opening in just over two weeks, she was not going to make it easy for the bride.

'I do need to verify dates with the owner,' Marianna said. 'We're expecting some VIP guests at the hotel in January so security will be particularly tight. I'm not sure we'll be able to accommodate you then. Alim has

asked to be informed before any dates are locked in…'
She paused and looked up. 'Oh, there he—'

Marianna halted, causing Gabi to glance up. Alim had just entered the foyer with the requisite stunning blonde.

Gabi guessed, and rightly so, that Alim did not like to be disturbed with minor details every time he made an appearance so Marianna did not alert Mona and Fleur to his presence.

Yet such was his charisma, both women looked over.

And while Marianna might be doing her best not to disrupt Alim's day, Gabi's had just been turned on its head.

In the nicest of ways.

He wore a slim dark coat and there was such an air of magnificence about him that he simply turned heads.

Not just for his dark looks—there was more to him than that—but they were rather wonderful to dwell on. His hair was black and glossy and swept back. He stood tall and his posture was so upright he always made Gabi want to pull back her own shoulders.

There was a shift that ran through her body whenever he was near, an awareness that made it difficult to focus on anything other than him, for all else seemed to move to the periphery of her consciousness to allow Alim centre stage.

'Quanti ospiti?'

Marianna's voice was coming from a distance and as she asked how many guests for the wedding, it was Mona who answered instead of Gabi.

For Alim had looked over and met her gaze.

He was beautiful.

Always.

Effortlessly elegant, supremely polite, he was the calm, still water to Gabi's fizz.

She was a dreamer, which meant that though he was out of her league, he was not out of bounds to her thoughts; innocent in body she may be, but not so in her mind.

And as for those eyes, they were a dark grey with silver flecks that spoke silently of the night.

His gaze was a dangerous thing to be held in, Gabi knew, and she was trapped in it now. There was a fire crackling in the grate and there was heat low, low in her stomach and rising to her neck.

She wanted to excuse herself from the conversation and walk over in response to his silent command. She wanted work to be gone, for his lover to disappear, and for Alim to lower her down onto a silken bed.

Just that.

'Gabi…' Marianna intruded.

'Alim,' his lover called.

But he was making his way over.

'Va tuto bene?'

He asked if everything was okay, and though his Italian was excellent, it was laced in his own rich accent and rendered Gabi incapable of response, for she had not expected him to come over.

It was Marianna who responded and told him the preferred date for the wedding.

'That would be fine.' Alim nodded to Marianna and to the other guests and then he looked directly at Gabi; she found herself staring at his mouth as he spoke, for it was just a little safer than to stare into his eyes. 'How are you, Gabi?'

'I am well.'

'That is good.'

He turned and walked away and she held her breath.

It was nothing—just an exchange so tiny that the others had not even noticed its significance, yet Gabi would survive on it for weeks.

He knew her name.

'Perhaps you could take Mona to see the ballroom while I discuss details with Fleur,' Marianna suggested.

Details being money.

'Of course.'

Gabi stood and smoothed her skirt.

Oh, she loathed the black suit with a gold logo and the heavy, cowl-necked cream top. It was the perfect outfit for a funeral director, not a wedding planner.

If it were her own business she would wear a willow-green check with a hint of pink. Gabi had already chosen the fabric.

And she would not wear the black high heels that Bernadetta insisted on, for she felt too tall and bulky as she walked through the foyer alongside the future bride.

And then she saw Alim and Ms Blonde stepping into his private elevator, and Gabi scowled at his departing back, for she envied the intimate experience they were about to share. Ms Blonde was coiling herself around him and whispering into his ear.

Thank God for gated elevators.

They were excellent for regaining self-control, for they slammed shut on the couple and as the world came back from the peripheries Gabi recalled that there was a wedding to be arranged.

There were large double doors to the ballroom and Gabi opened them both so that Mona could get the full effect as she stepped in.

It truly was stunning.

Huge crystal chandeliers first drew the eye, but it was a feast in all directions.

'*Molto bello...*' Mona breathed, and it was a relief to

slip back into speaking Italian. 'The ballroom is nothing like I remember it.'

'Alim, the owner, had it completely refurbished. The floor was sanded back, the chandeliers repaired. The Grande Lucia is once again *the* place for a wedding.'

'I know it is,' Mona admitted. 'It is actually where James and I met. I was here for my grandparents' anniversary. James was here, visiting…' Mona stopped herself from voicing whatever it was she had been about to say. 'I just don't like it that Fleur is calling all the shots just because her…' Mona clapped her lips together. Clearly she didn't want to say too much.

Gabi, curious by nature, wished that she would.

Fleur was being very elusive.

From the draft guest list, the groom's side seemed incredibly sparse. Just a best man from Scotland would be flying in and that was all. There was no mention of James's father.

Gabi wondered if Fleur was widowed.

But Gabi wasn't there to wonder and her mind turned, as it always did, into making this the very best of weddings.

'Imagine dancing under those lights at night,' Mona said.

'There is nothing more beautiful,' Gabi assured her, and then pointed up to a small gallery that ran the length of the westerly wall and imagined the select audience watching the proceedings in days long gone.

'The photographer can get some amazing overhead shots of the dance floor from up there. A photographer I…I mean Matrimoni di Bernadetta regularly uses does the most marvellous time-lapse shots from the gallery. They are stunning.'

She could see that Mona was starting to get excited.

'When you say you were here for your grandparents' anniversary,' Gabi probed, because the thought of time-lapse photos had got her thinking…

'My grandparents were married here,' Mona told her. 'Sometimes they take out the record they danced to on their wedding night.'

'Really?'

'I even recognise the floor from their wedding photos. It's like stepping back in time.'

Yes, even the ballroom floor was stunning—a parquet of mahogany, oak and redwood, all highly polished to reveal a subtle floral mosaic.

'Your grandparents still dance to their wedding song…'

Mona nodded and Gabi could see that she was already sold on the venue.

There would be a string quartet, but Mona loved Gabi's suggestion that she and James dance their first dance to the same record that her grandparents had.

And a wedding, a very beautiful one, was finally starting to be born.

It was a rather more glowing bride-to-be who returned to the lounge area and now chatted happily with Fleur and Marianna about plans.

And it was a bemused Gabi who looked up and saw Ms Blonde angrily striding through the foyer; she didn't know why, but she would bet her life's savings that Alim had uncoiled her, unwilling, from his arms.

Then later, much later, when plans were starting to be put more firmly in place, Gabi called Rosa with the official dates.

'I'm already working on the dress,' Rosa said. 'She's cutting it terribly fine to wear one of my gowns, even ready-to-wear.'

And, after a long, tiring day taking care of others, Gabi did something for herself.

She was all glowing and happy from that tiny exchange with Alim. Of course his lover's departure could have nothing to do with her, but Gabi was a dreamer, and already her mind was turning things around.

'Can I come and try on the silver dress?' she asked.

It was wonderful to dream of Alim.

CHAPTER TWO

IT TRULY WAS a beautiful wedding.

Not that Gabi had a second to enjoy it.

Resplendent in his kilt, the best man was being actively pursued by the matron of honour and doing his best to get away. Fleur was tense and asking that they hurry. The little flower girls were teary and cold as they stood in the snow for photos and Gabi felt like a bedraggled shepherdess as she juggled umbrellas for the bridal party and tried to herd the guests.

She was wearing boots, but that was the only concession to the cold.

Finally they were all in cars and heading off for the reception as Gabi ensured that the choir had been paid.

Bernadetta sat in her car, smoking, as Gabi shivered her way down the church steps.

And then it happened.

Gabi slipped on the ice and bumped down the last three stairs in the most ungainly fashion imaginable.

Not that anyone came over to help.

She sat for a moment, trying to catch her breath and assess the damage.

From the feel of things her bottom was bruised.

Pulling herself to a stand, Gabi saw that her skirt was

filthy and sodden and, removing her jacket, she saw that it had split along the back seam.

To make things just a little bit more miserable than they already were, Bernadetta was furious, especially that Gabi had no change of clothes.

'Why haven't you got a spare suit with you?' she demanded. 'You're supposed to be a planner after all.'

Because you only give me two suits, Gabi wanted to answer, but she knew it wouldn't help. 'It's at the dry-cleaner's.'

And, of course, Bernadetta spitefully pointed out that no one else had one that would fit Gabi.

'Go home and get changed,' she hissed. 'Wear something…' And she took her hands and sort of exasperatedly pushed them together, as if Gabi was supposed to produce something that might contract her size.

And Bernadetta didn't add, as she always did to her other staff, *Don't outshine the bride*.

Gabi, it was assumed, hadn't a hope of that.

Oh, she wanted to resign, so very much.

Gabi was close to tears as she arrived back at her tiny flat and, of course, there was nothing in her wardrobe she could possibly wear.

Well, there was one thing.

The silver-grey dress made by Rosa's magical hands, though Bernadetta would consider her grossly overdressed.

Yet it was a very simple design…

Gabi undressed and saw that, yes, she indeed had a bruise on her bottom and on the left of her thigh.

In fact, she ached and was cold to the bone.

A quick shower warmed her up and Gabi was, by the time she stepped out of it, actually a lot more relaxed for the brief reprieve.

Wedding days were always so full on and it was actually nice to take a short break.

When she had her own business, Gabi decided, she would organise a rota so that all of her staff were able to take some time between the formal service and the reception. Perhaps there could be a change of outfit for them too...

Gabi halted.

She was back to hoping and dreaming that one day she might be working for herself.

How, though, when Bernadetta had her securely locked in?

Still there wasn't time to dwell on it now.

The dress had been a gift from Rosa but, feeling guilty simply accepting it, Gabi had splurged on the right bra to go with it and, of course, matching silver knickers, which she quickly put on before wriggling into the dress.

Rosa really was a magician with fabric—the dress was cut on the bias and fell beautifully over her curves.

And it deserved more effort than her usual lack.

Sitting at her small dressing table, Gabi twisted her hair and piled it up on her head, rather than leaving it down. She put on some lip-gloss and mascara and then worried that it might be too much because usually she didn't bother with such things.

Yet she didn't wipe them off.

Instead, she dressed to look her best.

Tonight she didn't want to be the dowdy funeral director version of Gabi, or the clumsy, fall-down-the-stairs, eternally rushed wedding planner she appeared at times.

It was a split-second decision, a choice that she made.

Gabi looked in the mirror. This was the person she would be if she worked for herself and was orchestrating a high-class function tonight.

This was actually the closest she had ever looked to the woman she was inside.

Gabi arrived back at the hotel, her stunning dress hidden by a coat and wearing boots with her pretty shoes held in a bag. Security was tight and Ronaldo, the doorman, even though he knew her well, apologised but said that she had to show ID. 'There are VIP's staying at the hotel,' he explained as he stamped his feet against the cold.

'There often are,' Gabi said.

'Royalty,' Ronaldo grumbled, because royalty in residence meant a whole lot of extra work!

'Who?'

'Gabi,' Ronaldo warned, for he was under strict instruction, but then smiled as he chose to reveal—it was just to Gabi after all! 'The Sultan of Sultans and his daughter.'

'Wow!'

Oh, she hoped for a glimpse of them—it sounded amazing!

Gabi handed over her coat at Reception and pursed her lips when she saw the large crimson floral display in the foyer.

The Grande Lucia was a wonderful hotel but it was like turning the *Titanic* to effect change at times.

Nervous, a little shy, and doing her best not to show it, Gabi returned to the wedding and walked straight into Bernadetta's spiteful reproach.

'If the bride had wanted a Christmas tree arrangement in the corner, I would have charged her for one,' Bernadetta hissed, and Gabi felt her tiny drop of confidence in her newfound self drain away.

'We need to check that the gramophone has been properly set up,' Bernadetta told her. 'And we need to find the key to the gallery for the photographer.'

'*We*' being Gabi.

She hit the ballroom floor running, or rather working away to make the night go as smoothly as possible for the happy couple.

Indeed, they looked happy.

Mona's dress was sublime and her groom was handsome and relaxed and...

Gabi frowned.

James reminded her of someone, but she could not place him.

Or was it just the fact that he was tall and blond, like his mother, that made him stand out a touch more amongst the many Italian guests?

There was no time to dwell on it, though, and no time to acknowledge the ache of disappointment that Alim was nowhere to be seen.

And she admitted it to herself then, as she let the photographer up to the gallery and walked back through the foyer.

The dress, the pretty heels, the hair and the make-up...

In part they had been on the off chance that Alim might see her.

Alim was, in fact, in the building, but for once his presence was low key.

'I *hate* that we can't be at the wedding,' Yasmin moaned for the hundredth time, and pushed her dessert aside unfinished.

Alim said nothing in response.

He was very used to his sister's histrionics.

'We are shooed away like vermin,' Yasmin snarled, and threw down her napkin.

'Hardly vermin,' Alim drawled, refusing to be drawn

in—they were sitting in the private area of the sumptuous restaurant at the Grande Lucia after all.

Their father did not join them for it would only draw attention, and that was everything Alim was doing his best to avoid.

At least for tonight.

The staff at the Grande Lucia were very used to esteemed guests but, Alim knew, they were starting to comprehend that Oman, the Sultan of Sultans, was in fact Alim's father.

Alim did not use his title in the workplace—Sultan Alim al-Lehan of Zethlehan.

Neither did he use it in his personal life, for it was a risqué personal life indeed. Diamonds paid for silence and there was the slick machine of the palace PR to wash indiscretions away.

Oman's main indiscretion was the reason they were here in the dining room tonight.

Close to the wedding but not present.

Tonight, when the happy couple headed to the bridal suite, Fleur, the groom's mother, would head to her own sumptuous suite of rooms.

Violetta, who dealt with palace PR and external arrangements, had taken over the arrangements of the guest rooms from Marianna.

Alim did not need to know, though of course he did, that Fleur's suite adjoined his father's.

Fleur was Oman's mistress of long standing.

She had borne the Sultan of Sultans his first son.

James had had a seemingly privileged life. He had been schooled at Windsor, had attended university in Scotland, and had a trust fund that would make most people's eyes water.

But his father's name did not appear on his birth certificate and he bore no title. To the people of Zethlehan he simply did not exist.

Yet he was Alim, Kaleb and Yasmin's half-brother, and they loved him so.

Kaleb, who was younger than Alim, would instead see the happy couple in Paris, where he currently lived.

The three of them together would turn heads indeed but subtlety was the aim on this night.

Yasmin, who lived a very sheltered life in Zethlehan, had pleaded to be a part of the proceedings.

Those fervent pleas from Yasmin had been declined by their father and so Alim had stepped in and offered to do what he could to enable Yasmin to observe the wedding from a distance.

Alim had arranged it so that he and Yasmin had been taking refreshments in the lounge when the bridal party had arrived back from the church, so that Yasmin could see the dress and everything.

Yasmin had enjoyed it immensely. 'What on earth is he wearing?' she asked about the best man.

'A kilt,' Alim explained. 'He's from Scotland.'

'Oh, it's so exciting,' Yasmin breathed.

A glimpse of the bridal party wasn't enough for her, though.

And though Alim had arranged that they eat the same meal and drink the same wines as the bridal party, it was a somewhat muted celebration.

The speeches would be wrapping up now, Alim explained, and he actually ached that he was not able to hear them.

'I want to see them dance.' Yasmin pouted.

She was very used to getting her own way.

But not in this, Alim promised.

There were volumes of intricate and ancient laws and,

until he himself ruled, Alim had no choice but to adhere to them.

Alim loved his country fiercely, and respected many of the traditions, yet from childhood he had seen the need for change.

For now, though, he tried to placate his young sister.

'You will see James and Mona tomorrow for breakfast; you can congratulate them then.'

'It's not the same, though!' Yasmin refused to be mollified. 'Why can't I slip into the ballroom for just a few moments and see them? You shall, Alim.'

'I shall only because I own the hotel and I often check in on functions. You would be noticed.'

Yasmin, like her brothers, had her share of the al-Lehan good looks and her entrance would be noted.

It would not take much for people to work things out.

Even so, Alim could not bear to see his sister unhappy—he knew how much Yasmin had been looking forward to such a rare occasion as a trip overseas.

'Listen,' Alim said. 'There is a viewing gallery in the ballroom.' He watched Yasmin's eyes widen. 'The photographer will be there now, setting up for photos, but after he comes down, you could watch things from there for a short while. I can give you a master key and you can go in a separate entrance from him and wait.'

'Yes!' Her eyes shone with excitement.

'Just for a little while,' Alim warned. 'The photographer will be back towards the end of the celebrations so keep an eye on him for when he leaves to come back up.'

'I shall.'

He gave her the key and further instructions and pretended not to notice that she swiped a bottle of champagne as they walked from the dining room.

Yasmin was very protected and afforded none of the freedom that Alim and Kaleb had been.

She deserved a little fun during her time in Rome, Alim thought.

So he led her to the stairwell and warned her *again* to stay low and to be quiet.

'Thank you, Alim!'

'Don't make trouble! Watch for a little while and then go to bed.'

Alone now, it was Alim who wanted to see his brother on this his wedding day.

And he also wanted to speak with Gabi.

Alim was a very astute businessman and he recognised Gabi's talent. He had worked very hard to bring the hotel up to standard but was aware that there was still much to be done. Marianna was very set in her ways and the more he thought about it, the more he wanted Gabi to be a part of his team.

Alim did not use the main entrance to the ballroom, for he wished to be discreet. Instead, he walked out through a courtyard and breathed in the cold air.

It was snowing and he stood for a moment listening to the applause as the speeches ended. The master of ceremonies was telling the guests that there had been another couple who had married here some sixty years ago and was leading into the first dance for the newlyweds.

Holding the wedding here and all that entailed had been the least he could do for his half-brother.

The staff might discover his royal status perhaps, but that was a small price to pay for being able to be somewhat involved in this day.

He wondered how his father felt, upstairs in the Royal Suite, as his eldest son married downstairs.

Alim walked in through the French windows and

looked over at Fleur, who sat, a part of the bridal party yet somehow remote.

Alim held nothing against her—in fact, he felt for her. She had been a good mother to James and had never caused any problems for his family.

He, himself, was causing problems for a certain some-one, though.

His entrance, however unobtrusive, could not have come at a worse time for Gabi.

Of all the moments that Alim could have chosen to check on proceedings, Gabi would have preferred that it was not this particular one.

Often he arrived with an entourage, but on this night he had slipped quietly into the ballroom just as the happy couple were about to take to the floor.

And *that* was the problem.

An old-fashioned gramophone had been set up and a microphone discreetly placed over it so that in this de-licious old ballroom history would tonight be repeated.

Of course, there was a back-up recording to hand should the needle skid across the vinyl or start to jump, or should the assistant wedding planner's hand be shak-ing so much just at the sight of Alim.

He made her a quivering wreck simply by his pres-ence.

He came in from the cold and, though impossible from this distance, she felt as if the cool air followed him in, for she shivered.

Do not look over, Gabi told herself. *Just ignore that he has come in.*

Under Bernadetta's less-than-reassuring glare, Gabi placed the needle on the vinyl and the sounds of yester-year crackled into life. It was not the bride and groom who took to the dance floor—it was the bride's grand-parents.

Tenderly, the elderly man held his wife and it was the perfect pastiche as the younger couple joined them.

It was an incredibly moving passing of the baton and just so utterly romantic to watch the elderly couple and the newlyweds dance side by side that it brought a tear to Gabi's eyes.

Oh, it made all the sleepless nights worth it, just for this.

She glanced up and saw that the photographer was snapping away.

They would be beautiful photos indeed.

Gabi went through her list on her tablet and saw that for now she was up to date.

Everything really had gone seamlessly.

'Another Matrimoni di Bernadetta success,' Bernadetta said, and Gabi's jaw gritted as her boss came and stood by her side. 'I hope that I can trust you to take it from here.'

Bernadetta made it sound as if she was bestowing a great favour when in truth she was skiving off early and leaving it all to Gabi.

All of it had been left to Gabi.

Bernadetta had flown back from her vacation just this morning and had spent most of the day staying warm in her luxurious car.

Gabi stood there, biting back tears as Bernadetta waltzed off, though of course she took time to network. Bernadetta knew very well which side her bread was buttered on, and was sweet and charming to anyone who might assist her ascent. She walked up to Alim, and Gabi saw her put her hands up in false modesty as she no doubt accepted congratulations from Alim for another hugely successful wedding.

And Gabi stood there, dreaming of one day going it alone.

Just dreaming of the day when she could call a night such as this *her* success and be the one Alim congratulated.

And that was how he saw her.

Lost in a dream.

Alim walked towards her and as she turned and looked towards him he smiled. She felt that she shone.

Criticism and fault were gone when she was held in his gaze.

No man had ever made her feel like that, no man had ever made her feel as if there was nothing, but nothing, that she needed to change.

He did that with just one look.

'I was wondering…' Alim said in that smoky voice of his, and so lost in her dream was Gabi that she put down the tablet she held and stepped towards him on instinct.

'I'd love to.'

And then she wished the ground would open up and swallow her.

Of course his arms were not waiting for her. Gabi had thought, stupidly thought, that he was asking her to dance, but instead, as he sidestepped, it was just a cringe-inducing faux pas.

Of all the embarrassing moments she had lived through, this was Gabi's worst.

'We're working, Gabi,' Alim said politely.

But no matter how skilfully he deflected or made light of her gaffe, not even he could save her from her shame as he told her the real reason that he had approached.

Of course he hadn't been about to ask her for this dance.

'I was wondering,' Alim repeated, 'if I might have a word.'

CHAPTER THREE

Oh, THE SHAME!

Gabi wanted the dance floor to open up and swallow her whole.

Instead, she stood there as Alim gestured with his head, indicating that they move out from the ballroom.

When Alim asked to speak with someone, they tended to say yes, even if they would have preferred to run.

'The bride might need me.' Gabi floundered for an excuse. 'Bernadetta just left.'

'I know that.'

Alim had a word with one of the staff as they made their way out and told them where they could be found. 'If anyone is looking for you, you will be told.'

She retrieved her tablet and he led them out of the ballroom to a table and chairs, and as she took a seat he put up his hand to halt a waiter as he approached.

This was business.

Yet her navy eyes were shining with embarrassed tears and there was a mottle to her chest from the mother of all burning blushes.

Poor thing, Alim thought.

He was terribly used to women liking him, even if it was a more sophisticated sandpit where he usually played.

Gabi would know that.

Surely?

'The wedding and the celebrations have gone very well,' Alim said.

'Matrimoni di Bernadetta put a lot of effort into it,' Gabi duly responded.

'I think we both know,' Alim said, 'that Bernadetta put precisely zero effort into this wedding.'

Gabi blinked at his forthrightness.

'Bernadetta isn't here,' Alim interrupted, 'so speak to me, Gabi.'

'Why?'

'Because I might be able to help. I appreciate hard work, I like to see talent rewarded.'

'I am well rewarded.'

He raised an eyebrow slightly.

The pay, they both knew, was terrible.

'I know that the gramophone was your idea,' Alim told her.

'How could you know that?'

'I know the groom. That is why I had to drop in and check that everything was going well.'

'Oh.'

'And he told me how impressed they were with you.'

Actually, the information hadn't been that forthcoming, James hadn't raced to tell Alim how wonderful the assistant wedding planner was.

Alim had specifically asked.

His success had come, not by accident, or by acquired wealth or by flouting his title. He kept his royal status as private as he could, and while his impossible wealth had been a starting point, it was his attention to detail that caused his ventures to thrive.

Alim did not merely accept findings, he dug deeper. And while he knew that Matrimoni di Bernadetta was amongst the top tier of wedding planners, he was very aware of the mechanics of the business.

Bernadetta had chosen well!

'Tell me.'

He could tell she was nervous.

'Why did you choose this career?' he asked.

'Because I love weddings.'

'Even now?' Alim asked. 'Even after...?' He asked a question. 'How old are you?'

'Twenty-four and, yes, I still love weddings. I always have, since I was a little girl.'

'And you've worked for Bernadetta for how long?'

'Six years,' Gabi said. 'Before that I worked for a local seamstress. And when I was at school...' She halted, not wanting to bore him.

'Go on.'

'I worked for a local florist. I used to work through Friday night to have the bouquets ready for weddings. I would get up to go to the markets before school...'

This was the passion Alim wanted in his staff.

'I was very lucky that Bernadetta took me on.'

'Why is that?' he asked.

'Well, I had no qualifications. My mother needed me to work so I left school at sixteen and Matromoni di Bernadetta has a good reputation.'

'So how did you get an interview?'

'I wrote to her,' Gabi admitted. 'Many times. After a year she finally agreed to give me an interview, though she warned me the competition was extremely tough. I had my friend Rosa make me a suit and I...' Gabi gave a tight shrug. 'I asked for a trial.'

'I see.'

'Bernadetta showed me a brief she had for a very important wedding and asked for my ideas.' Gabi gave him a smile. 'You've heard of fake it till you make it…'

'Fake what?' Alim asked.

'I pretended that I knew what I was doing.'

'But you *did* know what you were doing,' Alim said, and Gabi swallowed. 'You had already worked for a seamstress and a florist…'

'Yes, but…'

'And what happened with the ideas you gave her for this very important wedding?'

'She incorporated some of them.'

'So what part were you faking?'

Gabi frowned. 'I've learnt an awful lot working for Bernadetta.'

'Of course,' Alim agreed. 'She is at the top of her game. I have no hesitation recommending her. Still, I know that lately most of the credit should fall to you. Have you ever thought about moving out on your own?'

Her blush had all but faded and now it returned, though not to her chest. He watched as her cheeks darkened and her jaw tightened and Gabi was angry indeed, Alim knew.

'I can't.'

'Why not?'

'Alim…' Gabi shook her head. She was loyal, even if it was misplaced, and she had also got into trouble for dreaming out loud before.

'Talk to me,' he said.

'Why?'

'Because I may be able to help.'

'Bernadetta found out that I one day hoped to go out on my own, and she reminded me of a clause in my contract.'

'Which is?'

'That I can't use any of the firms that she does for six months after leaving. I'd have to make new contacts.'

'But you already use only the best.'

'Yes.' Gabi nodded, glad that he immediately got it. She had spent hours trying to explain it to her mother, who'd said she should just be glad to have a job. It was so nice to discuss it with Alim! 'Those contacts weren't all Bernadetta's to start off with.' Gabi had held it in for so long that it was a relief to vent some of her frustration. 'The bride tonight is wearing Rosa's creation. It was her lounge floor that I used to cut fabric on.'

'Tell me,' he urged.

So Gabi did.

'When I first worked for Bernadetta we had a bride to dress and she had only one arm. So many of the designers shunned her, they did not want her wearing one of their creations. I was furious so I suggested that Bernadetta try Rosa. She scoffed at the idea at first but in the end agreed to give her a try—Rosa made the bride a princess on her day. It was a very high-profile wedding and so in came the orders. Now Rosa works in the best street in Rome. Rosa is *my* contact but of course I did not think to get that in writing at the time.'

Alim watched as Gabi slumped a little in her seat.

Defeated.

And then he fought not to smile as her hand went to her hair and she coiled a strand around her finger.

For after a moment's pause she rose again.

Now she had started to air her grievances, Gabi found that she could not stop. 'The flowers today, the gardenias—it was the florist's idea to replicate the grandmother's bouquet.' Alim noted that Gabi did not take credit where it was not due and he liked that. 'The florist,

Angela, is the woman I worked with when I was at school. We used to work in a tiny store, now she is known as one of the finest bridal florists in Rome.'

'So the best contacts are off limits,' Alim said, and Gabi nodded.

'For six months after I leave—and I doubt I could hold off for that long. That is assuming anyone will hire me as their wedding planner. I doubt Bernadetta will give a good reference.'

'She'll bad-mouth you.'

He said it as fact.

He was right.

Alim had thought he had the solution.

Right now, he could be wrapping the conversation up with the offer that Gabi come and work for him.

It was rather more complicated now, though, and not just because she liked him. Alim was very used to that.

It was that he liked her.

He acknowledged it then. Just a little, he assured himself.

But, yes, for two years the hotel had seemed warmer when Gabi was here. For two years he had smiled to himself as she clipped across the foyer in those awful heels, or muttered a swear word now and then under her breath.

He had never allowed himself to acknowledge her beauty but he could not deny it now.

She looked stunning.

Her hair was falling from its confines, her dress shimmered over her curves and how the hell had he not swept her into his arms to dance? Alim pondered. But the answer, though he denied it, was becoming clearer the longer they spoke—he had been resisting her for a long time.

The other week his mood had not been great.

Christmas was always busy in the hotel industry but it wasn't just that that had accounted for his dark mood.

Issues back home were becoming more pressing.

But it wasn't that either.

There had been a vague air of discontent that he could not place, though admittedly he had avoided seeking its source.

Alim had not wanted to give voice to it.

So he hadn't.

Outside work he had been his usual reprobate self, but some time between Christmas and New Year he had walked into the foyer of the Grande Lucia and seen that Fleur had taken him up on his suggestion that they use Matrimoni di Bernadetta to plan the wedding. They hadn't held a wedding here in a very long while and Alim had found that he missed Gabi's presence. The air felt different when she was around.

He fought to bring his thoughts back to work.

'What would you do differently from Bernadetta?'

Gabi frowned, for it felt like an interview, but she answered his question.

'I'd ditch the black suit.'

'You already have.' His eyes did not leave hers as he said it but he let her know that the change from her usual attire had been noted.

Oh, it had.

It no longer felt like an interview.

Their minds actually fought not to flirt—Gabi because she did not want to make a fool of herself again, and Alim because he kept work at work.

'There was a wardrobe malfunction back at the church,' Gabi carefully answered.

'Malfunction?'

'I fell,' Gabi said. 'Thankfully it was after the bridal party had left, but I tore my suit.'

'Did you hurt yourself?'

'A bit.'

He wanted to peel off her dress and examine her bruises; he wanted to bring her now to his lap.

But still his eyes never left hers and the conversation remained polite.

'So you would ditch the black suit in favour of what?

'I've seen this fabric, it's a willow-green and pink check, more a tartan. It sounds terrible but…'

'No,' Alim said. 'It sounds different. Do you have a picture?'

Of course she did, and she took only a moment to bring it up on her tablet and hand it to Alim.

He looked at the picture of the fabric she had chosen. It was more subtle than she had described and, yes, it would be the perfect choice.

'What would you change here at the Grande Lucia?' he asked as he handed back the tablet. He expected her to flounder, given that she'd had no time to prepare.

Gabi though knew exactly what the first change would be.

'There would be a blanket ban on red carnations throughout the hotel.'

She watched the slight twitch of his very beautiful lips. Alim had many areas of expertise but flowers were not amongst them. 'I don't tend to get involved with the floral displays,' he said.

'I do.' Gabi smiled. 'I obsess about such things.'

'Really?'

'Really.'

'What would you choose?'

'Sahara roses are always nice, though I think it should

vary through the week, and at weekends I would change the theme to tie in with the main function being held.'

'Would you, now?'

'You did ask.'

'Are Sahara roses your favourite flower?'

'No,' Gabi said.

'What is?'

'Sweet peas.' She gave him a smile. 'Marianna would faint at the idea and deny that they are sophisticated enough for the Grande Lucia, but, honestly, when arranged right…'

Her face lit up and he smiled.

Gabi was all fresh ideas and the zing of youth, and coupled with Marianna's wisdom…

But it was getting harder to think of business.

Very hard.

'Would you like a drink?' Alim offered.

'I'm working.'

And there was a slight ironic smile that dusted his lips as she mirrored his own words from earlier.

'Gabi…' Alim said, and then halted.

He needed to think this through before he offered her this role; she had already been dragged over the coals. If she were to work for him, it could get messy. One-night stands were his usual fare and that was why he kept his personal life where it belonged.

In bed.

He wanted the best for his business and yet, rarely for Alim, he found that he wanted what was best for her, so he came up with an alternative.

'Have you thought of going into partnership with Bernadetta?'

'Partnership?' Gabi shot him an incredulous look. 'She would laugh me out of her office if I suggested it.'

'And when she had stopped laughing, you would tell her that you'd make a better partner than rival.'

It had never even crossed her mind.

'Or, if you continue to work for her you set your limits, you tell Bernadetta only what you are prepared to do. What works for you…'

He did not want to lose her though.

Oh, this could get messy, yet the closer he examined it, the more it appealed.

'There is another option…'

'Gabi!' Her name was said again and she turned as one of the waiters came over. 'The photographer wants to speak with you.'

'Excuse me,' Gabi said, and, ever the gentleman, Alim stood as she left.

Alim went back into the ballroom and looked up. He saw the westerly door open and smiled at the thought of Yasmin creeping in.

And then he turned and saw his brother.

There were no halves where love was concerned.

'Congratulations,' Alim said.

'Thank you.'

And that was all he could offer in public.

James's complexion and hair were lighter but standing side by side it would be hard to miss the similarities. They had to step apart before someone made the connection.

Alim took a call from Violetta and was told that the Sultan of Sultans would like to speak with him.

Things were already tense between Alim and Oman.

Oman resented Alim's freedom, and was bitter with his lot for Fleur was the love of his life. And, in turn, Alim, though respectful with words, was silently disapproving, for he loved his mother and loathed how she had been treated.

Alim bowed as he entered the Royal Suite and then told his father about the wedding's progress.

'Everything is going smoothly,' Alim informed him, though that knowledge did not make things better for Oman since he could not be there to see his son marry for himself.

'Where is Yasmin?' he snapped.

'We had dinner,' Alim calmly answered, 'and she is now in her suite. The reception will finish shortly; you will see James and Mona in the morning.'

No doubt, Alim thought, Fleur would be here soon.

He thought he would now be dismissed but, instead, Oman brought up an argument of old.

One that had never really left them.

'I want you home.'

Alim was in no mood for this but he did not show his irritation. 'I was in Zethlehan last month and I shall be back for a formal visit in—'

'I mean permanently.' Oman interrupted.

'That isn't going to happen.'

They had had this argument many times before.

Alim refused to act as caretaker to his country just so that his father could travel abroad more.

He would not facilitate the shaming of his mother.

Although he was happy for James and Mona and wished he could participate more in the celebration, to-night still felt like a betrayal to his mother.

'You are thirty-two years old, Alim. Surely it is time that you marry?'

Alim stayed silent but his eyes told his father that he did not need marriage guidance from a man who had a wife and a mistress. Alim never cheated. He was upfront in all his relationships, and there could be no confusion that what he offered was a temporary affair. Arrogant, some might say, but better that than leading someone on.

'I shall select a bride for you,' Oman said in threat. 'Then you shall have no choice but to marry.'

'We always have choices.'

The advice he had so recently given to Gabi had been tested over and over by Alim—he had long ago set his limits with his father and told him what he was and was not willing to do.

'To choose a bride without my agreement could only serve to embarrass not just the bride but our country when the groom does not show,' Alim warned. 'I will not be pushed into marriage,'

'Alim, I am not well.'

'How unwell?' Alim asked, for he did not trust his father not to exaggerate for gain.

'I require treatment. I am going to have to stay out of the public eye for six months at least.'

Alim listened as his father went into detail about his health issues and Alim had to concede grudgingly that there was a battle ahead.

'I will step in,' Alim responded. 'You know that.'

It wasn't the response his father wanted, though, and he pressed his son further. 'Our people need good news, a wedding would be pleasing for them.'

Alim would not be manipulated and stood up to his father just as he always had. 'Our people would surely want to see the Sultan of Sultans at such a celebration. A son's wedding without his father's presence would send the message that the father did not approve of his son's choice of bride, and this could surely cause our people anxiety.' Alim watched his father's jaw grit. 'Let us discuss this again when you are well.'

His father would have argued further, but suddenly

Alim sensed distraction as he saw Oman glance towards the adjoining door, and he guessed that his father's lover had just arrived.

'I shall see you in the morning for breakfast,' Alim said, and then bowed and left.

As he walked along the corridor, though outwardly calm, inside his mood was dark. No, he could not put off choosing a bride for ever, but he had no desire to live the life that his parents did—he thought of his mother alone tonight in the palace. Always she had put on a brave face and smiled at her children as if things were just fine.

How could they be?

Alim did not want a bride chosen for him by his father.

He wanted...

What?

The maudlin feeling would not shift. Alim reminded himself that his friend Bastiano would be in town next week and that would likely cheer him up. But Bastiano was just another rich playboy, and the casinos and clubs did not hold their usual allure for Alim.

In truth, he was tired of his exhausting private life. The thrill of the chase no longer existed, for after two years in Rome women sought *him* out.

He walked through the foyer and, sure enough, the last of the guests were leaving.

Alim went up the stairwell and, unlocking the door, he went onto the gallery.

There were no signs of his sister and Alim assumed she was safely in her suite. The photographer had left some equipment so Alim made a mental note to lock the door as he left.

Alim glanced down at the stunning ballroom.

The staff were clearing the glasses and tables away but most of it would wait for the morning.

It was done.

The wedding had been *his* gift to the couple and Fleur had engineered things so that it was held at the Grande Lucia. Yet he had not taken any significant part in the proceedings.

Yes, it had been a wonderful wedding but for Alim it had been a wretched day and night.

Apart from the time spent with Gabi.

He looked down at her standing in the now-empty ballroom.

Alim had been going to ask her to work for him but had decided that, given how he felt, at best it would be foolish to get overly involved.

Then he smiled when he recalled her blush when she had thought he was about to ask her to dance.

And, as of now, he was no longer working.

CHAPTER FOUR

GABI WANTED TO go home and hide her shame.

Over and over she replayed it in her head—that awful moment when she had thought the suave Alim had been asking her to dance.

She stood in the empty ballroom and surveyed the slight chaos that a successful wedding reception left in its wake.

The staff had been in and cleared the plates and glasses, the tables had been stripped and the chairs stacked away. All Gabi had to do tonight was take the old gramophone out to her car and safely put away the grandparents' vinyl record that the bride and groom had danced to.

It could wait a few moments, though, and Gabi paused to look around.

It was *such* a magnificent ballroom.

The chandeliers had been switched off and it was lit now by the harsh white downlights that had come on when the music had ended and it had been time for the guests to leave.

And, because she could, Gabi headed to the power box and one by one flicked the switches until all the lights were off.

She did not turn on the chandeliers.

They didn't need electricity to be beautiful, for the

moonlight came in through the high windows and it was as if the snow outside was now falling within. Even unseen trees made an appearance because the shadows of branches crept along the silver walls.

It was like standing in an icy forest, so much so that she could imagine her breath blowing white.

What had Alim been about to say to her?

It might be weeks or months before she was here at the Grande Lucia again.

Maybe she would never know.

Gabi heard the door open and turned, assuming it was one of the staff to clear the remnants of the wedding away.

Instead, it was Alim.

'I was just...'

Just what?

Thinking about you.

Gabi didn't say that, of course.

'It went very well tonight,' he said.

'Thank you.'

And now she should collect her things and go home, yet she made no move to leave.

She was one burning blush as he walked across the room, and she did not know where to go or what to do with herself as he approached the old gramophone.

And then she shivered.

Not because it was cold, for the air was perfectly warm; instead, she shivered in silent delight as she heard the slight scratch of the needle hitting the vinyl. The sounds of old were given life again and etched on her heart for ever as he turned around, walked towards her and, without a word, offered her a dance.

And, without a word, she accepted.

His embrace was tender but firm and, close up, the

heady, musky sent of him held a peregrine note that she could not place. But, then, nothing about tonight was familiar.

Usually his greetings were polite; tonight things had changed and, Gabi thought, even the suave Alim seemed to accept they were on the edge of something.

'Listen.' He spoke into her ear and his low voice offered a delicious warning. 'I am trouble.'

'I know that.'

He felt her head nod against his chest and her words were accepting rather than resigned so he made things clearer. 'If you like me, then doubly so.'

'I know all of that,' Gabi said.

The trouble was, right now, here in his arms, Gabi didn't care and she lifted her face to his.

Tonight was her night.

Gabi knew his reputation and accepted it would never be anything more than a night, yet she had carried a torch for Alim for years.

The consequences she could live with.

It was regret she could do without.

His body she had craved and imagined for so long, and she rested against it now. He was lean and strong and he moved her so skilfully to the music that for the first time in her life Gabi felt not just co-ordinated but light.

They stared deep into each other's eyes. She never wanted to leave the warmth of his gaze, and for now she did not have to.

They stared and they swayed and they ached within.

His whole life, Alim had fought to keep his business and personal life separate. It had seemed the sensible thing to do, yet nothing made more sense than the thoughts that were now forming in his mind.

One woman.

He thought of the many upcoming trips home and he thought of returning to the Grande Lucia and to Gabi in his bed.

Alim thought of them working together and still it did not deter him, for there would be benefits for them both.

His head lowered, his lips brushed hers, and on contact Gabi knew she would never regret this.

A gentle kiss had been her fantasy, perhaps one on the cheek that changed midway.

Yet his kiss was decisive as his mouth met hers and he delivered her first kiss. She melted at the sheer bliss of it.

It actually felt as if her lips seemed to know what to do, for they moved and melded to the soft caress of Alim's.

He was used to slenderness yet his hands now ran over luscious curves; he felt the press of her breasts against his chest and suddenly there was less reason for caution than he had ever known.

He wanted Gabi in bed—and not just for this night—so he moved his mouth from hers.

'Are you seeing someone?' he asked.

And though she was held in his arms, though he was hard against her soft stomach, his question was so matter-of-fact and so direct that it felt again, to Gabi, like an interview.

'When does a wedding planner get time for a social life?' she murmured, keen to get back to his kiss.

'So it causes problems in your relationships?'

He was fishing, shamelessly so.

She was honest.

And not to her detriment.

'There have been no relationships.'

Her words went straight to his groin, and Gabi felt him further harden in response to them while his hands on her hips moved her further in.

As he met her mouth again, she felt the odd sensation of panic devoid of fear.

The intimate taste of him was briefly shocking, the intensity and the thoroughness of his kiss was better in the flesh than in dreams. There, in imaginings, she did not know quite what to do, but here, with him, she held his breath in her mouth and swallowed it as he accepted hers.

They made hunger.

Illicit.

That was the taste they made.

The tip of her tongue was surely nectar for he savoured it, and the scratch of his jaw was a new hurt for her to relish.

Her breasts ached against fabric as his hands roamed her curves, and she felt the dig of his fingers in her hips and the grind of him against her.

Dignity was not Gabi's forte.

She slipped and fell on so many occasions.

Tonight, though, she danced with the man of her dreams.

It was just a dance, she told herself. Her body denied it.

Oh, it was so much more than a dance.

He moved her an inch, a dangerous inch for it felt as if their heat met and she was scared to let go, scared to misread the situation again, but it felt as if they were headed for bed.

As she opened her eyes to the coolness of his cheek Gabi was ready for more.

It was the eyes of insatiable heat that met his.

'What the hell was I thinking?' Alim asked, for he still could not believe he had sidestepped that dance.

She did not understand the question, and since he offered no clarification Gabi did not attempt a reply.

Alim spoke for both of them.

'Come to bed.'

CHAPTER FIVE

HE TOOK HER hand and led her from the dance floor but as they reached the double doors he dropped it.

'For this to work,' he told her, 'we must be discreet.'

Alim was talking of the weeks and months ahead while Gabi was thinking just of this night, but nevertheless she nodded. Her cheeks were flushed and her mind was flurried with hormones like a snow-globe, and so she was grateful that he could think of sparing her blushes in the morning.

His thoughtfulness spurred her to think of tomorrow also.

'I need to get my coat, or they'll know that I stayed the night.'

'Do so, then,' Alim told her. 'Just say goodnight and that you are collecting some dresses…'

He knew her routines for he *had* noticed her… Often, before she went home, Gabi would head up to the dressing suite, where bridesmaids and such got changed, and leave the hotel with her arms filled with tulle.

She blinked at the fact that he knew.

'I'll head up,' Alim said. 'I have a private elevator…'

'I know that you do.'

'I shall send it back down.'

Alim left the ballroom and a moment later so too did she.

It was like any other night.

He walked to his elevator and pulled open the antique gate as Gabi smiled at Silvia, the receptionist on duty tonight.

'I just have to get some dresses and then I'm done,' Gabi said. 'Can I just get my coat?'

'Sure.'

Gabi slipped behind the desk and into the small staff cloakroom, where she collected her coat and put it on.

And just like on any other night she walked through the foyer.

There was a loud couple by the lifts who Gabi recognised as guests from the wedding and as she turned her head she saw a polished group coming in through the brass revolving doors.

No one was looking at Gabi.

The doors to the elevator were heavy and for a moment they did not budge and she wondered if he had forgotten to unlock them.

She was almost frantic, but suddenly they slid to one side and she stepped in and closed them.

His exotic fragrance lingered in the air and she leant against the soft cushioned wall.

The light was dim and she took a second, or maybe ten, just to imprint this moment for, she knew, things between them could never be the same again.

Oh, she accepted this was just one night, but it would be the absolute night of her life and she would never regret it, Gabi swore.

She went to press the button but before she did so the elevator jolted, and she guessed Alim would have known she was inside and was impatient for her to arrive.

It *was* he who had pressed the summons.

For he *was* impatient.

Alim was an ordered person.

Even as the elevator lifted her towards him, he made plans. Tonight was not the time to offer her a position here at the hotel and as his lover; he would wait until tomorrow when his head was clearer.

For now, he would take her to the bedroom and make very slow love to her, for he knew she was inexperienced and deserved due care.

And for once there was tomorrow.

Yes, Alim made plans…but then he saw her. She was flushed in the face and her hands moved with his to open the gated doors. Their fingers met, and haste was born.

Gated elevators were not so good for self-control, for they started to kiss through the gates. Dirty, fevered kisses as their hands reached through the bars.

It was ridiculous—one second apart and they could open them and be together, but even a second apart felt too long.

For the greater good she stepped back as Alim wrenched open the gate and rather than behaving shyly and reticently, as in her dreams she had been, she simply toppled into his arms.

How, he wondered, had he resisted her for so long?

'I hated it when you came up here with her…'

They were jealous words but she felt free to say them and he knew exactly the time Gabi referred to.

'You will recall that I sent her back down,' Alim said as he kissed her hard against the wall.

'Why?' she demanded.

'I was at risk of saying your name.'

'Why?'

'You know why,' Alim said, and mid-hallway, a long

way from the entrance to his lounge, let alone the bedroom door, he recalled that incident. 'Because I was hard for you.'

He was hard for her now.

Her hands were in his hair and though she was unskilled in her kiss, so untamed and frantic was her mouth it was effort that was rewarded.

His hands dug hard into her bottom as they kissed; he felt her wriggle and Gabi let out an 'Ow' as he dug into her bruise.

'It's sore there,' she said, for all her senses felt heightened and she saw him frown in concern that he had hurt her. 'Where I fell,' she further explained.

Oh, yes.

His apartment might just as well be in Venice, for the corridor was simply too long for both of them; he would have to drag her, like a marathon runner across the finishing line. Oh, her determination was there but her willpower had gone at the same moment as his.

Still he kissed her hard against the wall, his tongue forcing apart her lips and his hands holding Gabi's wrists by her sides.

She ached to touch him, but he held her tight as he kissed her hard. Her arms attempted to flex, but his grip tightened and then suddenly released.

'Bed,' he said.

'Please,' she told him.

They fell through the door and were greeted by warmth and the scent of wood and pine and a fire lit in the grate.

It surprised Gabi, for she had expected opulence but not warmth.

He was behind her and the intention was bed but so

warm was the room and so wanting the flesh that his hand came to her zipper.

'Show me where you hurt,' he said.

Gabi screwed her eyes closed for she wanted pitch blackness before she was naked but her dress was already sliding down.

She had felt beautiful in it, but now she was scared that the unwrapping of the parcel might reveal less than delicious contents.

Instead, she heard a low moan as he ran a finger down her spine.

'Alim…' Gabi breathed as she felt his fingers in her knickers, sliding them down.

Then he knelt and she felt his breath on her bottom and then his mouth soft and warm, and she thought she might fold over.

Her thighs were shaking as she stepped out of her knickers.

His hands splayed her thighs so that she stood in her lovely high heels with her legs spread a little apart. He kissed the sensitive flesh of her inner thigh, then kissed the new purple bruise and it was bliss, but a bliss that could not last, for either of them, for more was needed for such pleasure to be sustained.

He stood then, undid her bra and turned her around.

He was completely dressed.

As if he had just come in to check on his staff.

You could not tell he had been on his knees between her thighs.

'I feel at a disadvantage,' she admitted, for she was naked apart from her shoes.

'Yet you have the complete advantage,' Alim said, for she could bring him back to his knees if she so chose.

Instead, she took off her shoes.

They made her unsteady—or was that Alim?—for his eyes never left her face as he shrugged off his jacket.

Gabi stood perfectly still, yet her breath came in pants as if she had been sprinting. His fingers reached for a nipple, taking it between finger and thumb, and then he looked down. Gabi swallowed as he lowered his head and took a leisurely taste; to steady herself, her hand went for his head.

But he removed it.

Her breast was wet and cool from his mouth as he removed his tie and shirt.

Oh, she had wanted to see him for so long. His skin was like burnt caramel and his chest was wide, his arms strong. She looked at the fan of hair and the dark puckered skin of his nipples, and she too wanted her taste. For a moment she resisted, for there were other feasts to be had.

She ran a hand along his upper arm and it was an unexpected move for Alim but he liked the soft touch of her hands and the slight pinch of her fingers.

Then she looked down at the snake of hair and the swell beneath and she bit on her lip because she knew tonight was going to hurt.

'I'll be gentle.'

'Really?'

And there was a dry edge to her voice, a smoky provocative edge that even Gabi had not heard in herself before.

She was stroking the crinkle of hair on his stomach and then her mouth went to his flat nipple; she licked the salty skin and this time it was Alim who held her head and moaned at the soft nip of her teeth. And it was Gabi who slid down his zipper.

Alim had anticipated reticence, yet her touch was eager.

They both stood naked now, so there was no disadvantage, not a single one.

She could see and feel and touch his desire, which she did, stroking him at first then abandoning him erect so that she could reclaim his kiss.

He was damp and hard against her stomach and she was burning on the inside. She had dreamed of being kissed on his bed.

Instead, they did not make it past the fire.

They knelt, though their mouths remained engaged, sharing hot, wet kisses as they sank back onto their heels. His body was magnificent, his shoulders were wide as she ran her hands over them.

Always, she had felt cumbersome.

Not tonight.

He felt her lips stretch into a smile.

'What?' he asked, and pulled his head back a fraction.

'You always make me want to sit up straighter.'

'Sit up straighter, then.'

She had to fight to do so because, as he traced her clavicle with his tongue, she wanted to fold in two. Then down to her breast and he tasted it again, only slowly and deeply while massaging the other, rolling the swollen nipple between finger and thumb.

'Sit up straight,' he warned, as she started to sink into his skilled caress, which crept lower and lower.

She rested her arms on his shoulders as his fingers slipped into her tight hollow; she let out a sob of both pain and pleasure as he stretched and probed her, readying her for him.

She could sit up straight no more so he laid her down on the floor, stroking her and kissing her all the while.

His fingers did not rush, though his hand was insistent.

She went to push it away at one point for he made her want to scream, but instead Gabi clenched her jaw. He spoke in Arabic and his words, though not understood, matched her urgent desire.

He was passionate, sensual and far from cold as he coached her those final steps home.

'Come,' he told her, licking his lips, and she felt that if she did not then his lips would ensure that she did. Gabi succumbed to the pleasure, simply letting go.

She was tight around his fingers as her thighs clamped and her bottom lifted. Watching her pleasure was intense for Alim, and he fought his urgent need to take her.

Alim too was breathless as she lay there, temporarily sated, her hand over her mound.

She had not lied as others had, for there was blood on his fingers as he removed them.

Now they would retreat to the bedroom, yet still his hand roamed her thighs. Unwittingly, Gabi parted them for him, her mouth awaiting his kiss.

He fought with temptation and lost.

A little way, he decided, because he ached for her.

'It's going to hurt,' Gabi said, torn between fear and desire.

'A little,' he accepted, but despite his size her wetness eased him in.

It was *nothing* like her imaginings.

In her dreams it was a seamless, tender dance as he gently took her while telling her he loved her. In reality it was the tearing of flesh and the rising of pain as he inched into her.

Gabi found that she preferred the latter.

'Gabi…'

He had sworn *just a little way in*, but the grip was too

inviting, the scent of sex urged him on and he thrust in deeply.

She sobbed, loudly, and he cursed his lack of care. Alim stilled. It took a moment for her to acclimatise, to regroup, and then she begged him to do it again.

Alim obliged.

Over and over.

They rolled and they kissed, they dragged from each other pleasure beyond imagining, and she, the virgin, pushed him to extremes, for he fought hard not to come.

His life, his identity, even his seed was always protected.

Yet his abdomen was tight and he was lifting.

He did not withdraw and she did not resist. Instead, she coiled her legs tighter around his loins, and this time, when Gabi came, it was around his thick length.

He felt the throb of her demand.

'Alim…' Her voice told him *now*, in fact it pleaded, and Alim bade farewell to restraint and rained deep into her.

The rush of his release and the moan he made procured a tiny cry from Gabi that abruptly died, for she was back to his mouth, being consumed by his kiss and a slave to their bliss.

They lay there a while, until both the room and their bodies were cool. But the fires of passion had not dimmed.

'Bed,' Alim said, and he stood and helped her up.

For still it beckoned.

CHAPTER SIX

ALIM HAD ALWAYS been careful.

Always!

Until now.

There was nothing about this night that compared with others, for they made love again and then, instead of sleeping, lay in his bed, talking, thirstily drinking iced sparkling water.

It was refreshing.

Even mistakes were forgiven.

'Tomorrow I shall arrange for a doctor to see you,' he told Gabi as they discussed the morning-after pill.

'I'll sort it,' Gabi said, for she was not seeing a doctor here!

'I apologise,' he told her.

'Please don't.'

She would not change it, or, if she could, Gabi would only have been better prepared and been on the Pill, but nothing could have forewarned her that on this night her dreams would come true.

She had craved Alim from a distance for years. Now he was here and it was better even than she had dreamt.

Gabi might be inexperienced but she knew enough about Alim to be surprised by their ease in conversation afterwards.

She had known that he would be a brilliant lover; the surprise was that afterwards she felt like she was lying with a friend, for they chatted.

And she had never imagined that might happen with Alim.

Yet they spoke about their lack of thought earlier and made plans to remedy it later that day.

'I will sort it,' she told him. 'Believe me, I have no intention of ending up like—' She halted.

'Like who?'

'My mother,' Gabi said. 'I don't mean that I don't want to be like her, I mean I don't want to resent...'

Whatever way she said it made it sound wrong.

'Tell me,' Alim said, just as he had when they had spoken outside the ballroom, only this time she was wrapped in his arms.

'I was an accident,' Gabi explained. 'One she still pays for to this day.'

'Surely not,' Alim said. 'What about your father?'

'I don't know who he is.' Gabi admitted. 'It doesn't matter, I don't need to know...'

But she did.

Often, the need to know was so acute that she could not bear it, yet she played it down as she always had.

'My mother had been accepted to study at university but had to give it up to raise me.'

'It is not your fault that she did not follow her dreams.'

'It feels like it,' Gabi admitted. 'If she hadn't had me...'

'Then she would have found another excuse.'

'That's harsh,' Gabi said.

'Perhaps,' Alim conceded, and he smiled as she looked at him.

'Are you always so direct?'

'Always.'

Now it was Gabi who smiled.

'So planning weddings is your dream?' he asked.

Gabi nodded. She told him about when she had been a little girl and the flour and sugar that had driven her mother wild. 'I would pick flowers at the park for the bouquet and spend the whole day making sure that everything was perfect.' She thought for a moment. 'I was so worried about this wedding. It was so incredibly rushed but when I saw James and Mona dance last night I knew that they'd be okay.'

'How did you know that?'

'You can tell,' Gabi said. 'She was a very difficult bride, but together they seem so happy.'

He liked hearing that, for Alim wanted happiness for his brother.

It was not something he sought for himself.

Alim did not believe in happy marriages. He had been raised with the model that marriage was a business arrangement and a duty, and that happiness was sought elsewhere.

Things were different, of course, for James for he did not have the burden of being his father's heir.

Yes, he admitted in that moment, at times it felt like a burden.

Night was fading but there was no real thought of sleeping as they lay together chatting, Gabi idly running her fingers in circles on his chest.

And for Alim it was very relaxing, too, as well as a bit of a turn-on. He liked her curiosity about his body and her conversation made him smile as she moaned about Bernadetta, and the hell of getting this wedding sorted. But then Gabi crossed the line.

'The groom's mother is paying.'

'Gabi!' he scolded.

'What?'

Alim was considering her for a very senior role, yet she dropped confidential information like a shower of rain.

'You should not discuss such things.'

'Oh, come on,' Gabi said. 'I'm not down at the bar talking about it, I'm in bed with the boss. And it's you she's paying, so you must already know.' And then she smiled and it was like a rainbow and Alim found himself smiling back.

'Okay,' he conceded, and he pulled her in so that she lay with her head on his chest.

'It *is* odd, though,' Gabi said, though she was more thinking out loud, and it was so easy to do so with his hand stroking her hair. 'Usually it's the bride's parents who pay, or half and half...'

Alim shrugged. 'Perhaps Mona's parents are not wealthy.'

'Perhaps.' Gabi yawned. 'Though Fleur clearly is. She intrigues me.'

'Who?'

'Fleur,' Gabi said. 'The mother of the groom.'

Alim said nothing.

'I can't work out if she's divorced or widowed or just single like my mother.'

'Does it matter?' Alim asked.

'Probably not.'

Of course it did, Alim thought. Or it soon would.

He knew how the staff gossiped and very soon Gabi would know his title and it would be clear that the royal guests in residence tonight were related to him.

Or perhaps it would be the wedding photos that would be his undoing when Gabi saw them, for they had made love now and had stared deep into each other's eyes.

Alim knew he was a darker version of James.

Gabi might well see it too.

She was perceptive enough that soon she might work things out.

Alim did not enlighten her now, though.

There would be time for all that tomorrow.

It was more than one night he wanted, yet he was aware that he needed to think things through carefully.

And anyway, for now, Gabi was sleeping.

The more he tried to talk himself out of the plans he was making, the more sense they made. With his father unwell, the months ahead would be trying—that much Alim knew.

He could not put off marriage for ever, but he could certainly delay things.

And what nicer delay than this?

Alim did not expect Gabi to be at his beck and call as he carried on in the usual way; he would be faithful.

A year, perhaps.

It would work for both of them.

Alim's assessment was based on practicalities. Away from Bernadetta, her career would only flourish, he would see to that. And, during this difficult year, he could come back to Rome and to Gabi. There would be no scandal for the palace to deal with, particularly when he began taking a more prominent role while his father sought treatment.

Alim was arrogant enough to assume that Gabi would have no issues with what he was about to propose; after all, women never said no to him, and he was offering more to Gabi then he had to any woman in his life before.

Aside from his commitment to his country, it was the biggest pledge he had made and Alim made it in the still of the night as she lay sleeping.

The sky was grey and silver as the sun rose on a very cold Rome and he thought of her dress on the floor in another room and the soft warm body he held.

Gabi felt the roam of his hands as she awoke and turned her face for a glimpse of Alim asleep but it was denied to her, for Alim was already awake and looking at her.

He watched her eyes flicker open and her face turn to him. He wondered if he would see a grimace or a startle of panic as she recalled their night, but instead he watched as a smile stretched her lips and her sleepy eyes met his.

'Best night,' she said.

It had been.

And those were exactly the words he wanted to hear, for there was no tinge of regret in her smile and no confusion in her eyes.

Only desire.

And Alim *still* felt the same.

During the hours Gabi had slept, Alim had been thinking.

Yes, he still wanted more than one night.

'Fleur did not pay for the wedding,' he said, and watched her frown at the odd choice of topic, wrapped as they were in each other's arms and a breath away from a deep morning kiss.

She did not get yet that this was the most intimate conversation in the whole of Alim's life.

'It was my gift to Mona and James.'

'Why?'

'Because James is my half-brother.'

Her frown deepened and she ran a tongue over her lips as she tried to work things out; now that he had said it, she could see that James and Alim were related.

Gabi had started to see that last night as she had watched the couple dance—or rather there had been something in James that had spoken to her.

Now that she knew, Gabi felt almost foolish that she had not seen it more readily.

'Fleur is my father's mistress,' Alim explained.

'I don't understand,' Gabi said.

'Listen to me.' Alim's eyes and his tone told her that what he was saying was very important. 'Fleur was my father's lover but his father did not consider her a suitable bride. When she got pregnant with James, my grandfather summoned my father home and arranged his marriage to my mother, even though my father loved Fleur.'

'Why did he agree to marry a woman if he loved another?'

'Because he had little choice. His father was the Sultan of Sultans and his word is law; now that title belongs to my father.'

He actually felt the goose-bumps rise on her arm. 'And so what does that make you?'

'A sultan, and one day I shall rule.'

'Why are you telling me this?'

'Because my father is here in the hotel and it won't be long before the staff work out our connection. Soon you would have too.'

'But why are you telling me now?' she persisted.

'Because things back home are changing. My father is unwell, so I am going to have to travel there a lot in the coming months…' Still she stared at him with a puzzled look in her eyes so he made things a little clearer. 'I want to spend more time with you when I am here in Rome. Last night I was going to ask you to work for me as the events co-ordinator at the Grande Lucia.'

It was the offer of a lifetime.

Stunning, in fact.

It was the gateway to a shiny future and, Gabi realised, she may well have blown it for one night in his bed.

But still, she thought, she would not change it for anything.

'Is that offer being reconsidered in the light of certain events?' Gabi asked.

He smiled. 'It is being amended.'

And seriously so.

'What about a one-year contract?' he said.

'One year?'

'That frees you from Bernadetta; you would make many contacts here during that time.'

'And is sleeping with me a part of that contract?'

'Gabi.' Alim heard her indignation but was calm in his response. 'I think from last night it is clear we are not going to be able to work together and keep things strictly business. Of course, we will be discreet in front of the staff but...'

'You've really got this all worked out, haven't you?'

'I've given it considerable thought, yes.'

Gabi had walked in here last night without a doubt that it would be over by the morning.

Certain of it.

Reassured by it, in fact.

For Alim was a self-confessed reprobate and her heart could not be dangled on elastic by him, waiting to be hauled to his bedroom one minute, ignored or discarded the next.

She was shaken, seriously so.

'What happens when someone else comes along?'

She was direct with her questions and he liked that.

'Alim, I take my career seriously...'

'And I admire that you do,' he responded. 'I shan't

mess with it. And,' he offered, which for Alim was a great concession, 'there will be no one else.'

'Why a year?'

'Because I will be called home to marry.'

How cruel that he held her as he said that.

'Gabi.' He had felt her stiffen. 'Please, listen to me now. When Fleur fell pregnant my grandfather invoked a pre-marital diktat on my father. It is a harsh law, one intended to bring a reluctant groom to heel. Once invoked there can be no lovers, save for in the desert.'

'The desert?' she asked. 'You mean a harem.'

'That is what it meant then; they could have worked around it, but Fleur refused to be his desert mistress.'

'I don't blame her for that.'

'By the time James was due to be born my mother was pregnant with me. Fleur gave birth in London; my father could not leave at the time. But later, once he had royal heirs, things were easier for them and my father was more free to travel…'

Gabi didn't want to hear it. She sat up and clutched the sheet around her 'This conversation is medieval.' She did not like what she was hearing—it unnerved her, in fact—but Alim calmly spoke on.

'Perhaps when you see the doctor this morning you should speak about going on the Pill. I can call and arrange for him to see you here…'

'I make my own appointments, Alim, and I don't need to be told what to ask for.' She shot him a look. 'I don't need to go on the Pill because I'm not going to be your mistress…'

'Lover,' Alim corrected, for they were two very different roles.

'I am not going to be your lover for a year until your father summons you home.'

'I have given it a lot of thought.'

'Have you, now?'

'I don't see the issue.'

'Your assumption, for a start.'

She got out of bed and headed for the shower.

Gabi was sore from last night and her head was whirling from all she had been told.

And he was wrong about not messing with careers, Gabi thought as she showered.

Wrapping a towel around her, she headed out and told him so.

'What about Marianna? She's given the Grande Lucia years of her life and you'd discard her like that.' She tried to snap wet fingers; it didn't work.

'She wants to wind down her hours,' Alim answered. 'I would offer her a consulting role.'

She looked at him and for a brief second he seemed not so ruthless but then his hand shot out, stripping off the towel, and she stood naked. He would be ruthless to her heart, she amended.

But her body craved him.

It would be foolish at best not to go on the Pill because all she wanted at this moment was to climb back into bed.

'I know it's a lot to take in,' Alim said. 'But at least give it some thought.'

He did not understand her anger; most women pleaded for more time with him after all. 'Would you prefer it to have been just a one-night stand?'

'Yes.' She actually laughed—somewhat incredulously. 'Yes,' she said again, for this was too much for her to deal with.

'Liar.'

She caught his eyes and her laughter died. Gabi swallowed, because he actually meant it, she was starting to realise.

No!

'A year at your bidding?' she mocked.

'It works both ways,' Alim responded. 'I would be at your bidding too.'

He watched the colour spread up her cheeks and across her chest as she attempted indignation. He watched as she stood to pull on her knickers then sat back down to put on her bra.

He sat up and did it up for her and then kissed the back of her neck.

His tongue was thorough and he moved so he sat naked behind Gabi and kissed her neck harder as his hands played with her breasts.

'Alim.'

She was hot in the face and unable to stand and he knew it. Now one hand came down and slipped into her knickers. She was sore and swollen from last night, and his fingers were not there with the intent to soothe.

This love would hurt.

And it would be love, it possibly already was, but a year at his beck and call would only cement that fact.

'Alim…' She wanted to turn in his arms, to wrap herself around him, but he just upped the beats of pressure and kept bruising her neck with his mouth as she came.

And then he released her.

Somehow Gabi stood.

'The offer's there,' he told her.

And the pleasure might have been hers, but Alim knew it had been worth the restraint from him, for now they ached for each other.

It was the greatest feat of her life to dress and leave,

yet she needed the ice of the winter morning just to learn how to breathe again, and somehow think.

But the confusion he'd spun her into was not yet complete.

Alim leant over and opened a drawer to his beside.

The rumours were true, for there, in a small dish, as one might display after-dinner mints, was a collection of diamonds.

They sparkled in the wintry light, they beguiled, and one alone could make the months ahead so much easier for Gabi.

'Choose one,' Alim said. 'And then tomorrow—'

'I shan't be your whore.'

'In my country the tradition is—'

'We're in Rome, Alim,' she interrupted, and her lips pressed together in anger. Gabi shot him a look and then walked into the lounge and straight to her purse.

He made her feel confident. She felt emboldened.

Somehow he gave her permission to be completely herself.

And that self was cross!

'Here…' She opened up her purse and emptied the entire contents onto the bed. It wasn't much—a lot of coins and a few notes—but she tipped them all out and made him the whore now. 'Treat yourself, baby,' Gabi said.

As she walked out, to the surprise of both of them, Alim laughed.

He never laughed, and certainly not in the morning, yet here he was doing just that.

And, as the door slammed, Alim knew but one thing.

He wanted her back in his bed.

CHAPTER SEVEN

'THE SULTAN OF SULTANS is ready to receive you.'

Alim thanked Violetta when she called to inform him that his father was finally ready for him.

He had showered and dressed in black linen trousers and a fitted white shirt and then impatiently awaited the summons.

Alim had been looking forward to breakfast with the newlyweds, to being able to speak more freely with them.

Now, though, he was also looking forward to the rest of the day.

To the upcoming year.

He knew he had overwhelmed Gabi and that it was all too much to take in, but once she had thought it through, Alim was certain there was hope for them.

Alim looked forward not just to the nights ahead but to the working days, for he had loved this hotel on sight. Shabby, cheaply renovated, he had poured much into it and breathed it back to life. With Gabi as the new functions co-ordinator there was much to look forward to on many levels.

Violetta was waiting outside the Royal Suite. She gave Alim a smile as he approached, then three short knocks on the door to announce Alim's arrival. He opened it and stepped in, expecting to greet his family, but instead there was only his father.

'Alim.' Oman's voice was not particularly welcoming.

'Where are James and Mona?' Alim asked once he had bowed.

'On their way to Paris,' Oman said. 'I asked that they join me a little earlier.'

'I am sure they would have appreciated the early morning call the day after their wedding.'

Sarcasm was wasted on his father, Alim knew.

Still, he had long since realised that if he wanted a relationship with James then he had to forge that for himself.

When Alim had found out he had a half-brother, instead of quietly ignoring it, as would have been his parents' preferred way of dealing with things, Alim had insisted that they meet.

He had kept alive the relationship with his brother with calls, messages and visits, and would continue to do so. Once the newlyweds were back in Rome, Alim would see them, or he might call in a few days and catch up with them in Paris.

It would be good to see Kaleb too.

'What about Yasmin?' Alim asked.

'Violetta told me that she is unwell,' Oman said. 'Apparently she has a migraine—too much excitement last night.'

Or too much champagne, Alim thought, but made no comment as his father spoke on. 'It is just as well for I wish to speak to you alone. With all I told you last night there is a lot to discuss.'

'Very well.'

A gleaming walnut table had been laid and a feast prepared. Alim looked over to where it stood waiting on a large silver trolley.

There were no staff present, Alim noted, as was the case when formal business was to be discussed.

Alim was not really in the mood for a breakfast briefing but given his father's illness he knew there would be a lot to sort out.

If they'd been in Zethlehan, there might be an elder present in case sensitive issues were raised, but for now it was just the two of them.

Alim first served his father and then himself.

Oman preferred fruit, and usually so too did Alim, but this morning he helped himself to a generous serving of *shakshuka*—baked eggs in a rich and spicy sauce. There were several chefs at the Grande Lucia, including two from Zethlehan that Alim had brought over. He made light conversation with his father as he sat down.

'The Middle Eastern brunch at this hotel is becoming increasingly popular. Now people have to book in advance.'

Oman made no comment; he did not approve of Alim having investments overseas, and he particularly loathed his son's passion for this one.

And then Oman said it.

He did not look up; he said it as easily as he might ask for more mint tea.

'For some time now I have been considering invoking the pre-marital diktat.'

Alim, who had anticipated many things for the year ahead, had never envisaged this.

Never.

His father loathed the diktat, since it had been forced upon him, and Alim could not believe that he would bring this harsh ruling to bear on his son.

'There is no need for that.' Alim kept his voice calm, though he was rarely unsettled.

'It would seem that there is. I have been asking to choose your bride for many years.'

'And I have told you—' Alim's voice was still silk, but laced with threat '—that I shall never be pushed into marriage.'

Alim stared at his father. Not only was this unexpected, it was vindictive. 'You loathe that diktat,' Alim pointed out.

'It has its merits. My father chose well for me—your mother is an exemplary queen and our people adore her. We have raised three heirs…'

'And you hate it that you could not marry Fleur.'

He'd said her name out loud.

Now was not the time for reticence.

'You hate that your first born bears no title and that the woman you love gets no recognition.' Alim tried to stare down his father but Oman refused to meet his glare. 'You cannot do this.'

'It is done,' Oman told him. 'I informed the elders this morning. As of now you are Sultan Elect.'

This meant Alim was a sultan in choosing.

From this point on he must remain celibate for he could bring no shame on any future bride. There could be no release save from discreet times in the desert.

Alim stood, his appetite totally gone.

'You cannot force me into marriage.'

He said it again, loudly this time, and Alim never shouted.

Ever.

But this morning he did.

Oman did not flinch. In fact, vindictive had been the right word to describe his father's mood for the Sultan of Sultans' smile was black when he offered his response.

'I can make single life hell for you, though. You've had your fun, Alim. It's time to grow up.'

A year.

Gabi had stamped her way home through the slush and cold, furious at his suggestion.

But her flat was cold when she entered and she thought of the warmth she had left and the bliss of last night.

It should be over with by now.

Right now, Gabi thought, she should be accepting that, though amazing, her time with Alim was done.

Yet her mind danced with the hope of more.

Even before she had made a quick coffee, Bernadetta called.

'I have a meeting with a bride this afternoon but my vertigo has come on and I'm not going to be able to get there...'

Gabi closed her eyes as Bernadetta dragged out one of her tired excuses.

'Can it be moved to tomorrow?' Gabi asked.

Aside from all that had happened with Alim, Gabi had worked through to midnight and still had a lot to get done today.

She had to take the gramophone and record back to the grandparents, which was a considerable drive, and there were the outfits to collect, and a hundred other jobs that would go unnoticed but ensured that yesterday's wedding was seamless for the family.

'I don't want to let down a prospective client,' Bernadetta said. 'Gabi, I really haven't got the energy for debate. It's a summer wedding to be held at the Grande Lucia; you're going to be there today anyway.'

'I don't have a suit,' Gabi reminded her boss. 'Bernadetta...' Gabi paused. She was about to say no to her,

Gabi realised. She had been about to stand up to Bernadetta and not just on the strength of Alim's offer this morning. Their conversation last night had resonated. She was tired of being pushed around and knew she was worth a whole lot more than the treatment Bernadetta served, but for now Gabi held her tongue.

Her next step required careful thought, and so, instead of standing her ground, Gabi brushed down her skirt and did the best repair job that she could on the torn seam of her jacket and then headed back to the Grande Lucia.

There was a lot of activity in the foyer as huge brass trolleys filled with expensive luggage were being moved out.

'Gabi!'

She turned and smiled when she saw that it was the photographer. 'How did things go with you last night?' Gabi asked.

'Probably not as well as you,' he said, and Gabi frowned as he held out one of his cameras. 'I left this running in the gallery,' he explained. 'I set it to take intermittent photos up until midnight.'

Now Gabi started to blush as she realised what might have been captured.

He held out the camera and Gabi could almost not bring herself to look at the screen, terrified what she might see. 'Not exactly part of the bridal package, though it's a very beautiful image.' The photographer said.

Oh, yet another gaffe! Gabi thought, cringing, but she forced herself to look.

And then all the magic of last night returned.

For it had been captured exquisitely.

On the stunning ballroom floor, there, swirling in Alim's arms, was Gabi.

It was as beautiful as any professional wedding photo,

though it was almost impossible to reconcile that this was their first night and that they had at that point not so much as kissed.

She knew the very second that the photo had been taken. It had been when Alim had warned her that he was trouble and she had lifted her face to his.

The moment had been captured perfectly, for she was looking up into his eyes and Alim was holding her tenderly but firmly.

'Would you like me to delete it?' the photographer checked.

'No.'

'I thought as much.'

They had worked together on many occasions and he had Gabi's contact details. 'I'll forward it to you.'

He headed off with all his equipment and Gabi wanted to call out to him not to forget to forward it, but instead Gabi caught sight of Fleur in one of the side lounges, giving her order to a maid.

The woman had always intrigued Gabi, but never more so than now.

Was it lonely to be Fleur? Gabi pondered.

Of course it must be, but Alim wasn't suggesting the same for her. This was a business plan almost, a manageable slice of time.

A year.

She said it again to herself, though with mounting excitement this time.

Gabi had never dated, but knew from her friends that most relationships didn't even last that long.

It was the way he had said it and the assumption that she would simply comply that had irked.

'Gabi!' Anya, the receptionist on today, called out to her, and as Gabi looked over she realised that the foyer had become very busy. 'Can I ask you to step back, please? We have some VIP's about to leave.'

'Sure.'

Some dark-suited men were walking through the foyer and Gabi knew they were the hotel's security.

And she was about to see the Sultan of Sultans, Gabi realised.

She watched as the entourage moved through the foyer.

There was a young woman with a long mane of black hair wearing a deep mustard-coloured velvet gown and jewelled slippers. She was very beautiful, Gabi thought, even if her eyes were hidden behind dark glasses.

And then she saw a man dressed in a robe of black with a silver *keffiyeh* and Gabi felt her breath burn as she held it in her lungs, for she knew it was Alim's father. He was a mature version of Alim and had the same air of authority and elegance.

The managing director was in the foyer to bid farewell to the royal guests.

Usually, of course, it would be the owner.

Except the owner happened to be his son.

It all made sense now.

Fleur's insistence on the venue, and the reason that there had been few guests on the groom's side.

And all too soon it was over.

The procession walked through the foyer and out to the waiting cars, and when the last of them had gone, Gabi looked over to the lounge and to Fleur, who sat dignified and straight but terribly, terribly alone.

Gabi watched as she reached into her purse and took out a handkerchief, pressing it to her lips for a moment to gather herself.

There had been no kiss goodbye, not even so much as

a glance aimed at her by the Sultan of Sultans. No public acknowledgement from the man to whom she had borne a son.

What Alim had proposed this morning was different, though, Gabi told herself.

It was a year of her life and until last night there had been no love life for her.

It had been work, work, work.

Which she loved, of course.

But for a year she could have both.

And then what?

She saw that Fleur was making her way to the elevators and for the first time Gabi saw this usually poised woman with her shoulders slumped.

Defeated.

But that would not happen to her, Gabi assured herself, for she knew exactly what she was getting into. And Alim himself had said she would be a lover rather than a mistress. She had been carrying a flame for Alim since she had first seen him; the difference now was that she would be not carrying it alone.

And then?

She could not think of that now.

She was going to say yes.

It hadn't taken days of consideration, just hours, to come to her decision, and now that she had, hope filled her heart.

And as if in answer to her decision she watched as the gated, private elevator that had taken her to his suite last night opened.

Alim stepped out and her heart squeezed in reaction.

He was clean shaven and immaculate. But instead of ignoring Fleur, as he had before, Gabi watched as he stood and spoke for a moment with the woman and the conversation appeared tense.

It was.

'I tried to stop him, Alim,' Fleur said, 'but we both know my word holds little sway.'

And Alim let out a mirthless laugh for he had just come off the phone with his mother, imploring her to try and change Oman's mind, but her response had been almost the same.

'You hold more sway than you know,' Alim said. 'You simply refuse to stand up to him.'

'You try, then!' Fleur said, and her voice was weary.

Oh, he would.

Alim respected his father's title but not always the man himself.

Yet he was the ruler and his word was law.

Alim had tried to tell himself that just because the diktat had been invoked it did not mean that *everything* had to change. He would take over more duties while his father had treatment, but his work could continue here. Then he saw Gabi, standing in the foyer, dressed in that awful suit, but now that he had bedded her, she looked more beautiful than ever before and he realised that *everything* had changed.

The true ramifications were starting to hit home.

It was not even just about sex, for there could be no intimate conversation, no working alongside a woman for whom he harboured such thoughts.

And perhaps, more pointedly, no hope of observing the laws when Gabi was around.

He could only hope that her mood with him was as dark as it had been when she had left his bed this morning, so there would be no need to speak.

Alim could only think in minutes at the moment, so

he focussed on getting through the next few and, ignoring her gaze, he walked across the foyer. He wanted to be outside and to walk the streets of Rome.

He had changed his mind by the time he reached the brass doors, for Alim did not, by nature, avoid issues. He turned and walked towards Gabi, and when he saw her smile Alim knew she was going to say yes to the chance for them.

He watched the smile die on her lips as he approached.

'That offer...' Alim said, and he hesitated. He had been right when he'd said it would be impossible to work alongside each other and not sleep together.

'Yes?'

Here was no place to explain the diktat, but they could not be alone. He thought of her in bed this morning, wrapping the sheet around herself when he had tried to explain the rules and how lovers could only be alone in the desert.

Medieval had been her word to describe it.

It would be kinder to simply end it now, Alim knew.

It was also necessary.

He could smell the slight apple scent of her shampoo and could see the soft swelling of her mouth, a remnant from last night's hot kisses. He thought of how swollen she had been in readiness for him, and he thought of the love they could so easily still make.

Their bodies were aware of each other, they were attuned and wanting but, as of this morning, they were forbidden.

And so he said it, simply ended any hope for them.

'The offer has been withdrawn.'

He watched the colour drain from her face. He watched her rapid blink, and there was nothing he could do to comfort her.

'I see,' Gabi said, even though she didn't.

Yet she fought for dignity.

And dignity felt like a trapeze that she must grab onto, only Gabi was no acrobat.

She had only just accepted hope, only just accepted the brief possibility of them, and now it had been snatched away.

By him.

Oh, she had known he would hurt her one day, but after the way he had treated her that morning Gabi had never thought it would be today.

She could not even ask why or demand an explanation for she was fighting not to break down. Her nails dug into her palms and her breath was so shallow it made her feel a little giddy.

'You'll take care of what we discussed?' Alim checked.

Gabi looked at him. He was a bastard to the core, she decided, for she would have happily settled for just one night, but he'd ruined that with the glimpse of a dream. So as the imaginary trapeze swung by, she grabbed onto it with one hand and hoped it would quickly carry her away from him and drop her where she could weep unseen.

'Of course,' she responded.

'Gabi…' His voice husked and he did not continue with whatever it was he had been about to say.

It was Gabi who filled the silence. 'I need to get on,' she said. 'Bernadetta has given me quite a list to get through today.'

And she completed it. Somehow she got through the first day. Gabi and Marianna met with the new bride-to-be and her mother.

'We have the last Saturday in July available,' Marianna informed them.

'No, I want August,' the bride-to-be said.

'I'm sorry.' Marianna shook her head. 'Summer weddings have to be booked a long way in advance.'

'It's more than six months away!' the bride insisted.

'You are lucky that we have this one available.'

And Gabi just sat there.

Usually she would make soothing noises to take the edge off Marianna's slightly scolding tone.

She had been about to throw in her job, Gabi thought in horror. So trusting had she been that she had almost given Bernadetta her notice.

The numbness was fading, replaced now by a burn of anger as she watched Alim walk through the foyer.

Elegant, beautiful, it looked as if he had not a care in the world.

The rumours were true. Cold and callous did suit him. Alim did not look in her direction. She had been, Gabi knew, dismissed from his life.

And then the anger faded as she began to feel bereft. Soon followed by fear.

CHAPTER EIGHT

GABI DID NOT take care of things as the Sultan had ordered.

Though not out of recklessness or spite.

The first few days had felt like a bereavement, though not one she could ring in to work and explain about.

What could she say? *Bernadetta, I slept with Alim and he promised me the world and then dumped me.*

At best, she was a fool to have believed at all. Yet his behaviour made no sense to Gabi, for he had not offered her anything in the heat of passion. It had all been in the calm coolness of the morning, after hours of thinking, he had said.

So Gabi had somehow remembered to breathe as she'd fought not to cry and had done her best to get on with her work.

And by the time the fog had if not lifted then parted enough to take care of anything other than the seconds ahead, she had gone to the *farmacia*, only to find out that she had left it too late.

Late.

It became her most used word.

She was a day late, but put it down to stress.

A week late, but that happened at times.

And then she was late for work two days in a row because even the scent of her favourite morning coffee had her hunched over the bathroom sink.

Terror was her new friend.

Not just that she was pregnant, but by whom.

The more she found out about Zethlehan and the more she discovered about the power of the royals there, the more acute her terror became.

'Pregnant?'

'Yes,' Gabi had said to her mother.

It was a gorgeous spring morning.

Gabi had come from a weekend at the stunning Castelli vineyard, where the wedding had gone off beautifully, and she had told herself it was time. It had taken three months for Gabi to finally find the courage to tell her mother.

'Who is the father?' Carmel had asked.

And when Gabi had not answered, her mother had slapped her cheek.

Carmel, herself a single mother, had never wanted the same struggle for her only child.

'There go your dreams,' Carmel had said.

'No.'

Gabi knew things would be difficult but she was determined that her dreams would continue. It was her lack of contact with Alim that felt like an insufferable loss.

She had not told him about the baby.

Her mother assumed that because Gabi did not say who the father of her child was, it meant that she did not know.

Now Gabi was almost glad that she had been unable to tell Alim.

She was scared.

Not so much of his reaction, more the repercussions.

Sultan Alim of Zethlehan.

Sultan Elect.

He was next in line to the throne and the more she read about his kingdom the more she feared him. Alim was more powerful than she could fathom. His country was rich, extremely prosperous, and the royalty adored. There was a brother and a sister. Alim was the eldest and one day he would be Sultan of Sultans.

Gabi did not know how an illegitimate baby would be dealt with.

Her only reference point was Fleur, and she would never allow herself to become her, Gabi swore.

Though perhaps she was doing Alim an injustice?

On several occasions, Gabi had walked past the Grande Lucia, trying to find the courage to go in. Sometimes she would speak with Ronaldo and pretend that she was merely passing.

A couple of times she had plucked up the courage to go in but now Alim's royal status was known, security around him was tighter.

'Is Alim here?' Gabi asked Anya.

'Do you have an appointment?' Anya checked, when once she would have simply nodded or shaken her head, or picked up the phone to alert him.

'No,' Gabi said. 'I don't.'

'Then I can see if Marianna is available.'

'It's fine.' Gabi shook her head and, turning, looked over to the lounge and thought of Fleur, sitting alone and unacknowledged, and she thought too of James.

She did not want that life for her child, though it probably wasn't even an option to them. The Sultan of Sultans loved Fleur, whereas Alim had coldly ended things the morning after a night in his bed.

He had also told her to take the morning-after pill, not once, not twice, but three times.

Gabi was scared but determined to cope, for now, alone.

And so the next person she had told was Bernadetta.

And Bernadetta's reaction had been one of pure spite.

She resented that she would be paying for maternity leave and decided to get her money's worth while she could.

Every wedding that Bernadetta could, she passed over to Gabi.

Each teary bride or stressed call from the mother of said bride, Gabi dealt with.

And the most recent couple had barely left the church before Bernadetta skived off. Gabi barely had time to think, she was so busy working as Bernadetta became increasingly demanding.

'I don't want you showing,' she said when Gabi asked about wearing a dress for work rather than the hated suit.

It was the middle of summer and the weight had fallen off Gabi—or rather she had not, to her doctor's concern, put any on. Always curvy, at close to seven months pregnant she barely showed, but that wasn't good enough for Bernadetta.

'Our clients want to think your mind is on the job, not on a baby.'

'It *is* on the job,' Gabi insisted.

But the heavy suit remained. The only concession was that she wore the cream cowl-necked top out of the waistband.

And concealing her pregnancy as best she could was perhaps wise, for all too soon it was the wedding at the Grande Lucia that she had taken on the day the bottom had fallen out of her world.

Not that Alim would notice her, and neither was she likely to see him.

He was barely around any more. Ronaldo had told

her that he had moved back to Zethlehan and, sadly, the Grande Lucia was now on the market.

The staff were all worried for their jobs.

It was still beautiful, though, Gabi thought as, on the Friday before the wedding, she went for a breakfast meeting with Marianna in her office.

First they spoke about the timings of the big day and the arrival of the cars and photographers and such things.

Gabi's main focus was the wedding.

For Marianna, although the wedding was important, she was also dealing with the comfort of the other hotel guests and ensuring that they were not inconvenienced too much.

Again, Gabi pushed for a change to the flowers in the foyer.

'No, there has always been a red floral display.' Marianna shook her head and refused to budge on the issue. 'Our return guests like the familiarity.'

'But don't you want to attract new guests?'

Marianna pursed her lips as Gabi pushed on. 'Some of the hotels I work with actually organise in advance for their floral displays to tie in with the bridal theme...'

'The Grande Lucia does not compete with other hotels,' Marianna said. 'We're already at the top.'

Thanks to Alim, Gabi thought.

And Marianna was arrogant in her assumption that just because they were successful they could ignore competition.

For a very long while, before Alim had taken over, the hotel had struggled. Mona had been right in her description—the hotel had looked tired and many a potential bride had turned up her nose when the venue had been suggested. Oh, it was because of Alim that the Grande Lucia was now thriving and everyone knew it.

'I hear it will soon be under new ownership,' Gabi said.

'Yes, Alim is bringing potential buyers through over the weekend.'

'He's here?' Gabi squeaked, and then quickly recovered. Her voice had sounded too urgent, her words a demand, and she fought to relax herself. 'I thought that he was back in the Middle East?'

'For the most part he is there,' Marianna agreed. 'But this an important weekend. Today Signor Raul Di Savo is in residence and has free rein to look around; tomorrow it will be Signor Bastiano Conti.'

Gabi felt her heart sink a little. Hotels often took ages to sell but these were two serious names in the industry. Matrimoni di Bernadetta had held many weddings at Raul's boutique hotel here in Rome, and Gabi knew that Bastiano was also a formidable player in the industry.

'If you come across either of them, please be polite,' Marianna said.

'Of course.'

'They may have questions for you.'

Gabi nodded.

'And, please, ensure that all deliveries are discreet and that there is minimal disturbance to our guests. Alim is soon to marry so he wants the Grande Lucia off his hands as quickly as possible.'

Gabi just sat there.

She had read about it, of course, but it hurt to hear it voiced.

Even Alim had said that they could only last for a year because he had commitments back home.

How she wished they had had that year.

Or maybe not, Gabi thought as she sat there, trying to fathom being closer to him than she had been that night, knowing him more, loving him more...

For, yes, despite the anger and pain, Gabi now knew that it was love.

At least on her side.

'Gabi?' Marianna frowned because it was clear their meeting was over yet Gabi had made no move to leave. 'Was there anything else?'

'I don't think so.'

There could be no hope for them.

It was a very busy day spent liaising with the florists and soothing a temperamental head chef when she informed him that there had been some last-minute food preferences called in.

'I already have the updated list,' he told her.

'No,' Gabi said. 'There are more.'

A lot more.

And the head chef was not happy, declaring, as if it were her fault, that the world had gone gluten-free.

The gowns and outfits arrived and it was for Gabi to organise that tomorrow they would be sent to the correct suites.

She spoke with the make-up artist and hairdressers too, ensuring that every detail for tomorrow was in place.

Oh, she was tired, and there was still so much to be done.

Gabi headed to the ballroom to check on the set-up.

'There are some more changes to be made to the seating,' Bernadetta said by way of greeting. 'The ex-wife doesn't want to be near the aunt...'

Gabi sighed; she had been working on the seating into the small hours of last night and the bride constantly rang in her changes.

'I'll leave you to take it from here,' Bernadetta told Gabi. She didn't even pretend now to be sick, or to be meeting with a client. She simply waltzed off and left it all to Gabi.

It was late Friday afternoon and most people were just finishing up for the weekend yet Gabi's work had barely begun. Bernadetta would appear tomorrow, around eleven, just as the guests started to arrive.

One benefit of Bernadetta being gone, though, was that she could take off her shoes, which Gabi did; the high heels were not ideal and after a day of wearing them her back was starting to ache.

This weekend would be, Gabi was sure, her last real chance to tell Alim she was pregnant before the baby was born. Matrimoni di Bernadetta did not have another wedding at the Lucia for three months. She would have had her baby by then and the Grande Lucia could well be sold.

Gabi honestly did not know what to do.

His power scared her and, if she was honest, Alim's cruel dismissal still angered her; furthermore, he had made it very clear that he did not want any consequence from that night.

A kick beneath her ribs made Gabi smile.

As tiny as her baby was, it certainly made itself known.

At her ultrasound, Gabi had chosen not to find out what she was having. Not because she wasn't curious, more she did not want the baby's sex to have any bearing on the conversation, if she told Alim.

If she told him.

She was still troubled and unsure as to what to do.

Gabi stood in the ballroom and looked at the shower of stars that the chandelier created and recalled the bliss of dancing right here, alone with Alim, and how deeply happy she had been that night.

It brought her such pleasure to recall it.

The photographer had not forgotten and indeed the

image of the two of them that night now lived on her tablet. It had been her screensaver for a while but that had proved too painful, so she had taken it down and now Gabi barely looked at it.

It had always hurt too much to do so, but time perhaps *was* kind, because Gabi hadn't really been able to recall, with clarity, the bliss of them together.

Until now.

But on this afternoon, with her baby wriggling inside her, she remembered how the shadows of the branches outside had crept across the walls, how Alim had, without a word, asked her to dance.

Yes, Gabi was a dreamer, but it was a memory that she was lost in now.

And that was how he found her.

It had been a busy day for Alim.

And a hellish few months.

His sister Yasmin had created her own share of scandal at the wedding all those months ago, and Alim had been trying his best to sort that out.

Also, he had known the moment that diktat had been invoked that it would be impossible to be around Gabi and not want her. He took the laws of his land seriously. Now he walked into the ballroom with the first of the potential buyers and there was Gabi, holding her shoes and gazing up.

It was safer, far safer that she be gone.

'Is everything okay, Gabi?' Alim asked her, and his words were a touch stern.

'Oh!'

She turned and for the first time since that morning she saw him.

He was wearing a dark navy suit and looked stunning

as usual; she had never felt more drab, standing barefoot in an ill-fitting suit.

He was with a man she recognised as Raul Di Savo.

Gabi pushed out a smile and tried to be polite but her heart was hammering.

'Yes, everything is fine. I was just trying to work out the table plan for Saturday.'

'We have a large wedding coming up,' Alim explained to Raul.

'And both sets of parents are twice divorced.' Gabi gave a slight eye-roll, and then chatted away as she bent to put on her shoes, trying to keep things about work. 'Trying to work out where everyone should be seated is proving—'

'Gabi!' Alim scolded, and then turned to Raul. 'Gabi is not on my staff. *They* tend to be rather more discreet.' He waved his hand in dismissal. 'Excuse us, please.'

Just like that he dismissed her.

He knew that he had hurt her, for that morning she had left there had been so much promise between them and now she looked at him with funeral eyes. Alim could see the pain and bewildered confusion there.

He wanted to wave his hand to Raul and tell him to get the hell out of the ballroom. He wanted to take her to bed.

She did not leave quietly.

Gabi slammed the door on her way out and Alim and Raul stood in the ballroom with the lights dancing in the late afternoon sun.

'What is the real reason you are selling?' Raul asked him.

Raul knew the business was thriving and he wanted to know why Alim was letting it go. And Raul knew too that Alim could so easily outsource the management of the hotel as he moved his portfolio back to the Middle East.

Alim had brought him here to give the true answer, and now he tried to drag his mind back to the sale, yet Gabi's fragrance hung in the air, along with the memory of their dance.

'When I bought the hotel those had not been cleaned in years,' Alim said, gesturing to the magnificent lights and remembering when the moon had lit them. 'Now they are taken down regularly and cared for properly. It is a huge undertaking. The room has to be closed so no functions can be held, and it is all too easy to put it off.'

'I leave all that to my managers to organise,' Raul said.

Alim nodded. 'Usually I do too, but when I took over the Grande Lucia there had been many cost-cutting measures. It was slowly turning into just another hotel. It is not just the lighting in the ballroom, of course. What I am trying to explain is that this hotel has become more than an investment to me. Once I return to my homeland I shall not be able to give it the attention it deserves.'

'The next owner might not either,' Raul pointed out.

'That is his business. But while the hotel is mine I want no part in her demise.'

'Now you have given me pause for thought,' Raul admitted.

'Good.' Alim smiled. 'The Grande Lucia deserves the best caretaker. Please,' Alim said, indicating that their long day of meetings had come to an end, for he needed badly to be alone, 'take all the time you need to look around and to enjoy the rest of your stay.'

Alim walked out of the ballroom and he was conflicted.

So badly he wanted to seek her out. More worryingly, though, he wanted to work out a chance for them. The only place they could speak was the desert.

He could just imagine Gabi's reaction if he suggested that!

He was informed that Bastiano Conti, who had flown in from Sicily, had just arrived at the hotel. They were, in fact, friends, and would often hit the casinos and clubs together. Those carefree days were gone now, yet they were not the ones Alim craved.

It was one woman, and the hope for one more night with her that could be his undoing.

Alim went and greeted Bastiano and was grateful to hear that he had plans for tonight and would be entertaining guests.

'We will meet tomorrow?' Bastiano checked, and Alim was about to agree.

The hotel had to be sold after all and Raul seemed set to decline.

Yet Alim's problems were greater than real estate, and he watched his friend and potential buyer raise a surprised eyebrow as Alim, usually the consummate host, rearranged their plans.

'Bastiano, I deeply apologise, but I am going to have to reschedule the viewing. I have to return to my country tonight.'

There was not a hope of being in the same country, let alone the same building, as Gabi, and abiding by the rules.

His rapid departure from the Grande Lucia was unnecessary, though, because Gabi was no longer in the building.

By the time his private jet lifted into the sky, she was in the infirmary.

She had closed the ballroom door loudly on Alim, and at first had thought it was the shock of seeing him and being treated so coldly that had her doubling over.

It was then that her waters had broken.

The staff at the Grande Lucia were more than used to slight dramas unfolding and to handling them discreetly, though Anya was clearly shocked.

'You're pregnant?' she asked in surprise.

'Is there anyone I can call for you?' she continued as she ushered Gabi into a small room behind Reception.

'Not yet.'

Oh, she would have to let Bernadetta know but Gabi could not even think of her now.

And, yes, she would have to tell her mother, but Carmel's anger and resentment had hurt Gabi so much already.

She just wanted to be alone now.

They waited for the ambulance to arrive and as they did, need spoke for her as inadvertently she said his name.

'Alim…' Gabi gasped.

'Don't worry,' Anya reassured her, assuming that Gabi was upset that she might have created a problem for the smooth running of the hotel, especially when he was showing potential buyers around. 'No one saw what happened. Anyway, he has already left.'

'Left?'

'He flew back to his country a little while ago. Do you want me to call Marianna and let her know what is going on?'

Gabi didn't answer.

She was just trying to take in the news that Alim had gone.

A part of her had hoped that having seen her again in the ballroom he might later seek her out.

It would appear not.

Alim could not make it any clearer that he had no interest in her.

The ambulance did not come to the main entrance,

for that might be distressing or cause disruption to some of the guests.

Gabi left by the trade entrance, to bear the child of both the owner of the Grande Lucia and Sultan of Zethlehan.

'It's too soon,' she pleaded to the doctor at the hospital as she fought not to bear down, but time was no longer being kind.

Like endless waves submerging her, there was no pause, no time to catch her breath and calm her racing mind.

Alim.

She wanted his presence and to be held once again in his arms.

Yet she had chosen not to tell him, and whether it would have made a difference or not, this night she gave birth alone.

As she screamed, her mind flashed to Fleur, who had taken this lonely journey also.

And she would never be her, Gabi swore.

Her daughter was born a short while later.

She was delivered onto her stomach and, instead of being whisked away, her little girl was vigorous and Gabi was able to hold her to her chest and gaze down at her daughter.

Oh, she was beautiful, with silky black hair and dark eyes that were almond-shaped, like her father's.

'We have to take her now to the nursery,' the nurse informed Gabi, and it physically hurt to let her baby go.

Soon, though, her mother arrived and it was comforting to make up.

'You have me,' Carmel said.

'I know.'

It felt good to know that, and there were other things to be grateful for.

The baby was strong. So strong, the nurse told her when Gabi got in to see her, for she breathed with just a little oxygen for assistance.

'Do you have a name for her?' Gabi was asked.

Gabi had thought she was having a son; she had been so sure that history was about to repeat itself, and that, like Fleur, she would bear the Sultan's firstborn son.

But history had not repeated itself.

Still, she was absolutely beautiful, a little ray of light, and Gabi knew in that moment what to call her.

'Lucia.'

'That's such a pretty name,' the nurse said.

It was the place where love had been made.

Alim needed to know that he had a daughter, Gabi was painfully aware of that. But not now, not when she was so emotional and drained. Gabi was scared of what she might agree to. When she was stronger, she would work out how on earth to tell him.

Her mother came into the nursery to see her grand-daughter. It was close to midnight and Carmel had been running errands for Gabi—packing a case and also letting Bernadetta know that not only would her very efficient assistant wedding planner not be there tomorrow but that there had also been a lot left undone tonight.

'Bernadetta is not best pleased,' she told Gabi. 'She wants to know if you sorted out the table plan.'

'No,' Gabi said, and she got back to gazing at her daughter.

Bernadetta, for once, could sort it all out.

Lucia was Gabi's priority now.

And always would be.

Whatever the future held.

CHAPTER NINE

'THE CONTRACTS ARE *still* with Bastiano?' Alim frowned when Violetta gave him the news. 'This should all have been dealt with by now.'

Despite Alim's rapid departure, an offer on the Grande Lucia had been made and accepted, but nearly three months later the sale seemed to have stalled.

Alim needed the hotel gone!

He sat in his sumptuous office in the palace and tried to take care of business with a mind that was elsewhere.

Seeing Gabi again had proved to be his undoing.

Temptation beckoned more with each passing day but never more so than now.

A wedding was being held there this weekend and Matrimoni di Bernadetta was the company that had been hired for the event.

The itinerary was open on his computer and Alim scrolled through it, hoping for a glimpse of her name, or a note that she might have left in the margins, as Gabi often did.

There was none, though.

'Do you want me to contact his attorney?' Violetta asked, but Alim shook his head.

'I will speak with Bastiano myself,' Alim said.

He might even speak with him face to face.

Alim was sorely tempted to summon the royal jet, with the excuse of meeting with Bastiano, but really for the chance to see Gabi.

He was dangerously close to breaking the diktat.

'That will be all,' Alim said, and, having dismissed Violetta, he attempted to deal with the day's correspondence.

He didn't get very far.

It had been months since he had seen Gabi again but the feelings had not faded.

If anything, they had intensified for, despite the pressure his father and the elders exerted, Alim was no closer to agreeing to a wedding.

His mind was in Rome, rather than here in Zethlehan, where it should belong.

He thought of the days he had loved most at the Grande Lucia.

Gabi, arriving early in the morning, and how she would become increasingly frazzled throughout the working day.

And he thought too of the wedding nights, and how she would finally relax again and enjoy watching the show she had produced.

He missed her.

Not the risqué life he had once led, but the small moments that were now long gone—stepping through the brass doors and seeing her sitting in the lounge with Marianna. Knowing that there would be another wedding soon and the chance to see her again had brought him more pleasure than he had realised at the time.

His times at the hotel had been made better by her— the scent of flowers coming from the ballroom and Gabi directing brass trolleys laden with gifts and arrangements...

Alim missed those times.

And they would soon be gone for ever.

He had done all he could to sever his ties to Rome, yet it felt as if his heart had been left there.

He looked up as his mother knocked at his open office door and he shook his head.

'Not now,' Alim said.

'Yes, now,' Rina said and came in.

He had always been polite—if a little distant—with others, though now he was stone cold.

The vast palace felt too small, and there was no company that he wished to keep.

Unless it was Gabi's.

'How are you, Alim?'

Alim didn't even bother to lie and pretend that he was fine, he just gave a shrug. 'I am trying to chase up the contracts for the Grande Lucia. I think I might need to make a trip to Italy.'

'When?'

'Soon,' Alim said.

He would be courting temptation if he went back this weekend, Alim knew, yet he had to see Gabi.

'I have just held the morning meeting with your father. He thinks that a wedding would cheer Yasmin up.'

'I am not going to marry to provide a remedy for my sister's mood.'

'What about your mood, Alim?' Rina said. 'You are not happy.'

'No,' he admitted. 'But I do not need to be happy to do my work.' And there was indeed work to be done so he gestured for his mother to take a seat. 'Kaleb's thirtieth is coming up...'

But his mother was not here about that. 'I am concerned, Alim. I thought once you were home you might be happy, but it has been months now...'

'I love my land.'

'Yet you make no commitment to remain here?'

'You mean a bride?' Always the conversation led back to that. 'A bride is not the solution.'

'Then tell me the problem.'

'No.'

He did not share his thoughts, let alone his feelings, with others. In fact, until recently he had refused to examine them.

Life had always been about duty and work and solving problems logically.

Now, for the first time in his life, he could not come up with a solution to the dilemma he faced.

'Alim,' his mother implored. 'Speak to me.'

He did not know how to start.

'I might understand,' Rina insisted.

Yes, she just might, Alim thought, for there was no doubt that hers was a loveless marriage.

'Just before the diktat was invoked I met someone,' Alim said, but, even as he explained things, he knew that wasn't quite right. 'I have liked her for a couple of years but I always stayed back. Things got more serious just before I was summoned home. I left her without any real explanation and when I returned to Rome the other month…'

He didn't finish. Alim could not explain the sadness in Gabi's eyes, neither did he want to reveal the ache in his heart and the regret for the year together that had been denied them.

Alim knew it could never have been more than a year; his father would never give his approval to Gabi.

No, his bride would be from Zethlehan. In fact, his father had whittled it down to the final three—the one who would uphold tradition and best serve the country, and was deeply schooled in their ways, would be Oman's choice.

'I am thinking of going to Rome to see her.'

His mother was quiet for some considerable time and when she spoke her voice was strained and laced with fear. 'Have you broken the diktat, Alim?'

'No.'

He heard his mother breathe out in relief. 'That's good, then.'

'How can it be good?'

All that mattered to them was that he abided by the rules, no matter the cost to himself.

'There is a desert out there, Alim,' Rina said, and he stood and looked out the window; the reproach in his voice was aimed at himself, for of course he had considered it.

'Gabi will not be coming to the desert. She would never even entertain the thought.'

'She does not have to reside there,' Rina said. 'She could visit now and then and once you are married, once you have an heir...' It was a difficult conversation to have. 'Well, then the rules relax.'

And he threw his mother a look. 'Do you think I would do to my wife what my father did to you?'

The poorly kept secret was finally being discussed.

'I would never impose a loveless marriage on a bride,' Alim said, and then he closed his eyes because that was exactly what it would be, and the reason that, despite mounting pressure, still he refused marriage. 'I hate how you have been treated,' Alim told his mother.

He thought of them smiling on the palace balcony or waving and chatting as they arrived at a function.

Then the relative silence that would descend when

they returned to their private lives—his mother would retreat to her wing, his father to his.

'Do I look unhappy, Alim?' Rina asked.

He looked over. No, her features were relaxed and, as she often did, Rina smiled her gentle smile.

'You barely communicate,' Alim pointed out, but his mother shook her head. 'I have just come from a meeting with your father—we have one each working day.'

Alim accepted that, but that was for the running of the country—a private life between them did not exist. 'You sleep in a separate wing of the palace.'

'And we do so at my request,' Rina said. 'Alim, I love my country. Growing up, I always knew that I would likely be chosen and that I would one day be queen. I did my duty, I had three beautiful children who I have raised well; I continue to work hard for my country and I live a very privileged life.'

Rina knew she needed to say more.

Oh, she was very schooled in the rules, and had studied them closely.

Yes, Zethlehan was progressive in many ways, for *all* needs were served.

Save love, for it was not taken into consideration in the rules.

Still, it was a delicate topic and Rina took a moment to consider before she spoke on. 'Alim, just because I don't have a loving marriage, it does not mean that I don't know love.'

Distracted by his thoughts of Gabi, it took a moment for his mother's words to sink in and he looked up at her.

Was she telling him that she had a lover?

That the times her husband was away were not so lonely after all, that she had her own reasons for sleeping in a separate wing of the palace?

The silence between them was loaded but Rina gave a slight shake of her head. 'I am saying no more than that.'

It was as if every grain of desert sand had shifted as his mother told him without detail that she was happy. That somehow their relationship had been made to work for them.

'Your father and I have made it work for everyone...' Then she saw Alim's jaw tighten and amended, 'I do feel sorry for James,' she admitted. 'He deserves more of his father.' It was the first time his name had been spoken within these walls. 'That should have been handled better, but it is your father who makes the rules.'

Alim nodded.

'Talk to your love, Alim.'

'I did not say anything about love.'

'Talk to your lover, then. That is the one solution to all ills.'

'How?' he asked. 'She would never come to the desert.'

'I have studied this very closely.' Rina smiled and tapped the hated large, leather-bound file that sat on his desk. 'There is nowhere in the diktat that mentions phones.'

Alim smiled.

'If anyone can sort things out, it is you.'

Alim was not so sure but he knew that neither distance nor silence was working.

And it was for that reason that he picked up the phone and, rather than chase up Bastiano regarding the sale, he called the reception desk at the Grande Lucia.

'*Pronto.* May I speak with Gabi?'

'Gabi?' The female voice that answered was an unfamiliar one and didn't seem to know to whom Alim was referring.

'She is organising a wedding there,' he explained.

'Oh, that Gabi!' came the response, and it was clear that she now knew who Alim meant. 'I think she is still on maternity leave.'

'Maternity leave?'

The palace must be sitting on a fault line, Alim thought, because for the second time in an hour the sands seemed to shift.

'I think you have the wrong person,' he said, but the receptionist wasn't listening—she was talking to a colleague. Alim could hear his rapid breathing as in the background a male voice spoke and then the receptionist amended her words.

'No, no, my mistake.'

Alim didn't even have a chance to register relief before she spoke again.

'Apparently Gabi is back from her leave today.'

Alim's mind worked rapidly,

If indeed Gabi had been on maternity leave then the baby *had* to be his. It was practically nine months to the day since they had slept together and she had certainly been a virgin then.

Yet the dates confused him. Alim certainly wasn't an expert in pregnancy, but this woman was telling him that Gabi was already *back* from maternity leave.

Alim thought of the last time he had seen Gabi and she hadn't looked pregnant, but, then again, he had done all he could not to look at her.

Alim knew that he had to speak with Gabi.

Alone.

But how?

A possibility was starting to come to mind and when he spoke his voice was even and calm, for Alim rarely revealed his emotions.

'Actually, rather than Gabi, may I speak with Bernadetta?'

'Can I ask who is calling?'

'It is Alim.'

He heard her nervous gasp. 'Sultan al—'

Alim spoke over her, for his patience was running out. 'Just get Bernadetta on the line.'

He stood and, just as he had needed air the day his father had invoked the diktat, he walked out of the French windows and onto the large balcony.

Unlike then, the air was not cool, it was hot and dry, though it was calming to Alim and he gladly breathed it in, his eyes narrowing against the fierce sun as he looked out at the desert.

He could speak with Gabi there, unheard by others; only there could they discuss things fully.

There was no doubt a frantic search was under way at the Grande Lucia for the rather elusive Bernadetta and it gave time for Alim's plans to take better shape.

'Pronto,' he said when a nervous Bernadetta finally came to the phone.

'Sultan Alim...' Bernadetta attempted to purr into the phone but it was more of a croak. 'How lovely to hear from you. It's been a long time.'

'Indeed. I was wondering,' Alim said, 'if Matrimoni di Bernadetta had the necessary skills to co-organise a royal wedding here in Zethlehan.'

He heard her slight gasp. 'Of course. It would be not just an honour but a pleasure...' Bernadetta fawned but Alim swiftly broke in.

'Then I need Gabi here by tomorrow,'

'Gabi? Oh, no, I wouldn't be sending my assistant!' Bernadetta immediately responded. 'I would take care of every detail myself—'

'Bernadetta,' Alim interrupted her again. 'You have a good head for business and you hire only the best, but we both know that it is Gabi who turns a wedding into an unforgettable creation.'

He soothed her vast ego yet he got to the point.

'I want Gabi here.'

'Indeed, she's excellent, but Gabi might not be available to travel at short notice. You see, she has recently—'

Alim swiftly cut in. He did not want Bernadetta to reveal that Gabi had just had a baby. Alim was very well aware that should Gabi find out that he knew, there would not be a hope in hell of getting her to agree to come to Zethlehan.

Yet he wanted Gabi to tell him to his face.

'I don't care how busy she is with the current wedding. I do not care about her personal life and whether she has plans that she cannot change. If you want the contract for the wedding, then Gabi is to be here by tomorrow.'

Alim spoke like the Sultan he was and Bernadetta responded accordingly.

'And she shall be.'

Alim let out a breath and there followed a giddy sensation of relief that had nothing to do with what he had just discovered.

More that he would finally see Gabi.

She had been missed more than even Alim had wanted to admit.

'If, when you meet with Gabi,' Bernadetta said, 'you have any concerns…'

'I shan't be meeting with Gabi,' Alim said, anticipating Gabi's resistance to the suggestion that she come here. 'I am only making this initial contact. I don't want to be troubled with minor details. From now on, everything will be dealt with by the palace aide, Violetta.'

He gave Bernadetta a few more rapid details and then ended the call.

He looked out at the desert again and the golden sight soothed, for there solutions could more readily be found.

Alim walked back into his office, trying to take in that he could well be a father and trying to fathom all that Gabi would have been through.

He summoned Violetta.

She was more than used to dealing with scandal and had her work cut out for her in dealing with the al-Lehans.

And not just his father and James, Alim now knew, for it would seem that even his mother had a secret life of her own. One that Alim had had no clue about.

A baby.

He did not know if it was a boy or girl and Alim knew all the problems it could create.

Yet as he waited for Violetta to arrive, despite the news, his overriding feeling was relief.

Gabi would be here soon.

He looked up as Violetta came in and, without asking, she closed the door and came over to the desk.

'I require your discretion,' Alim said.

'You have it.'

Violetta, too, was brilliant at her job.

CHAPTER TEN

'GABI! GABI!'

Bernadetta was almost running through the foyer towards her.

Gabi was carrying a glass vase containing an array of Sahara roses to take up to the bridal suite.

Housekeeping should have already dealt with it but things at the Grande Lucia had got a little slack now that Alim wasn't around.

'Yes?' she answered wearily.

It was Gabi's first official day back at work and it felt as if she had never been away.

It had been hard leaving Lucia but her mother had promised to drop by with her at lunchtime so that Gabi could give her a cuddle.

Gabi could only hope there was time to actually take her lunch break!

There were so many boxes not ticked and a lot of things that should have long ago been taken care of which had been left for Gabi's return; she had just this minute come from a stand-up row with the very temperamental chef.

'I know this will come as a shock…' Bernadetta said, and Gabi stopped herself from rolling her eyes—there had been so many shocks this morning!

The cake had been confirmed for *next* Saturday, Gabi had found out.

The flowers had not, as Gabi had first thought, gone missing; instead, they had been delivered, as per Matrimoni di Bernadetta's instructions, to last week's wedding venue.

Chaos was all around.

The chef had not been informed that there were not only eighteen guests requiring the gluten-free option but that there were four vegans, two raw vegans, four kosher and five halal.

No, there was very little that might come as a shock, save that the groom had run off!

Gabi was about to be proved wrong.

'Matrimoni di Bernadetta has been invited to co-organise Sultan Alim's wedding...'

Gabi nearly dropped the vase.

What the hell was Alim thinking?

Or, more likely, he wasn't thinking, at least not about her.

His wedding needed to be organised and he had simply called on the best, without any consideration of the pain that it might cause her.

But then Bernadetta spoke on.

'Alim has asked that you fly there tomorrow and meet with his assistant.'

This time Gabi did drop the vase, for there was no one crueller in that moment than Alim.

It shattered loudly as it hit the floor and the water and crystal was strewn along with the gorgeous roses.

Gabi barely looked down and neither did Bernadetta.

'I can't,' Gabi said. 'It's impossible. I have a new baby...'

'I know that,' Bernadetta said.

'I can't leave her.' And then fear clutched at her heart because maybe Alim knew. Maybe he was planning for her to bring the baby… 'Lucia hasn't had all her inoculations.'

'Oh, for God's sake,' Bernadetta snorted. 'Do you really think I'd send you with a baby on such an important job?'

'Did you tell Alim about her?' Gabi was on her knees and trying not to cry as she scrabbled to pick up the crystal, her mind racing in fear as she thought of Alim plotting to whisk Lucia away.

Yes, Gabi was a dreamer, and some of them were nightmares.

'Of course I didn't tell the Sultan. Why would he care? This is a royal wedding he's asking us to organise.' Bernadetta was nearly shouting. 'He doesn't want to hear about your personal life.'

'I don't want to go,' Gabi said. 'Send someone else.'

'Alim wants you, though. He says you have an eye for attention and…' Bernadetta almost choked on her next words. 'He told me that he wants you adequately remunerated…' And then she told her the figure that Alim was offering just for this short trip.

Was this his way of apologising? Gabi wondered. Was this Alim's strange way of making amends?

As Sophie came over to help clear up the mess that had been made, Gabi sank back on her heels for a second and tried to make sense of things, not that Bernadetta gave her a moment to gather her thoughts.

'Gabi, if you cost me this contract, don't even bother turning up for work again. And don't think I shan't tell everyone that you were the one who blew the deal.'

Bernadetta stalked off and Gabi just sat there.

'I can mop around you.' Sophie smiled and then she helped Gabi up.

'I don't want to leave my baby.'

'Then don't go,' Sophie said. 'Tell her to get lost.'

And Gabi smiled because Sophie was Sicilian and rather feistier than she, but then Gabi's smile wavered and tears were dangerously close. 'I don't want to organise his wedding.'

She had said too much, Gabi knew, but Sophie was her dear, dear friend, though even she did not guess that Alim was Lucia's father.

'Did you have a crush on him?' Sophie asked.

Yes, he was as unattainable to the likes of Gabi as that.

Her mother, when she brought in Lucia, wasn't exactly gushing with excitement at the prospect of her daughter flying off to the Middle East.

They met in the foyer and there was only time for a very brief cuddle with Lucia as she told her mother the news.

'Gabi, isn't it time you looked for a more practical job?'

'I love my work,' Gabi said. 'I'm good at what I do.'

'Of course, but some dreams you have to let go of when you have a baby. When I found out I was pregnant with you I had to give up my studies...'

Gabi closed her eyes, she had heard it all many times before.

Only history wasn't repeating itself.

She held Lucia to her cheek and breathed in the soft baby scent.

If anything, Lucia made her want to achieve more; her love for her daughter drove Gabi to be better rather than less. And, yes, it would be hard to leave her, but the money would certainly help, as well as the boost to her career.

But more than that, so much more than that, she would be able to tell Lucia her history for she would have seen Alim's country first hand.

Gabi had grown up not knowing anything about her father; her daughter would not suffer the same fate.

'Are you able to look after Lucia for two nights?'

'You know I shall.'

Gabi thanked her mother. She knew Lucia would be beautifully taken care of, and though it was her first concern it wasn't the only one—Gabi wanted to be very sure she wasn't walking into a trap.

So, to be sure, she called the number she had been given by Bernadetta.

Violetta's voice was familiar and Gabi recalled that she had dealt with the hotel arrangements for Marianna when Mona and James had married.

Now Gabi knew why.

'Alim is concerned that his European guests will not understand Zethlehan ways,' Violetta explained. 'He said that you have a good eye for detail. We want the wedding to be seamless and all the guests' needs attended to.'

'Who shall I be liaising with?'

'Mainly me, but also the hotel manager at the venue where the commoner guests shall be housed. That is where you shall be staying during this visit, so you can work from a visual.'

'I see.'

There was no firm date yet but Violetta ran through the guest list. Some of the names were familiar. Bastiano Conti was amongst them and Gabi knew he was not just a friend of Alim's but about to be the new owner of the Grande Lucia.

It sounded legit.

Yes, it was more lavish and complex than anything she had dealt with before but, at the end of the day, it sounded like just another wedding to plan.

And so for now she dealt with it as such.

'Where will the service be held?'

'There will be two services,' Violetta explained. 'A small, very intimate gathering of family and elders, but we would take care of that. Following the formal service there will be a large reception back at the palace. We need you to help transport the guests and to ensure that they wear suitable attire.' She went through the dress codes with Gabi. 'Also, all dietary requirements from them must come through you.'

Yes, just like any other wedding!

'When you are here,' Violetta continued, 'you can speak with the palace head chef, so it might be helpful if you could bring some menu suggestions that he can incorporate. The banquet will be traditional but we want alternatives that can cater to all palates.'

'I see.' Gabi swallowed and forced herself to delve a little deeper. 'When I get there and speak to Sultan Alim I can ask him—'

'Oh, no,' Violetta quickly broke in. 'While I understand that you worked alongside the Sultan at the Grande Lucia, things are very different here. You will not have access to the Sultan; you will deal directly with me.'

And that was the real reason she agreed.

Gabi needed contacts, and not of the usual kind, and Violetta would be a very good one to have. One day she would be ready to tell Alim about Lucia and, as she was fast finding out, you didn't just call up a palace and ask to be put through to the Sultan.

And so, to Bernadetta's delight, Gabi said yes.

'You need to go home and prepare.' Bernadetta, for the first time ever, insisted that Gabi leave early. 'You have black trousers…?' she checked.

Gabi's curves had returned and she felt Bernadetta's disapproval as she looked over her figure.

'I do.'

She just hoped they would fit.

'What about this wedding?' Gabi asked Bernadetta. 'There's still so much to be done.'

'I think I can manage,' Bernadetta said, 'though if you could sort out the flowers before you go…'

Lazy to the last, Gabi thought.

Sophie found her a new vase and Gabi's hands were shaking as she rearranged the flowers. She heard an email ping in.

Gabi saw that it was from Violetta and picked up her tablet to read it. She would fly tomorrow at midday and the flight was first class.

It was all a little overwhelming.

Not the itinerary and not just leaving little Lucia but that the man she loved was getting married.

How? Gabi thought as she walked out of the office with the flowers. She did not know *how* her heart could still beat while planning his wedding.

'Hey.'

A man called out to her as she went to take the roses up to the bridal suite and, distracted, she nodded at the handsome stranger.

'Gabi!'

He called out her name.

'Oh!' She stopped when she realised that it was Raul, one of the potential buyers for the hotel, and then she remembered how he would know her. 'You were in the ballroom when Alim…' Her voice trailed off as she recalled how Alim had scolded and then dismissed her that day.

It had been the day Lucia had been born!

Oh, she had been cross, so cross with Alim, though this stranger was clearly not to blame for that!

'I'm hoping to meet with Alim.'

'Good luck!' Gabi rolled her eyes. 'He's back home.'

'Oh!'

'For his wedding.'

'I see.'

'I'm planning it, actually.'

She felt as if she was about to cry.

'Can you let him know I need to speak with him?'

'I'm a wedding planner,' Gabi said, and she let a little of her anger out before walking off. 'I don't get access to the Sultan.'

Saying goodbye to Lucia was incredibly hard.

She had already been staying at her mother's this weekend.

Going back to work yesterday and leaving little Lucia for twelve hours had seemed agony at the time but now she would be away for two days and two nights.

One day would be spent travelling to Zethlehan, then a night at a luxurious hotel followed by a day of meetings with Violetta.

The second night would be spent travelling back to Rome and then finally she would see Lucia again.

Gabi had been unable to feed Lucia herself, so there wasn't any problem with that, but it ached to see her little girl asleep in her crib and to know that she was about to leave.

'Don't wake her,' Carmel said, because she could see that Gabi was about to pick her up.

'I'm going to miss her.'

'Gabi, even if you weren't going to Zethlehan you would barely have seen her this weekend, what with the wedding and everything.'

'I know.'

Her hours were proving difficult and Gabi knew she was asking a lot from her mother just to keep her job. Carmel had raised one child alone and did not want to do it again. Right now, there were bills that needed to paid and so Carmel had agreed to help with Lucia for a few months, but after that…

'You could work with Rosa,' Carmel said.

Gabi had considered it, yet, as much as she cared for Rosa, Gabi did not want another boss. Still, it was the more practical solution and right now Gabi was beyond exhausted and could feel her grip loosening on her dreams.

Carmel went down to check if the taxi had arrived and Gabi kissed Lucia's little cheek and whispered that she was the sunshine of her life—*'Sei il sole della mia vita.'*

She wanted better for her, Gabi knew—which was part of the reason she was on her way to a new adventure.

What an adventure!

Gabi had flown before, but only within Italy and only for work.

Bernadetta, of course, would fly business class while Gabi sat way back in the bowels of the plane.

It was very different today!

Champagne was offered before they had even taken off but Gabi declined and took water as she was trying to be good. While the weight had fallen off while she'd been pregnant, Gabi had been thin for about two days after Lucia had been born and then her milk had come in, closely followed by the return of her curves.

A meal was served, then her bed prepared, while Gabi went and put on the pyjamas they offered her.

'Would you like to be woken for a meal before landing?'

It was a nine-hour flight to Zethlehan and Gabi was about to say that there was no chance of her *not* being woken, when again she was reminded that she was without Lucia.

'That would be lovely,' Gabi said.

The cabin lights were dimmed and Gabi lay there, sure, quite sure, that she would be too nervous to sleep.

Instead, she woke to a gentle shake of her shoulder and was informed that her meal would be served shortly; she had slept for seven hours. It wasn't just her first decent sleep since Lucia had been born, it was her first decent sleep since the morning Alim had so cruelly ended things.

Far from nervous, it was so nice to feel rested.

She made her way to the very nice bathroom where there was actually a shower. It felt wonderful to shower high in the sky and after she had washed and brushed her teeth and styled her hair, she took her Pill. Not that she would be needing it, but Gabi now took it every day. Not for this moment, and not to be ready for Alim, more because the absolute abandon between them that night had scared her.

In the cold light of day, she had realised that in bed with Alim she did not know her own mind.

In the deep of the night he had owned her so completely.

The absolute lack of thought and control had had her vow never to be so foolish again. No more chances.

Then she put on the heavy dark trouser suit and swore that if she ever did get her own business there would be a fitting, international choice.

Gabi returned to her seat and light refreshments and as she looked out over the ocean, Gabi amended that thought.

When she had her own business.

Sleep really was an amazing healer, and the distance from home combined with the white noise of the plane allowed her to think more clearly.

Alim had been harsh that morning when they had spoken and he had said that her mother used Gabi as an excuse. Yet he wasn't necessarily wrong.

Gabi didn't dwell on her mother's choices. She focussed instead on her own future, and her daughter's, for it was Lucia's future she wanted to improve upon too.

But first she had these days to get through.

Would she see him?

Gabi hoped so.

All the hurt, all the anger and the fact he was to marry should be enough to bury for good her feelings for him.

Yet they rose again and again, and more so since Lucia had been born, for every time she opened her eyes Gabi was reminded of the magic of him.

And the impossibility of them.

There were cross-winds, the pilot had warned them, and Gabi felt them as the plane came into land.

Her stomach lurched as she caught her first glimpse of the palace and it warned her of the might and power of the al-Lehan family.

It rose from a cliff edge, white and magnificent and looking out towards both ocean and city. And Zethlehan too was unexpected when seen from the air, for there was an eclectic mix of gleaming modern buildings that melded in with the old.

She had read up on the country's history and the royal

family's lineage that went as far back as when the country had first been named.

It was progressive in many ways—a firstborn daughter could—and had—ruled this stunning land. The desert princess's husband and children had taken the al-Lehan name. And while there were some mentions of children borne from the harem, the rulings were clear—they were not considered part of the al-Lehan dynasty.

Children like Lucia and James were simply sidelined. They were shadow families, hidden away and never formally recorded or mentioned. Lucia deserved better. So did Gabi.

And she must never lose sight of that, Gabi thought as the wheels hit the runway.

She had arrived in Zethlehan, where the time, she was informed, was five p.m.

Remembering Violetta's instructions, Gabi put a scarf she had brought over her head and shoulders but it didn't fall as nicely, or as effortlessly, as the other women's, who made it look so easy.

She opened her tablet and the first thing she saw was a message from her mother with the most gorgeous picture of Lucia attached.

She was lying on her stomach and lifting her head up and smiling widely. Oh, it was surely Gabi's favourite photo and she touched the screen and traced her daughter's beautiful smile.

Gabi was wearing heels, on Bernadetta's instructions, and felt a head above all the delicate beauties as she disembarked. A wall of heat hit her as soon as she stepped off the plane. The wind was hot on her cheeks and the air burned as she breathed it in, but soon she was in the cool of the airport and she made a quick call home.

'Lucia is fine,' Carmel told her. 'Did you get the picture that I sent?'

'I did.' Gabi smiled.

'The reception is terrible,' Carmel said. 'I can hardly hear you.'

'I'll call again tomorrow,' Gabi told her mother. 'Give Lucia a kiss for me.'

Customs was straightforward as she had a letter of introduction from the palace and, given she had travelled only with hand luggage, in no time she was walking through to the arrivals lounge.

'Gabi!'

She recognised Violetta immediately and though they had only worked together briefly it was nice to see a familiar friendly face.

'How was your journey?' Violetta asked.

'It was wonderful,' Gabi said. 'I slept most of the way.'

'Good.' Violetta nodded. 'It is good that you are well rested. We are heading this way,' she explained. 'We are taking a helicopter.'

'A helicopter?' Gabi checked.

'Of course.'

Violetta said it so casually and Gabi assumed that when you worked with royalty then taking a helicopter must be to Violetta the equivalent of taking a taxi.

The chopper was waiting and Gabi climbed in and fastened her seat belt and put on the headphones that Violetta handed to her.

'It's very windy,' she warned Gabi. 'We might be in for a bit of a bumpy ride.'

Gabi felt her stomach curl as she was lifted high into the sky.

The airport was a little way out from the city and Gabi

looked again at the amazing skyline that she had so recently seen from the plane.

The view was even more stunning than before. The sun was starting to set and the sky was such a blush pink that even the white palace in the distance seemed to have been painted rose. There was a haze over the city but then the helicopter banked to the right and she lost sight of it. Gabi craned her neck for a glimpse of the ocean to orientate herself but the view had disappeared from her window and so she turned her head to look for it on the other side.

It was way in the distance and Gabi felt her nostrils tighten as the palace faded from view.

Gabi looked over at Violetta, who was herself looking out of the window seemingly without concern.

Except even the city skyline had now faded and looking below there was only the occasional old building. 'Where are we going?' she asked Violetta.

There was no response.

Perhaps there were two cities, two palaces, Gabi told herself, while knowing that could not be right. Or maybe the pilot was diverting because of the wind?

Gabi had felt on high alert from the moment that she had agreed to come to Zethlehan but now she had her first taste of pure fear.

'Violetta,' Gabi said, more loudly this time.

Perhaps her microphone wasn't working, because Violetta did not respond to Gabi calling her name.

Now, as she looked out, there was nothing but desert. The sun was low in a burning sky and the endless sand looked like molten gold.

The ride seemed to take for ever, but finally coming into view she could see the billowing white of a desert abode.

* * *

And still Gabi fought for calm as she and Violetta disembarked.

What the hell had Bernadetta been thinking, making her wear heels? Gabi thought as she took off her shoes and then ran beneath the rotors.

'Is the service to be held in the desert?' Gabi asked, still fighting for an ordered reason, still hoping there was a sensible reason to explain why she had been brought here, but her voice was drowned by the rotors. 'Violetta?' she asked, and turned to see that Violetta was not by her side. She had run back under the rotors and was getting back into the chopper.

'Wait…' Gabi shouted.

Violetta did not.

The helicopter lifted into the blazing sky. The sand was a stinging blizzard of tiny, sharp pellets, and Gabi held her arms over her face to shield her eyes, eventually using her jacket to cover her nose and mouth. The soles of her feet were burning.

She had never felt more scared or alone, or more foolish for believing that she had been brought here for work.

And finally, when the helicopter was out of sight and the sands had somewhat settled she stood, windswept and scared but not alone.

There was Alim.

Only it was an Alim that Gabi had never seen.

Always he had been clean shaven, but not now.

Instead of the more familiar suits she was used to seeing him in, Alim wore a black robe and on his head was a *keffiyeh*; he stood utterly still, imposing and straight, and Gabi felt as if she were his prey.

She remembered his father walking through the foyer

and that moment of foreboding as she'd glimpsed the al-Lehans' power, and she felt the absolute full force of it now.

Yes, his prey was exactly what she was—he had sought her, found her and now she was within his grasp. As she stood there, waiting, they were plunged into darkness, for it was as if the desert had swallowed the fierce sun whole.

Gabi ran.

It was a rather stupid thing to do in a darkening desert but for now it didn't matter, she simply wanted to be away from him, only Gabi didn't get very far.

Alim caught up with her easily but so panicked was Gabi she shook off his hand from her arm and attempted to take off again, but she fell to the ground and lay with her head on her arm facing down, knowing that he stood over her.

Knowing there was nowhere to run.

'Gabi.'

His voice was annoyingly calm and terribly, achingly familiar.

Despite his attire, despite the unfamiliar surroundings, he was still the Alim she knew.

Gabi felt soothed when she should not, yet she could taste her panicked tears and feel the conflict for she wanted to turn around.

She wanted again to lift her face to him.

But anger won.

'You set me up,' she shouted, and thumped the ground.

'Come inside.'

'I don't want to come inside!'

Yet when he held out his hand she took it and she stood brushing herself down as the wind whipped her hair into her damp face.

So much for a sophisticated reunion!

'This is kidnap!'

'You are too dramatic.' Alim shrugged.

'Not where I come from. Your assistant told me I would not even have to see you…'

'Violetta ensured discretion,' Alim defended her. 'Don't you want a chance to be together for a while? I know that I do.' He had to shout to make himself heard over the wind. 'Don't you want a chance to speak and to catch up on all that has been going on?'

That was the very last thing that Gabi wanted!

Alim must not find out about Lucia while she was effectively stranded here.

'Come inside,' Alim said again, and the authoritarian note to his voice told her that he would not be argued with.

That did not stop Gabi. 'I don't want to.'

She shouted it but the wind whipped the words straight from her mouth and carried them into the night. Her mouth filled with sand and it was the most pointless argument ever, she knew, for she could not survive out here in this savage land.

Gabi had seen from the sky just how isolated they were.

He offered his hand to walk her back to the tent but Gabi declined it and for a few moments she stood her ground.

Alim would not stand in the fierce winds, attempting to persuade her. If she ran again he would find her in a matter of moments, for Alim knew the desert well and in her cumbersome clothes and winds such as these, Gabi would only manage a few steps.

Still, he was relieved to make it to the entrance and then turn around and sight her.

He waited, and after a short stand-off he could see that Gabi knew she was beaten.

There wasn't really a choice but to go inside and be with Alim.

The desert gave few options, she told herself.

The truth?

Gabi wanted to be with him.

CHAPTER ELEVEN

GABI WAS RELUCTANT to enter.

But for reasons of her own: she was scared she might like it.

Alim stood aside and Gabi stepped into relative silence.

She put down the shoes she carried in her hand, along with the small overnight bag, and felt him walk up behind her.

Her bare feet were caressed by soft rugs; oil lamps gave off a gentle glow that danced along the walls, though bore testimony to the fierce winds outside.

It was a haven indeed.

And she fought to keep her guard raised.

The peregrine note she had first breathed in when they'd danced was more prominent for Gabi now; it hung in the air and enveloped her from all around. It was hard to be scared with Alim so close by her side.

Gabi *was* angry, though.

'There is no one else here,' Alim informed her as he watched her walk through to the main living area.

She looked up at the high ceiling and felt terribly small. 'So there's no point screaming.'

Alim merely sighed. 'Gabi, you really are far too dramatic. What I meant when I said that we are alone is that there is no one here to disturb us and no one to overhear us when we are talking.'

He wanted to make it very clear to Gabi that whatever was said was just between them.

For now.

A baby certainly would change things—Violetta would have even more work cut out for her but at the very least he hoped by the end of this trip Gabi would leave knowing that both she and the baby would be taken care of.

Since he had found out that Gabi had been on maternity leave, Alim had been trying to find out what he could and using his best contacts to garner information.

It had proven surprisingly difficult.

Gabi did not work for the Grande Lucia; however, he had found out that indeed she had been on maternity leave. There was some recent CCTV footage of Gabi in the foyer of the Grande Lucia, speaking with a woman who handed Gabi a baby.

Alim had watched the grainy footage and had found himself holding his breath and zooming in on the image, desperate for a better glimpse of his child.

His child!

A fierce surge of protectiveness had hit him and his plans to bring Gabi to the desert had increased in their urgency.

He still did not know whether it was a boy or a girl.

And, from her silence, Alim was starting to realise that Gabi was in no rush to enlighten him with the news.

'I think,' Alim said, 'there is rather a lot to discuss, don't you?' But Gabi shook her head when he offered an opening for her to tell him.

'I have nothing to say to you.'

He was about to state that that was certainly not the case, but for now Alim chose to bide his time.

She was shocked, he accepted that, and angry too, so he offered her the chance to regroup.

'Why don't you go and get changed?' Alim suggested, and gestured to a curtained area.

'Changed?'

'Have a bath and get changed and then we can speak.'

'Alim, I'm stranded in the desert against my will and you expect me to go and slip into something more comfortable.'

'I don't like that suit.' Alim shrugged. 'And from memory neither do you.'

She just stood there.

The truth was, Gabi didn't really have anything more comfortable to put on.

Well, some pyjamas and another awful black suit and a small tube skirt and top.

Her packing really had been done in haste.

'My suits are all I've really got with me,' she admitted.

'I'm sure there will be alternatives in there.'

Again he gestured to the curtained area but still she did not move.

'Gabi, you are not stranded. If you want me to arrange the helicopter I shall do so, you just have to say the word.'

Gabi didn't, though.

She turned and walked to the area that Alim had gestured to and pulled aside heavy drapes.

It was like stepping inside a giant jewellery box.

The walls were lined with thick red velvet, which she ran her hand over, and jewelled lights dotted the ceiling.

It was a trove of exotic treasures with a huge, beautifully dressed bed in the centre.

She walked over and upon it lay a dark robe. It was

too dark to make out the colour but the fabric when she held it was as soft as the velvet walls.

There was more—a dressing table adorned with stoppered bottles. Gabi picked up one and inhaled the musky fragrance then caught sight of herself in a large gilded mirror.

She looked terrible. Her hair was wild and filled with sand and the mascara she had put on in the bathroom of the plane was halfway down her cheeks.

Gabi looked over to a screened area and curiosity beckoned her to investigate.

The lighting was subtle and it was even darker behind the screen, but she could see a deep bath and it had been filled most of the way. Gabi put in her hand, assuming that the water would be cold.

Yet it was not.

Her fingers lingered, feeling the oily warmth for a moment, and she simply didn't understand so she walked back out to Alim.

He was lying on some cushions, propped up on one elbow and completely unfazed by her rather angry approach.

'You said that there was no one else here.'

'There isn't.'

'So who filled my bath?'

He looked over to where she stood and smiled at the suspicion in her eyes and then the slight startle in them when he gave his response.

'Me.'

'You?'

'The water comes directly from hot desert springs and I added some oils that are supposed to aid in relaxation.'

A slight shiver went through her, albeit a pleasurable

one, as she thought of Alim here alone and readying the place for her arrival. But Gabi was in no mood to relax.

She wanted her wits about her, and knew that she needed to keep every one of them firing in his presence.

'Did you select the robe?' Gabi asked with a slight edge to her voice.

'No,' Alim responded. 'That would be Violetta.'

'So she lays out the clothes for your tarts?'

'Violetta has worked hard to ensure we are both comfortable and alone. We shall dine when you are ready to.'

'I ate on the plane.'

'Then there's no rush. Take your time.'

Gabi hadn't heard those words in a very long time; there simply weren't enough minutes in any day to get all she wanted to done.

Taking her time to get changed for dinner sounded like a reward on its own.

She wanted, for argument's sake, to say something scathing, but there was nothing that came to mind. Gabi wanted to point out that she was here against her wishes.

Yet her wishes said otherwise, for the truth was that she wanted to be there.

'Gabi.' He tried to capture her gaze but she would not let him. 'There is unfinished business between us.'

'I don't know what you mean.'

'Are you saying that you haven't thought of me?' Alim asked.

'I've tried everything I can not to.'

'Did it work?'

No.

Her silence said it for her, but then came the surprise when Alim spoke.

'It didn't work for me either.'

Her eyes flicked to his and she saw the burn of desire

there, and while she was angry it was tempered with relief. Absolute relief, not just at seeing him but that clearly
Alim had wanted to see her again too.

Gabi had ached not only because of the sudden end to
their affair but its lack of closure.

There was so much unanswered.

She'd felt as if she had been slowly going out of her
mind these past months.

Not just about the pregnancy but over and over she
had relived their night together, and the morning after,
like a perpetual film that restarted the moment it was
over, pausing, analysing and trying to work out where it
had all gone wrong.

And she wanted to know.

'Go,' Alim said.

He watched her turn and disappear and he was glad
of it, for there was such dark temptation between them
and that did not make for sensible conversation.

In their months apart he had told himself that possibly he looked back at their time through rose-coloured
glasses and that abstinence had made his memory of her
grow fonder.

Not so.

And consequently he dismissed her.

She turned, and as the drape swished closed behind her
it became a boudoir indeed, Gabi thought as she returned
to the dimly lit cavern.

She took off her suit and top and then her underwear
and there was no feeling of being rushed or concern that
she might be disturbed.

Oh, there were no locks or doors but this space was so
deeply feminine she just knew it had been assigned to her.

Assigned.

Gabi stepped into the bath. She did not like that word, though she knew that it was the correct one.

This mini desert kingdom was a lover's hideaway.

But she would not be his lover tonight.

Her anger at being brought here against her will served only to inflame her temper, and her blood was surely a full degree warmer as she could feel its warm passage through her veins and the weight and heat in her breasts and groin.

She wrenched herself from the bath but there were no towels or sheets to drape herself in and Gabi was certainly not going to ask him for one. And she did not put on the oils left out for her, or the rouge for her lips or kohl.

Instead, she ran a silver comb through her hair and still dripping wet she pulled on the robe over her naked body. It was a deep purple and the scooped neckline showed too much cleavage while the velvet clung to her skin. She could deny to herself her desire for Alim, but the reflection in the mirror stated otherwise.

Her eyes were glittering, her cheeks were flushed and it looked as if she had just come.

Or was about to.

Alim was sitting at a low table and watched as Gabi walked out.

The gown clung becomingly to her skin, her hair fell in one long damp coil and was twisted so that it fell over her right shoulder and dripped onto her breast.

'Oh, you didn't have to go to all this effort,' she teased as she took a seat opposite, assuming Violetta had prepared the treats and she simply hadn't noticed until now.

'Why wouldn't I?'

'I meant,' Gabi said, her voice a touch shrill, 'that clearly Violetta has been busy.'

'I selected the banquet,' Alim said. He picked up a jewelled flask and poured a clear-looking fluid into her glass. As he did so, a citrus scent coiled up in the air. 'And Violetta ensured it was all prepared, as best as it could be. However, while you were bathing I took care of the last-minute details.'

Her eye roll told her she did not believe him for a moment.

'You don't seem to understand the privacy afforded us here,' Alim said as he offered her delicacies. 'A woman is not brought here to work.'

Gabi peeled open the pastry she had selected; it was plump with succulent meat and ripe, pink pomegranate seeds. Gabi understood his words but she would not succumb to seduction. 'Why? Because you don't want her to be too tired for sex?'

He smiled that slow smile and she forgot his might, for he was Alim and they could just as easily be in the Grande Lucia, smiling across the foyer.

'Or too tired for conversation,' Alim said. 'Or too tired to lie on a clear night and look at the stars. There are many reasons other than sex to come deep into the desert. Let's explore them, shall we?'

And Gabi breathed out for he had done it again—just as she'd thought she had scored a point he trumped her.

Sex was the uncomplicated part.

'It has been a long time since we have spoken,' Alim said, inviting conversation.

'I don't think there's anything to discuss.' She gave him a smile then, but it was far from sweet. 'Apart from the reason I'm here—your wedding!' And then the bitter smile faded and for a moment she came close to crumbling and she revealed a little of her pain. 'How cruel you are!'

'Gabi, you are not here to plan my wedding. I invented that, just so that we could be alone.'

'Oh, so you ruin my career because you want a conversation…' She hesitated because the air between them was potent and she knew it was more than conversation they both craved. It was one of the reasons for her defensiveness because even after everything there remained desire. 'What is Bernadetta going to say when I return home without the contract?'

'You will think of something.'

She stared at him in anger and her lips twisted. 'You know how important work is to me.'

'As I said, I am sure you will think of something. So, how has it been?' he pushed for her to open up. 'Work?'

'Much the same.' Gabi selected a plump fig but as the questions began her appetite faded and she found that she was playing with her food.

'Is it still busy?' he asked, knowing she had just come back from leave.

'Extremely.'

She wasn't going to tell him about the baby, Alim realised. He was almost certain the baby must be his but he had to make sure.

'So what else have you been doing with your time?'

Gabi gave a small mirthless laugh before answering him. 'You've lost any right to ask about my personal life.'

'Have you met someone?' he asked. 'Is that why you are so uncomfortable to be here?'

A piece of fruit had just found its way to her mouth and he watched as she furiously swallowed, such was her haste to respond.

'I'm uncomfortable to be here because of what you did to me,' Gabi said, and she knew that tears flashed in her eyes. She wished she had found a more sophisticated answer but the fact was he had landed her in hell that morning. 'We don't all leap out of one bed and dive into the next. You hurt me, Alim, badly. I get that you might have been bored that night and just filling in time...'

'Never.'

'Don't!' Gabi said, and she stood from the table, tired of any attempt at being polite. She was glad, so glad that there were no staff and they were in the middle of the desert because she could say exactly what was on her mind and as loudly as she chose to! 'You'd had me already, Alim,' she shouted. 'I was fully prepared to leave it at that, to walk out the door and go back to being colleagues, yet you offered me a year. And a job. You made it more! And then you took it away. Did it give you a kick?'

'Gabi...' He tried to take her arms, to contain her, but she shook him off.

'And now you decide that you want to see me again. Well, tough, Alim, I don't want to see you.' Great thick tears were streaming down her cheeks, and they both knew that she lied.

It was torture not to see him and agony to be here. He did not move to hold her; instead, he drew her into his arms and it truly was the lesser of two evils because even resisting she sank into them.

'I did not set out to hurt you,' Alim told her.

He could feel her anger and the frantic beating of her heart and then she spoke. 'But you did.'

So badly.

'That morning I went for breakfast with my father and he told me the diktat had been invoked.'

Gabi frowned as she recalled a conversation that had taken place so many months ago. 'The same ruling that happened to your father and Fleur?'

'The same one.'

'Why couldn't you have told me this that morning, and saved all this hurt and pain?'

'Where?' Alim asked. 'In the hotel foyer?'

'No, you have an entire floor of the Grande Lucia at your disposal.'

'But the laws state that I cannot be alone with a woman I desire unless it is my future bride.'

Desire.

The word made her burn, it made her face feel hot and she wanted to press her cheek into the cool of his robe, so she did.

Yet she could feel the heat from his skin and the thud of his heart as he spoke.

'Even to work alongside you and want you would be forbidden. When I was showing Raul through the hotel and I came into the ballroom and you were there, I knew it was imperative that I leave or I would have broken the rules by which I have been raised. I can only take a lover here in the desert.'

'Are you camped out here, then?' she asked, and looked up. He smiled and for a moment so did Gabi. When she met his eyes, the problems of the world faded; when he smiled like that she forgot the hurt and how cross she was.

'I have been to the desert,' Alim said, 'alone.'

'Oh.'

He looked at her and her cheeks went a bit pink because she wanted to know about his alone time in the desert.

'And when I am here I think of you.'

'And the night we shared?' she asked, because when exhausted, when wretched, when aching for the memory to fade, the image of them taunted and sleep was no relief for he was there in her dreams.

'I think of that night,' Alim said, 'and I think of this.'

'This?'

'Us here together.'

He had been fighting not to bring her here for many months.

He pulled her in tighter so she could feel his arousal. His hand slipped to her back and his fingers explored the top of her spine while still his eyes held hers.

Gabi knew she should resist and not be drawn further under his spell, yet at the same time she told herself it would be the last time.

This was the only time she would be in the desert with him for she would never be tricked into being here again.

His mouth brushed hers and she tried to keep her lips pressed together but as their mouths met again she realised that the feel of him had never left her mind.

Alim's hand came to the back of her head and as he pressed her in he gave her his tongue.

She accepted. Deeply.

And she offered hers.

They tasted and claimed each other again, while his other hand slid to her breast and took its aching weight.

'Just once,' she told him.

And Gabi meant it.

This wasn't like a break in her diet, this was her absolute rule.

'Once?' Alim checked, and his fingers slid between her thighs, sliding along the velvet of her robe and then probing her softly.

He made her feel weak with the promise of more.

'I mean one night,' Gabi said as his tongue made indecent work of her ear as she amended her rules. 'One night and that's it. I shan't be your on-call desert lover, Alim.'

Gabi would be more than his desert lover, Alim thought, though he chose not to enlighten her.

With a child between them, once he married she would be his mistress.

Alim just had to tell her, though he felt no guilt withholding that information.

After all, Gabi held the biggest secret of all.

'Come to bed,' Alim said.

There, he had decided she would tell him.

Whatever it took.

CHAPTER TWELVE

THIS TIME THEY made it to the sleeping area, because Alim had decided it would be a more measured seduction.

He was not used to being lied to, or having vital information withheld from him. Not for long anyway.

Alim took her by the hand and led her there.

The wind played a seductive tune as she stepped into his chamber and they faced each other.

'Here,' Alim said, 'we are not forbidden.'

But it was a forbidden love.

His fingers traced her clavicle and moved the robe down so that her shoulder was bare, and then he did the same on the other side. Alim's hands roamed over her breasts and to the sides of her ribcage as her mouth ached for his kiss and the weight of him on her.

'I have missed you,' Alim told her.

And she could not confess to just how much she had missed him too, for that would leave her exposed and weak to his demands.

'I have thought about you,' Alim said, and he pointed to the bed. 'There, on that bed, I have thought about you a lot.'

She swallowed at the image he conjured and watched as he freed himself from his robe.

Gabi caught her breath for, to be kind, her mind had

dimmed his beauty a touch, but now it was hers to witness again.

She put a hand up and touched his chest—solid and warm. She pressed her fingers to his skin and then shared a deep kiss as her fingers pressed into the flesh of his torso.

'Have you thought of me?' he asked.

'At first,' Gabi said. 'But I'm over you now.'

'Not quite,' he said, pulling the robe down over her breasts and hips so that it fell to the floor. His hands were thorough and hungry for her body as they again felt her generous flesh.

'Tell me how you have been,' he said as he kissed her all over, gently lowering her so she lay naked on soft silks, 'since you got over me.'

'I've been...' She hesitated, and she wondered what he would say if she told him that each night she still cried herself to sleep. 'Fine.'

'Fine,' he said as he joined her and they lay with their fingers tracing each other's outlines. His muscular arms were as she remembered and his erection still responded to the trace of her finger on the hairs of his thigh. It was Alim who wavered from the sensual tracing and ran his hand along the soft insides of her thighs. He savoured them again with a teasing caress, then tortured her by halting her at the peak of the thrill.

'Did you ever think of contacting me?' he asked, and she bit on her lip in frustration. As he held back the pleasure, she became a little more truthful. 'I wanted to but, you moved to Zethlehan.'

'Not until recently.' He looked up. 'You had months when you could have made contact.'

'For the pleasure of being rejected again?' Gabi shot back, and her more honest response was rewarded by a deep kiss to her breast, one that hurt because it was so exquisite.

His fingers stroked her inside and it was his deep desire for her that made Gabi burn and want.

Yet as he removed his fingers and the deep contact of his mouth, she was reminded how abruptly he had ended things between them and as he went to part her legs, she drew them closed.

He parted them with his palm. Not even a hint of pressure, just the soft touch of his skin and she opened to Alim; he came to kneel between her calves.

She felt again like his prey.

He moved her knees and her legs up higher, and her throat was tight as he lowered his head.

'Gabi...' he said, and she felt his words in her most intimate space. 'Tell me...'

Tell him what?

That she loved him and that she was going out of her mind because she lay in the desert with a man who had brought her here on a lie? Yet she was fighting not to plead for him.

His tongue was subtle.

At first.

She considered that she might relax into the caress of his mouth and then his kiss strengthened and he moved down onto his stomach, his tongue slipping inside her. She heard the kiss and swallow of him and she moaned.

'Tell me...' he said again.

'I have thought of you.'

There, she had said it.

His tongue was making love to her and his fingers hurt her thighs but she would not have him lighten his touch, not even a fraction.

Gabi's hand was turning, searching, for a pillow, a

cushion, for an anchor but he was tasting her so deeply her fingers then tugged at his silky hair. His unshaven jaw was rough and delicious and she had never thought she would know such pleasure again.

'Alim…'

Inadvertently, as she had the night their baby had been born, she sobbed out his name.

Alim liked it.

He liked how she cried out his name as she started to come, and he drank her in, yet she frustrated him too for, even in the throes of passion she did not reveal the truth.

And so he rose from between her legs, left her in the middle of her climax, and reached for a sheath.

Gabi almost screamed in frustration at the sudden dearth of sensation. He rose over her and she ached for him to be inside her, yet he was busy taking the care he had not that first night.

'Please…' Gabi begged, and she was about to tell him she was covered, not to worry, for she was on the Pill, but it didn't matter now; he was over her and squeezing into where she was so swollen, aching and ripe.

'We don't want you getting pregnant…' he said, and she gave in to the bliss, but it was short-lived, for Gabi's eyes flew open to just one word from Alim.

'Again…'

He knew!

She was a ball of panic and he was taking her, a mire of sensation, for he was an assault on all of her senses.

His lovemaking was savage. Her pleasure he had taken care of already and now, when perhaps it should be just for him, she was taken to the edge of sanity as Alim unleashed himself.

He spoke words she did not understand but they were

harsh and scolding, yet his arms held her tight as he bucked within.

She was dragging her nails down his back and now it was Gabi's anger that was released. For he had left her, and she had had to fight to survive in a world that did not contain him.

Their teeth clashed, their bodies locked and she bit his shoulder; it felt primal and she was screaming. Her thighs burned now as her legs wrapped tightly around him, and his rapid thrusts had her high and coming so deeply as he shot into her.

'Never...' he said, and was about to tell her to never lie again, but as he came, as he felt her deep pulses drag him in, words did not matter.

He lay on top of her and they breathed in air that felt clear and cool, as if a storm had just passed.

It had.

Alim knew, Gabi thought as she lay there.

He kissed her back, a very soft kiss, for the storm really had passed.

She knew he knew now.

CHAPTER THIRTEEN

'WERE YOU EVER going to tell me?'

Alim had waited for her breath to even out before he asked her.

'Yes.'

'I don't believe you,' Alim said, and he turned his face to Gabi's. 'I gave you every opportunity and you said nothing.'

'I wanted to tell you from a distance.'

'Why?'

Gabi didn't answer that for she did not want to admit that being around him made her feel weak and that she'd been scared what she might agree to when she lay by his side.

Here, she felt they could do no wrong.

Here, in the desert, this love did not feel so forbidden, and the idea of being his desert lover felt rather wonderful, in fact.

'What did we have?'

His words said so much—that he accepted their baby as his and that the question was gently asked brought tears to her eyes.

'A little girl.'

She was back there again in those lonely hours, giving birth without Alim by her side, but now his hand found hers as she told him their daughter's name.

'I called her Lucia.'

'She is well?'

Gabi nodded for her words were strangled by tears as she heard the care behind his questions.

'You'll never forgive me, will you?'

'Gabi, I accept that the decision would have felt like an impossible one.'

Alim did not like it and maybe later he would resent the times denied to them but now was not that time; there were too many things he needed to know this moment.

'When did you have her?'

'The last time we met,' Gabi said. 'When you were showing Raul through the hotel.'

Alim frowned. 'The night I returned to Zethlehan?'

Gabi nodded.

'You didn't look pregnant,' Alim said. 'Though admittedly I was doing all I could not to look at you.'

'I lost a lot of weight,' Gabi told him. 'I've put it all back on, though.'

'Good.'

He was the most back-to-front man she knew, for he was playing with her stomach as if it was the most beautiful stomach in the world.

'I was sick a lot at first and then I was very busy with work. I was just about to go on leave when I went into labour.'

'That would have been far too soon.'

'She's done so well, though,' Gabi said. 'Lucia amazed the doctor and nurses; she was early but so strong.'

'The al-Lehans are.' One day he would tell her about the strong lineage; one day he would share in tales of babies that should not have survived but had lived to rule.

But not now.

For Alim ached with sadness that a desert princess had been born but his country would never know her name.

She did not exist as his daughter, except here in the desert.

Gabi had left the bed and had gone to her case in the hallway and retrieved her tablet.

There was something so splendid about her, Alim thought as she walked back to the bed. He knew Gabi was shy, yet here she was not and he loved how she slipped back to his side; he wrapped an arm around her as she opened up the latest image of Lucia—the one that her mother had sent her just as she had landed here in Zeth-lehan.

There had never been any real doubt in his mind, Alim had known she was his, but he had never expected to feel so moved by a photo.

Her eyes were almond shaped and she was a beautiful old soul, a true al-Lehan.

'When was this taken?' Alim asked.

'My mother sent it to me yesterday. I got it when we landed.'

'She is tiny,' he said, unable to take his eyes from his daughter and loathing that he could only see her on a screen.

'She's the size of a newborn now,' Gabi said. 'She caught up quickly.'

He scrolled through the images and Gabi explained each one. 'That was the day I brought her home from the hospital,' she said. 'And that's on the night she was born.'

He had been on his way here.

Alim looked at their fragile daughter and then at the mother who held her. Gabi had indeed lost weight; in the picture she looked drawn and pale, scared yet proud as she looked down at her very new daughter, and his heart twisted in fear and pain as he thought of how it could have gone.

'You have done well,' Alim said, and looked at Gabi.

She had expected him to be accusatory, to be furious for all she had denied him, yet his voice was kind and his words told her he was proud of her for the care that their daughter had received.

Yes, from the day she had met him he had enthralled her, for his responses were like no others; they threw her in new directions.

And then he turned back to the tablet and the photos of his daughter. 'That's all there are...' Gabi said.

Except there was another image that held his attention now—the one of Gabi and him dancing in the deserted ballroom.

She blushed. It felt as if he was looking through her diary and she hastily moved to play the image down.

'The photographer had left a time-lapse camera set up, there was this at the end...' She was a little embarrassed to have saved it, but how could she be when she now lay in his bed and from that night they had made a daughter?

'I'll send you the pictures of Lucia—'

'Already done,' Alim said, as he clicked on them.

They lay there in the dark with the wind an orchestra that seemed to play only for them.

'Will you bring her next time?' Alim asked, and Gabi went still, for there would not be a next time.

Nothing had changed for Gabi, except that he knew.

'Has James ever been to Zethlehan?' she asked, instead of answering.

'No.'

'In case it caused rumours to spread?'

'There are always rumours and they are dealt with by

the palace,' Alim said. 'No, James has never been here because Fleur always refused to come.'

'She's never been?'

'No. Fleur said that she deserved better than a tent in the desert so my father saw that she and James had a home in London and an apartment in Rome.'

'At the Grande Lucia?'

'No. They have only started to dine there since I bought it.' He gave her a smile. 'It is there that James and Mona met—she was there for her grandparents' wedding anniversary and Fleur and James were there with my father.'

That's right, she remembered Mona telling her that and it had seemed so inconsequential at the time.

'I don't want to be your lover, Alim.'

'You would be better than a lover,' Alim told her. 'You would be my mistress.'

He said it as if it were a reward.

'I don't want to be like Fleur,' Gabi said. 'I don't want to bring her here and...' Yet she fought with herself, for even as she said it, she lied.

There was nothing she wanted more right now than for Lucia to lie between them.

There was nothing that appealed more than the thought of visiting Alim, and their child growing up with the love of her father.

'Would it be such a terrible life?' he turned and asked her. 'I would take care of you two so well.'

She stared back at him.

'You could come here often and still have your career.'

'Career?' She gave a short, incredulous laugh. 'I seem to remember you offering me that once before; it didn't last very long.'

The hurt was still there—even recalling that moment

took her straight back to the pain he had caused her. 'Anyway, the Grande Lucia has been sold…'

'The contracts are not signed yet.'

And it didn't appease her—because Bastiano was his friend, but that meant little to Alim, she was sure.

He was ruthless and would get his own way.

Well, not in this.

'I don't want to work for you,' Gabi said, and her voice was certain. 'I want my own career.'

'And you could have it. I would see you often.'

'Where?'

'Mostly here,' Alim said. 'And once things were more settled for my country I could spend more time with you and Lucia in Rome…'

'You mean once you are married and have an heir?'

'Yes.'

And even if it appalled her, it was the life he had been born to, Gabi knew.

'You didn't approve when it was your father,' she pointed out.

'I did not know then that they had made things work.' And he told her a little about how he had found out his mother was happier than he had believed she was.

'I think we could do it even better than them.'

He made the unpalatable sweet, for now the winds buffeted the walls of the desert tent and she could almost imagine a little family here at times. But then her eyes closed on the madness that her mind proposed she consider; she saw the image of Fleur sitting taking refreshments alone; she thought of the other injured parties that an illicit love brought.

'I wouldn't do that to your wife,' Gabi said. 'And I shan't do it to our child.'

'You'd deny her a chance to be with her father?'

'Never,' Gabi said. 'You can come and see her whenever you choose.'

She was braver in words than in thought, not that he gave her a moment to think.

'I want you to move into the Grande Lucia.'

'It's about to be sold.'

'Bastiano isn't going to be kicking out the guests… you're to move there forthwith.'

'No.' He was pulling her into his world, and she would not allow it. 'I shan't be your lover and I shan't be your mistress.' She rolled onto her side and faced away from him.

'Gabi, just think about it.'

'No.' She was crying because he made her weaken. 'Haven't you heard a word I've said?'

'I heard all that you said,' Alim told her as he spooned in from behind, his hand on her stomach and his mouth at her ear, 'but I think we need to speak at more length.'

The only length she was certain of was the one that was nudging between her thighs and Gabi knew it would soon be the delicious experience all over again.

Not just now but for the rest of her life.

'No, I need to get back to my baby.'

She felt lost and reckless to be in the desert with him, and her mind was made up.

'I shan't be your mistress.'

Gabi's mind was *almost* made up but she was open to persuasion in his arms. And so she climbed out of the vast bed before she shattered again to his touch.

'Get back into bed,' Alim said.

He lay uncovered and beautiful and she had never fought harder not to simply give in to his demands. 'The only way I'll sleep with you again is as your wife.'

'Wife?' Alim's tone told her how impossible that was. 'I am offering you—'

'I don't want to be your mistress, Alim.'

'Please,' he angrily retorted. 'You want centuries of history wiped out just for you?'

A few months ago she would have backed down, almost apologised for being so bold.

Yet what they had found together had changed her, and for the better.

She had a baby to think of too.

His love, though not on offer, made her strong.

'I don't just want it,' Gabi hotly responded. 'I insist on it.'

'Oh, you do, do you?'

'Yes, and now I want to leave.'

He just lay there.

'I said—'

'I heard.'

He rolled over and the world was invading because here in their remote haven Alim retrieved his phone.

'The helicopter will be here within the hour.'

Gabi breathed out in relief, but her relief was short-lived.

'Now,' he said, 'get back to bed.'

CHAPTER FOURTEEN

OH, IT SHOULD feel wonderful to be back in Rome and to step into her mother's house and hold Lucia.

She brought her baby back to her flat and drew the drapes on the world to create her own little haven of peace.

But peace was fragile and, Gabi knew, at any moment it could be, *would* be, shattered.

That much Gabi was certain of.

The days passed and she heard nothing from Alim, but the lack of contact did not serve as relief.

She knew he was working his way towards them.

Indefinable, indescribable.

Gabi just knew.

For seven mornings, the sun rose as promised in the east and for seven nights it slipped away into the west, but distance and time did not soothe Gabi. She knew that Alim kept his family close—his insistence at maintaining ties to his half-brother James, despite his father's pressure to leave well alone, told Gabi that.

And Lucia was his daughter.

Always Alim seemed a step ahead of her, and Gabi, rather than trying to second-guess his next move, decided to focus on her own.

If she was going to be strong against Alim, then she

needed a life. She needed to be able to take care of her daughter enough that she did not solely depend on him, and that started now.

'I'd hoped for something more concrete!' Bernadetta was less than impressed with the rather sparse report Gabi offered as to her time in Zethlehan.

'When is the wedding?'

'Sultan Alim is not sure,' Gabi answered, and then she looked at Bernadetta. 'I've been thinking, Berna-detta...' Except that sounded unsure. 'As you know,' Gabi amended, 'for a long time I've wanted to go out on my own...'

'Oh, not this again.' Bernadetta rolled her eyes. 'Do I have to remind you of the terms—?'

'Bernadetta,' Gabi broke in, 'I cannot hire any of your contacts for six months, I'm very aware of that, but they can still hire me.'

'Hire you?' Bernadetta gave a condescending laugh.

'Rosa would hire me in an instant. I worked for her for ages and, to be honest, with Lucia so young the thought of more regular hours for a few months is appealing. And, of course, some of Rosa's brides-to-be might not yet have found a wedding planner...' She could see Bernadetta's rapid blink but she quickly recovered.

'You wouldn't last five minutes in this industry with-out me.'

'I think I'll last a whole lot longer,' Gabi said. 'I guess we're going to find out, but not for a while, though. I've just returned from maternity leave so I'm legally obliged—'

'Gabi,' Bernadetta broke in, 'this is nonsense. We've got a royal wedding coming up—'

'We?' Gabi checked. It was the first time she had ever included Gabi in the business and it had taken a threat to resign to hear it. 'Matrimoni di Bernadetta has a potential contract. I have a child to raise. Bernadetta, I think we could make a very strong partnership but obviously it has to be something that would work for you too.'

'Gabi,' Bernadetta said, 'you're getting ideas above your station.'

'No.' Gabi shook her head. 'I've got ideas and plenty of them, and they're exactly where they ought to be.'

It didn't go well.

She wasn't exactly laughed out of the office, as Gabi had predicted she would be; instead Bernadetta sulked and ignored her.

In Zethlehan it wasn't business as usual either.

Violetta asked to see Alim and broke the news.

'Bastiano Conti has withdrawn his offer.'

Usually Alim would hold onto a hiss of indignation when a sale fell through at this late stage. He never revealed his emotions, even to the most trusted staff or those closest in his circle.

Now, though, he let out an audible sigh.

One of relief.

He did not want the Grande Lucia to be sold.

Alim loved that building; there had been more than memories made there and he did not want that chapter of his life closed.

Lucia.

He had to see her.

'What was his reason?' Alim asked Violetta.

'Apparently one of your chambermaids has light fingers. A family heirloom was stolen from Bastiano.'

'I will deal with that,' Alim said.

He and Bastiano were friends, and a deal falling through would not mar that.

Business was kept separate, but still he rang the hotel and asked to be put through to the head of Housekeeping to find out things for himself before calling Bastiano.

'Young Sophie…' Benita told him. 'I wanted to give her the benefit of the doubt but a ring was found when she turned out the pockets of her uniform so there was no choice but to let her go.'

Sophie was a friend of Gabi's, Alim knew.

He had often seen them chatting; in days long gone he had seen them with their coats on at the end of the day, heading out for supper.

And, on Gabi's behalf, he probed further.

'Did she admit to it?' Alim checked.

'Of course not,' Benita said. 'I've yet to find a thief who would.'

'Yes but—'

'Alim,' Benita said, 'I think there might have been something between our esteemed guest and maid.'

'Oh.'

'It's been dealt with.'

'Okay.'

Yet he could not let his thoughts of the Grande Lucia go.

He was flicking through his phone, looking at pictures of Lucia, and then he came to the photo of him with Lucia's mother.

It was a magnificent portrait of a couple gazing at each other, on the edge of a future together…

And Alim felt his heart quicken.

He reached for the leather-bound folder on his desk and read the pertinent parts of the diktat.

And then he read the rest.

Violetta brought in refreshments but instead of waving her out he had her bring him more files.

Ancient files with ancient rulings that he had been forced to learn as a child.

Alim studied them as a man now.

He read the ancient teachings and pored over the laws of his land, and as he turned the pages Alim glanced up and saw his father standing there.

They were barely speaking.

His father considered Alim to be stubborn.

'I have chosen my bride,' Alim told his father.

'That decision belongs to me,' Oman said, for he knew the laws well.

'Then you had better make sure that it is the right one,' Alim responded coolly, but his voice held a silk-clad threat, 'or there shall be no wedding.'

Oman's assessment was the correct one.

Sultan Alim al-Lehan of Zethlehan was the most stubborn man in this land.

He would not succumb to rules of old, as his father had.

Alim would work within them.

CHAPTER FIFTEEN

GABI NEVER FORGOT.

Even as she sat in her tiny flat, consoling poor Sophie, Alim was not far from her mind.

For nearly a week, Sophie had been around every day bemoaning the loss of her job and the man who had caused it—Bastiano Conti.

'I would never steal,' Sophie said. 'But if I did, I would not steal some stupid emerald and pearl ring. It would be diamonds.'

She made Gabi laugh, and in the second that the world felt lighter, Alim invaded, for her phone rang and the fragile peace was shattered.

'Why,' Alim asked, 'are you still living in that flat, when there is an apartment at the Grande Lucia at your disposal?'

She gave an apologetic smile to Sophie and went through to her bedroom to take the call.

Lucia was asleep in her crib and Gabi kept her voice down so as not to disturb her, and also because she did not want Sophie to hear.

'Because I refuse to be kept by you.'

'Your daughter has a father who will provide for her.' Alim gave in, he refused to argue on the phone when he would see Gabi soon, but there was something he badly needed to know.

'How is Lucia?'

'She slept through last night for the first time.'

'That is good. I am in Rome and I would like to meet her.'

Gabi screwed her eyes closed.

She had been dreading this, had been preparing herself for this moment. He had told her that nothing would stop him from seeing his child, and yet again Alim was a step ahead for she had at least thought there would be time to prepare for their meeting.

'When?'

'This afternoon. Is that a problem for you?'

'No,' Gabi admitted. 'I've got a couple of days off.'

'Really?'

'Bernadetta told me not to come in this weekend,' Gabi said. 'I'm not sure if I've been fired. I asked Bernadetta for a partnership...'

Alim, it would seem, had lost interest in her career plans for he spoke over Gabi. 'Can you bring Lucia to me at the Grande Lucia at one?'

She looked around her home; no, she could not imagine him here.

'For how long?'

'The afternoon,' Alim answered calmly. 'Say, until five?'

No, *that* was the part she dreaded, for Gabi knew she would have to get over him all over again.

Sophie was terribly hard to get rid of, but Gabi pulled out an excuse and, sounding like Bernadetta, told her friend that she had a migraine.

'That came on quickly,' Sophie said.

'Yes, they tend to.'

Thankfully Sophie soon left and, wishing she could lie down in a darkened room and hide from the world for a while, Gabi bathed her slippery baby and washed her hair and then she fed her.

'You're going to meet your daddy,' Gabi told her.

And though Gabi was worried for herself, and her absolute drop-knickers reaction to Alim, at least today she had the shield of her daughter. Alim would be far too besotted with Lucia to worry about other things.

And, more importantly, she was so happy for Lucia.

No, history was not repeating itself—this little girl would have a dad.

Of sorts.

And so, just before one, Gabi walked into the foyer of the Grande Lucia, as she had done many, many times, but then she stopped in her tracks.

The pillar display in the middle of the foyer was no longer its trademark red. Instead, there was a stunning display of sweet peas.

Pinks, lilacs and creams, they were absolutely stunning and she stood for a moment, enjoying the wonderful change.

'They're for you,' Gabi said to her daughter. 'He did this for you!'

Her happiness soon evaporated, though. She was met by Violetta, and it would seem that both baby and mother required preparation to enter the Sultan's world.

Pride had ensured that Gabi had dressed as well as she could for today, and little Lucia was wearing a gorgeous outfit and was wrapped in a new muslin square.

It wasn't enough.

And it wasn't just Lucia who had to be prepared.

There was a silver robe laid out for Gabi and, she quickly realised, Violetta had an assistant to do her makeup and hair.

'That won't be necessary,' Gabi said. 'I'm here so that Alim can see his baby.'

'The Sultan—' Violetta started, but Gabi would not hear it.

'He didn't tell me he was a sultan when he took me to bed,' Gabi interrupted. 'And I am not here as his mistress. I am here as the mother of his child.'

Violetta blinked, clearly more used to people bending over backwards to please the Sultan. Well, no bending over would be happening today.

'This is Hannan,' Violetta introduced them. 'She is a royal nanny of considerable standing and will help get the baby ready to meet Sultan Alim.'

'Her name is Lucia,' Gabi said. 'And she *is* ready.'

This time Violetta paid no attention.

The muslin was replaced with a cashmere wrap and Gabi bit her lip as Hannan dared check that her baby was clean enough for the Sultan's eyes.

It incensed Gabi but for now she stayed quiet.

Lucia did not.

She let out a cry of protest as her face was wiped.

'Perhaps we will wait till after she is fed so that she is content when she sees the Sultan,' Hannan suggested.

'She isn't due to be fed for another three hours.' Gabi said. 'And, given I'm due to leave at five, it would make it a very short first visit with her father.'

'Perhaps just a small feed,' Hannan suggested. 'The Sultan is not yet here.'

Gabi clutched her daughter, and already ached for her, unable to believe that Alim could be late for his first meeting with his daughter.

The wait was awful.

But finally the words were said. 'The Sultan is ready for you.'

The real question was, was *she* ready to face Alim?

His offer that she be his mistress had been met with the contempt it deserved.

Yet talking to herself was easy when Alim wasn't close.

She picked up little Lucia and held her close and when Hannan came over to check again that her baby was sweet and clean enough to meet her father for the first time, Gabi shot her a look.

Wisely, Hannan stepped back.

The small entourage walked along the long carpeted corridor and Gabi did her best not to think of the last time she had been here—being kissed up against these walls, falling together through the door that Violetta now knocked on.

Making love.

She walked in, holding Lucia to her chest, with Violetta and Hannan by her side.

Alim stood by a window in his immaculate reception room. The fire that had blazed as he'd stripped her naked was now devoid of flames and filled with an autumnal floral display.

A tamed version of itself.

Just like Alim.

He was wearing a suit and was clean shaven, and though he looked somewhat less formidable out of traditional robes, not for a moment would she forget his power.

'I apologise for keeping you waiting,' he said by way of introduction, but offered no explanation for the reason he had done so. He looked over at Violetta and Hannan. 'Excuse us, please.' Polite, in all dealings *outside* the bedroom, Alim dismissed his staff and Gabi stood, a little awkwardly, as Alim's eyes flicked down to the baby she held in her arms, though he did not approach.

'She's just been fed,' Gabi said with a distinct edge to her voice, 'to ensure that she's no trouble for you.'

'Did they feed you too?' Alim asked, implying he knew full well that it was the mother who was trouble, and he saw that she resisted a smile.

'No,' Gabi said.

'Then I had better watch out.'

Indeed he had, for Gabi made her own rules, and that, his father had pointed out, might make her an unwise choice for a sultan's bride.

He walked over and peered at the bundle that she held—their tiny baby hidden in a swathe of cashmere.

Gabi watched as his hand moved back the fabric. She heard the slight hitch in his breath as, for the first time, he met his daughter.

She had dark hair, like her parents', and her dark lashes swept over round cheeks. Her little rosebud mouth was pink and her skin as pale as Gabi's.

And she was beautiful.

Alim had been raised knowing he would one day be Sultan of Sultans, yet he met true responsibility now, for he would move mountains for his daughter and she had not even opened her eyes to look at him.

He looked up to Gabi and saw that *her* eyes were angry.

Though she held Lucia tenderly, Gabi's stance was almost confrontational, and he loved that she would do anything to protect not just her daughter but herself.

She was a wise choice indeed.

And for Gabi he *had* moved mountains.

Though Alim would tell her that later, right now he was overwhelmed to see Lucia.

'Can I hold her?'

Gabi handed him their child and it was the first awkward move she had ever seen him make.

Indeed, it was awkward at first, for Lucia was so light and she moved and stirred as she went into her father's arms, and he held her perhaps a little too firmly.

Gabi said nothing; she did not tell him to watch her head and she did not move to hush her daughter, who was starting to wakeup; instead, she walked over and took a seat.

She was close to tears, watching him hold their daughter so tenderly and witnessing the obvious love he had for Lucia.

It didn't feel fair that they could never be a family. She wanted to go over to where he took a seat, she wanted to be with the two people she loved.

His part-time lover.

The desert still tempted her. Alim always would.

Then Lucia opened her eyes.

Alim had never doubted that Lucia was his—had he, though, he would have been proved a fool, for her eyes were navy, turning to grey, and there were the same silver flecks that greeted him in the mirror each morning.

He hoped she might cry so that he could hand her back to her mother, for he had never felt more moved than now; there was guilt too for the months Gabi had dealt with this alone, and fear about how tiny Lucia was, even though she was more than three months old.

But Lucia did not cry or whimper. She looked straight at her daddy and smiled and completely won his heart.

'I could have lived my entire life not knowing about her.'

'No,' Gabi said. 'I lived my life without knowing my father so I would never do that to my child. I was going to wait till I felt a little better, and then tell you.'

'Better?' He frowned, worried that she had been ill.

'Stronger.'

'Stronger?' Alim checked.

'To say no to you.'

His eyes raised just a fraction, as if doubting she could.

'I meant what I said—I shan't be your mistress, Alim. I will always let you see your daughter whenever you come here to Rome but there will be no trips to the desert.'

'Really?'

'Yes.'

She must be stronger because she almost believed that she could say no to him.

'So you are going to be single and—'

'I didn't say that,' Gabi corrected. 'You will marry the bride of the Sultan of Sultans's choosing and I will get on with my life. I won't be like Fleur, living a lonely life with you as my occasional, discreet lover.'

'Oh, so you hope to meet someone else?'

'Yes.'

He stared at her and she tried not to meet his gaze because she just could not imagine being with another man.

Ever.

She could not imagine anyone after him, yet she had to believe it, for she would not be his mistress, neither would she be alone.

The minutes passed so slowly they were half an hour in with three more to go.

He picked up a phone and soon Hannan appeared; Gabi's lips tightened as she scooped up Lucia and took her away, and soon it was just the two of them.

'I thought you wanted to see her.'

'I don't need to stare at her for the entire visit to love her. I will call for refreshments for you.'

They made small talk as they waited for afternoon tea to arrive.

'Bernadetta is being weird,' Gabi said. 'She won't take my calls.'

He just shrugged and then told her his news. 'I have withdrawn the Grande Lucia from sale.'

'I thought the contracts were signed.'

'No. Bastiano returned to the Grande Lucia for a visit and apparently some jewellery was stolen from his suite—your friend apparently.'

Gabi wasn't going to blush or apologise for Sophie. She just gave a shrug.

'He's withdrawn his offer.'

And now Gabi rolled her eyes because Alim would be here in Rome so much more.

Her desire was safer from a distance.

Arabian teas, coffees and pastries arrived and as the maid poured Alim declined.

'Enjoy,' Alim said to Gabi as the maid left.

'Where are you going?'

'Bed,' Alim answered. 'I read that you should try and sleep when the baby does.'

Her mouth twisted into an incredulous smile when she thought of the hours she had paced the floor with her baby and snatched twenty-minute naps on the sofa.

He had not a clue!

'Half an hour of fatherhood and you're already tired?' Gabi accused.

'Months of fatherhood, had I but known,' Alim corrected. 'And months of abstinence, apart from one night in the desert.'

And he took her back in her mind to where she had been trying to avoid going.

Gabi looked ahead and tried not to think of her time in his bed.

And Alim, as he stepped into the bedroom where he had had so much planned, instead was incensed by her words.

Pride perhaps was at fault, but there was also this need to know not that Lucia was his but that *Gabi* was his—that he was and always would be her one and only.

He started to undress and then remembered he should be dressed for the planned proposal and standing when Gabi inevitably walked in.

Surprise!

Yet she did not walk in.

Alim rarely got angry, he rarely cared enough to be so.

And he was also jealous.

Gabi had riled him.

On what should be the most romantic of days she spoke of other men!

Oh, Alim wanted to prove her wrong. There would *never* be others.

So, instead of the plans he had made, Alim opened the bedside drawer and there they lay his collection of diamonds; he selected the best, then he closed the drapes and turned off the lights.

He would not be brought to his knees until Gabi was.

And so he walked out.

She sat, drinking tea.

Her foot was tapping, Alim noticed, but apart from that she seemed calm, like a guest sitting in the foyer, waiting for her car to arrive, or to be told that her suite was now ready.

Gabi was not calm.

She had been fighting with herself not to follow him in.

To 'Keep Calm and Drink Tea', as suggested.

Yet her hands were shaking and her desire was fierce and she ached for these visiting hours to be over.

For an imaginary nurse to come in and ring a bell so that she could leave.

Then he walked out.

The jacket was off, the tie gone and his shirt half-undone, as if he had been undressing and had suddenly remembered something.

Indeed he had. 'There will be others?' Alim questioned, and even though his voice was dark it held a slightly mocking edge, for he was sure there could be no other.

And what was said now would define their future, Gabi knew.

She would not be Fleur, sitting in the foyer of this very hotel and ignored. She would not be his mistress and make love and then not make a fuss when he returned to his wife.

How bloody dare he?

And so she met his eyes and she played a very dangerous game with a sultan who was already not best pleased.

'Maybe just *one* other,' Gabi said. 'Perhaps I will find the love of my life.'

'What if you have already found him?' Alim said.

'How can I have,' Gabi countered, 'when he speaks of a future wife?'

And she found out then just how strong she was because now she could look him in the eye and tell him things she would once never have dared. Now she stood her ground and it felt firm beneath her feet, for she was resolute.

She watched as he reached into his pocket and beside her teacup he placed a stone.

A magnificent one.

'You shall be kept in splendour,' Alim said, and when every other woman would reach for the stone, she had the nerve to take a sip of her tea. 'Never again speak of other men. Now,' Alim said by way of parting, 'come to bed.'

She would not succumb.

Gabi stood, walked across the lounge and looked out of the window.

A bridal car was pulling up outside the church further down the street and she watched as a bride was helped out and her dress arranged.

The little flower girl stood patiently as Gabi's heart impatiently beat for the day that it might be her.

Never the bride.

She had never been able to envisage herself as one.

And now she knew why.

A mistress was all she would ever be.

No!

Gabi was torn for as she watched the bride walk into the church she told herself that a mistress was surely better than being a virtual spinster, holding onto just two perfect nights for the rest of her life.

That was all her love life would be.

For, despite brave words she might say to Alim, in truth, there would never be another man—Gabi had already found the love of her life.

Yet agreeing to be his mistress went against everything she believed in, and if even the thought of it was eating her up, living it would be unbearable.

Neither was she cut out to keep secrets, for she would want to sing their love to the world, and she was hardly of a size that faded neatly into the background.

No, Gabi would not be his mistress, but that did not stop the door to his bedroom calling her.

Set your limits.

Alim's words now replayed to her.

Do only what you are prepared to do. What works for you...

And Gabi knew what did.

Alim.

CHAPTER SIXTEEN

GABI WALKED OVER to a dresser and took some paper and wrote down three little words.

No, thank you.

She placed them by the stone that Alim had left out for her.

Gabi would not be kept.

She would not be another Fleur, paid for in diamonds, rich in everything save respect.

Then she undressed and, naked, walked to the closed doors of the bedroom.

She would not cry and she would not be a martyr as she took those final steps, for Gabi wanted this.

Gabi stepped into darkness. The air was fragrant and sweet but there was the now familiar musky note of Alim and the pull of arousal as she came to the side of the bed.

'What kept you?' Alim asked.

'My thoughts.'

'And they are?'

'That I'll never be your mistress.'

'Then why *are* you here?' Alim asked as his hands roamed her naked body.

'I shall be your lover,' Gabi told him, and she knelt on

the bed and kissed his salty chest. 'I will be your lover in the desert at times and at others I will be your lover in Rome.'

And when once she had been demure, she was not so much now, for she wanted to intimately taste every inch of him. Gabi kissed down his stomach and between hot kisses she told him how it would be.

'I don't want your diamonds, I owe you nothing.'

And in the dark she could not see his smile, for he loved it that she stood up to him.

'But I do want the contract for your wedding,' Gabi said, and she blew onto his wet skin as his fingers dug into her thigh. 'I'm going to stand there and you can damn well watch what you're saying goodbye to, because your mistress I shall never be.'

His scent was her addiction and her undoing; she could feel him against her cheek and so she took him in her hand and tasted him.

She took him deep; his hands went into her hair and his hips rose at the bliss of unskilled but willing lips and to the heat of her tongue.

And then he pulled her up before he came, yet still she told him how it would be.

'The day your bride is chosen I'll cease to be your lover.'

Gabi had not finished school, neither was she versed in the rules, yet she, Alim knew, was as clever and as powerful as he.

He pulled her up to his kiss and as their tongues touched he lowered Gabi onto him.

The relief of him inside her was unrivalled.

A future she could now see.

He held her hips and they found their rhythm. She

danced as if free, for that was how she felt when they were together.

She wanted the light on, she ached to see him, but as she leant and reached for the bedside lamp his hand grabbed at hers. Gabi lost her stride and toppled forward. There was a tussle and he flipped her and then entered her again, and she lay in the dark, being taken.

Gabi did not bring him to his knees but to his forearms.

'Yes,' Alim said as he thrust into her. 'You *shall* be at my wedding.'

'Alim…' Gabi sobbed, for she had meant it as a threat yet it seemed to turn him on.

It was the way she said his name that called to him. Like a plea from the soul. And when Gabi said it again he came hard into her. She fought not to, Gabi really did— fought not to cave to the flood of warmth and want and the orbit of them.

She lost.

Near spent, Alim had the pleasure of the full clutch of her passion and his body pinned her as she writhed, and when she wanted to breathe it was the only need his body denied her, for he then took the air from the room.

'You shall be at my wedding…as my bride.'

She was always a little dizzy when Alim was close— for Gabi it was a constant state of affairs. Held in his arms, breathing his scent, and her body still coming down from the high he so readily gave, she told herself she had misheard him.

And then light invaded for Alim reached over and turned on the bedside lamp and his bedroom was not as she recalled it.

There were flowers.

Sweet peas.

Ten thousand of them, she was sure, and the flowers in the foyer had, in fact, been for her.

But that was not all.

A stunning portrait had been blown up and set on an easel beside the bed.

It was the image of them.

Alim had moved more than mountains, he had turned back the hands of time. For days he had pored over the rules he had studied for years, searching, discounting and trying to find a way to make it work for them.

'You and Lucia are the most wonderful things that have ever happened to me,' Alim told her.

'According to your land, we *never* happened.'

'No.' Alim shook his head. 'When the Sultan offers a commitment it is to be taken seriously…' He took her in his arms. 'I committed to you that night.'

'You offered a year.'

'I vowed fidelity.'

He had.

'And unless it has been broken, you are still mine.'

'Alim?'

'There has been no one else,' Alim said. 'There could be no one else. Had you not spoken of other men you would have walked into this room and I would have got down on my knees and asked you to be my wife.'

Gabi laughed.

Still dizzy, still confused, she laughed, because even if he had planned the perfect proposal she would not change how it had transpired.

There was nothing about them she would change.

Even now, could she go back to their first night and be on the Pill, she would not. There was nothing she would change save for the cruel rules of his land, and now her laughter died.

'Your father will never agree.'

'Reluctantly, very reluctantly, he already has.' Now it was Alim who smiled. 'I am more stubborn than he. I went through the rules and the diktat and then I showed him this image. I told my father that there had been no one else and that that would remain the case, for the rest of my life if need be.'

'I don't understand.'

'My father caved in to the Sultan of Sultans' demands when Fleur would not come to the desert. I told him that I would not.'

And still she did not understand.

'We think the same, Gabi. For the decision you reached was mine too. We would have more than made it as lovers. I would have come to Italy regularly, and brought you on occasion to the desert, and you would have remained the one and only woman in my life.'

And she stared back at him as he told her just how deep his love was.

'I told my father that if he did not choose you as my bride, then I would never marry. Kaleb is next in line, Yasmin after that, and they will one day have children. The country is not short of heirs…'

'You told him that you'd give up your throne?'

'No.' Alim shook his head. 'I would still rule, but they would be my heirs.'

He had thought every detail through and he had presented it to his father, just as he would in any business meeting.

Only this one involved his heart.

'He knows I am strong, and he knows his own regrets. He agreed.'

'And Lucia…' Gabi asked. 'What will your people think?'

'My father has been unwell, that is enough reason to have refrained from announcements and celebrations. This photo, of the night I made a commitment to you, is enough testimony of our love.'

It *was* love.

She had never truly thought she would know it.

Not fully.

An unrequited version perhaps, if she remained with Alim. Or a diluted version if she attempted to move on and meet someone else.

Yet the man she loved had changed his world for a chance for them. And he told her now why he had.

'Gabi, I never considered love important. I grew up in a loveless, albeit privileged home. I saw first-hand the pain love caused for my father and Fleur…'

He thought back to when love had first started to arrive in his heart.

'When I came to buy the Grande Lucia you were setting up for a wedding. It was the first time I saw you.'

Gabi thought back.

'No, the first time we saw each other was the day after a wedding. You had come back for a second viewing of the hotel…'

'No.'

And Gabi realised then that he had memories of her that she did not know, that the days she had felt so invisible had been days when she had, in fact, been noticed.

'Marry me?' he said, and she nodded.

'Oh, yes.'

'There is only one problem.'

And here it came, Gabi thought, the downside, for she could not remain on this cloud for ever. She braced herself for impact.

'It has to be now.'

Gabi frowned. 'Now?'

'We're already late for our own wedding.'

'You mean *now*!'

'The Sultan of Sultans has chosen. I was lucky to buy us even a few days. I have my family gathered, and I went and spoke with your mother; she has given her blessing if you say yes.'

'When did you speak with my mother?'

'That is why I was late to meet Lucia.'

Gabi was lying in bed on her wedding day when surely there was so much to be done.

'Alim…' She sat up. 'I haven't…'

There was panic, because she was a wedding planner after all and this wedding was her very own.

'There is nothing for you to do. I know you would have dreamed of this day and that it might not be quite what you had planned…'

'No.' Gabi shook her head. 'I never thought of my own.'

'There will be a bigger celebration in Zethlehan but for today everything is under control.'

Except the bride!

For instead of answering her million questions Alim got dressed and then, having read her note with a smile, he left.

Gabi sat in the unmade bed, unsure what she was supposed to do, so she called her mum.

'I am so happy for you,' Carmel said. 'It meant everything that he came and spoke with me…'

'You'll be there?'

'Of course,' her mother said. 'I'm at the hotel now with Lucia and we're both being very spoiled. I shall see you at the wedding.'

It seemed everyone knew what was happening except

Gabi and just when she was starting to think she must have misunderstood the bedside phone rang.

'Gabi…'

Gabi rolled her eyes at the familiar voice.

'I can't work today,' Gabi started, but then realised that Bernadetta wasn't calling her to ask her to work.

'If you'd like to put on a robe, the bridal suite is ready for you.'

'For me?'

'Gabi, I haven't been avoiding your calls. Well perhaps a bit, but I've been very busy arranging a royal wedding in Rome, with only five days' notice. Thank goodness I'm good at my job!'

Gabi had always resented that Alim seemed one step ahead of her.

She didn't today.

Yes, Bernadetta was a right royal pain, but she was the best in the business.

Gabi almost felt sorry for Bernadetta for the panic she must have had to arrange such a rapid wedding.

Almost!

CHAPTER SEVENTEEN

GABI KNOCKED ON the door of the Grande Lucia's bridal suite.

She knew it very well, but usually she was carrying flowers or had her arms piled high with a wedding dress.

Today she had nothing, not even her purse, for in the confusion she had left it all behind.

The door to the suite opened and there stood Bernadetta. Gabi's nerves didn't quite disappear but they faded as, even from a distance, Alim made her smile.

Gone was the black suit.

Bernadetta looked amazing in a willow-green and pale pink check suit—and, yes, Alim really had thought of it all.

'You have nothing to worry about,' Bernadetta said as Gabi stepped in. 'I've been working closely with Alim and Violetta and everything is under control. But first I have something for you from me.'

Bernadetta handed her a box, and when Gabi opened it she saw that they were business cards. They were the palest blush-pink with a trail of willow-green ivy and the lettering was in gold.

Matrimoni Internazionali di Gabriella.

'No.' Gabi went to put the card back in its box; this wasn't how she wanted it to be. 'I don't want Alim buying me a career.'

'Gabi,' Bernadetta said, 'I had a long think after our discussion. Of course I was furious at the suggestion, but when I had calmed down I thought about it properly. It is too much for one person. I was going to offer you a junior partnership. I don't want to lose you and when Alim called and asked if I would arrange the wedding, well, I knew I was about to so I had to think on my feet. I came up with this. Gabi, you're going to be overseas a lot and I hope back here often…'

Gabi nodded.

'We can work all the details out, but together we can make a success of it.'

And her heart started to soar because Bernadetta was right—married to a sultan, a career would be hard without back-up, but in a partnership, well, perhaps it could work for them both.

And there was something else too.

'It's been a tough few years in the industry,' Bernadetta said, 'but things have been starting to turn around and it's in no small part thanks to you.'

Oh, it wasn't just the suit, but Bernadetta looked lighter, younger and more relaxed. Maybe this partnership would take some of the pressure from her too.

But as exciting as the future was, there was really only one partnership on Gabi's mind today.

The door opened to hair and make-up artists and while they set up Gabi went and had a bath.

It was so wonderful to relax, knowing that Lucia was being taken care of and that soon she and Alim would be married. That on the day he met his daughter for the first time, a family they became for real.

After the bath she unwrapped some packages to discover the underwear was a soft white gauze and just what Gabi would have chosen.

It was subtle but terribly sexy and she was glad to hide it under a robe when she stepped out.

Gabi's hair was curled and pinned up, leaving a few long coils to fall, and then the make-up artist got to work under instruction from Bernadetta as Gabi closed her eyes.

'Not too much!' Gabi warned, because she wasn't big on make-up and it felt as if it was being piled on.

'Perfetto,' Bernadetta said, and Gabi opened her eyes. But sheets had been put over the many mirrors. 'I want you to see the full effect all at once.'

'What if I don't like it?'

'Then we keep the groom waiting until you do.' Bernadetta shrugged. 'But I know you are going to love it.'

The door opened again and this time it was Rosa, and Gabi found that she was nervous as the dress was unveiled.

There was no need to be.

Rosa had worked magic indeed.

It was a pale ivory and reminded her of the robe she had worn in the desert.

As Bernadetta did up the row of tiny buttons at the back, Gabi found she was shaking. It was starting to sink in that she would soon be Alim's wife.

The shoes chosen for her had just a little heel and then the door opened and it was Angela with the flowers.

Gabi had to fight not to cry when she saw them.

A bunch of sweet peas and all paper white.

'I wanted to add some gardenias but Alim was adamant. Do you know,' Angela said as she looked at the exquisite trail of blooms, 'I think this is the best I have ever made.'

Each bloom was so delicate and fragrant and perfect that there was nothing—not a single wisp of anything—that Gabi would add to them.

And then Bernadetta took the sheet from the full-length mirror and Gabi, who had never dared to even imagine herself as one, looked back at the bride.

'Oh, Gabi,' Bernadetta said.

And Gabi just stared. The dress hung beautifully and did nothing to play down her curves; her eyes were smoky and her lipstick pale and, no, she could not have chosen better.

'Are you ready?' Bernadetta asked.

'So ready—I would run if I could.'

'You would fall,' Bernadetta said. 'And I don't have a spare dress for you to change into.'

It was a smiling bride who turned heads as she walked through the foyer of the Grande Lucia and stood outside the double doors of the ballroom.

And then nerves caught up with her.

'Just walk straight ahead,' Bernadetta told her. 'Gabi, all you have to do is enjoy every moment.'

She stepped in and there in that ballroom was everyone she loved, and for a moment she looked and tried to take it all in.

Her mother looked gorgeous and was holding Lucia, who wore a little mink-coloured dress and showed one little dark curl.

And when she got over her joy, and when they had made love as man and wife, there would be questions—so many of them.

Fleur was there and she stood next to James and Mona

and, a couple of rows ahead, sat a very handsome, exotic-looking middle-aged man.

Oh, there were secrets in every family and mysteries too, but there was now no shame in the al-Lehans.

Alim did not want to know if this man was the reason his mother knew love.

Gabi, curious by nature, would be certain to find out!

Yes, Violetta had her work cut out with this family and, Gabi suspected, the adjoining rooms at the Grande Lucia would be creaking tonight.

Bastiano was there, and Sophie was too.

It dawned on Gabi then the reason she had been around so much these past days, she had been keeping an eye on the bride while so many plans were underway.

'You knew!' she mouthed to her dear friend as she walked past, and Sophie laughed.

The only person missing was the groom.

And then nerves caught up.

There was his errant sister and Alim's brother, Kaleb, and beside them was the queen, but most intimidating of all was the Sultan of Sultans, who, as Gabi nervously approached, stepped forward.

He spoke first in Arabic, which Gabi did not understand, but then he spoke again.

'The Sultan of Sultans has chosen.'

Gabi saw Alim then.

He wore a robe of silver, but it was the love for her in his eyes that brought tears to hers.

He took her hands and she felt the warmth of his fingers as they caressed hers; his voice was low and for Gabi's ears only.

'He chose wisely.'

Gabi always felt that she shone under Alim's gaze, and this moment was no exception.

They knelt on the gorgeous floor and were blessed, and then they rose as man and wife.

'Are you happy?' he asked.

'So happy,' Gabi said, and then she smiled. 'What if I'd said no?'

'Are you cross now at my assumption that you would agree to marry me?'

'No.'

For it told her of his certainty in them.

And as he moved in to kiss his bride Alim told her a truth.

'This is love,' he whispered, 'and it's ours for ever.'

* * * * *

Don't forget to read the first part of
Carol Marinelli's
BILLIONAIRES AND ONE-NIGHT HEIRS
miniseries

THE INNOCENT'S SECRET BABY
Available now!

And look out for the third and final instalment—
coming soon!

'His Highness, Azim al Bahjat,' the attendant intoned, and with fear coating her insides with ice Johara stepped into the room.

The man she was meant to marry stood in the centre of the room, his body erect and still, his face grave and unsmiling. Johara could see how black and opaque his eyes were—like a starless night in the desert. His dark hair was cut so close she could see the powerful bones of his skull, and a scar snaked from the corner of his left eye to the curve of his mouth, clearly long since healed over, although the wounded flesh still looked red and livid.

The whole effect was beyond intimidating, and she had to fight not to take an instinctive step back towards the doors, towards safety, away from this man whose face even in repose looked frightening.

If she looked at his features reasonably, Johara told herself, fighting off panic, she could see that he was an attractive man—his features even, his nose a straight slash, his mouth a mobile, sensual curve.

Then Azim inclined his head in what Johara supposed was a greeting. His voice, when he spoke was clipped, cold.

'We will marry in one week's time.'

Seduced by a Sheikh

*Two heirs to a desert kingdom
need brides to secure their legacies!*

Brothers Malik and Azim al Bahjat are the two Princes
of Alazar, wielding enormous power with iron control.
They have no interest in love—but duty demands they
take convenient wives, and these ruthless royals
always get what they want!

Read Malik's story in
The Secret Heir of Alazar
April 2017

&

Read Azim's story in
The Forced Bride of Alazar
May 2017

Don't miss this sensational new duet from Kate Hewitt!

THE
FORCED BRIDE
OF ALAZAR

BY
KATE HEWITT

First Published in Great Britain 2017
By Mills & Boon, an imprint of HarperCollins*Publishers*
1 London Bridge Street, London, SE1 9GF

© 2017 Kate Hewitt

ISBN: 978-0-263-92521-0

Printed and bound in Spain
by CPI, Barcelona

After spending three years as a die-hard New Yorker, **Kate Hewitt** now lives in a small village in the English Lake District with her husband, their five children and a golden retriever. In addition to writing intensely emotional stories she loves reading, baking, and playing chess with her son—she has yet to win against him, but she continues to try. Learn more about Kate at kate-hewitt.com.

Visit the Author Profile page
at millsandboon.co.uk for more titles.

To Jenna, thanks for all your encouragement
and chats-by-text.
See you in Orlando?!
Love, K.

CHAPTER ONE

'I HAVE GOOD NEWS, *habibti*.'

Johara Behwar gazed in surprise at her father striding towards her. She was standing in the garden of the family villa in Provence, the dusty-sweet smell of lavender scenting the air, the sun shining benevolently down on a world on the cusp of summer. Her father's visits to their villa in France were precious and rare, and he'd only been there last week. To see him again was indeed unexpected. 'Good news—' She almost said *again* but then she thought better of it. Her father had not viewed the end of her engagement last week in the same shining light that she had.

'Yes, I think you will be very pleased,' Arif continued. 'And I, of course, am pleased when you are pleased.' He walked towards her, a smile creasing his weathered face, his hands outstretched. Johara smiled back, caught up in his cheerful mood.

'I'm pleased simply to see you, Father. That alone is a treat.'

'You are so kind, *habibti*. And in return here is a treat for you.' He took a small velvet pouch from his breast pocket and handed it to Johara.

She drew a diamond pendant from within the blue velvet, the jewels winking in the bright sunlight. 'It's lovely. Thank you, Father.' Obediently, because she knew her fa-

ther expected it, she clasped it around her neck, the heart
shape encrusted with diamonds nestling in the hollow of
her throat. It was indeed lovely, but, considering how quiet
her life was, she had little need or place to wear it. Still,
she appreciated the thought he'd given.

'What is this good news?' she asked as Arif took hold
of her hands.

'I have renegotiated your marriage.' Arif squeezed her
hands as his smile widened, triumph glinting in his eyes.
Johara stared at her father, confusion making her mind
spin even as sudden dread seeped like acid into her stomach. The diamond pendant felt cold against her skin. This
was not the good news he'd said it was. This wasn't good
news at all.

'Renegotiated?' she repeated faintly. Her hands felt icy
encased in her father's. 'But you told me barely a week
ago that Malik—I mean His Highness—had ended our
engagement.' She'd had six days first for that news to
sink in—and then to revel in the glorious freedom she'd
never thought to possess. The marriage she'd been trying
not to think about and dreading at the same time would
no longer happen. She'd felt as if the shackles she hadn't
realised she'd been wearing had suddenly fallen off, leaving her feeling light, as if she could fly. She was *free*—free
to do as she liked, and in a heady moment she'd let herself
think about an independent future, maybe even going to
university. The whole world had beckoned, shining and
wide open for the first time in her life.

And now... 'How can it be renegotiated? You told me
that His Highness was...was infertile.' It seemed indeli-
cate to mention such a thing, but her father had not spared
her the details last week, when he'd flown to France to
inform her that Malik al Bahjat, heir to the Sultanate of
Alazar, had called off their wedding. He'd been furious

on her behalf, storming and stomping around, and he had ignored Johara's stammering attempts to placate him and explain that she really didn't mind not getting married to Malik, or, in fact, not getting married at all. She hadn't quite dared to tell her father that she preferred it. After a lifetime of being reminded where her duty lay that seemed a step too far, even as she'd told herself her father surely only wanted her happiness.

'Yes, yes,' Arif said now with a touch of impatience. 'But Malik is no longer the heir, and we thank heaven that you did not marry him before this happened. *That* would have been a disaster.'

Johara agreed, but she doubted it was for the same reason as her father. A week of freedom had made her realise how unwelcome an arranged marriage was. Malik was a virtual stranger and a life bound in duty had lost any lustre it might have possessed. But she knew her father would not agree. So what was going on? If not Malik, then…?

Arif dropped her hands to rub his own together in obvious satisfaction. 'It has all worked out so well for us, Jojo,' he said, using the childhood nickname she hadn't heard in years. 'For you.'

An instant and instinctive disagreement was on the tip of her tongue, but Johara swallowed it down. She never disagreed with her father. She hated to see the smile fade from her father's face, the shadows of disappointment enter his eyes.

Invoking her father's displeasure always felt like the sun disappearing behind a cloud, a sudden chill entering the air and her heart. Her mother's love had long since gone, and taking away her father's attention was a further blow she knew she could not withstand. 'Tell me what has happened, please,' she said instead, trying to inject a note of interest in her voice that she was far from feeling.

'Azim has returned!' Arif spoke with a joy Johara didn't understand. The name was familiar, and yet…

'Azim…?'

'The true heir of Alazar. He has returned from the dead, or so we all thought him.' Arif shook his head in happy disbelief. 'Truly it is a miracle.'

'Azim.' Of course, Azim al Bahjat, Malik's older brother. Stupidly she had not made the association. Azim had been kidnapped twenty years ago, when Johara had only been two. There never had been a ransom note delivered or a body found, and so Azim had remained missing, presumed dead, for two decades. Malik had become the heir, had been the only heir in Johara's mind. Until now.

'Azim,' she said again, the name sounding strange on her tongue. 'What…what happened? How has he returned?'

'He had amnesia, apparently, after the kidnapping. He's been living in Italy for twenty years, not knowing who he was. But then he saw a mention of Alazar on the news and it all came flooding back. He has returned to claim his throne.'

'But…' A realisation was growing in her mind like a sandstorm kicking up in the desert, obliterating rational thought just as the sand blotted out the sky. Surely her father wouldn't…to a complete stranger… 'But what does that have to do with me?' She was afraid she knew the answer.

Arif's smile hardened at the edges. Johara knew that look. She quailed at that look.

'Surely you have guessed, Jojo,' he said, his voice jovial yet with a warning hint of underlying iron. 'Azim is to be your husband.'

Johara's stomach swooped. 'But…but I have never even met him,' she protested, her voice faltering.

'He is the heir.' Arif spoke as if it were obvious. 'Since birth you have been pledged to the heir to the Sultanate. In fact you were meant for Azim before you were betrothed to Malik.'

Shock rippled through her in icy waves. *Meant for Azim.* 'I didn't know that. No one ever said.'

Arif shrugged. 'Why would you know it? He disappeared when you were but a child. But now he has returned, and he shall claim you as his bride.'

It would have seemed romantic in a story or film, the kind of sweeping, fairy-tale gesture, a knight riding on his white steed, to make a girlish heart flutter. Johara's heart felt as if it were made of lead, weighing her down. She didn't want to be *claimed*, and certainly not by this stranger. Not when she'd had the whole world open to her moments ago, when she'd felt free for the first time in her life, able to make her own choices, live her own life.

'This seems rather sudden,' she said, trying not to sound quite as horrified as she felt, because she knew that would displease her father. 'My engagement to Malik al Bahjat only ended a week ago. Perhaps we should wait a little.'

Her father shook his head. 'Wait? Azim is determined to secure his throne, and that includes marriage as soon as possible. In fact he expects you in Alazar by tomorrow afternoon.'

Johara gazed at her father's face, the fixed smile, his bushy eyebrows drawn together, and felt her spirits start a precipitous descent. She'd known where her duty lay as long as she could remember. She'd been told it again and again, reminded that she had been given so much, and this was the way—the only way—she could repay her family.

And she'd *wanted* to repay it, had longed to please the father she rarely saw. She'd been prepared to marry Malik, even if hadn't quite felt real. She'd met him only twice, and spent only a handful of days in Alazar. And then for one brief and tantalising week, she'd imagined a different kind of life. One with choice and opportunity and freedom, where she could pursue her interests, dare to nurture her dreams.

Now, looking at her father's stern face, she realised how foolish and naïve she'd been. Her father was never going to let his only daughter go unmarried. He was a traditional man from a traditional country, and he would see her wed…this time to a man she'd never so much as laid eyes on. A man she knew nothing about, that *no one* knew anything about, because he'd been gone for twenty years.

'Johara?' Arif's voice had turned sharp. 'This is not unwelcome, I trust?'

Johara gazed helplessly at the father she'd always adored. She'd lived a sheltered life, educated at home, her pursuits solitary save for some charitable works her father approved of. Her mother had been distant for years, beset by illness and unhappiness, and so it had been her father's love, his sudden smile, his indulgent chuckle, that she had craved. She could not refuse him this even if she had the opportunity to do so, which she knew she did not.

'No, Father,' she whispered. 'Of course not.'

Azim al Bahjat watched from a window as the sedan with blacked-out windows came up the curving drive of Alazar's palace. The car contained his bride. He had not seen a picture of Johara Behwar, had told himself her looks were irrelevant. She was the intended bride of the future Sultan; the people of Alazar expected him to marry her. Any other choice would be less than second best, and therefore impossible. Nothing would prevent him from securing his inheritance and destiny, from proving himself to the people who had more than half forgotten that he was the real heir, the true Sultan.

A servant rushed forward to open the car door, and Azim leaned closer, curious in spite of himself for this first glimpse of his future bride, the next Sultana of Alazar. He saw a slippered foot first, small and dainty, and then a slim, golden ankle emerging from underneath traditional embroidered robes. Then the whole form appeared, willowy and enticing even beneath the shapeless garment, hair as dark as ink peeking from beneath a brightly coloured hijab.

Johara Behwar tilted her head to gaze up at the palace, and from the window Azim could see her whole face, and appreciate its striking beauty. Large, clear grey eyes framed by sooty lashes and gently arched brows. A pert nose, delicate cheekbones and full, pouty, kissable lips. He registered it only for an instant, for the delectable symmetry of her face was marred by its expression. *Revulsion*. Her eyes were wide and shadowed with it, her mouth thinning to a puckered line of distaste. As she gazed at the palace, a shudder went through her, her shoulders jerking, and for a second she wrapped her arms around herself, as if she needed to hold herself together in order to endure what was to come. *Him*. Then she straightened, steel entering her spine, and started towards the palace like a condemned woman ascending to the gallows.

Quickly Azim stepped away from the window. His stomach clenched and pain stabbed his head in two lightning-like slices. He pressed his fingers to his temples and tried to will it away even though he knew from far too much experience what a pointless exercise that was. So Johara Behwar was disgusted by the prospect of marrying him. It was not really a surprise, and yet...

No, he could not think like that. He had no use for sentiment of any kind, the naïve, youthful longings for some sort of connection with the woman who would be his Sultana. He'd made sure to live his life independently, needing no one. Being dependent on someone, much less actually *caring*, led to weakness and vulnerability. Shame and pain. He knew it too well and he had no intention of courting those awful emotions again.

This was a marriage of convenience and expediency, to secure an alliance and produce an heir. Nothing else mattered. Nothing at all.

Taking a deep breath, Azim dropped his hands from his temples and turned to face the door—and to greet his bride.

Each step down the marble corridor felt like a step towards her doom. Johara told herself she was being fanciful, it couldn't possibly be that bad, but her body disagreed. Nausea churned in her stomach and with a sudden lurch of alarm she turned to the attendant who was escorting her to meet His Royal Highness Azim al Bahjat. 'I think I'm going to be sick.'

The attendant backed away from her as if she'd already thrown up onto his shoes.

'Sick—'

She took a deep breath, doing her best to stay her stomach. She could not lose her breakfast moments before meeting her intended husband. Icy sweat prickled on her forehead and her palms were slick. She felt light-headed, as if the world around her were moving closer and then farther away. Another deep breath. She could do this. She had to do this.

She'd done it before, after all, although she'd been a child when she'd first met Malik, and hadn't realised the import of what was happening. The subsequent few meetings had been brief and businesslike, and Johara had managed not to actually think about what they were discussing, and its lifelong consequences, a wilful ignorance that in hindsight seemed both childish and foolish.

Now she couldn't keep from thinking of them. Azim was an utter stranger, and she'd been passed from one brother to the next like some sort of human parcel. The thought made her stomach churn again.

She'd spent the eight-hour flight from Nice telling herself that she and Azim could, perhaps, come to an amenable agreement. An arrangement, which was what all convenient marriages were. She would present him with a proposal, a sensible suggestion to live mainly separate lives that would, she hoped, be to both of their advantage. If she'd had the foresight and presence of mind, she would have done the same with Malik when they'd first discussed their engagement several years ago. Or perhaps she wouldn't have…it was only since she'd tasted freedom that she'd acquired a desperate appetite for it.

'Are you well, Sadiyyah Behwar?' the attendant asked, all solicitude now that he'd ascertained she wasn't really going to vomit.

Johara lifted her chin and forced a smile. 'Yes, thank you. Please lead on.'

She followed the man down the hallway, her trailing robes whispering against the slick marble floor. Her father had insisted she wear traditional formal dress for the first meeting with Azim, although she had never stood on such ceremony with Malik. She found the garment, with its intricately embroidered and jewelled hem and cuffs, stiff, heavy and uncomfortable, the unfamiliar hijab hot on her head. One more element of this whole affair that felt alien and unwelcome.

The attendant paused before a set of double doors that looked as if they were made of solid gold. Johara had been in the palace a few times before, for her brief meetings with Malik, but they'd always taken place in a small, comfortable room. Azim had chosen far more opulent surroundings for this initial introduction.

'His Highness, Azim al Bahjat,' the attendant intoned, and, with fear coating her insides with ice, Johara stepped into the room.

Sunlight poured from several arched windows, nearly blinding her so she had to blink several times before she caught sight of the man she was meant to marry. He stood in the centre of the room, his body erect and still, his face grave and unsmiling. Even from across the room Johara could see how black and opaque his eyes were, like a starless night in the desert. His dark hair was cut so close she could see the powerful bones of his skull, and a scar snaked from the corner of his left eye to the curve of his mouth, clearly long since healed over although the wounded flesh still looked red and livid. He wore an embroidered linen thobe, the material emphasising his lean, muscular form, broad shoulders tapering to narrow hips and long, powerful legs.

The whole effect was beyond intimidating. Terrifying was the word that came to mind, and she had to fight not to take an instinctive step back towards the doors, towards safety, away from this man whose face even in repose looked frightening. Looked cruel, although perhaps that was simply the darkness of his eyes, the livid red of the scar.

If she looked at his features reasonably, Johara told herself, fighting off the panic, she could see that he was an attractive man, his features even, his nose a straight slash, his mouth a mobile, sensual curve. Underneath his linen thobe his body was powerful and he moved with a graceful fluidity, taking a few steps towards her before stopping to survey her as she was surveying him, those dark eyes sweeping from the crown of her head to the soles of her feet, giving away nothing of what he felt or thought.

Then Azim inclined his head in what Johara supposed was a greeting. His voice, when he spoke, was clipped, cold. 'We will marry in one week's time.'

CHAPTER TWO

JOHARA'S MOUTH DROPPED open as Azim's words reverberated through the grand room. *Those* were the first words out of his mouth—not hello, nice to meet you, or any of the other forms of basic introduction acceptable to civilised society? Just this chilling dictate that the clenching of her stomach made her fear she would have no choice but to obey.

'I am glad you are agreeable,' he added shortly, turning away, and Johara realised he'd taken her silence for acquiescence—and was now effectively dismissing her. As far as her future husband was concerned, their conversation was over, and they hadn't even said hello.

'Wait—Your Highness!' Her voice was a hoarse whisper, and Johara cleared her throat, frustrated by her fear. This was too important a moment to act the shocked maiden. Azim turned back to her, his eyes narrowed, his mouth a hard, flat line that looked as if it never saw a smile.

'Yes?'

'It is only…' Johara gulped as she collected her scattered thoughts, the fragments of her dashed hopes. Their conversation—if she could use that word—had been so abrupt she could hardly believe it was over. She hadn't even had a chance to *think*. 'This has all happened so quickly. And we had never met before today—'

'We have met now.'

Johara stared at him, searching for some glimmer of warmth in those starless eyes, a hint of a smile in the uncompromising line of his mouth. She saw neither. 'Yes, but we do not know one another,' she continued, trying to make her tone both light and reasonable. 'And...*marriage.*' She spread her hands, tried for a smile. The pep talk she'd given herself on the plane seemed woefully improbable now, and yet she had no other plans, no other weapon. 'It is a large step to take for two people who have not laid eyes on one another before this moment.'

'Yet one you have, I have been told, been prepared to make for some time. I do not see any reason for your objection now?' The lilt of his voice suggested a question but Johara was wary of answering it. He did not seem as if he was waiting for a response.

When she dared to look into his eyes, she wished she hadn't. They felt like two black holes she could tip right into and fall for ever. 'I only meant...' she tried, 'shouldn't we get to know one another first? In order to—'

Azim's expression did not change a modicum as he answered, cutting her off. 'No.'

Johara took a deep breath, clinging to the remnants of her composure that was now in shreds. Even in her worst imaginings she hadn't expected Azim to be this unrelentingly cold. His expression was pitiless and impatient, his arms folded over his chest, as if she was wasting his time. How could she marry a man such as this? And yet she had to. Her only hope was some kind of negotiation as to the terms.

'Our marriage then will be one of convenience,' she stated.

His mouth twisted, drawing the puckered flesh of the

scar along his cheek tight. 'Surely you had already come to that conclusion.'

'Yes, but I mean…' She faltered, unsure how to present the suggestion that had seemed so logical, so amenable, on the journey here. She had not anticipated Azim al Bahjat's attitude of stony indifference, underlaid by a hostility she didn't understand. Unless she was being paranoid? Perhaps he was like this with everyone. Or perhaps he was simply nervous, as she was.

The prospect was laughable. Azim al Bahjat did not look remotely uncertain or nervous. He was a man utterly in command of the situation—and her. Still Johara persevered. 'Malik and I had discussed—'

'I do not wish to talk about Malik.' Azim's voice was the quiet snick of a drawn blade. 'Do not mention him to me again.'

Johara fell silent, chastened by this dictate. Her father had told her Malik was acting as Azim's advisor, but the lethal warning in his voice made her wonder if their relationship was fraught. Or perhaps it was the relationship with *her* that was fraught. 'I'm sorry. I only meant it would make sense for our marriage to be an arrangement that is convenient to both of us.'

'Make sense?' For a moment Azim looked coldly amused. 'How so?'

Encouraged by the mere fact that he'd asked a question, Johara plunged into her explanation. 'As you might know, I have spent most of my life in France. I am not as familiar with Alazar as you are—'

'You are Alazaran-born, with your bloodline able to be traced back nearly a thousand years.'

Yes, she knew of her precious ancestry, descended hundreds of years ago from the sister of a sultan. 'All I meant is,' she explained, 'France is my home, and has been since

I was a young child. I've only been to Alazar a handful of times in my whole life.'

Azim's mouth twisted in contempt. 'A notable lack in your upbringing. You will have to familiarise yourself with its customs immediately.'

This wasn't going at all the way she'd intended. *Hoped.* 'What I mean to say is,' Johara tried yet again, 'I would like to live in France for as much of the year as possible. Of course, I would come to Alazar when needed, for state functions and the like.' She spoke quickly, tripping over her words, desperate to come to an agreement. 'Whenever I'm needed, of course. It seems a suitable arrangement to us both—'

'Does it?' Azim cocked his head, his narrowed gaze sweeping over her, a dark searchlight. 'It does not seem so to me. Far from it, in fact.'

Frustrations warred with despair and Johara clenched her fists, hiding them in the stiff skirts of her dress. 'May I ask why?'

'My wife belongs with me, not pursuing her own interests in another country,' Azim stated, a hint of a sneer in his voice. 'The Sultana of Alazar must be by the Sultan's side, or in the palace, showing the country what an exemplary, modest and honourable woman she is. That is where you belong, Sadiyyah Behwar,' he finished in a ringing, final tone of a judge delivering his sentence. 'By my side, in the palace harem—or in my bed.'

Azim noted the way Johara's pupils flared even as her face paled. Was she disgusted by the thought of sharing his bed? He'd had his fair share of women over the years, and they had all been more than willing to be there. In any case it didn't matter whether Johara was or not. He was not looking for companionship or even pleasure from this arrangement. After a lifetime of being denied such things, he had schooled himself not to want them.

'You are very blunt,' she managed, two bright spots of colour now visible high on each cheekbone, the delicate skin around her pouty mouth nearly white.

'I am merely stating facts.'

Johara shook her head slowly. 'So you want me with you all the time, and yet you have no interest in getting to know me?'

'What is there to know?' Azim returned. The pain in his temples was becoming too much to indulge her in such a sentimental conversation. He didn't care about her feelings, or even his own. This was a matter of state, nothing more. 'You are young, healthy and eminently suitable,' he clarified. 'You can trace your bloodline back almost as far as I can. That is all I need to know.'

She lifted her chin, her eyes flaring now with anger. Arif had assured him his daughter was extremely biddable, but from this conversation alone Azim knew the man had exaggerated—and her defiance was both an aggravation and an insult he didn't need.

'There must be a dozen women like me,' she said, her chin lifted, 'with suitable breeding and bloodlines. Why are you so determined to marry a stranger you don't even want to get to know?'

Because she'd been intended for Malik. Because choosing anyone else when his entire country had been expecting her as Sultana would be an admission of failure, a sign of defeat, and something he refused to consider. He had suffered too much, sacrificed too much, to fail in this. 'You are my chosen Sultana,' he stated coldly. 'Most women would consider that an honour.'

Her eyes flashed. 'But I am not most women.'

'So I am beginning to realise.'

'I just don't understand—'

'You don't need to understand,' Azim snapped. He took a steadying breath, pain stabbing his temples once more. He could feel a full-fledged migraine coming on, the black spots starting to dance before his eyes, the nausea churning in his stomach. He had five minutes, if that, to get to a dark, quiet room and wait out the agony. 'All you need to do,' he stated in a tone of utter finality, 'is to obey.'

Her mouth dropped open as Azim turned away. He walked blindly from the room, his vision starting to grey at the edges. He could not manage any more. From behind him he heard a ragged gasp.

'Your Highness…' It was a cross between a protest and a plea, a sorrowful sound that grated on his nerves even as it plucked at the broken strings of his compassion. He had been abrupt with his fiancée, he could acknowledge that. If he hadn't been in pain, if he hadn't seen her shudder…perhaps things might have been a little different. But it was too late now to make amends, if he even wanted to, which he didn't think he did. Better for his bride to accept the hard reality, just as he'd had to do time and time again. Life was hard. People turned on you, betrayed you, used you. She could learn the same life lessons he had, albeit in far more comfortable circumstances.

'An attendant will show you to your room,' he stated, forcing the words out past the pain that was building like a towering wall in his head. 'You may spend the next few days preparing for our wedding.' He didn't wait to hear her reply. He knew Arif would force her to comply, and in any case he didn't trust himself to stay standing for much longer. He pushed through the doors, doubling over the moment they'd swung behind him, his hands braced on his knees.

'Your Highness…' An attendant hurried forward, and

with immense effort Azim straightened, throwing off the servant's arm. He couldn't be seen as weak, not even by a servant.

'I'm fine,' he grated. Then he walked on leaden legs to his bedroom, and its welcoming darkness.

Johara stood in the audience chamber for a full five minutes before she felt composed enough to leave its privacy for the prying eyes of the many palace staff. The abruptness of her conversation with Azim had bordered on the surreal, and yet it had possessed the stomach-clenching realisation of hard reality. This man, who had not spared her so much as an introduction, who barked commands, whose smile seemed cruel, was going to be her husband.

She tried to find one redeeming quality in the man she was meant to spend her life with and came up empty. He possessed a strong sense of duty, she supposed, her thoughts laced with desperation and flat-out panic. He wasn't bad-looking; in fact, if his expression hadn't been so severe, his manner so terse, she might have thought him quite handsome. His form was certainly powerful, and even in the shock and tension of their conversation she'd noticed his muscled shoulders, the dark slashes of his eyebrows.

He had a compelling look about him, possessing the kind of bearing that made you want to both stare and look away at the same time. He was too much. Too hard, too cold, too cruel. He hadn't offered her one simple civility in their first meeting. What on earth would their life together look like?

She *couldn't* marry him.

Johara pressed her hands to her cheeks, distantly noting their iciness, as she gazed out of the arched window at the desert vista. A hard blue sky and an unrelenting sun framed the endless, undulating desert. Looking at it hurt Johara's eyes, and made her long for the rolling hills and lavender fields of Provence, the dear familiarity of her book-lined bedroom, her kitchen garden with its pots of herbs, the stillroom where she'd pottered about experimenting with salves and tinctures, pursuing her interest in natural medicine. Made her wish, yet again, that everything about her meeting with Azim had been different. Better. Or preferably, hadn't happened at all.

She dropped her hands and took a deep breath. What recourse did she have now? She was powerless, a woman in a man's world, a sultan's world. Her only option was to run to her father and beg him to release her. Hope flickered faintly as she considered this.

Her father loved her, she knew he did. Yes, he'd been planning for her marriage to the Sultan of Alazar for years, but...he *loved* her. Perhaps her father had not realised what kind of man Azim was. Perhaps when she told him just how cold and hard her husband-to-be seemed, he'd renegotiate yet again. Or at least ask for a delay, months or even years...

Taking a deep breath, Johara turned from the room. A palace attendant was waiting by the door as she came through. 'His Highness wished me to show you your rooms.'

'Thank you, but I'd like to see my father first.'

The attendant's face was blank, his voice polite as he answered, 'Many pardons, but that is not possible.'

The anxiety that had been coiling in her stomach like a serpent about to strike reared up, hissing. 'What do you mean? Why can I not see my own father?'

'He is in a meeting, Sadiyyah Behwar,' the man answered smoothly. 'But I will, of course, let him know you wish to speak with him.'

Johara nodded, the panic receding a little. Perhaps she was overreacting, seeing conspiracy or coercion at every turn. Her father would surely come to her when he was able. He would listen to her. He would understand. He might be ambitious and sometimes a little bit hard, but she had never, not once, doubted his love for her. 'Thank you.'

She followed the man silently down a long marble corridor to a suite of rooms nearly as opulent as the audience chamber where she'd met Azim. She gazed round at all the luxury, the huge bed on its own dais with silk and satin covers, the sunken marble tub in a bathroom that was nearly as large as her bedroom at home, the spacious balcony that overlooked the palace's lush gardens. It was lovely, but all she could see was a gilded prison, invisible bars that would hold her there for the rest of her life.

What would she *do* here, as Azim's wife? Lie on a bed with her face to the wall, as her mother had these many years, trapped by her own endless despair? Johara resisted that with a deep, frightened instinct. She had long ago vowed never to be like her mother, had chosen a cheerful, optimistic approach to life as a matter of principle, because to give in to doubt or despair was no life at all. Yet optimism was hard to find now.

So then would she devote herself to her children, if they came, and try to forget the unending loneliness of being yoked to a man who had no interest in her beyond her bloodline? Would she be able to make friends, make a *life*? There was so much she didn't know, so much she couldn't imagine and didn't even want to imagine. She wanted more for her life than what Azim was offering. She wanted more for her life than any arranged marriage could provide. It had taken a fleeting week of precious freedom to make her realise that.

She sank onto a divan by the window, her body aching with both emotional and physical fatigue. It had been a little more than twelve hours since her father had told her she was marrying Azim. And only a week until she would be forced to say her vows…unless she could find some way out of this disaster—seek her father and try to persuade him to end the engagement. He had to listen to her. He loved her, she reminded herself. She was his *habibti*, his treasure, his little pearl. He wouldn't let her suffer a fate such as this.

Azim blinked in the gloom of his bedchamber, the migraine having finally lessened to a dull, endurable throb, the fragments of a dream still piercing his brain in poignant shards. He'd been back in Naples, hiding from Paolo, cowering and afraid. He hated that dream. He hated how it made him feel.

With determined effort Azim shook it off, banishing the memories of his confusion and fear. He was a sultan-in-waiting now, restored to his rightful place, a man of power and authority. He would not allow himself to be bested by his old nightmares, even if he'd had more and more of them since returning to Alazar.

He had no idea what time it was, but he noted the moonlight sliding between the shutters and knew it had been many hours. He closed his eyes, his whole body aching with the effort of having battled the pain—and won.

The headaches that had plagued him since he was fourteen years old had been getting worse since he'd returned to Alazar, no doubt from the unrelieved tension of being back in a place with so many bitter memories, as well as his legacy hanging by no more than a slender thread. He hated the fragility of his position, the powerlessness it made him feel. No wonder he'd had that old dream. He had no idea if the old tribes of the desert would accept him as a leader when he had been gone from his country, from his people's memory, for so long. He had only been a boy when he'd been taken, an event he couldn't actually remember. He had not yet had a chance to prove himself capable and worthy of command, no matter that his grandfather had been preparing him for it for years. Marrying Johara, as unwilling as she was, would help to cement his position as the next Sultan. He needed her compliance…or at least her perceived compliance. How she felt didn't matter at all as long as she obeyed.

Sighing heavily, he rose from his bed, the room see-sawing around him until he was able to blink it back into balanced focus. It wasn't only the pressures and tenuousness of his role that weighed on him now. It was the look of shocked hurt in Johara's clear grey eyes when he'd issued his flat commands earlier that day. He had not attempted to soften them with the merest modicum of kindness or compassion; he'd been in too much pain as well as too angry at her own unguarded reaction, when she'd looked up at the palace and he alone had seen the truth in her face.

He supposed he would need to remedy the situation somehow, but he was not a man prone to apologies. In the world he inhabited an apology was weakness, the admission of any guilt a mistake. He could not afford to do that now, even if he wanted to, which he did not. It was better for his new bride not to have any expectations except obedience.

'Azim?' Malik spoke softly from behind the bedroom door. Quickly Azim grabbed his shirt and pulled it on. He'd shucked it off in the worst throes of the migraine, when he'd been covered in icy sweat, but he was always careful to keep his back covered. No one, not even his infrequent lovers, had seen his scars. No one would know of his shame.

He flicked on the lights even though the flash of brightness sliced through his head like a laser. He straightened his clothes and ran a hand over his closely cropped hair, determined that Malik not see any sign of his weakness.

'Enter.'

Malik came in, closing the door quietly behind him. 'You are well?'

'Yes, of course. What is it?' He spoke more tersely than he'd intended, and saw the flash of bruised recognition in his brother's eyes. Once, a lifetime ago, they'd been close, leaning on each other when the adults in their lives had failed them, but now Azim had no idea how to navigate that old, once-precious relationship. For too long everyone had felt like an enemy, someone who would break the trust he now refused to give.

'You spoke to Johara?'

'Yes. She is not as compliant as her father indicated.'

Malik leaned one powerful shoulder against the doorframe, his arms folded. 'She knows her duty.'

'I would hope so.' Azim reached for his trousers, preferring the Western dress he was far more comfortable in after twenty years in Italy, at least in private. 'I told her we would marry in a week's time.'

Malik's eyebrows rose. 'So soon?'

'I do not have time to waste.'

'Still, that is rather quick,' Malik said mildly. 'Considering only a week ago she was meant to marry me.'

'She was meant,' Azim clarified with clipped precision, 'to marry the heir to the Sultanate, whoever that was.'

Malik inclined his head. 'You are right, of course. But she is very young, and she is not as used to our ways as you might—'

'I thought you did not know her.' Azim heard the edge to his voice and turned away from his brother. The knowledge that Johara had been meant for Malik gave him a deep-seated sense of resentment that he did not fully understand. He knew Malik and Johara had never so much as kissed, and yet still he resisted the notion of them together. So much had been taken from him, including his bride. He was more determined than ever to gain it all back, no matter what the cost—or who paid the price.

'She said she has spent most of her time in France,' he remarked to Malik. 'Why is that?'

Malik shrugged. 'Her mother has been ill for a long time. Arif has kept her away from Alazar.'

'Simply because she is ill? That does not seem sensible.'

'I am not quite sure of the details,' Malik answered. 'Arif never speaks of her.' He paused. 'That seems intentional.'

Azim frowned. 'I was assured Johara's bloodline was impeccable—'

'It is. But even impeccable bloodlines contain people with problems, with illness or suffering.'

Azim did not answer. God knew he had his own share of suffering, and he was descended from kings. 'Well,' he said after a moment. 'She will comply. She has no choice.'

'A little kindness might go a long way,' Malik suggested mildly. 'Considering her youth and inexperience.'

Azim had come to that conclusion himself, but he didn't particularly like hearing it from Malik. And what kindness could he offer her? He had no time or interest, not to mention ability, in wooing, paying court or offering flattery. He was a man of action, not words. He always had been. And in the world he'd lived in these last twenty years, flattery got you nowhere.

'I can manage my own bride,' he told Malik, his tone curt. Malik nodded, his mouth a pressed line. Tension simmered between them. Once they'd been as close as brothers could be, sharing everything, including sorrow, and now—what? Reluctant allies, perhaps, but even that was a step of faith for him, a level of trust he wasn't comfortable with, not even with Malik.

After Malik had left Azim summoned an attendant to his room. 'Send some fabric to Sadiyyah Behwar,' he instructed. 'Brocade and satin, spare no expense. As a gift from me, for her wedding dress. And ensure there are seamstresses on hand to do her bidding.' He knew she already possessed a gown from her intended wedding to Malik, but he wanted her to have a new one, one that was just for him. A new start for a new marriage. He hoped Johara appreciated his gesture.

CHAPTER THREE

JOHARA WRAPPED HER arms around herself, suppressing a shiver despite the sultry summer air, as she looked out on the steep roofs and steeples of Paris's Latin Quarter. She'd arrived back in Nice that morning and she was still trying to ignore the icy panic creeping coldly over her—and to convince herself that she'd made the right decision.

In the end it had been both easy and heartbreaking. She closed her eyes against the look of icy disbelief in her father's eyes when she'd asked him to delay the wedding. The memory of the conversation caused pain to lance through her again.

'F-F-F... Father,' she'd stammered, inwardly cringing at the look of barely concealed impatience in her father's face. She'd caught him leaving a meeting, and the other diplomats and dignitaries had eyed her with cold disapproval, a woman trying to break into a man's world.

'What are you doing here, Johara?' Arif asked. He glanced back at his colleagues. 'She is to marry His Highness Azim next week.'

'That's what I wanted to talk about,' Johara said, trying to gather the tattered remnants of her courage. 'About the marriage...'

'What is it?' Arif grabbed her elbow and steered her to a private alcove. 'You are humiliating me in public,' he snapped, his eyes narrowed to dark slits, everything in him radiating icy disapproval. Johara shrank back, shocked. He'd never looked at her like this back in France, even when she'd dared to risk his displeasure.

'Azim is…very cold.'

'Cold?' Arif looked nonplussed.

'He seems almost cruel,' Johara whispered, losing courage by the second. 'I…I don't want to marry him. I can't!'

Arif stared at her, his lips thinned, the skin around them white. 'Clearly I have spoiled you,' he stated in a hard voice. 'For you to be speaking this way to me now.'

'Father, please—'

'You have been petted and indulged your whole life,' Arif cut her off. 'And I have asked only one thing of you, something that is a great honour and privilege. And now you tell me to humiliate myself and my family, risk my career and livelihood, because you find him a little cold?' He shook his head slowly. 'I will do my best to pretend this conversation has not happened.'

'But, Father, if you love me…' Johara began, her voice shaking. 'Then surely you wouldn't…'

'Nothing about this has to do with love,' Arif stated. 'It has to do with duty and honour. Never forget that, Johara. Love is a facile emotion for fools and weaklings. Your mother is a testament to that.' Without waiting for her reply he stalked off, leaving her reeling.

Love is a facile emotion. She could hardly believe he'd dismissed her concerns, her feelings so easily. And worse, seemed to have none of his own. Like a naïve child she'd believed her father loved her. Now she knew the terrible truth that he didn't, and never had.

Baubles, presents, a careless pat or smile—these things cost her father nothing. They'd been sops to appease her, not expressions of his love. It was so obvious now, so awful.

For when his ambition was at stake, Johara's happiness was a sacrifice he didn't even have to think about making.

Her father had arranged her flight back to Provence that afternoon, so she could pack her things and collect her mother before returning for the wedding. Naima Behwar rarely left her bed, much less the villa in Provence, and Arif didn't want the trouble of having to coax her out of either. Amazing, really, how Johara could now see how self-serving he was. Kindness only came when it was free. Why hadn't she considered his father's treatment of her mother—his indifference and impatience—as a true reflection of his character, rather than the presents and smiles he carelessly tossed her way? Why had she been so stupid and shallow?

All during the flight to Nice her mind had raced in hopeless circles, trying to find a way out. A way forward. She was by nature an optimist, but her innate cheerfulness had taken a critical hit. She'd barely been able to summon a smile for the chauffeur, Thomas, who'd met her at the airport; he had been in the family's employ for two decades, and had once taught her to ride a bicycle. His wife Lucille had worked as their cook and first showed Johara how to distil oil from plants, the beginning of her interest in natural medicine. She'd miss them both, and the quiet, simple contentment of the life she'd had, the life she realised now she'd taken for granted.

Then, while Thomas had been getting the car, Johara had made a split-second decision, acting on desperate impulse, something she never did. She'd run.

Her mind had been a blur of panic as she'd walked away from where Thomas had told her to wait, towards the shuttle bus that went to the train station in Nice Ville. Within an hour she'd been on a train to Paris, amazed that she'd actually done it. She'd run away. She'd freed herself.

And now that she'd booked into a shabby, anonymous-looking hotel on a side alley in the Latin Quarter, she wondered what on earth she was going to do next. She had her freedom, but she knew she was ill-equipped to deal with it. Taking the train and navigating the crowded streets of Paris by herself had already felt overwhelming, more than she'd ever dealt with before. How was she going to survive, get a job, make a life for herself?

And, she wondered with a shiver that this time she couldn't suppress, how was she going to keep from being found? She shuddered to think of both her father and her husband-to-be's reactions when they learned she'd run. Perhaps they already knew. Thomas, their driver, had probably already sounded the alarm.

Outside a church bell began to toll and a flock of sparrows rose in a dark flurry. Laughter from the streets below floated up, and all the sounds and sights, the sheer normalcy of them, lightened Johara's spirits a little.

She could do this. She *would* do this. How hard could it be, to find some menial job that would keep a roof over her head and food on the table? Her needs were small and although she didn't have much life experience she knew she was smart as well as a quick learner. Surely any life, no matter how small, was better than being forced into a marriage she didn't want. Taking a deep breath, she turned from the window and went to get ready to look for a job.

Fifteen minutes later she was easing her way along the crowded streets of the Latin Quarter, clutching her bag to her chest as people moved past her in an indifferent stream. She hadn't realised how noisy and crowded the city was. Her few experiences of Paris had been from behind the tinted windows of a limousine, and then she'd been ushered into one boutique or another with her mother, everything exclusive and private. And even those trips had been a long time ago—her mother had not roused herself to go to Paris, or anywhere, in years.

Spotting a sign for a small café, Johara decided to take the necessary plunge. She ducked into the tiny restaurant and stammered a question to the hassled-looking manager by the kitchen door, asking if he was hiring.

'Do you have any waitressing experience?' he asked, his voice full of scepticism as he eyed her up and down.

'No, but—'

'Sorry, no.'

Dejectedly she turned away. She repeated the same cringing experience in the next four cafés. All of the managers had looked at her with either doubt or disbelief when she'd asked for work, and Johara wondered how they could tell she was inexperienced. Was it the way she dressed? Spoke? Or was her naiveté that obvious, like a beacon above her head?

Her feet ached and her stomach rumbled—she hadn't eaten since she'd been on the plane hours ago. Worse than either of those afflictions was the plunging sense of despair that she wasn't going to be able to make it in the real world. And what would she do then? Slink back to Azim with her tail tucked firmly between her legs, her head lowered in guilty remorse, and accept a cold, loveless marriage with a man she didn't like or even know?

No. She would rather pound every street in Paris looking for work than submit to a man as cold and cruel as Azim al Bahjat.

'*Salut, chérie,*' a man's low, purring voice carried over the sounds of the crowd, and Johara turned, startled to realise he was talking to her.

'*Salut,*' she said cautiously. The man's smile was wide as he lounged in the doorway of the shabbiest café Johara had ever seen, just a few tiny, dirty tables on a floor of cracked tiles.

'Are you looking for work?' He made a moue of sympathy. 'Finding it difficult?'

'A bit,' Johara admitted. 'Why?' She nodded to the café. 'Are you hiring?'

The man's smile widened. 'As it happens, yes. Do you know how to be nice to customers?'

It seemed a strange question, and Johara shrugged. 'I think so.'

The man eyed her up and down in a way that made her blush and shift uncomfortably, her bag clutched to her chest. 'Then you can start tonight. Can you be back here at nine?'

Johara swallowed, hardly daring to believe that she'd actually found a job. She didn't particularly like the look of the greasy man or the shabby café, but she was hardly in a position to choose. 'Yes, of course.'

Back at the hotel she ate, showered and changed, trying to ignore the sense of unease she felt about the man and his offer of work. As she headed out into the sultry summer evening butterflies flitted in her stomach and she tried to walk as she saw other women walking, with their heads tilted at a proud angle, their hips swaying, as if they knew who they were and where they were going. Johara felt as if she knew neither and had no idea how to find out.

The café was full of noisy customers when she approached, relieved that she'd managed to get herself to the right place. So many of the narrow, cobbled streets of the Latin Quarter looked the same. The same beady-eyed man who had hired her met her at the doorway.

'Ah, *chérie*. I'm so glad you came.' He drew her by the hand into the hot press of people, one arm snaking around her waist. Alarm bells started clanging in Johara's head as she tensed, her body arching instinctively away from him. No man had ever touched her so intimately, their hips bumping, her breasts brushing his shoulder.

'Don't be shy,' he said with a laugh, pulling her closer, one hand brushing her breast. 'Remember I said you had to be nice.'

Johara glanced around at the crowded café, and all the faces looked sweaty and leering. The man's hand was still on her waist, the side of her body pressed tightly to his. The acrid smell of alcohol and sweat stung her nostrils and made her head swim.

She opened her mouth to say something, to explain this wasn't quite what she'd thought it would be, but no words came out. And then someone else was speaking.

'Get your hands off her right now.' The words were clipped, the tone utterly lethal. The sneering smile on the man's face slid right off when he caught sight of whoever was standing behind Johara. He held up his hands as he backed away.

'*Pardon, monsieur*, I didn't know she was taken.'

'Now you know.'

Slowly Johara turned, her heart beating so hard she could feel the blood roaring in her ears. It couldn't be… but of course it was. Azim stood in the doorway of the café, his eyes blazing black fire, his hands clenched into fists at his sides. With his powerful frame, the scar snaking down his cheek and his air of barely leashed fury, he was utterly terrifying. No wonder the man backed away. She wanted to run.

'Don't think of trying it,' Azim said in a low, dangerous voice, and Johara knew he'd read her thoughts.

'How did you find me?' she asked in a shaky whisper.

'Easily. Come with me. Now.' As his strong, lean fingers circled her wrist and pulled her towards him Johara had no choice but to comply. She stumbled as he drew her from the café, throwing one hand out to the doorframe to keep from falling.

'Stop, you're hurting me.'

Azim slowed, his fingers loosening around her wrist, even as his expression remained icily furious.

'My car is waiting.'

'I'm not going with you.' Johara wished she'd sounded more firm.

'Don't be ridiculous,' Azim snapped. 'You can't stay here.'

'Why not?'

'Because,' he gritted between clenched teeth, stepping closer to her, 'I just took you out of a whorehouse.'

'A…' Her jaw dropped.

'You do know what that is?' Azim inquired. 'I presume you're not that innocent?'

A fiery blush rose from her throat to the crown of her head. 'Yes, I know what that is,' Johara muttered. 'I've read books.'

'Oh, well, then. You're the voice of experience, I suppose.' He shook his head, clearly disgusted, and pulled her, gently at least, towards the waiting limousine. This time Johara went without a murmur.

She clambered into the luxurious interior, the leather sumptuous and soft against her bare legs. Azim climbed in next to her and barked out an address to the driver before slamming the door and leaning back against the seat.

Realisations were firing through Johara, short-circuiting her synapses. 'Was it really…?' she began through trembling lips.

'Yes,' Azim stated flatly. 'It was.'

Her teeth started to chatter as she realised how close she'd come to utter disaster. She could have been raped.

She could have been sold into sexual slavery. She could have been... She closed her eyes as a wave of nausea hit her. She could hardly bear to think of it.

'Are you cold?' Azim demanded, and Johara shook her head. She wasn't cold, but she couldn't seem to stop shaking.

He eyed her for a moment, his expression utterly fierce, before he reached forward to the limo's minibar and poured a generous shot of whisky into a glass. 'Here. Drink this. It will help.'

Her numb fingers curled around the glass. 'Help...?'

'You're in shock.'

She glanced down at the amber liquid, its pungent smell making her grimace. 'I've never drunk hard alcohol before.'

'Now is as good a time as any.' Azim watched her, his very gaze commanding her to drink, and Johara raised the glass to her lips.

The whisky burned down her throat and lit a fire in her belly. Somehow she managed not to sputter, but she wiped her mouth with the back of her hand, thrusting the glass back at Azim.

'No more.'

A tiny smile curved his mouth, making his scar pucker. 'Not bad for the first time. You didn't cough.'

'I wanted to.'

'You have strength of spirit.' From his tone she couldn't tell if that was a good or bad thing.

She turned to look out of the window, unsettled by the sudden and overwhelming turn of events. Outside the limo the streets of Paris streamed by in an electric blur.

'Where are we going?' she asked after a few tense, silent minutes had ticked by.

'To my flat.'

'How did you find me? Easily, I know, but…'

'Your driver alerted your father, who told me.'

So her father had betrayed her yet again. She wasn't surprised, but it still hurt. 'Was he angry?'

'Furious,' Azim answered shortly. 'What did you expect?'

For someone who loved her to think about her happiness. But of course her father had never really loved her. How long, she wondered, was that going to hurt? 'I don't know,' she mumbled. She felt tired and near tears, trapped and humiliated, as if she were a naughty child being marched to the corner.

'Even I did not think you would be so stupid and selfish as to run away,' Azim said. Anger thrummed through his voice. 'Even though you had made it clear what you thought of our forthcoming marriage.'

'As did you,' Johara returned, half amazed by her own audacity. She never spoke to her father, or anyone, like this. It felt good to speak her mind to someone, even if she'd regret it later.

'So I did.' Azim was silent for a moment and Johara found herself suddenly conscious of his nearness, the powerful length of his thigh brushing hers on the seat. She could smell his aftershave, the mingled aromas of sandalwood and cedar. Her senses stirred in a way that felt unfamiliar and intriguing. She had a bizarre desire to shift closer, to feel the length of his leg against her own, a prospect that horrified her. This man was her enemy. He was also, unless she managed a miracle, going to be her husband.

Azim turned to look out of the window, his gaze hooded as he looked out at the blur of traffic. 'Our first meeting,' he said finally, 'did not go as I had intended.'

'Oh? What had you intended?' She was curious but she

couldn't keep a sarcastic edge from her voice. Disconcerted now by his nearness, she found the memory of their first conversation—such as it had been—still stung. How had he thought any sane woman would respond to his unemotional, autocratic dictates?

'That you would be the compliant woman your father indicated that you were,' he replied as he turned back to her. 'But so far you have disappointed me at every turn.'

'And you have disappointed me,' Johara snapped, and then drew a ragged breath, pressing herself against the seat, as she realised from the look of cold fury on Azim's face that she'd gone too far.

'Then we shall both have to learn to live with disappointment,' he answered after a moment, his voice dangerously even. 'Hardly a tragedy.' He turned his head away once more and they did not talk again until the limo had stopped in front of an elegant building off the Champs-élysées.

'Is there where you live?'

'It is one of my homes.' The driver opened the door and Azim slid out, extending a hand back towards Johara. With the awkward angle of the seat, as well as Azim's body barring the door, she had no choice but to take it.

The slide of his strong hand against hers was an unexpected jolt, as if she'd touched a live wire. Shocked by the sensation, she let out a gasp, and then registered Azim's cool smile of satisfaction with wary confusion.

The smile disappeared as soon as she'd noted it, their gazes locking in a taut battle of wills before Azim dropped her hand and turned towards the building. On legs as shaky as the rest of her, Johara followed.

CHAPTER FOUR

A THOUSAND THOUGHTS and feelings whirled through Azim as he stalked through the foyer of the apartment building, ignoring the concierge's murmured pleasantries. Foremost was fury, that Johara had shamed him in such a way by publicly absconding days before their marriage. After that came disgust, that he'd led her to do such a thing. As angry as he was about her runaway attempt, he knew he'd handled their first meeting badly. He just didn't know if he had it in him to make amends.

Beyond those two negative emotions was a deep-seated relief that he'd saved Johara from, at best, a very unpleasant evening, and at worst, a lifetime of enforced prostitution—and then finally primal, masculine satisfaction, for in the moment when their hands had touched he'd felt her reaction, like a spark travelling up his arm, igniting in his belly. She desired him.

Perhaps she didn't want to, perhaps she didn't even realise it, but he knew. He'd seen it in the flare of her pupils, heard it in her surprised gasp and felt it in the shudder that had gone through her, just as he'd felt his own body's response. Their marriage, then, would at least have sexual chemistry—and that was no small thing.

They didn't speak in the tiny, enclosed space of the antique lift that juddered up towards the penthouse. Johara pressed herself against the grate, her grey eyes startlingly wide and looking almost silver in the dim light. He'd seen her only in the shapeless robes, and now he noted the slender and enticing curves highlighted by the sundress she wore. The thin, gauzy material clung to her small, pert breasts and tiny waist, flaring out about her long, slender legs. No wonder that disgusting pimp had wanted her for his whorehouse. She was gorgeous, innocence and sensuality in one jaw-dropping package, and she didn't even realise how alluring she was.

'Does your father know you wear clothes like these?' he demanded and Johara pressed back even farther away from him.

'My father lets me wear what I like.'

Wasn't around to notice or care, Azim filled in silently. He'd taken Arif's measure at their first meeting; the older man had been more than eager to have his daughter exchange grooms weeks before the wedding. While it suited Azim's purposes admirably, it did not endear him to the man. He was the worst combination of weakness and lust for power, just as Caivano had been. It had led to his tormentor's downfall, and it would eventually lead to Arif's. He would not have such a man in his cabinet.

The lift jolted to a stop and the doors opened. Azim ushered Johara out to his flat, a soaring, open space that took up the entire top floor of the building.

Johara stepped out, craning her neck to take in the vaulted ceiling and huge windows. The doors of the lift closed behind Azim and he stood watching her, noticing the way her dress clung to her hips, the fabric whispering about her shapely legs as she moved. A dark, curling tendril of hair lay against the nape of her neck and he had the absurd urge to lift it and see the delicate skin beneath.

She turned to face him, her trembling lips pressed together, her chin raised in challenge. Even though her rebellion tried him sorely, he could not help but admire her courage. He hadn't thought she'd possessed the audacity to make a run for it. He was, perversely and annoyingly, pleased that she'd been that daring, even if he was still furious that she'd tried.

'So?' Johara asked, her voice managing to be both strident and shaky at the same time. 'What now?'

Azim folded his arms. 'You will marry me.'

'Of course.' She let out a high, trembling laugh. 'Of course, I have no say in the matter.'

Irritation, and something deeper and rawer, rippled through him. 'If I am not mistaken, you have known about your arranged marriage for nearly your whole life. Why are you resisting now?'

'Because.' Johara looked away and said nothing more.

Azim regarded her coolly. 'Because of me, you mean.'

She shot him one wild glance before turning away again, giving him a view of her profile, the high forehead, the smooth curve of her cheek, the heavy mass of hair pulled back in an elegant chignon. 'You have made your intentions clear,' she said. 'You have no interest in getting to know me.'

'Did Malik?' He hadn't wanted to mention his brother, hated even thinking about Johara married to him, sharing his bed. Quickly Azim banished the image. 'Well?' he demanded when Johara did not answer. 'Did he?'

Johara glared at him, the lift of her chin now seeming stubborn rather than courageous, and entirely aggravating. 'Not particularly,' she said after a moment, the words drawn from her reluctantly and yet ringing with stark honesty.

'Well, then.' Azim didn't know what point he'd been trying to prove. That his bride-to-be objected to wedding him more than his brother? That she was repelled by him, by the scar on his face? What would she think if she saw the scars on the rest of his body? Not, of course, that she ever would.

'If I'm honest,' Johara said after a moment, her voice quiet, 'I wasn't looking forward to marrying Malik, either. What woman wants to marry a stranger for the sake of a crown?'

'I imagine there are many.'

'I am not one of them.'

'But you agreed.' He cocked his head. 'Your father insisted on that.'

'He would.' A new bitterness spiked her words and she looked away again. 'I agreed because I've known nothing else. Because...' She shook her head, clearly not wanting to say more.

'If you were so reluctant, why did you not say something to my brother?'

'I just didn't want to think of it. I... I pretended it wasn't going to happen and I told myself I could carry on with my life as normal afterwards. It was easier to do that, since I hardly ever saw him. We only met a couple of times, for no more than a few minutes. And I had my life in France.'

A life she seemed desperate to get back to. Was someone waiting for her there? Perhaps his bride was not as innocent as her father claimed, although considering her obvious naiveté he found that a difficult notion to entertain. 'It seems remarkably shortsighted,' he remarked. 'Your marriage was in a matter of months.'

'I know.' She hunched her shoulders. 'The closer it got, the less I tried to think of it. A child's response, but perhaps I was a child.' Her lips trembled again and to Azim's horror he saw a single, silvery tear slip down her cheek. She dashed it away with a grimace. 'Perhaps I still am.'

'You are not a child.' The response he'd felt in her earlier, the woman's body he saw now, told him as much. 'But you are innocent and have lived a sheltered life. That is not a bad thing.'

'Except that it caused me to walk into a whorehouse tonight, thinking I was going to be a waitress.' Azim saw the glimmer of a smile through her sadness, and felt a flicker of admiration for her bravery, facing a future she didn't want, even as he rebelled against the knowledge that *he* was that future. 'What must you think of me?'

'I think,' he said, his voice low and gravelly, 'that I am very thankful I found you in time.'

Johara closed her eyes, shaking her head. Another tear slipped down her cheek and Azim had an urge to comfort her, an instinct that seemed absurd. He was her captor, the person she was fighting against. Her enemy, or so she seemed to think. How could he comfort her? He'd never comforted anyone.

And yet as he watched her turn to the window, looking out at the wash of lights that was Paris at night, he could not keep from feeling a sharp pang of sympathy for her. He knew what it was like to feel trapped. He'd felt the invisible walls of a prison surrounding him, suffocating him for too many years, just as he suspected she was feeling now.

Johara let out a soft, sorrowful sigh, a sound of resignation and even despair, and the wave of sympathy he'd felt receded. His bride-to-be's prison was luxurious, with every comfort to hand. She was poised to become a woman of respect and power, not some lackey or near-slave. She had nothing to complain about.

'You should rest,' he said, his tone abrupt. She turned back to him, startled and wary. 'Tomorrow is going to be a big day.'

'Why…?'

He shook his head, not willing to say more then. It was time that his future wife started to obey him, no questions asked. 'Go to bed,' he commanded. 'You may have any one of the guest rooms down the hall.' He nodded towards a dark corridor leading away from the open-plan living area. 'And don't even think of trying to escape. The apartment is locked and alarmed, and the doorman has orders not to assist you in any way.'

Johara blinked, clearly shocked by both the information and his tone, and Azim hardened his resolve. Johara had shown him just how loyal she could be. He would not trust her an inch. Considering he'd never trusted anyone, it was hardly a loss. Turning on his heel, he left her alone in the room without waiting to see whether she would obey. He knew she would.

Johara woke to bright sunlight spilling through the tall, sashed windows and for an instant she felt cheerful, her old, optimistic self, intent on a new, sunny day. Then the memories of the last forty-eight hours played on a loop through her brain and she sagged against her pillows, exhausted before the day had begun. She was Azim's prisoner, and soon she would be his wife. Her one desperate bid for freedom had utterly failed. She saw no way to mount another, and Azim seemed utterly determined to marry her.

Did she have any options at all? With a heavy heart Johara ran through the possibilities. She had a feeling it would be near-impossible to run away again, and once she was back in Alazar it would be even harder. And even if she did manage to get away, what would she do? Where would she go? Her one foray into independence had shown her how ill-equipped she was for it.

Her heart heavier than ever, she rose from the bed,

knowing she needed to face the day—and Azim—at some point. Would they fly back to Alazar today? Would she see her father? The thought brought a lightning strike of pain. Her father had shown his true colours. The relationship she'd thought she'd had, that she'd counted on, had never really existed. Her father didn't love her. No one did. The best and only thing she could do was face her future, her chin lifted high.

Last night she'd stumbled into the first bedroom she'd found, smarting from Azim's set-down and aching from the trials of the day. Now she looked around the room properly, admiring its clean lines, the cool colours. A huge window overlooked the city, the Seine winding its green-blue way through the narrow streets and wide boulevards. And her suitcase was by the door.

Johara registered it with a mixture of bemusement and apprehension. Azim had moved quickly in this, as he had with everything else, finding out where she was staying and getting her things. What would he do next? What demand would he make of her?

She showered and dressed slowly, taking her time, wanting to postpone the moment when she opened her bedroom door and faced Azim. Eventually she decided it would be better simply to get it over with, and in any case she was hungry. She came into the living area to find him dressed in a sharply tailored Italian suit, sitting at the dining table with a computer tablet and a cup of coffee. He looked up as she entered the room, and in that second Johara's whole body blazed with an awareness that shocked her, his dark gaze seeming to see right inside her, peel away all her protective layers.

She stopped where she stood, everything tingling from Azim's single, blazing look. Had his cheekbones always been so blade-sharp? Had his lips really been that full? And why on earth was she thinking this way now?

'Are you going to work?' she asked uncertainly, for he looked brisk and businesslike, poised for action. But perhaps he always looked like that. She really didn't know this man at all.

'No.' He nodded towards the silver coffee pot on the table, along with a tray of croissants and pastries. 'You should eat.'

'Are you always going to tell me what to do?' Johara returned, more out of curiosity than pique, and Azim arched an eyebrow.

'Are you not hungry?'

'Yes, but…' She shrugged, not wanting to pick a fight over pastries. She didn't like the way Azim barked out commands, but she supposed she'd have to get used to it. Their impending wedding loomed, a dark cloud on the horizon coming ever closer, impossible to ignore and too big to flee, even if her mind still raced to find possibilities.

Azim sat back in his chair, watching her as she came to the table and poured herself a cup of coffee. She sat down, conscious of his brooding look, the long brown fingers wrapped around his coffee cup. For some reason seeing him this morning, freshly showered and wearing a suit, felt different than before, when she'd been greeting a stranger dressed in ceremonial robes in an opulent room in the palace. As for last night…she'd been so shocked by the turn in events that she'd barely registered what he looked like.

Now she couldn't seem to keep her gaze from darting to him, noting the play of muscles under the crisp white shirt, the steely glint in his fathomless eyes, the barest hint of stubble on his freshly shaven jaw. Each detail imprinted itself on her senses and made it hard to focus. She'd never noticed such things about Malik. Why was she reacting this way to Azim now? Was it simply because her wedding was closer than ever and impossible to ignore—or because Azim seemed more dangerous, more primal than Malik ever had? She could hardly believe they were brothers.

'Is it strange?' she asked abruptly, following the train of her thought without considering the consequences. 'To be back?'

Azim lowered his coffee cup, his eyes narrowing to dark slits. 'Strange? What do you mean?'

Johara shrugged, realising again how little she knew this man. And yet, in that moment, she wanted to know a little more. 'You have been gone from Alazar for a long time.'

'And I'm not in Alazar now.'

'But…you know what I mean.'

Azim rose from the table, taking his computer tablet and slipping it into an expensive-looking leather attaché. 'Yes, it is strange, but only in that it is not strange. If that makes sense to you.'

'I suppose it does.' She paused, toying with her pastry with the tines of her fork. 'My father said you had lost your memory.'

Azim stilled, his hands resting on the attaché. 'Yes.'

She glanced up, saw the wary, almost hunted look on his face and wondered at it. 'Have you gained all your memory back? Of everything?'

'No. Of most things. Most of my childhood, at any rate.' He zipped up the case and straightened, his expression closed now, as if it had been wiped clean.

Johara nodded slowly. She could tell the conversation was over, and yet she was still curious. 'If we are to be married, we should know things about one another,' she blurted.

'If?' Azim repeated with a sardonic lift of one eyebrow. 'There is no if.'

She looked away, hopelessness warring with something else, something indefinable that she didn't recognise, an emotion that stirred inside her like something long dormant coming to life.

'I don't understand why you must marry me and not someone more suitable.'

'There is no one more suitable.'

Johara let out a hollow laugh. 'I am not the only young woman with impressive Alazaran lineage.'

Azim was silent for a moment, his arms folded across his chest, biceps bulging. 'No, but you are the only one who was engaged to my brother,' he said at last.

'Why does that matter?'

'You have been known as the next Sultana for fifteen years. To choose someone else would be to disappoint expectations and sow doubt among my people. I do not wish to do either.'

'Why would they doubt?'

Azim's mouth tightened, his eyes flashing darkly. 'I have been gone a long time.'

So marrying her would help to stabilise the country, or at least his rule. Johara sighed and shook her head. 'It is hard to believe I am that important.'

'Be flattered,' Azim returned dryly.

'I would rather be free.'

Something flashed across his face, so quickly that Johara almost missed it. She thought it might be pity, or perhaps compassion. As if he understood what she meant, how she felt. But she could tell by the iron set of his jaw and the steel in his eyes that any momentary flicker of compassion would not change his decision or set her free.

'You have had plenty of time to get used to the idea of

an arranged marriage,' Azim said with a dismissive flick of his fingers. 'And in any case, if you did not marry me, what would you do? Where would you go?' She stared at him mutely, not wanting to admit how few options she had, but Azim didn't need her to answer anyway. 'You almost stumbled into a life of prostitution when you'd only been on your own for a few hours,' he continued, his tone reminding her of the relentless growl of a steamroller, flattening every argument, every opposition. 'You are not suited for work, and you have very little experience of the world. You have no choice.'

'How can you say I am not suited for work?' Johara protested. 'You don't know me.'

Azim shrugged. 'I admit I assume, but have you ever done a day's work?'

She spent hours in her garden and stillroom in France, or in her bedroom studying books on herbal and natural medicine. Maybe that wasn't the same as an eight-hour shift working as a waitress, but she resented the implication that she was lazy or spoiled. Still she said nothing, because to trot out her list of meagre accomplishments now felt both pathetic and pointless. Azim had already told her he wasn't interested in getting to know her beyond her bloodline and breeding.

'I have very little experience of this world,' she said, addressing his second point, 'and I am unlikely to get more stuck in a palace, hardly ever able to go out.'

'Now you are the one making assumptions.'

'Am I? You told me yourself that my only place was by your side, in the harem, or...' She trailed off, her cheeks going pink as she realised the trap she'd stupidly set for herself, and then walked right into.

'Or in my bed,' Azim filled in, his voice a soft, beguiling purr. 'There are worse places to be than those.'

'I wouldn't know,' Johara muttered, looking away. She was utterly out of her depth.

'No, you wouldn't,' Azim agreed in that same quiet voice. He had prowled as stealthily as a panther up to her chair, close enough so she could breathe in the sandalwood-and-cedar scent of his aftershave. 'But that is at least one area of marriage that could prove interesting to us both.'

Her breath came out in a shaky rush. 'Interesting…?'

'Pleasurable.' One hand reached down to her own nerveless fingers and drew her up so she was facing him, their bodies only inches apart. Unable to bear the look of sensual intensity on his face, Johara looked down, conscious of his fingers twined with hers, his body so close she could feel the heat rolling off him. She'd never been so close to a man before. If she moved so much as an inch, she'd be touching him. Her head swam.

'Perhaps we should see how pleasurable,' he suggested softly. 'So we are not taken by surprise on our wedding night.'

'I don't…' Johara found she couldn't say anything else. Her head felt as if it were full of cotton wool, and yet every sense was achingly, exquisitely alive. Azim nudged her closer so their hips bumped and she let out a gasp of shock. Malik had not touched her once, save for a formal handshake. This felt like tangling with electricity.

'You don't…?' Azim prompted, tilting her chin up with his other hand so she was forced to meet his eyes. They were as black as ever, yet somehow they no longer seemed menacing or cruel. She felt as if she could lose herself in them, in him. Fall into their dark depths and never come out. 'Or you do?'

She had no idea what to say, and so she simply shook her head helplessly, parted her lips although no words emerged. Azim laughed softly,

'You are sending out mixed signals, Johara,' he breathed as his fingertips trailed sparks up the side of her face, a tiny, tingling caress. 'I think you are scared, but I think you also want me to kiss you.'

Kiss. She'd never even come close to being kissed. Yet now her gaze dropped of its own accord to Azim's mouth, those full, mobile lips that she'd noticed that morning. Lips that were coming closer to hers, and made her heart race. She did want to kiss him. She didn't understand it, and a distant, panicky part of her brain insisted she didn't really want that, she couldn't possibly, but her body was saying otherwise. Her body was clamouring for Azim to close the mere inch between their mouths so she could feel the taste and touch of him on her lips.

And then she did. Azim brushed a kiss over her lips, as soft as a whisper, so Johara was left wondering if it had really happened. And then another brush that made her whole body tense like a violin that had experienced the first swipe of a bow across its strings, before his mouth settled firmly on hers and a symphony of sensation began.

She felt as if fireworks were popping in her mind, all over her body, as Azim explored the soft contours of her mouth with gentle assurance, fitting her body close to his, hips bumping, breasts pressed against the hard wall of his chest. Her hands tangled in his hair as her head fell back and he sweetly plundered her mouth.

She had had no idea that kissing felt like this. Could be this...*wonderful.* Her body was tingling, pleasure zinging through her like bubbles in champagne. She barely knew what she was doing, only that she desperately wanted more. Her hands drifted from his hair to his face, her fingertips trailing down his cheek and then brushing the raised, puckered flesh of his scar.

Azim stilled for a second and then broke the kiss. Johara blinked up at him, her lips swollen, her mind reeling. Azim gazed down at her, his expression as inscrutable and unchanged as ever, save for a faint flush on his sharp cheekbones, a hint of smug triumph in his dark eyes.

'That was a good start,' he said, and moved away from her. Johara simply stared. She didn't know what had happened, or why. That kiss, with its passion and promise, was the last thing she'd expected. No, she acknowledged with a plunging realisation, her *response* was the last thing she'd expected.

Azim had short-circuited her senses, utterly overwhelmed them. She'd never felt that blaze of desire streaking through her body before, lighting everything up, burning away common sense or rational thought. For those few blissful moments it had taken over everything, made her act like someone she couldn't recognise, didn't even know.

'Do you make a habit of kissing people like that?' she asked shakily.

'No,' Azim answered. 'Only my bride.'

'I'm not your bride yet.'

'No,' he agreed, 'but you will be.' He paused, turning back to level her with a single, assured look. 'Today.'

For a second Johara, her mind still spinning from Azim's kiss, couldn't make sense of the words. Finally her brain kicked into belated gear. 'What do you mean, *today*?'

'Exactly that. I have arranged a civil service at a courthouse nearby.' He spoke matter-of-factly, as if this were an everyday occurrence. 'We're expected there in a little over an hour.'

'An hour?' Johara goggled. 'You expect me to marry you in an *hour*?'

Azim's stare was flat and uncompromising. 'Yes, that is my expectation, and it is yours as well.'

'But…' Her mouth was dry, her heart pounding. *And she'd thought one week was fast.* 'What about my parents? And your people?'

'They are your people too, Johara.'

That might have been so, but they didn't feel like her people. Alazar was a strange country, a place she went to on rare occasions to play-act at being a sultana-in-waiting for her father's sake. And Azim, no matter how he'd just kissed her, was still a strange man. She wasn't ready to marry him. She wasn't ready emotionally and as for *physically*—

Her insides lurched like a ship in a gale. Was he expecting a wedding night along with the wedding? Images, blurred by ignorance and yet shockingly specific in parts, danced through her mind. Candlelight on burnished skin. Limbs twined among satin sheets. Kisses like the one she'd experienced, but even more explosive. And yet *marriage*, in a matter of minutes.

'Why?' she asked, the word bursting out of her like a bullet from a gun, reverberating through the room, shattering the taut stillness. 'Why are you rushing things? Don't you want a proper wedding, a real ceremony, back in Alazar?' She snatched a trump card and threw it down. 'Don't your people?'

'Yes, and they will get one. This is but a civil service. In five days the wedding ceremony, a religious occasion, will still go ahead. But make no mistake,' he finished, a warning glint in his eyes. 'The ceremony today will be valid.'

Johara stared at him, caught between despondency, fear and a new, dangerous excitement she didn't want to examine too closely. 'I'm not ready,' she said, even though she knew Azim wouldn't care.

'I can't trust you not to run away again,' he answered flatly. 'Not that you'll have much opportunity.'

'If I promise…?'

'I don't trust your promises,' he returned. 'And I will not change my mind.'

A last bid, desperate, pathetic. 'Does my father know you're doing this—?'

'Yes,' Azim said, and it was the flicker of pity in his eyes that sealed her fate. Made her realise how hopeless it all was. 'He does.'

So her father had no objection to Azim spiriting her away and essentially forcing her to the altar. Of course not.

She couldn't escape marriage. If she ran away, Azim would find her again. And even if he didn't, she wasn't at all sure she could survive on her own. She hadn't done a great job of it in her few hours of freedom.

Besides, she acknowledged bleakly, what about her duty and honour? They were concepts she still believed in even if her father had flung them at her like insults. Perhaps as the wife of the Sultan she could carve out a life for herself, do good in the world. Certainly she'd have more opportunity for it than a life on the run, penniless and destitute.

And maybe Azim's lack of interest could be a good thing. *Love is a facile emotion.* At least she would have no reason to go chasing after it, and be hurt again, the way her father had hurt her.

She'd made a desperate, childish bid for freedom, but now she needed to grow up and face her future. She would not shirk her responsibility simply because her father had not been the man she'd thought he was. The realisation was like swallowing lead. It rested in the pit of her stomach, heavy and poisonous.

'It won't be all bad,' Azim said, and Johara let out a huff of despairing laughter.

'Is that supposed to make me feel better?'

'Why shouldn't it? You look,' he informed her with a

touch of acid, 'as if you are about to head to the gallows. I'm simply reminding you that becoming the queen of a country and enjoying a life of luxury and means is hardly a prison sentence.'

'No,' Johara agreed, because he was making her sound rather spoiled, 'but it is a life sentence.'

Something flashed in his eyes and she had the bizarre sense that she'd hurt him with her words. It hardly seemed possible, and before she could process whatever that flash had been he'd turned away.

'Yes,' he agreed tonelessly. 'It is that. Now I suggest you go and prepare for your wedding day.'

CHAPTER FIVE

Azim spared a sideways glance for his new bride, noting her pale face and downcast gaze as she slid into the limousine. She'd been silent since he'd told her to prepare for their wedding day, offering only monosyllabic answers to the few attempts at conversation he'd made, and saying even less during their brief wedding ceremony.

She had looked lovely, if subdued, in a pale pink dress with an overlay of pearl-encrusted gauze, her heavy, dark hair pulled back in a low chignon. Azim had instructed a nearby boutique to send several appropriate gowns to his flat, and he'd been gratified that Johara had chosen one.

A few days ago he'd told himself he hadn't cared what Johara thought, that her opinion didn't matter. Now he realised it *had* to matter, at least for now, because constant hostility was simply too aggravating to deal with. Of course, once they were in Alazar he would simply send her to the harem and see her only as required. That had always been his plan, but now, glancing at her subdued profile, he felt a twinge of…what? Not quite regret. But something, an emotion he wasn't used to, and one that did not feel comfortable. Pain twanged through his head and he leaned back against the seat and closed his eyes, taking a deep, even breath. He could not afford to have a migraine now.

'Are you all right?' Johara asked quietly and Azim cracked open an eye.

'I'm fine.'

Her soft grey gaze moved over him, without rancour or bitterness, which pierced him in a bittersweet way, like a honey-tipped arrow finding a crack to slide through. 'It's only that you looked as if you were in pain.'

Azim tensed against another laser-strike in his head. 'I'm fine,' he repeated more firmly and closed his eyes again. Johara let out a soft sigh.

He had no idea what she was thinking. He realised he was curious, and that annoyed him further. He hadn't meant to get involved. He didn't get involved with anyone. He'd long ago learned the hard lesson of trust and when it was misplaced—*always*.

No, trust was most certainly not going to be part of his relationship with Johara. In fact, relationship was the wrong word entirely. They had an arrangement, nothing more, and he really didn't care what she thought—about anything.

'I don't even know where we're going,' Johara said. 'Are we flying back to Alazar today?'

'No, we are going to Italy. I have business in Naples.'

'Business…?' She turned to him, eyes wide with curiosity. 'What kind of business?'

'I need to review the accounts of my company before I return to Alazar.' As reluctant as he was to hand over that responsibility, he knew he needed to. He had to focus on his country now. His crown.

'I didn't know you had your own company. What is it?'

'A real estate company. Olivieri Holdings.'

Her brow creased. 'Olivieri…?'

'I went by the name Rafael Olivieri before I remembered who I was.' And Rafael Olivieri was dead now. Dead and buried, at last, with all of his shame.

'That must have felt so strange.' Her features softened and Azim looked away.

'It was what it was.'

'What about the people who knew you as Rafael? The life you left behind?'

He tensed, his gaze remaining on the window as Paris traffic streamed by. Memories came, unbidden, of those years of hard work and fruitless fighting. Fury and shame. Pain and then finally, sweetly, so sweetly—revenge. Ruining the man who had ruined him still hadn't felt like enough. It didn't make up for all the wasted years. Only claiming his inheritance, his destiny, would do that. 'What about it?' he asked tonelessly.

'Don't you miss it? Them?'

He slid his phone out of his pocket and began to scroll through messages. 'No.' There wasn't a single person he missed from his old life. Not one. Enemies, employees and meaningless liaisons. He'd easily turned his back on them all. Twenty years of striving and success reduced to nothing.

Everything had been centred on gaining his revenge against Paolo Caivano—and when he'd done that he'd re-alised it hadn't been enough. It was only when he'd seen his grandfather on the news, when he'd remembered about Alazar, that he'd realised what he needed to do. What would make up for all he'd endured.

Johara was silent for a few minutes and Azim thumbed a few buttons on his phone, answering some quick emails.

'How long will we stay in Naples?' she finally asked.

'A few days.' He glanced up, giving her a cool smile of intent. 'We need to be in Alazar this weekend for our proper wedding.'

Azim kept himself immersed in work on the short flight to Naples, and then for the drive to his villa on the city's outskirts. Johara hadn't attempted to engage him in conversation, and Azim had told himself he preferred it, although he'd been unsettlingly aware of her presence next to him, every draw and sigh of her breathing, the subtle vanilla and almond scent that wafted towards him whenever she moved. Her hair was so dark it almost had a deep blue sheen, and it made Azim wonder how soft it felt. He hadn't got as much work done as he would have wished, the realisation of what a distraction his bride was a further aggravation.

By the time they arrived at his villa Johara looked pale and drawn. She didn't say anything as she stepped into the house, glancing around at the luxurious furnishings, the soaring ceilings and marble floors, the French windows open to the terrace bathed in twilight.

His butler, Antonio, hurried forward to take their bags, and Johara gave the man a genuine smile that made Azim realise she had never smiled at him like that. He felt annoyed for noticing—and caring.

She stood in the centre of the foyer, a solitary figure, her eyes luminous, her hair dark against her pale face, her slender body swathed in pink. In spite of every determination to remain unattached, Azim found he was strangely moved by the sight.

'We should eat. I rang ahead for my chef to prepare something.'

'Oh.' Johara turned, seeming startled by this simple act of practical kindness. 'That would be nice.'

Azim nodded tersely, feeling as uncomfortable as she obviously was. Neither of them knew the protocol. It would be easier simply to leave her, busy himself with work as he had done for the last few hours, but for some absurd reason he was reluctant to do so. She looked so nervous, so fragile, and he wanted to do something about it. The

trouble was, he just didn't know what. He was not a gentle man. He was not accustomed to kindness. Everything
about this situation felt strange, and yet he still could not
keep from wanting to soften the blow for his new bride,
or at least the landing.

Johara looked around the foyer, her glazed eyes barely
taking in all the luxurious details. Her body was buzzing
with nervous energy, her mind a spinning maelstrom of
both anxiety and expectation.

Everything had happened so *quickly*—she'd felt as if
she'd been watching a film of someone else's life rather
than taking part in the major action of her own. She was
married. How had that happened? And more importantly,
what happened now?

She had no idea what to expect. Oh, she knew the lo-
gistics of a wedding night—she wasn't *that* innocent. But
as for Azim…there had been moments, unexpected and
startling, when he'd almost seemed kind. He'd ordered
several gorgeous dresses for her to wear for the ceremony,
and at times he'd seemed concerned for her, his forehead
furrowed as he glanced at her, dark eyes sweeping over
her as if checking for injuries. And of course there had
been that kiss…

But maybe that kiss hadn't been kind. Perhaps it had
simply been a display of the power he had over her, the
power he intended to wield, maybe even tonight.

'The food will be ready shortly.'

Johara turned to see Azim standing in the doorway of
the enormous sitting room she'd wandered into, his expression as grim as ever. Was he expecting to consummate
their marriage tonight? She couldn't bring herself to ask.

'That's good,' she managed, struggling to find even the
simplest words. 'Thank you.'

He nodded towards her dress. 'Would you like to change?'

Into what? Johara glanced down at the lovely dress she'd worn for the wedding. It had made her feel beautiful, with its gauzy, pearl-encrusted fabric swishing gently about her legs. It was one of the prettiest things she'd ever worn, and she'd been touched that Azim had thought to provide it for her. Stupidly touched, perhaps. As with her father, it had cost him nothing, or at least very little. It didn't *mean* anything.

'I thought you might be more comfortable in something else,' Azim explained when she didn't reply. 'There are clothes upstairs. I had them sent from several boutiques. They will provide a wardrobe for you until we return to Alazar.'

Johara couldn't tell if this was another one of his autocratic commands or an act of kind consideration. Maybe both. 'All right, thank you.'

'I'll show you.'

She followed him up the sweeping staircase to a bedroom decorated in shades of cream and gold, everything sumptuous, at least a dozen pillows of silk and satin piled high on the king-sized bed.

Glancing at that huge bed, she couldn't keep from imagining it occupied, and a sudden, shocking image of naked bodies twined and flickering with candlelight burst into her brain...where had *that* fantasy come from? Their wedding night wasn't about fantasy. It was about expediency. Even so all the oxygen seemed to have been sucked from the air, and she felt light-headed and dizzy.

'The clothes are in the dressing room.' Azim gestured to an adjoining room that looked to be nearly as large as the bedroom.

'Thank you.' Johara could feel her skin heat with embarrassment. Had Azim seen something of what she'd been thinking in her eyes, her face? His expression was as inscrutable as ever.

'I'll be downstairs. You may join me in the dining room when you are ready.'

'All right—'

He left the room without waiting for her reply, and Johara let out the breath she'd been holding. Every exchange they'd had had been punctuated by abrupt stops and sudden silences, so Johara felt as if they were jolting along, her psyche forced to absorb every juddering bump. She wondered if talking to this man, her *husband*, would ever seem natural. Would they ever chat or laugh together? Share anything other than a bed? Or would it be better, safer, for her not to want those things? Even if they didn't love each other, she reflected, she hoped they could get along. Enmity was exhausting, especially when it was coupled with enforced intimacy.

She eyed the king-sized bed again in front of her with a shiver of apprehension and then went into the dressing room, stopping in amazement at the sight of at least a dozen dresses hanging in the huge wardrobe, and tops and trousers, as well as a host of gauzy, silky underthings, folded in the drawers. A wardrobe, indeed. There were more clothes in there than she'd ever had in her life. She could hardly believe that Azim had bought her so many things. How did he even know her size? Her *bra* size?

It was thoughtful and yet at the same time it wasn't. Was she never going to be able to choose her own clothes, or anything, ever again? Was Azim going to dictate everything about her life? So far he seemed to expect to, and the thought of fighting, no doubt uselessly, over every little thing made Johara want to both weep and sag in exhaustion.

And what was she supposed to pick to wear? One of the cocktail dresses? Or a silky negligee? Letting out a groan of frustration, she finally settled on a pair of flowing palazzo pants in soft jersey and a matching loose top in aquamarine. Then, taking a deep breath, she headed down to the dining room.

Azim was standing by the window, his back to her, when she came in. He turned as he heard her, his eyes flaring as he took in her appearance, his gaze moving slowly over her, leaving a warm ripple of awareness in its wake. She felt suddenly, achingly conscious of the smooth jersey sliding over her skin, the peaks of her breasts and the heat between her thighs. How did he create such a reaction in her by just a look? It scared her, how her body responded to him even when her mind was trying to maintain a cool distance. She wasn't ready for this. She had no experience, nothing to give her some perspective or simply some calm.

'That smells good.' She nodded towards the table laden with dishes, still conscious of Azim's presence, feeling his gaze like a brand on her skin. Blindly she surveyed the table, barely taking in the different options.

'What would you like?' Azim asked, his shoulder brushing her breast as he reached for a plate. Johara had to suppress the urge to shiver.

'I...I don't know.' Her voice came out in a humiliating, hoarse stammer.

'You can relax,' Azim told her as he began to fill up the plate with a variety of succulent dishes—a risotto with vegetables, pasta with ragu sauce, stuffed peppers. It all looked mouth-watering and yet with the way her stomach was churning Johara didn't know if she'd be able to eat a single mouthful.

She let out a shaky, uncertain laugh. 'Can I?'

'I'm not going to ravish you over the dining room table,'

Azim informed her flatly. 'Or even tonight at all. Our wedding night will happen after our wedding in Alazar.'

'Oh...well...' She had no idea what to say. The flood of relief she felt was mingled with an unsettling trickle of disappointment.

'Relieved?' Azim's voice rang with the sharp note of cynicism. 'I can assure you, when it comes time to consummate our marriage, you'll be as eager for it as I will.'

That arrogant statement felt like both a promise and a threat, and it brought a flush to her cheeks and a skip to her heartbeat. She still didn't know whether to be thrilled or terrified by the prospect. 'Why wait, then?' she dared to ask, then wished she hadn't. She'd sounded as if she was disappointed in the delay, and she wasn't. She couldn't be.

'Because our people will be waiting to see a sign that you're a virgin,' Azim stated baldly. 'And if we cannot provide it, we will both be shamed.'

'Really?' Johara blinked. 'That seems a bit...archaic.'

He shrugged. 'It is the reality.' His smile was twisted as he added, 'But at least you have a few days' reprieve.' He nodded towards the open French doors, the gauzy curtains billowing in the evening breeze. 'We will eat out on the terrace.'

'All right.' Although the reason for it was practically medieval, the reprieve, Johara realised, was needed. The fact that she now had at least a few days to unwind made the tension unknot in her shoulders, and gave her the confidence to suggest, 'Maybe then we could...talk.'

'Talk?' He sounded both surprised and appalled by the suggestion. 'About what?'

'About ourselves. Since we're married, shouldn't we get to know one another?' Azim stared at her blankly and Johara remembered that he had already informed her he didn't want to get to know her. He knew everything he needed to already. The look on his face reminded her of that all too well; he looked completely nonplussed by the suggestion, as if she'd suggested something both outrageous and pointless. 'Never mind,' she muttered, feeling stupid, and she took her full plate and headed out to the terrace, the cool breeze and stunning view of the surrounding hills cloaked in violet restoring her spirits only a little.

How on earth was she going to make this marriage work? She picked at her salad, her appetite receding. She was by nature optimistic; she'd made herself be, after living with her mother's endless sadness for so long. She'd always chosen to see the bright side, to choose a smile over a frown. But right now she had a glimmer of understanding of the despondency her mother had felt, the years yawning in front of her, barren and hopeless. Azim didn't want to know her. He didn't want any kind of relationship. He simply wanted her as his bride—and in his bed.

'What exactly do you want to talk about?' Azim stood in the doorway, a plate balanced in one hand, his expression drawn in lines of taut resignation.

'It's not meant to be some form of torture,' Johara answered tartly.

'I am not used to talking about myself.' Azim sat down across from her at the small wrought-iron table and squinted at the horizon. His profile reminded Johara of the bust of a Roman consul or emperor, the smooth curve of his skull, the patrician nose, the strong jaw. The only blemish to the perfection of his face was the scar snaking its way down one cheek. Johara wondered how he'd got it, and knew she wouldn't ask. Not yet anyway, and at this rate probably not ever. 'In fact,' Azim continued without looking at her, 'I am not used to making much conversation at all.'

That, at least, was something. 'Why not?' Johara asked.

He shrugged powerful shoulders, muscles rippling. 'As a child it was not encouraged. And then…' He stopped, as if he'd said all she needed to know.

Johara's stomach turned over. She was afraid to probe too much, afraid of Azim's sudden anger or stinging setdowns, and yet she was intensely curious. This man was her husband now. She wanted to understand him. She wanted to have some kind of relationship, *any* kind, even if he didn't. 'Do you mean after you were kidnapped…?' A terse nod was all the confirmation she got and even though he was clearly discouraging her from continuing, she made herself ask, 'You said you remembered some things…?'

'I do not remember the kidnapping.' His voice was flat, his shuttered gaze still on the horizon. 'All I remember is waking up in a hospital bed in Italy, not knowing who I was or what had happened.'

'That sounds awful.' He'd only been fourteen, a mere boy. She could not even imagine enduring such a thing. 'But someone must have taken care of you, since you were only a boy. And you had your company eventually…' Azim did not reply, and Johara shook her head slowly, absorbing the enormity of the seismic shifts he'd experienced in his life. 'Where were you for all that time? Who was taking care of you?'

He smiled slightly at that, a bitter twisting of his lips that drew at his scar. 'No one.'

'But you were only fourteen. Someone must have been… I mean, what were you doing?'

His gaze had turned even more distant, focused inward, making him seem more inscrutable and inaccessible than ever. 'Surviving,' he finally said, and there was a terrible bleakness in his voice that made Johara ache even though she didn't understand why.

* * *

Why did people talk about themselves? It was torture, like peeling back a layer of skin, exposing the raw nerves to air and sunlight. He didn't want to tell Johara anything about his past. He didn't want to have that kind of relationship with her; he didn't want her to have that kind of knowledge and power over him. And yet in just a few short sentences he'd told her more than he'd told anyone else.

Surviving. And sometimes barely, at that. It was just a word, and yet from the way her lush mouth turned down, her eyes crinkling at the corners, he knew he'd said too much. She pitied him, and he couldn't stand the notion. He'd been pitied before, and, worse, he'd *deserved* to be pitied. He hated the thought of enduring such a thing again. He shouldn't have said anything at all.

'What about you? How have you filled your time in the south of France?' He imagined a life of leisure, lounging by the pool, attending endless parties. Johara was innocent, but that didn't mean she was unspoiled.

'I've lived a very quiet life. I helped my mother, and I gardened.' She shrugged, smiling. 'Not very interesting.'

'You must have gone out to parties and things.'

'No. My mother is often unwell and so we lived just the two of us, very quietly. I went to the village sometimes, and I had a tutor for a few years, and of course my garden to keep me company.'

It was not the life he'd expected her to have. 'What about friends?'

'I don't really have any friends.' She shrugged, her smile philosophical and yet touched with sadness. 'Some of our staff. Lucille, the cook, and her husband, Thomas. I'll miss them.'

'And yet this was the life you were desperate to maintain?' He heard a note of contempt creep into his voice,

and saw Johara flinch. Still he could not keep himself
from continuing. 'This was what you were running away
from me for? A garden and a sick mother, with only the
cook as your friend?'

Johara lifted her chin, her slender shoulders straightening. 'No. I was running away from you because I wanted
my freedom to choose to live as I wanted. To decide my
own destiny.'

'Even I do not have that freedom.'

She frowned. 'What do you mean?'

'It is both my duty and destiny to be the next Sultan.
To shirk it would be unconscionable.'

'And yet you still have a choice.'

A choice? No. The Sultanate was more than a birthright;
it was a necessity. To validate who he was and what had
happened to him, all he'd endured. Sometimes it felt like
the only way he could save his soul, if indeed that was a
possibility at all. 'You had a choice as well,' Azim pointed
out. 'You said the vows of your own accord, Johara. If
you'd really wanted out of this marriage, you could have
told the judge you were being coerced.'

She flushed and looked away. Azim wondered why he
was pressing the point. He'd been intending to use this
time together as a way to help her to relax, and instead
he was practically picking a fight. Aggression was more
familiar to him, keeping in control a necessity he could
not relinquish. Johara's innocent questions had touched
him too rawly, made him feel too unsure. And the truth
was he wanted to know. 'Why didn't you, at that?' he demanded. 'A word to the judge…it could have been simple.' Although not that simple, considering he'd paid the
judge beforehand to keep things straightforward. But she
hadn't known that.

Johara's face remained averted. 'Because it seemed

pointless,' she answered quietly. 'As well as dishonour-able. Like you I have a duty. I have been told it my whole life. To walk away from it...and for what? A chance to really screw up my life, to live in poverty or worse?' She wrinkled her nose. 'This seemed like the lesser evil.'

'Is that supposed to make me feel better?' he asked, parroting her own question from earlier.

'No, not really. You asked me, and I answered honestly.' She took a deep breath and met his gaze unflinchingly, her eyes shining like silver with courage and determination. 'But now that we are married, I would like to get along with you, Azim. I would like to get to know you. I would like us to be...friends, at least.'

'Friends?' He repeated the word disbelievingly, every-thing inside him resisting such a suggestion. He didn't have *friends*.

'Why shouldn't we?' Johara pressed. 'We're married. We're going to share our lives together, have children one day, God willing. Wouldn't it be better for both of us if we could actually like each other a little bit? Share with each other our concerns, our fears, our hopes...?'

Azim stared at her in appalled amazement. Johara's view of marriage was entirely at odds with his own. He had no intention of sharing those things with anyone, of giving anyone that kind of power over him, exposing him-self to scrutiny and judgement.

And yet...for a second, he could almost picture how it could be. He thought of his brother Malik, who had found that kind of relationship with his fiancée, Gracie. He imag-ined himself as Malik now was with Gracie, smiling, re-laxed, easily affectionate. *Weak*.

He was not his brother. He couldn't be that man. His life experience had hardened him, ossified any natural craving for such closeness. Despite that one treacherous flicker of yearning, the possibility horrified him. He could not seek it now, and he did not want to.

'We are not friends,' he stated flatly. 'We are husband and wife. I told you what I needed from you,' he reminded her, ignoring the hurt look on her face as he continued relentlessly, 'And that is all I want.'

CHAPTER SIX

BY THE TIME Johara woke the next morning Azim had already left for work. She hadn't seen him after dinner; Azim had closeted himself in his study and then they'd retired to separate bedrooms. She spent the morning wandering aimlessly around the large, elegant rooms of the villa; none of them possessed a single personal memento or photograph, nothing to give her a better idea of who her husband was. Yet according to the butler, Antonio, who had warmed up to her after the first few taciturn hours, this was Azim's main residence.

It looked, Johara thought, as if every sign of individuality or interest had been removed, scrubbed away, but perhaps it hadn't been there to begin with. It was as if, in having amnesia for twenty years, Azim had simply not existed for all that time. Where were his friends, his memories, his pictures and keepsakes? Books, even? There wasn't a single one in the house beyond some hand-tooled leather volumes that looked as if they'd never been opened.

Perhaps he kept his more personal items in a private room, his bedroom or study. She didn't dare look for such a room, not with the staff seeming to watch her every move. In the end Johara retreated to the gardens, vast and ruthlessly landscaped, simply for some privacy from the stultifying silence and watching eyes.

The sun was hot on her head, the sky a deep, pure blue, but Johara took little pleasure in her surroundings. She wanted to get to know her husband, at least a little; she wanted to find some chink in his inscrutable armour, some glimpse into the mind and maybe even the heart of this man she had just pledged to spend all her days with. She didn't want to spend the rest of her life with a stranger.

She wasn't looking for love or even much affection. She'd learned the dangers of believing someone loved you, hoping for it, trusting it. No, she wasn't about to go down that route again. But why couldn't they be friends?

Johara thought she could be patient, if she felt it was simply a matter of time for Azim and her to get to know one another. But she feared with a leaden and growing certainty that it wasn't. She would never get to know Azim, because he did not want to be known. He had locked himself like a vault, and he had no intention of giving Johara, or anyone, the key.

From the French doors Antonio called her for lunch, and with a sigh Johara rose from the bench. She ate alone at a table that seated twenty, working her way through three courses and wondering if this was what the rest of her life was going to look like.

It wasn't as if she even cared for Azim, she told herself. She knew she didn't. She barely knew the man, after all, and what she knew she wasn't sure she particularly liked. And yet she *wanted* to know him. She was married, and yet she felt more isolated than ever, and that felt wrong.

After lunch she plucked up the courage to go out. She got her coat and her bag and asked Antonio to fetch the driver.

'But…*signora* is not going out?' Antonio asked, his forehead creased with concern.

'I thought I'd see some of Naples's sights.' Whatever those were.

Antonio was looking troubled, shaking his head, and Johara kept her sunny smile with effort.

'Perhaps you can recommend…?' she began, only to have Antonio shake his head more vigorously.

'No, no, I am sorry, *signora*. The *signor* does not permit you to leave the estate.'

Her heart started a slow, steady descent towards her toes. 'Even with the driver…?'

Antonio looked regretful but very firm. 'I am sorry, but no.'

Johara stared at him, feeling frustrated and, worse, humiliated. So she really was a prisoner. Did Azim really think she was going to make a run for it, now that they were wed? She accepted that he had little reason to trust her, but her enforced imprisonment still rankled. She supposed it would only be worse in Alazar, when she was banished to the palace's harem, only to be brought out like a trophy.

Holding her head high with effort, she left Antonio and retreated again to the garden. She'd always taken solace in nature, but the manicured hedges and sterile-looking flowers were far from the wild and unruly garden she'd cultivated back in Provence. Quite suddenly, she missed her home with a ferocity that left her breathless and winded. She wanted her garden, her stillroom with its stoppered bottles and jars, the kitchen with sunbeams slanting on the floor and Lucille humming tunelessly as she cooked.

She wanted her big grey cat, Gavroche, and her favourite books, and the freedom that her life, small and simple as it had been, had possessed. She even missed her mother, who had been nothing but a sullen, silent presence for years, hardly ever coming out of her bedroom. Anything but this—this loneliness and isolation, wandering around empty rooms with no company, no purpose.

She'd been married but one day and she was already regretting it. Deeply. Johara sank onto a garden bench under a cypress tree and closed her eyes. This time there was no escape.

Azim scrolled through the latest accounts in his office in downtown Naples, barely able to keep his mind on the columns of figures on his screen. He had important business to attend to, checking the accounts of his real estate interests in Italy before returning to Alazar, and he couldn't concentrate for more than a few minutes at a time. He kept thinking of Johara, wondering what she was doing. Thinking. *Feeling*, which was extraordinarily aggravating, because he wasn't like that. His marriage wasn't like that. Yet for some reason he kept picturing her in his mind's eye as she'd been after their wedding, looking solitary and lonely, her slender body encased in pink, her dark, heavy hair pulled back, a few tendrils framing a face that held such an expression of sorrow and resignation he was torn between regret and frustration. He knew how she felt. He understood that kind of loneliness and desperation, the resignation to a fate you never, ever would have chosen.

And yet…her marriage to him did not have to be such a *wake*. Nobody had died. And he knew what real suffering looked like, felt like. It wasn't this.

Even so she stayed in his thoughts, and sometimes he felt as if he could almost catch a whiff of her vanilla and almond scent, which was ridiculous.

By four o'clock he gave up on the day's work, knowing he was too distracted. Impatiently he pressed the intercom on his phone. 'Send Signor Andretti here to discuss the last month's accounts.' He'd hand everything over to Andretti, something he wouldn't normally do, and go home. See what Johara was up to. Hell, maybe he'd even talk to her, the way she'd wanted him to last night.

While that prospect of her getting to know him still had his insides shrinking in horror, he wondered if perhaps *he* could get to know *her*.

He had too many secrets, too many darknesses, to reveal them to Johara. If he'd disgusted her already, what on earth would she think when she learned just how low he'd been brought? How low he'd stooped? The idea of anyone, but especially his wife, learning his weaknesses made him tense with horror. He would never give someone that kind of insight or power. Never again.

But he could ask her questions. Learn more about his bride, and then perhaps when his curiosity—and lust— were satisfied, he could concentrate on the far more pressing business of securing his throne.

An hour later he left the office for the sprawling villa on the outskirts of Naples. He quickened his step, scanning the marble foyer for a sight of his bride, half-expecting her to be waiting for him there.

'Where is Signora Bahjat?' he demanded of Antonio, his butler.

'She is out, *signor,*' the man replied with a short bow.

'Out?' Azim stared at him in disbelief. Had Johara defied him even in this? And what about his staff? 'Out where? I gave strict instructions that she was to stay in the villa.'

'Only—only out to the garden,' the old man stammered, clearly alarmed by Azim's ferocious expression. 'She has been sitting out there for hours.'

'She has?' Azim frowned, not liking that for some reason. 'I'll go find her now.'

Too late he realised how that sounded, as if he were so

besotted by his bride that he had to see her the moment he came through the door. He decided he didn't care.

He strode through the palatial rooms of the villa, all of them gorgeously decorated and glaringly empty. He felt a tightening in his midsection, an anxiety he didn't understand.

He threw open the French doors that led to the garden, breathing in the scents of jasmine and oleander. The sun was just starting its descent, bathing the terraced gardens in golden light, the sky turning to violet, the colour of a bruise. He surveyed the expanse of lawn, the landscaped shrubs and carefully tended flowerbeds, but he didn't see Johara. His anxiety increased. He had top-notch security on his estate, out of necessity. Paolo Caivano, broken as he was, still wanted revenge, and always would, as long as Azim was alive. And he wanted his villa back.

Azim's mouth curved in a cold smile as he thought about how unlikely that was. He'd utterly destroyed his one-time tormentor, at least financially. Still, the man had friends in ugly places.

Slowly he strolled through the gardens, his gaze narrowed as he looked for Johara. He didn't actually think Caivano could have got to her, but the possibility was enough to make his muscles clench. Maybe he'd forbid her from coming outside.

Then he saw her, sitting on a wrought-iron garden bench under a cypress tree. She looked peaceful, her head resting against the trunk of the tree, her eyes closed, a slight smile on her face. The sight of her made something in Azim twist painfully, a sensation he didn't particularly like.

'What have you been doing out here for so long?' His voice grated on his own ears, harsh and demanding, too much, and definitely not the tone he'd meant to take. But he'd been *worried*. She didn't realise the dangers the way he did. She didn't understand how much was at stake.

Johara opened her eyes, the instinctive smile that had started to bloom across her face sliding off as she caught sight of his expression, registered his tone. 'I was simply enjoying the garden,' she informed him stiffly. 'Is that a crime?'

'Antonio said you've been out here for hours.'

She lifted her chin. 'So?'

This was not going to plan at all, Azim realised with frustration. He was making a mess of what he'd intended to be a friendly conversation. He tried again. 'Why?' It came out sounding like an interrogation.

Johara's gaze narrowed. 'Because I enjoy being out of doors, and I was bored inside. The comforts of your home only last so long, and, as I was forbidden from venturing outside the estate, I decided to come out here.' Her voice was touched with acid and Azim drew back, needled.

'You know why those measures are in place.' Although her running away wasn't the real reason, at least not the main one. She would be foolish to try to flee from him here in Naples, and in any case he knew she wouldn't get very far.

'I'm married to you now. What's the point of my running away? In any case I've already accepted my life sentence.' She leaned her head back against the seat and closed her eyes, effectively dismissing him.

Azim stared at her, silently fuming. He'd come out here to talk to her, to do what she'd been wanting him to do and get to know her. What a waste of time that had been. They'd only ended up trading accusations and insults.

'Don't go out to the garden any more,' he said abruptly.

Her eyes opened, anger sparking in their silvery depths. 'You're forbidding me from spending time outside? In a

walled garden with security cameras all over the place?
What do you think is going to happen?'

A muscle ticced in his jaw, and he felt the first flickers
of a headache at his temples. He knew he was being over-
bearing and unreasonable, but he'd been pushed into it by
her insouciant indifference.

'I am speaking for your safety,' he bit out.

'How thoughtful of you,' she drawled. 'Because it seems
like you're simply trying to show me your power. Again.'

'I have enemies in this city,' Azim said, the words
drawn from him with terse reluctance. Johara's eyes widened in surprised alarm.

'Enemies? What kind of enemies?'

He shrugged, having no intention of giving her any
of the grim details. 'Power and wealth breed envy and
malice,' he answered repressively. 'That is all you need
to know.'

'Am I really in danger?' Her tongue darted out and
touched her lips, causing an entirely inappropriate arrow
of lust to dart through him. Their wedding night could
not come soon enough. That, at least, he hoped would be
simple.

'I don't know,' he admitted gruffly. He didn't know
what Caivano was capable of anymore, or how much
power he had, if any, but he certainly didn't intend to
take chances. In the many years since he'd escaped the
man, he'd always watched his back. Hired bodyguards
and taken bullet-proof cars—but that was no more than
what many Neopolitan businessmen did these days. 'I'm
not willing to take the risk. Any risk.'

'So I have to stay in the villa all the time?' Johara said.
'And not even go out to the garden?'

'We're only here for a few days.'

She glanced at the walls topped with barbed wire, her

scornful gaze taking in the many security cameras, and Azim knew she was doubting the truth of what he said. Hell, so was he. His estate was safe. He knew that much. He'd been foolish to restrict her so much, but he'd been piqued by her seeming indifference. This, he supposed, was why he did not attempt relationships of any kind. This and a lot of other reasons.

'Fine,' Johara said as she rose from the bench, a lovely vision of wounded dignity. 'I don't mind. These are the most boring, soulless gardens I've ever seen.'

And with that last insult she turned and strode back to the villa, her cheeks bright with angry colour, her head held high.

No matter how much she tried, how much she pretended, Johara knew she couldn't escape the truth. This place was a prison. Her *life* was a prison, and her new husband seemed intent on proving it to her again and again.

The stupid thing was, she'd actually been looking forward to him coming home. To seeing him again. She'd hoped they might talk again, at least a little. They'd share a meal, figure out some kind of new normal.

And then she'd seen him, and he'd been furious, punishing her to no purpose. Not being able to go out in the garden was a ridiculous restriction. The walls surrounding the estate were a foot thick and twelve feet high, with barbed wire on top. She'd counted a dozen security cameras on her stroll around the gardens. What kind of enemies did Azim have, anyway?

That, Johara realised with a chill, was a question she didn't really want to ask—or have answered. What could he have possibly done to create such enmity? It was another awful reminder that she didn't know this man, and yet she was married to him.

With her feelings in a ferment, she headed back into the villa. Its palatial rooms and sumptuous decorations left her cold; the place was as soulless as the gardens, all professionally decorated perfection without any heart or humour, or any personality. Just like its owner.

No, that wasn't fair. She was sure Azim had plenty of personality. He even, she thought, had a glimmer of humour. But heart? Just when she thought she'd found a chink in his iron armour, he behaved in a way that made Johara fear there was nothing beneath that cold exterior but more ice.

She ate dinner alone in the cavernous dining room; Antonio had informed her that Azim was working again that evening. The elderly man looked tired, stooping to serve her, and so Johara told him she could look after herself.

'But that is surely not appropriate—' Antonio protested in broken English, the only language they shared.

Johara waved a hand. 'I'm fine, Antonio, honestly. I'll go to bed soon, anyway.'

Alone in the dining room, the clink of her cutlery sounding overly loud in the spacious room, she forked a few more mouthfuls before she lost both interest and appetite. She'd spent most of her life in virtual isolation, but she had never felt as alone as this. She wasn't even sure why—in Provence she'd had the servants for company, but it wasn't all that different, really. She'd spent most of her time alone.

The difference, she supposed, was Azim. Knowing he was near and yet choosing to stay away. She'd never realised before how another person could make you feel lonely.

The restrictions he'd placed on her bothered her too—at least in Provence she'd had her garden and stillroom, the opportunity to walk into the village, experience a little bit of life. She'd had freedom, as limited as it was. Here she had nothing but the promise of long, empty days of waiting. She doubted things would change once they reached Alazar. They were more likely to get worse.

Johara pushed away from the table, determined not to give in to the despair that threatened. She couldn't think like that. She wouldn't let herself. She'd always chosen hope over despair, joy after sadness. Even when it had been hard. Even when it had hurt. Why couldn't she do the same now? Why did this feel so different, so much more?

Slowly she strolled through the spacious rooms of the villa, and then, feeling a bit as if she were venturing into Bluebeard's castle, she went upstairs and then down a shadowy corridor she thought led to Azim's bedroom. The whole villa was silent save for the occasional creak of wood or the restless slap of a shutter.

Johara walked on tiptoes, holding her breath, wondering what or who exactly she was looking for. Azim? What on earth would she say to him if she found him?

She came to the end of the corridor, and a firmly closed door she supposed led to Azim's bedroom. No light spilled from underneath it, and she could hear no sound from within. Even so she raised her hand, her closed fist hovering in front of the door to knock, yet she did not possess the courage to do it. He probably wasn't there anyway. He was most likely in a study somewhere, closeted away with business papers and his laptop.

Then she heard a sound inside the bedroom—something that almost sounded like a groan. Her whole body tensed, every muscle straining as she sought to hear more. Should she knock? Could he be hurt or ill?

The room fell silent again and Johara wavered. Azim

would be undoubtedly angry if she violated his privacy in this way. Enraged, even. But if she didn't dare to now, she never would.

Taking a deep breath, she pushed open the door.

The room was awash in shadow, the only light from the moonlight spilling through the windows. It took Johara a few moments for her eyes to adjust, and then she saw Azim sprawled in a chair by the window, his head leaning back against it, his eyes closed.

'Antonio, I told you I did not wish to be disturbed,' he said, his voice taut with suppressed pain.

'It's me.' Azim's eyes flickered open and Johara closed the door softly behind her. 'Johara.'

He closed his eyes again, his jaw clenched. 'What are you doing here?'

'You're in pain.' She moved quickly to him, her healer's instinct wanting only to help and soothe. Azim jerked away from the touch of her hand on his.

'I'm fine.' His eyes were still closed, sweat beading on his brow. He was so clearly not fine that Johara would have laughed if the situation weren't so serious, and the sight of Azim struggling against his suffering so achingly poignant.

'Is it a headache?' she asked quietly and with obvious effort he opened his eyes.

'It's nothing.'

'Why won't you tell me?' He did not reply, and Johara stared at him, her hands on her hips. He was the most insufferably stubborn man she'd ever met, arrogant and unyielding, and she wasn't even sure she liked him very much. But she didn't want to see him in pain. 'Fine. I'll be back in a moment.'

Azim's eyes fluttered closed. It only took a few moments to go to her bedroom and fetch some of the essential oils she always carried with her. Back in Azim's room she knocked softly once and then slipped inside; he hadn't moved from his chair.

Quickly she prepared a handkerchief with drops of lavender and peppermint oils. 'This should help,' she said quietly, and pressed the cloth into his hand. Azim took it without opening his eyes. His jaw was still clenched against the pain and his ashen skin looked as if it had been stretched tautly over his bones.

'What am I meant to do?' he asked after a moment, the words forced out.

'Press it to your forehead, or wherever the pain is worst.' Azim didn't move and Johara realised he was in too much pain even for that. 'Here, let me,' she said, and, kneeling in front of him, she took the cloth from his slack hand and pressed it against his temples.

'Does it hurt here?' she asked softly and Azim did not reply for a moment.

'Yes, my temples,' he finally said. 'It is always my temples.'

Gently she pressed the cloth against his head, releasing the sharp, fragrant smell of the oil. There was something startlingly intimate about the moment; she'd never been so close to a man except when Azim had kissed her. She began to massage his temples, rubbing her fingers in slow, gentle circles. Azim let out a groan.

'Does that hurt?'

'No.' A shudder went through his powerful body. 'No, it feels good.'

A dart of fierce pleasure went through her at his admission. She liked the realisation that she was helping him. It made her want something indefinable and yet more from him—what, she could not say. She continued to massage his temples, her fingers learning the feel of his skin, the ridges of bone. 'You get headaches often,' she remarked softly. She left the cloth draped across his forehead as her fingers continued to learn the shape of Azim's skull, the gentle abrasion of the stubble on his cheeks, the strong line of his jaw, moving rhythmically to relax his muscles. Every touch felt as if it brought her closer to him, an intimacy she'd never expected but now found she craved. The thought of him pushing her away now was awful. She wouldn't let him.

'Yes,' Azim admitted, the single word clearly reluctant.

'Tension makes it worse. You keep a lot of tension in your facial muscles and your jaw.' Her fingers were working their way down the side of his face, finding and unknotting the tension of muscles clenched for far too long, her thumbs brushing against his scar, the texture of it surprisingly smooth and silky. She held her breath, hoping he wouldn't pull away, everything in her singing as he relaxed into her touch.

'Probably,' Azim murmured. His voice sounded slightly slurred, his muscles loosening under her fingers. His head was back, his eyes still closed, giving Johara the freedom to study his face in leisure—the strong nose, the full lips, the surprisingly long eyelashes. The scar, which snaked its way like a river down one cheek, bisecting his face, ending right at the corner of his mouth. He was beautiful, in a hard-hewn, rugged way. Beautiful and, for the first time, accessible, at least a little.

'How long have you had the headaches?'

'Twenty years.'

The maths was easy. 'Since your kidnapping?'

He nodded, the movement barely noticeable.

'Are they caused by an injury?'

A long pause, with the only sound their breathing, the

whisper of her fingers across his skin. 'Yes. I was beaten. At least, that is assumed. I don't actually remember it.'

'Oh.' The sound was a soft gasp of sorrow. He'd said, she remembered, that he'd ended up in a hospital. 'I'm so sorry.'

'The doctors told me I'd received a concussion, which caused the amnesia. The headaches come and go.'

'But they're very painful,' Johara remarked. Things were clicking into place—the times she'd seen Azim close his eyes or clench his jaw, the way his gaze sometimes became hooded and unfocused. A sudden thought occurred to her. 'Did you have a headache at our first meeting?'

Another pause, and then he sighed, the sound long and weary. 'Yes.'

She worked her way back up to his temples, massaging in slow, rhythmic circles. She could smell his aftershave, and she was conscious of his powerful body so near to hers. She had a deep urge to press even closer, to feel the hard muscles of his chest against the softness of her own, a desire that shocked her. She was already as close to a man as she'd ever been—and yet she wanted more? 'Why didn't you tell me, then?' she asked.

'It is not something I tell anyone.' Azim hesitated before continuing, 'Pain is weakness, especially in a world leader.'

'It would have helped me to understand.'

A small, cynical smile curved his mouth, his eyes remaining closed. 'You think you would have been more predisposed to marry me if you knew I suffered from headaches?'

Johara sighed, recognising the folly of her logic. 'I don't know,' she admitted. 'But I have told you before, I want to know you. Understand you. I am your wife now, Azim.'

She wasn't prepared for the sudden electric jolt as he opened his eyes and gazed up into her face. She'd forgotten how close they were, and how fierce and dark his expression could be. 'Yes,' he agreed, his voice a low growl of sensual intent. 'You are.'

CHAPTER SEVEN

AZIM STARED UP at Johara, noting the way her pupils had dilated, her breathing turning uneven. Her breasts were brushing his chest, and had been for the last fifteen minutes, as she'd massaged his temples and face. He'd felt each point of contact with an exquisite ache, the brush of her breasts and the gentle touch of her fingers, desire warring with pain, lust with something far deeper.

He'd never experienced anything so erotic, so *emotional*, as her touching him in this way. Every brush of her fingers against his scar had jolted him with an intense emotion, made him almost want to weep even as he yearned for something he could not even name.

With her now-startled gaze fastened on his, Johara began to ease away. Azim reached out and circled her wrist with his fingers, his touch gentle but completely secure, holding her in place.

'Is the pain better?' she whispered, her tongue touching her lips and inflaming him further.

'Much.' It usually took hours for a migraine to recede, and, while the pain still lapped at his senses, it was definitely bearable. 'Thank you.'

'My pleasure.' She glanced down at his fingers on her wrist, and then up at his face again. He saw uncertainty but also excitement in her eyes, and knew she was feeling the same inexorable, magnetic pull of desire that he was. 'You're still holding me.'

'That's because I find I don't want to let you go.'

A tiny, uncertain smile curved her mouth. 'You...don't?'

He reached out with his other hand and brushed a stray tendril of hair from her face, tucking it behind her ear, letting his fingers caress her cheek as hers had caressed his. Her skin was soft and cool, like dipping his fingers in water or silk. 'No,' he said softly. 'I don't.'

In one easy movement he anchored his hands on her waist and lifted her up onto his lap. She gasped, her eyes wide with the shock of it. It only took another quick movement to adjust her legs so she was straddling him, her dress rucked up to her thighs, revealing slender, golden legs that were now clasping his.

'There,' Azim said as he settled her more firmly on his lap, his arousal brushing the juncture of her thighs, tantalising him even further. 'That's better.'

'I...' Johara shook her head slowly, her expression dazed but also, Azim thought, inflamed. She gazed down at their bodies pressed together. 'I thought we had to wait until Alazar for...'

'Our wedding night? We do. But that doesn't mean we can't get to know each other a little beforehand.' And he found he wanted to get to know his bride very much. Slowly, being careful not to spook her, he arched his hips so his arousal pressed against her. Johara gasped, clearly shocked by the sensation.

'Does that feel good?' Azim asked, his voice a growl of wanting.

'Yes...' Her breath came out in a shudder and she placed her hands on his shoulders to balance herself, her cheeks flushed, her eyes bright. Azim rocked again and Johara's hands clenched on his shoulders.

'That feels very good,' she admitted in a jagged whisper. 'I don't even know why.' She pressed back against him, her eyes fluttering closed as they rocked against each other for a few incredible seconds, their breathing ragged as they found their rhythm, their bodies pressing into one another in silent, hungry demand.

They'd hardly done anything and yet Azim found he was already close to losing control. Even more intoxicatingly, so was Johara. He wondered how much it would take to push her over the edge, and wanted to do it. He needed to see her fall, to feel her come apart in his arms, under his hands, helpless in her desire for him.

But as much as he longed for that, he knew he had to wait. Wait for the wedding night his country and his position demanded they have. Still, he couldn't keep from sliding one hand along her thigh, the other anchoring her hip, his fingers brushing against her soft centre. Johara's body tensed, her eyes widening.

'*Oh…but…*'

'I do not want to ruin our wedding night,' Azim said in a hoarse voice. 'Merely give you a taste of what we can both look forward to.'

'Oh…' He touched her again, watching as her lips parted, her expression becoming glazed, her hips moving to invite a further caress. She was so open and eager, and it thrilled him. Still he knew he could not risk either of their shame tonight.

Regretfully Azim withdrew his hand, everything in him aching with the desperate need to finish what they'd started, and bury himself deep inside her. He slid his hands up to her face and drew her forward for a thorough, lingering kiss.

Johara melted against him, her body wonderfully pliant and yielding. Azim drew back. 'We will save the rest for our wedding night.' Johara nodded, biting her lip, and Azim saw she could hardly look at him, her face already turning fiery. 'Johara, there is no shame in what we are doing,' he stated, surprised and discomfited by her embarrassment. 'We are married.'

'I know, but…' She shook her head, still not looking at him. 'I didn't know it felt like that.'

'Like what?' Azim asked, bemused. She had a lot more experience ahead of her.

'So…intimate.' She made a face. 'I know I must seem appallingly naïve.'

'Naiveté is no bad thing.' Sometimes he wished he still possessed a little optimistic innocence, the belief that things might actually get better. He'd lost it long, long ago.

'I suppose it's not in a bride who must be a virgin on her wedding night,' she answered with a touch of tartness.

'You still chafe at such restrictions?' The intimacy of the moment was making him feel languidly curious. He wanted to know what she thought as much as he wanted to prolong the moment, the feel of her against him.

'I don't know.' She shifted on his lap, making Azim suppress a groan of sheer longing as her body brushed intimately against him once more. 'Not necessarily, I suppose, but I want more from my life than being an ornament.'

He arched an eyebrow. 'An ornament?'

'The only purpose I have as your wife is to decorate your arm and to secure your throne with my suitability.'

'And to provide an heir.' Azim shifted against her, noting the way her eyes flared with satisfaction. 'That is something we will both enjoy, I think.'

'And yet there can be more to a marriage than this. There should be, anyway.' She gestured to their bodies, a look of confused hurt dawning in her eyes that made him both wary and tense. The warm, drowsy intimacy that had cocooned them started to melt away like a morning mist.

He'd been stupid, he realised. He'd let her in too close, allowed her to see too much. And now, of course, she wanted things. Expected things. Things he had no intention of giving, even if he had the emotional capacity to give them, which he knew he did not.

'It's late.' With only a flicker of regret he straightened her dress and then slid her off his lap. 'You should go.'

'You're dismissing me,' she said, and now he definitely heard the hurt.

'Yes.' With effort he rose from the chair and turned his back on her. 'I am.'

Johara stared at Azim's taut back and knew whatever they had shared was over. Her body was still buzzing from the way he'd touched her, and, far worse, her heart was aching. He'd started to open up to her, told her things, and now he was withdrawing again, becoming as cold and autocratic as ever. He'd touched her as only a husband should and yet now was acting like a stranger. She felt torn between anger and sadness, tears and fury. She'd been stupid to want more from him, to look for it. She'd opened herself up to the kind of rejection she'd told herself she wouldn't let herself feel. *Idiot*.

Slowly she gathered the little bottles of oils and put them back in the case, delaying the moment when she slunk out of here like a scolded servant. After what they'd done, the way he'd touched her body, it felt like an ever worse humiliation, a deeper sorrow.

She couldn't postpone it for ever, though, and Azim clearly had no intention of making it any easier. His back was still to her as he checked his phone; as far as he was concerned, she'd already left. And so, with no other real choice, she did.

Back in her bedroom she got ready for bed, her heart aching even as her body thrummed with remembered pleasure. Every brush of her hands against her over-sensitised skin as she pulled her pyjamas on reminded her of the way Azim had touched her, with such knowing yet gentle expertise. Would their wedding night be like that? Or would Azim act the cold stranger again? Perhaps it would be better for her if he did. Then she wouldn't start hoping again, that crazy optimism inside her insisting they could have more of a relationship than they did—or ever would.

The next morning Azim left for work again before Johara had even arisen. At breakfast she toyed with the eggs on her plate, sipping coffee she didn't really want to drink. It was a gorgeous day, sunny and warm, the sky a brilliant blue. Perfect for sightseeing or simply being in the garden, and Azim had forbidden both. The hours stretched emptily in front of her, made more so by Azim's determined absence.

'Signora Bahjat?'

Johara looked up, startled to see Azim's driver standing in the doorway of the dining room, his cap in his hands. 'Yes?'

'Signor Bahjat asked me to accompany you today. If you would like to see some of Naples's sights.'

'He did?' Johara's jaw nearly dropped in astonishment. Then a smile bloomed across her face as excitement took hold, along with hope. Despite his autocratic dictates of yesterday, he'd chosen to give her this. Perhaps he had softened after last night, even if he had not wanted to act as if he had. And of course that sent her hope soaring again, like a balloon floating into the sky. Still, she wasn't going to question it, at least not now. 'I certainly do,' she said. 'Let me just get my things.'

Azim stood by the front door, watching as the limo pulled up to the entrance. He'd spent a tense day wondering about Johara, hoping she was safe. The decision to allow her to sightsee had been an impulsive one, born of the realisation at how trapped she truly was—and, he acknowledged, the desire to please her. The memory of last night had stayed with him, making him both smile and yearn for more.

Throughout the day he'd wondered what she was doing, if she was enjoying the sights. He'd pictured her strolling through the city, her expression interested and vibrant as she examined a work of art or sipped espresso in a café. A day had never felt so long.

Now he tapped his foot impatiently, watching as Johara exited the car and then ran lightly up the steps, her eyes sparkling like silver stars, her cheeks flushed, a few tendrils of hair falling from her chignon to curl delicately about her face. She looked lovelier than ever, and the sight of her felt like a fist to his solar plexus, making his chest ache not just with desire but something deeper. Something he knew he could not afford to feel.

'Where have you been?' he demanded as she crossed the threshold. The light in her eyes winked out, and Azim cursed himself. He hadn't meant to sound so harsh, but he didn't know how else to be. She disarmed him without even trying, and that was a very unsettling thing. He did not want to give her that kind of power over him, and yet she seemed to take it without even realising.

'Sightseeing, as you instructed me to do.'

'Yes, but you're late.'

'Am I? I had a wonderful time. The frescoes in the cathedral were gorgeous.' She laid one slender hand on his arm, a touch that sent shocks ricocheting right up to his ribcage. 'Thank you, Azim. It was very thoughtful of you to arrange the car and driver.'

Completely disconcerted by her touch and the look in her eyes, he found he could only shrug. 'It was nothing.'

'Even so, it meant something to me.'

Azim stared at her, flummoxed, overwhelmed. It would have been easier to kiss her into silence than respond in kind. As it was he just nodded dismissively and said, 'You should get ready. I am finished my business and we leave for Alazar tonight.'

CHAPTER EIGHT

JOHARA GAZED OUT of the window of the royal jet as the bleak mountains and desert of Alazar's interior came into view. She'd woken up an hour ago in the plane's master bedroom, having spent a restless night wondering what the future held. Azim had remained remote, first immersed in work and then sleeping in the jet's smaller second bedroom. Johara had wondered if he was suffering from another headache, but when she'd asked he'd snapped at her that he was not.

Every terse word or deliberate silence of his felt like a step backwards. She'd been so full of hope, practically buoyant with it, after her day out in Naples. She'd thought Azim was softening, their shared intimacies bringing an even greater and more wonderful intimacy. She'd spun fairy tales in her mind of the two of them learning to get to know one another, being friends, and the hard reality of her cold, remote husband felt like a slap in the face. A stab wound to the heart.

When was she going to learn to stop thinking that way? She needed to set some boundaries, and yet she had no idea how. The things they'd done together, and the things they would do, made boundaries feel impossible. Irrelevant. Every time he touched her she yearned for more. Every time he smiled she started to hope. *Stupid, stupid Johara.*

She glanced at him now, sitting across from her in the main cabin's luxurious seating area, his expression settled in a frown as he scanned some official-looking documents.

'What happens after we leave the plane?' she asked. They were due to arrive in Teruk in less than an hour, and she felt completely unprepared.

Azim glanced up from his papers, his eyebrows still drawn together in a near-scowl. 'We go to the palace.'

'Will there be some…some presentation or ceremony? I mean, since we're formally arriving…'

'Do you want one?'

'No.' She'd rather sneak in without anyone noticing. 'But I want to know what to expect.'

Azim sat back, settling himself more comfortably. 'There will be some press waiting at the airport, no doubt, but I wanted to keep our arrival quiet. The real ceremony will be in two days' time.'

'And what will that look like?'

'One of my staff will brief you.' He returned to scanning his papers, leaving Johara blinking in hurt.

So this was another aspect of a convenient marriage, she supposed. Brisk and businesslike. Except the other night, when she'd been massaging his temples and he'd been touching her, it had been anything but. She told herself it was better this way; it was certainly safer. The trouble was, it didn't *feel* better.

'Why can't you brief me?' she asked, wincing inwardly at the slightly petulant note that had entered her voice.

Azim sighed and looked up from his papers. 'When you arrive at the palace, you will be taken to the harem, where you will remain in seclusion until you appear as a bride.'

She grimaced. 'That sounds about as archaic as everything else.'

'Alazar is a traditional country. You knew this.'

Yes, she had, but she hadn't let herself think about it. She'd pushed the thought of her marriage to Malik far away, pretended it wasn't going to happen. Now the reality was staring her in the face, imminent and unavoidable. 'Why the harem?' she asked. It was a point that had needled her since he'd first mentioned it at their introduction. 'Why can't I live in the normal part of the palace?'

'The harem *is* normal. That,' Azim enunciated, 'is what is normal for Alazar.'

'I thought you were trying to bring the country into the twenty-first century,' Johara shot back. 'Westernise it, at least in some ways. That's what Malik said.'

His eyes flashed and she knew she shouldn't have mentioned Malik. 'Not in that way.' His tone was so flat and final she fell silent, knowing that to ask more questions would be to pick a fight, and the last thing she wanted was more acrimony.

She thought that would be the unfortunate end of it but then Azim sighed and rubbed the bridge of his nose. 'I appreciate that you have essentially grown up in a culture different from the one you were born into. If your father had been sensible, he would have made sure you had spent more time in Alazar, got used to its ways.'

Her father had been so sure of her obedience, he hadn't thought she'd needed to spend time in Alazar. 'I don't understand why things have to be so traditional when you are, by your own admission, trying to modernise the country.'

Azim looked as if he was going to deliver another setdown but then, to her surprise, he answered her question honestly. 'Because the interior of Alazar is controlled by desert tribes who are very traditional, and they are waiting to see how I treat my bride.'

Johara drew back. 'And how do they want you to treat me?'

'They will expect to see you modestly covered and walking several steps behind me when we are in public places, and residing in the women's quarters when you are at home.'

It sounded awful. 'So how exactly are you going to modernise the country, then?' she asked.

'Slowly, at least until the tribes have been appeased. The alternative is civil war, if the tribes start to revolt again.' He paused. 'My brother has been working tirelessly for ten years to keep the country stable. He had achieved that, but my arrival created tension and uncertainty. I must do my best to return the country to its previous stability, and then increase it.' Azim set his jaw, his eyes darkly opaque and hooded, his body radiating tense determination.

'I would have thought your arrival would have brought even more stability,' Johara said after a moment. 'Since you are the firstborn, the true heir.'

'Perhaps in time. But I have been gone a long while. And I spent the last twenty years in a Western country. Some of the tribes doubt my loyalty to Alazaran ways, which makes it even more important that I respect tradition in my personal life.'

Grudgingly Johara had to admit it made sense, even if she didn't quite want it to. 'I suppose I can understand that,' she said after a moment. 'But it would have helped if you'd told me this earlier.'

Azim inclined his head. 'Perhaps I should have.'

She widened her eyes, daring to joke. 'Wait, did you just admit you were wrong?'

'No, only the possibility of it.'

She laughed, even though she wasn't sure if Azim was joking, and then he gave her the glimmer of a smile that lightened her heart. 'So you do have a sense of humour. I was hoping, but I was starting to wonder.'

He rubbed his jaw as his gaze moved to the cerulean sky outside the jet's windows. 'I haven't had much cause for laughing.'

'What did you mean,' Johara asked suddenly, her voice soft and yet intent, 'when you said you were surviving?' She realised she quite desperately wanted to know.

Azim stilled, and then dropped his hand, his gaze returning to his papers. 'Just that.'

'Where did you live?' Johara pressed. 'Who were you with? You were only fourteen, weren't you, when you were kidnapped? Who took care of you?'

'No one.'

'But…what do you mean? Someone must have…'

'Someone who did not do a very good job of it, then,' Azim answered repressively. He let out a long, low breath. 'It was…an unpleasant experience, and one I have no desire to discuss. Now, we are landing shortly, and I need you to change.'

'Change?'

'Wear a hijab and dress suited for your role.' He nodded towards the back of the cabin. 'You will find the appropriate clothes in the bedroom.' His expression was closed and obdurate in a way that was becoming depressingly familiar. Johara knew there was no point in trying to keep conversing now. Azim would give her no answers.

Wordlessly she rose from her seat and went to the bedroom. Laid out on the bed was a hijab of delicate cream lace, and a matching gown that was certainly modest, covering her from her neck to her ankles, but no less pretty for it. Thoughtfully Johara fingered the lace.

Before Azim had confided to her his concerns about Alazar's stability, she would have resisted wearing such a garment. She'd chafed at many of his restrictions, and yet now she could see that some of them at least made sense.

And she was tired of fighting against her fate—she was tired of trying to keep herself independent from the man who, by the dictates of the country he ruled, controlled her. What if she partnered with him instead? What if she gained Azim's trust and confidence by giving him hers? Maybe then they could have some sort of friendship, a way to get along that she could live with and enjoy without getting hurt.

Johara slipped on the dress, the heavy, lace-encrusted material falling about her feet, and adjusted the hijab so it completely covered her hair. She looked in the mirror and was started by her reflection; the lace hijab framed her face, making her eyes appear larger, her lips fuller. She took a deep breath and then went to show herself to Azim.

Approval flared in his eyes as he caught sight of her. 'You look lovely,' he said, and Johara sat back down across from him.

'I am not used to such heavy garments.'

'I know.' He paused. 'Thank you for wearing them.'

A thank you and apology in the course of one morning. Johara almost smiled. Maybe they were actually getting somewhere.

No matter what Johara wore, she looked beautiful and alluring, but Azim thought she looked particularly lovely in the lace hijab and dress, appropriate for a new royal bride. *His* bride. He felt a fierce sense of possession, a need and desire to show her to his country and mark her as his.

Yet thinking of Alazar made familiar tension knot his shoulder blades and pierce his temples. He closed his eyes, willing the pain away. They were going to land in a few minutes, and he could not betray any weakness, knowing his enemies and doubters would seize on it. Now more than ever he needed to be strong.

Then he felt Johara move to sit next to him, her slender, supple body close to his. She pressed something damp, its fragrance sharply familiar, into his hand and he opened his eyes.

'It helps, doesn't it?' she asked softly.

His first impulse was to toss the handkerchief away, to insist he had no need of it and wasn't in pain. It was what he'd done for his entire adult life, because to admit he was suffering was to admit he was weak, and that was one thing he couldn't stand. Not when he'd been forced to be weak, to be utterly pitiful, for so long. Strength, even if it was an illusion, was everything.

Yet sitting there now with Johara so close to him, close enough that he could breathe in her vanilla and almond scent and feel her alluring warmth, her eyes so full of kindness, he found he couldn't do that. He didn't want to, and there was no need, because she had seen him in pain before. She'd seen him in pain and she hadn't thought he was weak. The realisation was like missing a step in a staircase, jolting him, opening him to other, unsettling possibilities.

He pressed the handkerchief to his forehead, breathing in the sharp, clean scent of peppermint. 'Thank you,' he murmured. He was touched by her concern, more than he wanted to admit even to himself. Johara smiled at him, and he managed a smile back. It felt like more than he'd meant to give, as if he'd just declared something to her, and yet he couldn't take it back.

They landed a short while later, and the peppermint oil had, thankfully, staved off the worst symptoms of an oncoming migraine. A few press had gathered by the royal jet as the door opened and the stairs were lowered, poised with cameras and notepads. Johara peeked out of the window, her face pale.

'I've never faced the press before.'

'Haven't you? Your face has been in the Alazaran news enough.'

She stared at him in surprise. 'Has it?'

Azim shook his head slowly. 'You really have lived a sheltered life. Yes, of course it has. You've always been known as the next Sultana, and your wedding to my brother was imminent. Of course you were in the press on occasion.'

'I never knew.'

Which begged the question why her father had kept her so far from Alazar's limelight. Malik had mentioned something about her mother's illness, but Azim had not thought to ask her about it. He had so convinced himself he wasn't interested in getting to know her, didn't need to know. Now he found he wanted to, not just for mere expediency's sake but out of simple—and growing—interest in who she was.

The crowd was waiting, as were the security personnel and motorcade, and Azim knew he would need to leave it for another time.

'You don't need to say anything,' he advised her. 'In fact, you shouldn't. Wave once, keep your head lowered, and follow me to the car.'

The questions rained down on them as soon as they stepped out of the plane. *When was the wedding, what about the rumours they'd already wed and would there still be a ceremony in Alazar?* Azim kept his face politely neutral and said nothing as he stepped past the reporters to the waiting car. He held the door open for Johara and she scooted inside, breathing a sigh of relief when the door shut behind them.

'Will it always be like that?'

'You are a royal, Johara.'

She made a rueful face. 'I don't feel prepared. I know

I have the alleged bloodline—my mother's family is descended from the same princes and kings as yours. But a life in the spotlight is so far from what I've experienced.'

'You won't be in the spotlight very often. Only on certain public occasions.'

'Oh, right, of course.' She glanced out of the window, her wry expression turning into something darker. 'The rest of the time I'll be locked up in the harem.'

Admittedly he'd given her that impression, but now Azim regretted it, at least a little. 'There are no locks on the doors as far as I am aware.'

She managed a brief, tense smile. 'Thank you for putting my mind at ease.'

Irritation warred with sympathy. The sooner his wife accepted the constraints of her new life, the better off they'd both be. 'My pleasure,' he replied, and turned to stare out of the window.

CHAPTER NINE

EVERYTHING WAS A BLUR. It seemed only minutes that they were in the limousine on the way to the palace, and then its golden spires flashed before them. The car had barely stopped before the door was opened and Johara was ushered out to a row of waiting servants who then steered her through the main doors and down several marble corridors before she ended up in a suite of luxurious rooms, behind a set of latticed doors. The harem.

It wasn't as bad as all that, she told herself as she walked around the opulent rooms. Besides a lavish bedroom, she had sitting and dining rooms and a private pool and gym. A table had been set up with fruit, pastries and a pot of mint tea. A young girl, who looked only about fourteen, bobbed a nervous curtsey and asked her if she would like anything else.

'No, this is fine.' Johara gave the girl a reassuring smile. 'What is your name?'

'Aisha, *Sadiyyah*.'

'It is good to meet you.' Johara noticed the girl's chapped-looking fingers as she pleated her hands together. 'Your hands look sore.'

Aisha glanced down at her fingers, blushing. 'It's nothing. They're always like that.'

'Are they?' Johara reached out to examine the girl's hand, glancing up at her. 'May I?'

'Of—Of course, *Sadiyyah*.'

It looked like eczema, and could be treated with a salve of coconut oil and jojoba. Johara was about to offer to make some up when she realised that of course she couldn't. She didn't have her garden here, her stillroom with its stove and all her equipment for making oils and other natural concoctions. She gave Aisha a sympathetic smile. 'I'll see if I can get some proper salve for you.'

The girl beamed. 'Thank you, *Sadiyyah*.'

It wasn't going to be so bad here, Johara told herself as she readied for bed that night, trying to be as optimistic as she could. She'd eaten dinner by herself, served by Aisha, who had, after some shy hesitation, shared a little bit about herself. They'd had a pleasant chat about palace life, and Aisha had assured her she could order anything she wanted and she would have it almost instantly.

An ice cream sundae, a favourite book or DVD, a new dress. Anything, and yet nothing at all. The restrictions reminded her of her father's empty gifts, lovely, dazzling even, and yet ultimately costing nothing. The things she truly wanted—the freedom to choose her own destiny, the affection or at least the company of the man she'd married—were utterly beyond her request or reach.

She did not see Azim for two endless days. Days that were kept busy with preparations for her wedding and yet which felt far too long. She wanted to see Azim, needed to reassure herself that the man she'd had glimpses of before, a man who was taciturn but also kind, was still there, or had really existed at all.

When she'd asked Aisha about where Azim was, the girl had looked scandalised. 'He cannot see you before the wedding day!' she'd exclaimed, and then scurried off.

Johara had fought exasperation and even tears, and then chosen laughter instead. He couldn't see her, when he'd already kissed her senseless and far more? Just the memory of his hands on her made her blush. She'd never felt anything so intimate, so intense, before; she both thrilled and trembled to think of feeling it again—and more.

Even from behind the palace doors Johara could feel the buzz of the palace as the wedding drew closer. Servants came and went, chattering excitedly, bringing cloth and jewels and perfumes, trying out different necklaces and earrings, and in spite of her trepidation she found herself caught up in the mood.

She stood still for fittings of her ornate wedding dress, encrusted with pearls and trimmed with a yard of lace, that was appropriately modest and yet also the most gorgeous thing she'd ever seen.

'His Highness chose this cloth for you specially,' the seamstress told her, and Johara stared at her in surprise.

'He did?'

'Yes, on the day your engagement was announced, when you first came to Alazar.'

When she'd run away. Guilt curdled her insides. Azim had made a kind gesture and she'd essentially trampled on it. Now, gazing at her reflection in the mirror, she wondered what Azim would think when he saw her in it, if his eyes would flare with male appreciation and desire. She pictured him slipping the cream hijab from her head, unpinning her hair, taking off her dress…

'Don't fidget,' the seamstress reprimanded her, and Johara saw her reflection give a secret smile. As the days stretched on, she found she couldn't wait for her wedding, simply for this limbo to be over—and so she could see Azim again.

* * *

Today was his wedding day. Azim studied his reflection in the mirror, straightening the jewelled collar of the brocade *jubba* he wore, paired with matching trousers. It was the traditional wedding outfit for a sultan, and it felt heavy and stiff across his shoulders, reminding him of Johara's comment about her unfamiliar clothing.

There was much she wasn't used to here, and he wondered how she was receiving it all. How had she found the harem, after all her protestations? Was she looking forward to their wedding, now that she'd had a taste of the pleasures they both would know?

It had felt like an endless two days without her, busy as he'd been learning the politics of his kingdom with Malik at his right hand. His grandfather had become too ill to do much more than bark from his bed, for which Azim was grateful. He tried to avoid the old man as much as possible. The memories he had of him were nearly all bitter.

Although he knew the separation was an important part of the Alazaran wedding tradition, he wished he'd had a chance to see Johara before the ceremony. Why, he couldn't even say. It seemed as if every attempt to reassure her failed, and in any case it was far better to start the way they were meant to go on, living virtually separate lives. And yet since that encounter in his bedroom, when she'd touched him so gently, when he'd felt her unrestrained response, he wasn't at all sure that was what he wanted any more.

The trouble was, he didn't know what he wanted—or how to get it.

'Your Highness?' An attendant appeared at the doorway of his bedroom. 'It is time.'

Azim nodded and turned away from his reflection. Indeed, it was time.

The grand salon of the palace was full of dignitaries and diplomats as Azim took his place at the front, his expression grave as he looked towards the back of the room from where Johara would proceed. He wondered what she looked like, if she was excited or nervous or still, heaven help them both, reluctant. Today she would stand in front of all of Alazar and take him as her husband of her own free will, the *nikkah* ceremony that was an essential part of any marriage. Today he would truly claim his bride.

Johara took a deep breath and tried to stem the tide of nervousness that threatened to overwhelm her. There were so many people. After spending two days in virtual isolation in the harem, she wasn't prepared for the sheer noise and size of the wedding ceremony. Or the sight of Azim at the other end of the room, looking more remote than ever in a brocade *jubba* and trousers, his expression seeming as if it had been hewn from stone.

Everything in her resisted this step, even though she knew she had no choice. They were already married, after all. Still she hesitated, caught on the cusp of knowing she was starting down an irrevocable path that would lead on to for ever.

Then Azim caught sight of her, and for the merest second his mouth flicked upwards. A smile. Her husband, her groom, was smiling at her, offering her the reassurance she'd been craving. Relief poured through her, and, even though his expression had turned severe again, Johara kept that smile like a secret, tucked away in her heart. She started down the aisle.

Each step felt weighted down by the heavy dress as well as the stares of several hundred people. Trying not to notice, she kept her head held high, her gaze fixed on Azim. She willed him to smile again, but his expression did not change and she almost faltered. Then, at the last step, Azim reached out with his hand and drew her towards him. The feel of his palm sliding across and then encasing hers gave Johara the strength to stand tall as the ceremony began, the words washing over her, barely audible over the hard thud of her heart. Then a question, said a bit louder, reverberated through her.

'Do you consent to this marriage of your own free will?'

This was the *nikkah,* the required part of the ceremony where they both pledged their freely given commitment to the marriage. She glanced at Azim, who was staring straight ahead, his jaw tense, his gaze shuttered. Johara realised she knew that look. He was bracing himself, thinking she might refuse. And yet how could she?

For a second, no more, she considered what would happen if she *did* refuse. Scandal, humiliation for Azim, instability for Alazar. Could she request an annulment of their marriage? Would she be thrown out from her father's house, having to make her way on the street?

But she *could* do it, she realised, just as Azim had pointed out. She could refuse. In this moment the choice was hers. Her destiny was her own, even if it hadn't felt like it. She was free to do as she pleased. And she knew what she wanted. That smile had given her hope, had made her believe. *This could work.*

Azim squeezed her hand, the pressure gentle but firm, and she realised she was taking too long to answer the question. A question she knew the answer to, even as so much of her future remained uncertain. 'Yes,' she said. 'I do so consent.'

CHAPTER TEN

IT WAS HER wedding night. Servants chattered and giggled around her as they prepared Johara for Azim, giving her knowing smiles and winks, making her blush. She'd already been bathed like a baby, fragrant oils massaged into her skin, intricate patterns of henna painted on her hands and feet. Her hair had been arranged in heavy coils and loops, her face carefully painted. And then they'd presented her with a nightgown that looked nearly transparent, the scalloped lace barely covering her breasts. Johara had stared at it, fascinated and appalled.

'But…but there's hardly anything to it!'

Basima, Aisha's mother, had giggled. 'Exactly why your husband will like it so much,' she'd said, and slipped it over Johara's head.

Fortunately a much more modest robe of gold satin accompanied it, but Johara still felt terribly bare. She'd thought she would be better prepared for this, considering what she and Azim had already done together, and yet now that the moment had arrived she realised afresh how little she'd actually shared with him. One kiss, one caress. Intense experiences both, but hardly enough preparation for *this*. She'd barely spoken to him throughout the wedding ceremony and celebration; they'd sat on matching thrones, drinking *sharbat* as a dozen different people, all of them important and officious, had toasted their marriage, their health, even their fertility. But Azim had hardly said anything at all. He'd barely even looked at her, and Johara had kept sneaking him glances, craving reassurance, something more than the tiny smile he'd given her as she'd walked down the aisle. Something that assured her she'd made the right choice in consenting, in believing that they could actually have some sort of real marriage. A real friendship.

'And now it is time.' Basima clapped her hands and stepped aside, and Johara's mother approached her, her smile fixed, her eyes as blank as ever. Naima had long ago stopped registering any emotion or interest in the world, and she approached this momentous event as she would any other, small or large, with a staring face and a distant air, as if she weren't actually there.

Johara had not seen her since she'd arrived in Alazar, beyond a few distant glimpses at the wedding ceremony and celebration. She'd long ago stopped hoping for anything from Naima, a loving word or glance, had thought she'd come to terms with her emotional absence, but she felt it keenly now.

'May God bless your union,' Naima said, and kissed her, cool lips brushing her forehead. Johara gazed into her mother's face, wishing Naima would smile and reassure her. Wondering if her mother had felt this uncertain on her own wedding night. *Love is a facile emotion.* Had her mother known her father's thoughts on the matter when she'd married? If only Johara could ask her, seek some wisdom on how to navigate marriage without love.

'Thank you, Maman,' she whispered, and Naima stepped away, her duty dispatched. She was leaving for France in the morning, and Johara didn't know when she would see her again. Everything that felt familiar was gone. All that was left was Azim.

Taking a deep breath, accompanied by a host of female attendants, Johara started towards her husband's bedroom.

Azim heard the excited clamour of female voices coming from the hallway and he tensed. He'd been anticipating this moment ever since he'd first kissed Johara, had spent several sleepless nights imagining it in all of its enticing splendour, but now that he was here he felt as unsure as a boy.

The ceremony earlier had been rich in pomp and ritual, and Azim had played his part—but that was what it had felt like, a part. He'd been strangely detached from everything, watching Johara, seeing how young and nervous she had looked, noting his grandfather's narrowed gaze, the way Malik had held Gracie's hand. This was his life now, his home, his people, and yet he felt as if he were spinning in a void, alone. Always alone. He didn't know how to be anything else, and he wondered if he ever would. If he would ever dare to try for something different, something dangerous.

Tonight was about being as close to a person as you could possibly be, and yet he felt more isolated than ever, conscious of all the gaping years of loneliness and revenge that had consumed him, the scars on his back he still wouldn't allow Johara to see, the wounds in his heart. He'd barricaded himself from the rest of humanity because letting people in was giving them access to your weakness, showing them how to slip the knife between the ribs, into the heart.

Yet so far Johara had seen glimpses and she hadn't shied away. She hadn't thought he was weak. No, she'd wanted *more*. She'd asked more questions, craved more closeness. The knowledge surprised him, alarmed him too.

And pleased him, because part of him knew he wanted to be known. However stupid that was.

The women knocked at the door and tersely Azim bid them to enter. They spilled in, laughing and giggling, eyes downcast, pushing Johara forward. She stumbled slightly on the hem of her robe and then righted herself, looking up, blushing, at Azim, her gaze darting away before he'd had time to offer a smile, although in truth he didn't know if he could.

The women were backing away, flapping their hands, offering encouragement, their only chance to be ribald. Finally one of the older women shooed them out, and the door closed with a decisive click. They were alone.

Johara was still staring at her feet, her slender body encased in a satin robe, her hair done up in intricate loops of shining blue-black.

Azim cleared his throat. 'You look lovely.'

'Thank you.' Her voice was a husky whisper. Azim could see her body tremble. If he felt unsure and a little nervous, he could not begin to imagine how his bride might be feeling, having been pushed into the room like a human sacrifice, as innocent in this as in everything else.

'A drink,' he said decisively. He'd ordered a bottle of champagne, and now he popped the cork and poured them two glasses. They both needed to relax.

Johara looked up, her eyes widening, wide and silvery and as clear as glacier lakes. 'I've never tasted champagne.'

'Surely now is the perfect opportunity.'

She nodded, accepting a glass, and then taking a sip and wrinkling her nose. 'Fizzy.'

He smiled, amused and also touched by her honest, unhidden responses to everything. 'Indeed.'

She looked up, her expression heartbreakingly candid. 'This all feels so strange.'

'Yes.'

'Look.' She showed him one palm, hennaed with intricate designs. 'It took hours.'

'It is beautiful.'

'I feel as if I've been trussed up like a chicken.' She laughed, and the sound, so tinkling and genuine, made him smile again. 'It's all a bit ridiculous, isn't it? All the ritual?'

'Traditions exist for a reason.'

'Yes.' She took another sip of champagne. 'I suppose they do. I suppose it makes people happy, to see it all done properly, the way it's been done for centuries. Will the Bedouin tribes be satisfied by all this, do you think?'

'I hope so.' When Azim had returned to the palace Malik had given him a report; the tribes were muttering, wondering if he was too European, displeased by his unexpected trip to France and Italy. They doubted whether he would continue to do things the old way. The negotiations with their leaders would require patience and discretion, otherwise Alazar could be plunged into civil unrest yet again. But he didn't want to think about Alazar now.

Johara wandered around the room, her robe swishing around her legs. He could see the outline of her breasts underneath the satin, and his body stirred insistently. 'Is this your bedroom?' she asked.

'Yes.'

She glanced at the canopied king-sized bed on its dais, piled high with satin coverlets embroidered in rich colours. Her gaze swept over it and then the whole room thoughtfully. 'Nothing about this room reveals you.'

He started, disconcerted by her remark. The last thing he wanted to be was *revealed*. 'Why should it?'

She turned to him with a little shrug. 'Because it's your bedroom. Your private room.'

'I've only been in the palace for a matter of weeks.'

'Yes, but a book or a picture, at least? Something. Most people would have something.'

He shrugged, feeling uncomfortably exposed by her perception. He was not most people.

'And there wasn't anything personal that I could see in Naples, either.'

'It is true, I do not have a lot of personal effects.'

For those first few years in Naples he'd had nothing but the ragged clothes on his back. Afterwards, he had never seen the point of keepsakes, mementoes, meaningful trinkets. Houses, cars, yachts—these things he possessed, because they had value in of themselves. They could be bought or sold, assessed and admired. And none of them were special. If you didn't let things become important, it wouldn't matter if they were taken away. And he'd had everything taken away, once.

'I can't decide,' Johara said slowly, 'if you are hiding yourself, or if it is simply that there is nothing to hide.' She stared at him openly, waiting for him to respond. Azim had no idea what to say.

Nothing to hide? He had far too much to hide. Scars, wounds, darkness, shame. Nothing he wanted Johara to see, and yet as she looked at him with that soft, silvery gaze he felt as if she saw it already, she was already starting to know him, and in that moment he didn't know how that made him feel.

'I don't have photographs,' he said, 'because there has been no one in my life worth remembering.'

Her eyes widened, her mouth turning down in surprised sympathy. 'No one?' He shrugged. 'What about your parents?'

'My father was a weak man who fell apart after my mother died.'

'She died when you were young,' Johara recalled slowly.

'When I was six. But I rarely saw her, or my father.'

'You were raised by your grandfather.'

'Yes.'

'He seems a hard man.'

Azim felt his jaw tense. 'Yes.'

'And your brother?' she asked softly. 'Were you ever close to him?'

For a moment he pictured Malik as a boy, all floppy dark hair and soulful eyes. He could see them both, lying on their stomachs, building a model aeroplane together. He could hear the laughter carried on the breeze, and he could almost, *almost* feel the lightness inside him that he'd felt then. But then it was as if a dark cloud hovering on the horizon moved closer, blotting everything out.

'Once.'

'Do you think you could be again?'

'Perhaps.' He didn't want to admit that he didn't know if he had it in him. If the softness and sympathy had been leached out of him by so many years alone.

Johara put her hands on slender hips. 'So no photos. What about books?'

'I don't read,' he said, and her eyebrows rose.

'Don't...?'

'I can read,' he clarified impatiently, 'but I try not to. Reading for business is about all I can manage. For pleasure...' He shook his head.

Realisation dawned in her eyes. 'Your headaches.'

'Yes.' He had no idea why he'd told her all that. Perhaps because he'd wanted her to understand something of him, to know that he wasn't a cipher, someone who wasn't interesting or alive or fully human. For too long he'd lived like a ghost or a shadow, but tonight he wanted to be real. He wanted to feel.

'Have you seen a doctor about it?' she asked.

'They say there is nothing they can do. In any case I have learned to live with the pain. Sometimes it feels like a part of me. Something that were it to stop, I would no longer be myself.' He could hardly believe he was saying the words, revealing so much, and yet bizarrely he wanted her to understand. To know. *Him.*

'Experience defines and shapes us,' she agreed quietly. 'But its end surely does not mean our own.'

'Perhaps.' He wasn't sure about that; if he took away the pain, the suffering, the hardship, what would be left? Not much, he feared. His success, his wealth, his whole self had been built on those foundations. They had defined him for too long.

She cocked her head. 'You are not convinced.'

'Perhaps you need to convince me.' He had an overwhelming desire to touch her, to feel that connection they'd once experienced before. 'Come here,' he said, and then he reached for her.

Her hand felt soft and small in his as he drew her slowly to him. She stood in front of him, the rise and fall of her breasts as she breathed visible beneath the thin satin of her robe and gown. She looked up at him, her eyes wide and clear, full of trust—trust he didn't know if he deserved, but in that moment he wanted to earn it.

He lifted her hand, his thumb sliding along her palm, and kissed the delicate skin of her inner wrist. He felt a tremor go through her—and himself. 'I've been wanting to touch you again. Very much.'

Johara's wrist flexed under his lips, and when she spoke her voice was a breathy whisper. 'I've been wanting to be touched.'

'You're not afraid?'

'No. Not afraid.' A shudder went through her. 'Nervous, perhaps.'

'You do not need to be nervous.' He touched her fingers to her chin, tilting her face upwards so he could meet her gaze. 'I will not hurt you.'

'But it does hurt, doesn't it?' She spoke practically, looking to him for both honesty and reassurance.

'A little, or so I've been told.' He gave her the glimmer of a smile. 'I do not know myself.'

'When did you lose your virginity?'

He laughed, disconcerted and yet also a little charmed by the blunt question. 'A long time ago.'

'I shouldn't have asked.' She bit her lip. 'Sorry.'

'No, no.' He shrugged. 'Sadly, it wasn't memorable. A single encounter.'

'Do you remember her?'

He pictured a knowing smile, a sultry look, nothing more. 'Barely.'

She nodded slowly, accepting, and he felt strangely shamed by the admission, as if it were something to be sad about, to regret. Perhaps it was. Heaven knew he hadn't experienced much of women beyond what they could provide him for a few brief hours. This experience was, in some ways, as new to him as it was to Johara, and the depth of it entirely unexpected.

'More champagne,' he said, and filled both their glasses.

She let out a shaky laugh as she took a sip. 'You're going to get me drunk.'

'Two glasses of champagne shouldn't accomplish that.' He definitely did not want her drunk. A little buzzy and relaxed, yes.

She twirled the flute between her fingers. 'I've never had much alcohol before. A glass of wine, perhaps, when my father visited.'

Which made him remember what he'd wanted to ask. 'Your mother is ill,' he said, phrasing it somewhere between a statement and a question as he drew her to a set of comfortable chairs by the window.

'Ill? Yes.' Her gaze was shadowed, a little wary, as she looked out at the palace now lost in twilit shadows. 'You could say that.'

'What is the illness?'

Her throat worked for a moment and she rotated the fragile stem of her champagne flute with slender fingers. 'Depression.'

'Ah.' He paused, the realisation sinking into him. He'd seen Naima Behwar only briefly at the ceremony, and it occurred to him now how little she'd engaged with her daughter, her only child, or in fact with anyone. He hadn't remarked it at the time because who was he to notice such things? He'd had an utter lack of loving relationships in his life. But now, looking at Johara's sad face, her thoughtful frown, he thought he understood, at least a little. 'That is why your father sent you both to France?'

'She prefers it there,' Johara answered quickly, instantly defensive, and then she sighed, her shoulders slumping a little. 'Yes, I suppose. He never said exactly, but…' She shrugged, staring down into the popping bubbles of her champagne. 'I suppose it became apparent. Obvious. She was an embarrassment to him, a liability to his ambition. We were never to talk about it.'

'And that is why you have not returned to Alazar very often.'

'Only for the most formal, necessary occasions.' Her smile was both sad and wry, and it reached him like a fist around his heart. 'I didn't realise it for a long time. Why he kept us in France. I didn't see it that way, that it was…a banishment. I simply accepted it as the way things were. I was so *trusting*.' A savage note of despair had entered her voice, torn on the last word, and she shook her head, her eyes full of recrimination and memory.

'Your father was not worthy of your trust?' Azim surmised, and Johara shook her head again, harder this time. 'No.'

From what he'd experienced of Arif Behwar he wasn't exactly surprised, but he was curious all the same as to how Johara had arrived at that conclusion. 'Why do you say this now?'

'Because...' She froze, her expression turning trapped, her eyes wide with sudden realisation.

'Johara...?' His voice was gentle but a cold finger of realisation had begun a relentless creep along his spine.

'Because,' she whispered, 'he insisted I marry you.' The smile she gave him was lopsided, uncertain, as if hoping he'd see the funny side of it. Or not.

Azim felt his expression iron out, like a mask slipping over his face, over his true self. 'You asked him to reconsider our marriage.' It was a statement, coolly given. Why it should hurt or even surprise him, he did not know. He knew how reluctant she'd been. She'd run away, for heaven's sake. And yet stupidly perhaps, it still stung.

'Yes, but only because...because I didn't know you.'

And she didn't know him now, not really. Azim leaned back in his chair. 'I see.'

'You don't, not really,' Johara insisted. 'Because...because I feel differently now.'

Of course she would say that. And of course she would confuse lust with something deeper, something like love. Hell, this evening he'd practically been doing it as well. And yet at the same time the soft and stupidly tender feelings he'd been nurturing for these last few moments were rapidly evaporating, replaced by a determination to keep this what it was supposed to be—and nothing more.

'Well.' He plucked the glass out of her hand and put it with his own on a nearby table. 'It is done, at any rate.'

Johara gazed at him, anxious now. 'Are you angry?'

'No, why should I be? Your reluctance to this marriage was clear, Johara.' He smiled at her, determined to stay both relaxed and unmoved. What she'd felt about their marriage didn't matter. He wouldn't let it matter. 'But I think,' he continued in an inexorable tone, 'the time has come for us to put words aside.'

CHAPTER ELEVEN

AZIM'S EXPRESSION WAS OBDURATE, his smile like steel. The warm feeling that had enveloped Johara, of relaxation and comfort, of understanding and being understood, had evaporated, replaced by something that both alarmed and thrilled her.

'Already…?'

'It is our wedding night, Johara.' Azim's eyes blazed darkly. 'This has to happen.'

'I know.' Still she didn't move. She couldn't. She was paralyzed by anxiety, even as a strange, surprising excitement licked along her veins. She remembered his kiss, the way his mouth had plundered hers so thoroughly, the sparks of pleasure he'd ignited inside her, the roaring flame that had only just begun to burn.

And then when he'd touched her…his fingers so knowing, so *intimate*. Yet what had been amazing and intense now made her blush in remembrance.

'Johara.' Azim's voice was rough and gentle at the same time. He looked devastatingly attractive, stubble glinting on his jaw, the loose linen shirt he wore open at the throat, revealing a column of brown throat and a tantalising glimpse of his muscular chest, sprinkled with springy dark hair. 'I promised you, I will not hurt you.' He held out his hand and Johara stared at the callused palm, the long, lean fingers, knowing she would have to take this step and yet still resisting.

They'd only just begun to talk. She'd only just begun to know him—and to start to like what she knew. And then she'd ruined it by admitting she hadn't wanted to marry him. Something he knew, of course, and yet it had spoiled the mood, or at least created another one. One of sensual, sexual expectation. She saw the heat in Azim's eyes and felt burned by it.

She wasn't ready for this. To give herself to him, to bare herself so utterly, felt like a leap into the unknown, and she had no idea how high the drop or hard the fall. And yet he was her *husband*. She knew her duty. This was his right, just as it was hers. Just as he'd said, this had to happen.

Slowly she reached out and took his hand. She felt as if she were sleepwalking as he drew her from her chair and led her slowly to the bed, his dark, hot gaze not leaving hers. Her pulse hammered wildly in her throat and her breath came in shallow pants even though he had barely touched her. They'd barely begun.

Her feet sank into thick, plush carpet as she stared at him, waiting for him to touch her. To tell her what to do, because she had no idea.

Gently Azim touched the pulse at her throat with one finger. 'You are scared.'

'A little,' she admitted in a whisper.

'May I?' He reached for the sash of her robe. Holding her breath, Johara nodded. He tugged at the sash and the robe opened, revealing her negligee, which was near-transparent, the sexiest and most revealing thing she'd ever worn, the deep V neckline plunging low enough to reveal most of her breasts, her nipple visible through the scalloped lace. The silk was gossamer-thin and showed every shadow and curve. She might as well be naked. Soon she would be.

Azim had dimmed the lights and drawn the curtains across the oncoming twilight, so the room was bathed in warm light and comforting shadows. Even so she felt exposed, her body open to his intense gaze. Johara swallowed audibly.

Slowly his eyes swept over her, and his mouth tightened and a muscle flickered in his cheek as he finished his thorough inspection, missing nothing. It felt as he were physically touching her with his gaze, burning the secret places barely concealed. His gaze finally moved to her face and settled there. 'Will you undo your hair?'

Self-consciously she reached up to the heavy mass of hair pinned at the back of her neck with its intricate loops and whorls. She started to withdraw a pin and then stopped. 'It is a husband's privilege to undo his wife's hair.'

'So it is.' He didn't move and Johara looked at him uncertainly, finding it hard to dare even in this.

'Do you want to…?'

'Yes,' he said, the word simple and sincere, and he moved towards her. Johara remained still, her breathing going shallow again as he stood before her and lifted his hands to her hair. His breath fanned her face and she closed her eyes, bowing her head a little so he could take out the pins more easily.

Each brush of his fingers against her skin sent tiny electric shocks skittering along her nerve endings. Each slide of a pin from her hair felt incredibly intimate, strangely erotic, causing a tendril of hair to uncoil and fall down her back.

He plucked one pin out after another, tossing them onto the top of the bureau where they scattered, the only sound in the room besides their increasingly ragged breathing.

Another pin and then her hair was free, and all of it fell down her back in a dark river of tumbled waves and curls, well past her waist.

Azim picked it up in two handfuls, bringing it to his face to breathe in the vanilla scent of her shampoo. 'It's so long.'

'It's never been cut.'

He looked up in surprise. 'Never?'

She shook her head. 'My mother thought it should grow longer. When she married her hair fell to her knees. But mine stopped growing.'

'It is more than long enough for me.' He drew it back over her shoulders, smoothing one hand down its shining length. 'It's beautiful.' The words sounded stilted, as if he wasn't used to paying compliments. Johara certainly wasn't used to receiving them.

She liked her face well enough, but she didn't think she was traditionally beautiful, at least not by Alazar's standards of feminine beauty. She was too tall, her nose too long, her mouth too wide, her jaw too firm.

'Thank you,' she whispered. She thought he must be able to see her heart pounding through the thin nightgown. She could certainly feel it.

Azim wrapped one thick tendril of hair around his wrist and pulled her closer to him. Their hips bumped and she drew her breath in sharply at the feel of his arousal pressing insistently against the softness of her belly.

He released her hair, moving it so her neck was bare. Then he bent his head and pressed a kiss to the sensitive curve of her neck, making her gasp again. He nipped her skin softly with his teeth, the tiny sting of pain somehow making the pleasure all the sweeter. Her knees buckled and she grabbed onto his shoulder for balance.

He laughed softly, the sound full of satisfaction. 'I like how you respond to me.'

'I don't know what I'm doing,' she confessed in a rush. 'What I'm feeling.' It was the same torrent of sensations she'd felt before, only stronger. She felt as if she were melting from the middle, a deep, instinctive longing rising up inside her, controlling her actions, begging for more.

Azim kissed her again, light, butterfly kisses up to her ear, and then he sucked gently on her earlobe, which seemed the strangest and yet most wonderful thing. Her fingernails dug into his shoulder as she tilted her head to give him better access.

'You don't need to know,' Azim told her. He was working his way round to her mouth, and Johara was possessed with the sudden, intense need, a craving she'd felt like no other, to have his lips on hers. 'Just let yourself feel it.' He paused, his lips almost brushing hers. 'Feel it all,' he said, and then his mouth was on hers, claiming it, claiming her, her very soul seeming sucked into that kiss.

She grabbed onto his shirt to anchor herself, drowning in his kiss, revelling in the feel of him even as her senses exploded. It was too much. She felt as if he were possessing her, as if she'd lost who she was apart from that kiss.

Azim broke the kiss, his gaze hot and hard on hers, to slide the straps of her nightgown off her shoulders and down her arms, and Johara shivered in the cool night air as the garment pooled at her feet.

She was naked, every part of her bare to him. A rosy blush spread across her entire body and Johara looked down, embarrassed by her own nudity, feeling more vulnerable than she ever had in her life.

Azim cupped her breast in one large palm, running his thumb gently over the peak. The touch felt shocking, as if he were taking hold not just of one part but her whole self. Owning her. 'You are beautiful.'

Johara released the breath she'd been holding in a relieved shudder. His hand was warm and sure on her breast, his thumb moving in lazy circles that created tremors through her whole body. She wanted to back away; she wanted him to touch her more. 'I'm glad you think so,' she whispered.

Azim cupped both of her breasts in his palms and Johara closed her eyes, amazed at how his touch could turn her to liquid, everything in her melting and straining at the same time. He slid his hands to her waist, spanning it easily, and pulled her more closely to him, so his erection throbbed and pulsed against her, an insistent life force.

Another shudder went through her, and her hips moved of their own accord, pressing back against him, welcoming him into the juncture of her thighs. Wanting him there. She was learning the steps of a dance she'd never known, and yet her body seemed to know them clumsily, instinctively.

Azim let out a groan as he fastened his hands on her hips, anchoring her in place, his arousal throbbing against her.

'Slowly,' he murmured, and then, placing one strong arm under her knees, he scooped her up as if she were no more than a handful of air and laid her on the bed.

Johara pressed back against the silken sheets, conscious of how naked she was, how on display. Then her eyes widened as Azim began to undress, lean fingers flicking open the buttons of his shirt, revealing more and more bronzed chest. The buttons finished, he shrugged off the garment, showing a torso that rivalled any Grecian statue in its perfect musculature, his burnished skin sprinkled with dark hair that veed downwards. The trousers came off next, in a gentle snick of sound, and he kicked them away. His hips were slim, his legs muscular and sprinkled with dark hair, and when he slid his boxers off she averted her eyes, overwhelmed by the sight of him wholly naked.

'You have nothing to fear,' he murmured, and joined her on the bed.

The collision of their naked bodies as he drew her into his arms was both sweet and strange, soft meeting hard, smooth touching rough. She felt each aching point of contact, her nipples brushing the hard wall of his chest, her hip bone pressing into his thigh, their legs loosely twined.

He slid his hand from her shoulder to her hip, smoothing his way across her skin, and then his fingers drifted to her leg, stroking the tender flesh of her inner thigh, creating quivers of sensation. Johara tensed, remembering how glorious this had felt before. It felt even better now, combined with the heady sensations of his naked body against hers. His fingers brushed her centre and she felt as if she'd been electrocuted. She jumped and Azim laughed softly.

'Why does it feel so good?' she murmured, dazed by the way his fingers moved with such knowing deftness, creating ripples of pleasure so intense Johara let out a mewling sound she'd never heard herself make before.

'I don't think many people care about that answer,' Azim murmured. He spread her thighs farther apart, his touch becoming deeper and more knowing, each stroke bringing Johara another stronger wave of pleasure.

Then he lowered his head and to her utter shock she felt his lips on her, his tongue touching her with the same deft surety. Her hips arched instinctively and she closed her eyes, embarrassed at how exposed she was, how revealing the act even as pleasure overwhelmed her. How did people do this and then look each other in the face?

How could she face Azim when he knew how he affected her, how he played her body like an instrument and only he knew the tune?

Her legs were splayed wide open, Azim's mouth exploring her most intimate folds. Johara let out a sound that was half moan, half sob. The sensations were building inside her, like a towering wave that was about to come crashing down, more intense than anything she'd ever felt before. She didn't know whether to welcome the deluge or run away from it.

'Let yourself feel it, Johara,' Azim instructed, his voice harsh with his own wanting. 'Let yourself go.'

'How...?' The word was a cry, everything inside her coiled so tightly she felt as if she might come apart, and she was afraid what would happen if she did. She could see a shining light but it felt too hot, too bright, and Azim was commanding that she walk towards it. That she let it burn her up.

'Trust me,' Azim murmured, his mouth and fingers continuing to work their magic, touching her more deeply, and her body pulsed around him as her hips arched and the sensations exploded inside her.

Her mind blanked with bright light as her body took over, the pleasure exquisite and almost painful in its intensity, wave after wave crashing over her until they were mere ripples, her body juddering with each one. She let out a gasp as she clutched at Azim, pressing her damp forehead against his shoulder. She felt weak, her muscles loose and relaxed, her body limp and pulsing with the aftershocks of a climax far stronger than anything she'd ever experienced before.

She felt overcome and emotional, weirdly near tears, moved by the entire experience. She craved Azim's closeness, not just his body, but his mind and even his heart.

How could anyone do this and not crave that kind of closeness? One without the other felt absurd, wrong.

'There is much more to it than that,' Azim told her, a hint of humour in his voice, a note of raw, sexual satisfaction. He rolled her onto her back, bracing himself above her. Johara blinked up at him, saw the look of harsh and sensual intent in his face, and felt herself quail.

There was no softening in Azim's features, no breaching of his mind or heart in this moment. This was a physical exercise of intense pleasure, nothing more. Her body might be ready, slick and wanting, but her mind felt suspended emotionally, needing more from Azim than his assured ability to awaken her to desire.

She tensed, her hands clutching his shoulders, as his arousal nudged her entrance. She clamped her lips together as he began to enter her, the invasion so unexpected, so *much*, it brought tears stinging to her eyes. Films and novels didn't do this justice. No one said how intimate it all was, how exposing and overwhelming. He was invading her soul. She bit her lip, her eyes scrunched closed.

'Am I hurting you?' Azim asked, his voice a growl of barely held self-control.

'No.' He wasn't, not in that way. The feel of him inside her was strange, parts of her stretching in a way that felt utterly alien, but it didn't *hurt*. And yet something did, because she felt nearer to tears than ever before, her mind resisting this closeness, her body demanding it, her hips arching up to receive and welcome him.

Azim slid all the way inside her, taking her over. In that moment he owned her, and he knew it. She saw it in the way he smiled, the satisfaction and triumph that blazed in his eyes as he began to move. She moved her hips in rhythm with his, needing to, finding it clumsily, and then becoming more assured. Each stroke brought a fresh wave of pleasure until that was all there was, all she could feel, her body's need obliterating her mind's protest. Her cry, when she came, was a jagged plea that broke on the still air, left her in splinters.

Azim sagged on top of her for one moment and Johara stroked his damp, spiky hair, still trying for the kind of intimacy that she knew Azim didn't want to give. He'd made her body sing but her heart yearned—and his was cold.

Her hands began to drift down his back and in one fluid movement Azim rolled off the bed and away from her, shrugging on a dressing gown before Johara could blink, and then disappearing into the bathroom, leaving her feeling achingly alone even as her body still hummed with her sated desire.

CHAPTER TWELVE

AZIM GAZED IN the bathroom mirror at his own flushed face, eyes glittering, and wondered why he didn't feel more satisfied. He'd made Johara respond, just as he'd known she would. Watching her come apart under his touch had been a sweet satisfaction. And afterwards…he'd found his own pleasure, deeply, and he knew she had as well. He'd got exactly what he'd wanted from the experience.

And yet, as his heart rate slowed and his breathing evened, it wasn't the memory of the savage, intense pleasure he'd just enjoyed that pulsed through his brain. It was the memory of Johara looking up at him with such innocence and trust as he'd taken down her hair. It was the feel of her heavy hair in his hands, knowing no other man had had the privilege or right to see her as he was seeing her. It was the way she'd rested her forehead against his shoulder, how she'd touched his face and hair as they lay in each other's arms.

Somehow those moments had felt more intimate than anything else. It made him ache in a way he didn't like, opened up a deep well of yearning that had been dry and empty for as long as he could remember.

Azim turned on the taps and washed his face, scrubbing away that memory and the unsettling thoughts and feeling that came with it. So they had chemistry, undeniable and overwhelming. That was good. It would serve them well in their marriage. That was all he needed to concern himself with now.

When he returned to the bedroom Johara had retrieved her nightgown and put it on, her cloud of dark hair hiding her face. She lay on her side, her back to him, her knees tucked up to her chest under the covers.

Azim hesitated, not wanting to prolong the moment but recognising just how innocent she'd been. 'You're all right?' he asked in a low voice. 'You're not…sore?'

She shook her head, her hair flying about her face, and before he could question or rethink the action Azim sat next to her and stroked her hair, tucking a few unruly tendrils behind her ear so he could see her face. The silvery tracks of tears shone on her cheeks. He drew his hand back, appalled.

'You said I didn't hurt you.'

'You didn't.' Her voice was muffled by the blankets she'd drawn up to her chin.

'Then why are you crying?' Azim demanded.

'I don't know.' Johara's voice sounded small, and she let out a hiccupy laugh. 'Isn't that silly?'

He didn't know if he would call it *silly*. He didn't like it, that was for certain. 'I do not appreciate a woman crying after I have made love to her,' he said, wincing inwardly at how cool he sounded. But he'd *felt* her passionate response. To cry afterwards was both idiotic and insulting.

'But we didn't make love, did we?' Johara pointed out. Azim stilled, even more appalled by her implication. She rolled onto her back to gaze at him openly, the tears still glistening on her cheeks.

'I know I'm being stupid,' she said. 'I know you don't love me. How could you? We barely know each other. And

I don't love you,' she added, which, infuriatingly, both re-assured and irritated him. 'I don't even want to.'

'Then what is the problem?' he asked in a clipped voice.

'I really don't know.' She sighed and swiped at her cheeks. 'I just feel sad for some reason.'

Impatient now, Azim rolled away from her. He couldn't deal with such emotional antics. Johara sighed softly, the sound one of weary resignation, and for a reason he could not fathom Azim felt compelled to say, his voice gruff, 'It is an emotional experience for any woman, I suppose.' It hadn't been for any of the women he'd slept with previously, but Johara was different—a virgin, innocent and naïve. *Hopeful.* Of course she would embroider romantic notions onto what they'd just done.

'Yes,' Johara agreed slowly. 'And it isn't for a man.'

'Not often.' Not ever, at least for him.

'Have you ever been in love?' she asked softly. 'Do you know what that feels like?'

'No.' The word was flat and uncompromising. As reluctant as he was to quash her completely, Azim knew what needed to be said. 'And I won't love you, Johara, if that is what you are hoping for. You are young and inexperienced, so it is natural perhaps for you to dream of romance. But you won't have it with me.'

'I wasn't asking,' she said with a spark that improbably made him smile. He was glad she hadn't lost her spirit.

'Good.'

'I've known that since you informed me we were going to marry,' Johara answered tartly. 'It was hardly a *romantic* proposal. And in any case, I don't want to love you. Why would I want to fall in love with someone who has no intention of loving me back?' Her voice was strident but also jagged, hiding pain. 'That's a recipe for disaster if there ever was one.'

'I'm pleased we're clear,' Azim returned, and they both lapsed into a tense silence. Azim rolled onto his back and stared at the ceiling; Johara turned back on her side, her back to him, her knees tucked up. He listened to her breathe, finding the gentle draw and tear strangely comforting. He had never actually slept with a woman before, the whole night through. Yet as tired as he was, it was an aggravatingly long time before he fell asleep.

Johara gave herself a stern talking-to when she readied and dressed the next morning. She and Azim had been woken up by attendants who had brought in a huge breakfast on a trolley of silver dishes and platters. A palace official had accompanied them, and Johara had blushed and retreated to the bathroom while he inspected the sheets for the needed proof of her virginity. Satisfied, he'd left them alone, as had the servants.

They'd eaten breakfast in bed, something that could have been romantic or even erotic but felt more like a business meeting.

'Your attendants will come shortly to take you back to the harem,' Azim said as he poured them both coffee.

'And that's where I stay?' She couldn't keep a note of ire and, worse, hurt from her voice.

'I am sure you will be entirely comfortable.'

Johara shook her head slowly. 'Am I really going to spend the rest of my life in a couple of rooms?'

'No, of course not. Why must you be so melodramatic?' Azim sounded irritated.

Johara lowered her coffee cup. 'I didn't realise I was being melodramatic.'

'You will accompany me on events around the city, and you will attend many dinners and other formal occasions in the palace. You are not a prisoner, Johara, and if you feel like you are, you do not know what real imprisonment feels like.'

Something about his tone made her ask, 'And you do?'

His expression closed, like a fan snapping shut. 'I know what it is to feel trapped.'

'How?'

He hesitated, and Johara held her breath waiting, hoping for more. 'The years after my kidnapping were not easy.' He took a sip of coffee, looking away, as if that was the end of the matter.

'You said they were unpleasant, but what do you mean by *trapped*?'

He pressed his lips together. 'It does not matter. I fought hard to survive and triumph, and I did. But there were years where I felt trapped, when there seemed no way out, no end to the suffering, and that experience was not like this.' With one impatient hand he gestured to their opulent surroundings, making Johara wince. It sounded as if he'd had a truly terrible experience, and here she was whingeing about all the luxury she was surrounded with.

'I'm sorry, Azim.'

He shrugged her words aside. 'This is not an imprisonment, Johara. You are free to do what you like in the women's quarters, to make friends among your attendants, to devote yourself to causes appropriate to your station. You have more freedom than most likely any other woman in Alazar.'

When he put it like that she felt petty and spoiled for complaining. And yet the life he was outlining still held a lack—a lack of companionship with her husband, a lack of friendship and, dared she think it, love. She'd told him last night that she didn't want love, but after what they'd done it was near impossible not to think of it. How could anyone not think of love when you gave your body, your whole self, so freely? It felt inconceivable to separate the two, and yet Azim obviously did, easily.

She'd been stupid to talk to him about love at all, Johara told herself as she returned to the harem to dress and ready for the day. What had she been expecting him to say? To do? Take her in his arms and whisper how much he cared, shower her with kisses and compliments? She was ridiculous for imagining that sex changed anything for him. She'd been pathetic, and that was one thing she did not intend to be again.

She had no wish to replicate the same kind of eager-to-please neediness she'd shown with her father. He'd only been kind to her when he'd wanted something, and in the bright, hard light of morning Johara recognised that Azim was essentially the same. Yes, he could give her lovely dresses and even lovelier kisses—but they cost him nothing. Nothing emotionally, anyway, which was what mattered.

And she was not going to fall in the trap of longing to love someone, *anyone*, who wouldn't love her back. *Love is a facile emotion.* No, she wouldn't give into it, or the desire for it.

Besides, she didn't even know Azim very well, although the more she knew, the more she realised how much he must have endured, how strong he was. The more she wanted to know him, and even now a little voice was whispering that perhaps if she was just patient, if she just waited for his hard heart to thaw, for him to learn to trust again, things could be different. He could love her, and she could love him, and it wouldn't be like her father said, facile, for fools and weaklings. Talk about being naïve.

Johara gazed at her reflection in exasperation. Pink cheeks, sparkling eyes, the look of a woman who had been thoroughly loved when she hadn't been. She'd been *en-*

joyed. Nothing emotional had happened last night, at least not for Azim.

And not, she determined, for her. From now on she was going to be like Azim, at least in his approach to their marriage. Briskly practical, enjoying the chemistry they obviously shared. Nothing more. Nothing that would make her feel hurt and used, and in a far worse way than she ever had with her father.

She spent the morning organising the women's quarters to her liking, getting rid of some of the fussy furniture and unpacking her own books and clothes and photographs, feeling better about having the space more personalised. At lunchtime she ate with Aisha and Basima, enjoying their friendly chatter.

In the afternoon she wandered out to the harem gardens, appreciating the pretty courtyard with its fountain and benches, and a larger terrace of landscaped shrubs and flowers. It was bigger than her garden back in France, and remembering what Azim had said, how much freedom she had, she turned to Aisha with a determined glint in her eye.

'Aisha, do you think you could bring me a spade?'

Azim spent the day in his office, meeting with Malik and other officials, trying to concentrate on the business at hand and finding it difficult. He kept thinking of Johara, reliving the best moments of their night together, and found himself so distracted he had to ask Malik to repeat things more than once.

'You must be tired,' Malik remarked with a mischievous glint in his eye, and Azim shook his head impatiently.

'I am fine.'

'It was your wedding night, brother. It is perfectly acceptable to admit to a little fatigue. Expected, I would have thought.' Malik spoke mildly, reminding Azim of the camaraderie they'd once had. If he hadn't been kidnapped, hardened beyond all bearing, he would have shared a laugh and a smile with his brother, and admitted to just how tired he was. Now he found he could not summon the tone, the lightness, but instead of his brother's remarks irritating him and putting him on the defensive, he found himself both frustrated and saddened by his own inability. He wanted more for himself, and yet he had no idea how to go about getting it. This wasn't a business deal or property transaction; he couldn't buy his way into deeper relationships. No, this was far more difficult, more confusing.

'I admit I am a bit tired,' he said stiffly, his best attempt at banter. 'But it is from the jet lag as much as anything else.'

A smile lurked in Malik's eyes as he sat down across from him to discuss their new policies for the country's tourism industry. 'Of course.'

By late afternoon Azim decided he'd had enough. He'd told himself he would not seek out Johara for the rest of the day, and only summon her to his chamber at night, as was befitting of a sultan-in-waiting and his new bride. He would not show he needed her, because he didn't, and such a gesture would smack of a weakness he could not show to the palace informants of the desert tribes, who were already suspicious of him for being too European, married to a woman who had spent most of her life in France.

Even so, after finishing a meeting with several diplomats, he excused himself from his study and found himself walking from the official front rooms and offices of the palace to the women's quarters at the back. He had not actually been to the harem since he was a boy, visiting his mother.

A memory, long forgotten, stirred, of his mother in the harem garden, watching goldfish dart through the still, cool waters of the pond, her slender, golden arm around his thin boy's shoulders. She'd died when he was six, and the harem had been closed and shuttered. Life had changed completely as his grandfather had taken over his upbringing, determined to weed out any weakness or sentiment, and Malik had been banished to the nursery and a host of nannies. His father, lost in grief, had become a shadow of a man, uninterested in either of his sons. And so for the next eight years Azim had learned to be sharp, to be quick, to be tough. And then he'd been kidnapped and he'd learned a whole new kind of tough.

'Your Highness!' A servant girl opened the door to the women's quarters, fluttering around him with girlish titters and blushes. 'If you are looking for Her Highness...'

'I am.'

'She is out in the garden.'

'Ah.' This was becoming something of a habit. His step grew lighter as he strode towards the louvred doors open to the enclosed gardens. He stopped on the threshold, arrested by the sight of his wife kneeling in a flower bed, her skirt caught up around her knees, digging with enthusiasm.

'We'll need another bag of compost before we can plant, Aisha,' she called. 'I wish we had some sort of irrigation or sprinkler system. Watering is going to be difficult.'

Quietly Azim closed the doors behind them, ensuring their privacy. 'I am afraid I am not Aisha.'

'Oh.' Startled, she turned around, her surprised expression morphing into wary pleasure as she smiled at him, her cheeks and eyes both glowing. 'I wasn't expecting to see you.'

'Were you not?'

She gave a little grimace. 'Basima told me you would only summon me at night.'

That had indeed been his plan, but now Azim shrugged it aside. 'I wanted to know how you were.'

A smile lit her face, lit up his insides. 'I'm well.'

'Busy.' He nodded towards the dug-up flowerbed. 'These gardens were prized, you know. The roses in particular.'

'Oh.' Her eyed widened in dismay. 'Were they? I should have asked, I suppose, but you did say I was free to do what I liked in here. I kept the rosebushes. I'm going to plant them on the other side.'

'I don't care about the roses,' he told her. 'I am glad to see you so occupied.' He was, fiercely so. He wanted her to make a life for herself here. He wanted, he realised, for her to be happy. 'You mentioned you had a garden in France?'

'Yes, mainly to grow herbs and plants for natural medicine.'

'Like the peppermint oil you used for my headache.'

'Yes.' Wanting to touch her, he took her hand and drew her up from the flowerbed to the bench by the fountain. 'You have dirt on your nose.' He brushed it off and she ducked her head.

'I must look a mess.'

'You look lovely. Enchanting.' Her hair was tucked up under a scarf, a few unruly tendrils escaping to frame her flushed face. He had the urge to kiss her, and so he did, brushing his lips once across hers, and then again, in a hello kiss that made him want to settle there, go deeper.

She drew back, searching his face, a frown developing between her brows.

'What is it?'

'Nothing.' She shook her head, smiling. 'I'm pleased to see you.'

'Good.' And then, to indulge himself, he kissed her again, taking the time to savour her sweetness, exploring the delectable softness of her mouth, tracing the seam of her lips with his tongue. The kiss went on, endless and aching, until Johara melted in his arms, her body pliant under his.

The sweetness of the kiss bred a deeper, more urgent need. Azim slid one hand under her skirt and Johara let out a breathy laugh.

'Someone will see…'

'The doors are shut, and your attendants know better than to disturb us. The walls are too high for anyone else to see.'

His fingers climbed higher, brushing her underwear, teasing her sensitive flesh, and Johara bit back a moan. He loved that he only had to touch her for her to start coming apart.

But then, with seeming superhuman effort, she batted his hand away. 'No.'

He stared at her in disbelief, battling a dismay and even hurt at her apparent rejection. 'No?'

Johara's eyes glittered as she answered with only a hint of shyness, 'If we are going to…well, then I want to touch you.'

Relief poured through him, along with something even sweeter. She wanted him. She wanted him as much as he wanted her. He sat back against the bench, his heart full, his body throbbing. 'Then by all means, go ahead.'

Johara glanced at Azim from beneath her lashes, his powerful body sprawled on the seat, muscular thighs spread, practically inviting her caress. She wondered if she'd issued a challenge she did not have the courage to carry out.

Last night she'd been a passive recipient, and, while it had certainly been pleasurable, now she wanted to take some control in this aspect of her life. She had so little control in others. And, she knew, she wanted to touch Azim. She wanted to see if he responded the same way to her touch as she did to his. She wanted to give him pleasure, to know she affected him at least in this.

Yet how…? Where to start?

'Surely you're not scared, Johara.' His voice was gently mocking, his lips curved in a small smile. He looked devastating sitting there, his eyes and hair so dark, his skin like burnished bronze, the crisp white shirt he wore highlighting the perfect musculature of his chest and abdomen.

'No.' She spoke with bravado and then, deciding she needed to dare, she placed one hand on his chest. Felt the steady thud of his heart under her palm, the muscles leap and jerk under her questing fingers, and a smile of pure feminine power curved her mouth. She could enjoy this.

Azim's dark eyes met with her own, and his mouth curved in an answering smile. 'That's a beginning.'

'Yes.' Not quite able to look at him, she focused on unbuttoning his shirt. Azim remained still under her clumsy movements—wretched buttons that didn't seem to want to come out of their holes. Then finally she'd got it unbuttoned, and she spread the shirt so she had a full view of his chest.

He was truly glorious, his skin taut over sculpted muscles, a sprinkling of dark hair veeing down to his trousers. She trailed her fingertips down his bare skin, from his throat to his belly button, and her blood heated at the hot look of naked need in Azim's eyes.

'All you have to do is touch me to make me want you.' She trailed her fingers back up and he leaned his head against the bench, closing his eyes. 'You don't even have to touch me. All it takes is a look, a thought, and I'm yours.'

Yours. She wanted him to be hers. If she was honest

with herself, she wanted him to be hers more than in this, but she'd take this for now. She'd revel in it.

In one purposeful movement she slid onto his lap, lifting her skirt up to her hips so she could straddle his thighs.

Azim's eyes gleamed and colour appeared on his high cheekbones. She could feel his arousal pressing against her, and remembered when he'd brought her onto his lap before. When he'd touched her most intimately. Now it was her turn.

'I think I like this,' he murmured.

Now the brazen part. She tugged at the zip of his trousers, gasping a little at the feel of his arousal pressing so insistently against her hand. Then she freed him, and dared to stroke his full length, amazed at her own courage, the feel of his hot, satiny skin under her fingertips.

'Yes, I like this very much,' Azim murmured, his breath hissing between his teeth, his voice a husky growl of need. 'But make sure you finish what you started.'

Finish… Realisation dawned, and, with it, power. She could do this. She would do this, because the knowledge that Azim wanted her as much as she wanted him was heady and empowering. 'I intend to,' she said, and then she rose up on her knees and, pushing her clothing aside, sank slowly onto him, sheathing him inside her. *'Oh.'* She gasped as new sensations hit her synapses. 'It feels different than before.'

He laughed, the sound low and throaty as his hips began to move against hers. 'Different good?'

'Yes.' She was starting to lose the power of speech, her mind going blissfully blank as she matched his movements. 'Yes, definitely. *Definitely*.'

Later, after they'd tidied themselves up and Azim rang for refreshments, Johara marvelled at her audacity. Sitting in the sunshine with Azim's arm around her shoulders, she thought she was the happiest she'd been in a long time. The fact that he'd come to find her was like a song in her heart, a secret she hugged to herself, promising more. Never mind her resolutions of that morning; they'd scattered away with the first breath of hope. She didn't want to live like her father. She didn't want to guard her heart and stay isolated and alone, as Azim had been for so long. She wanted more, even if it hurt. Even if it meant risk of pain. Wasn't that what true optimism, true hope, was all about? And right now she felt more hopeful than ever that in time Azim could begin to care for her. Just as she could—and was already doing.

'Why natural medicine?' he asked as he toyed with a tendril of her hair. They were sitting together on the bench, sipping mint tea that Aisha had brought. Johara thought she'd detected a mischievous, knowing glint in the young girl's eye and wondered if her attendant had guessed what they'd been up to.

'Our cook, Lucille, introduced me to herbal remedies when I was trying to alleviate my mother's worst symptoms. I started a garden with her help and began to read books about it.'

'Did they work on your mother?'

'Sometimes.' Johara paused, not-so-pleasant memories invading and darkening the sunshine of the afternoon. 'She had terrible headaches, which is why I recognised when you had one. And she also was…lethargic.' Which was putting it mildly.

'Do you know what caused it?'

Johara hesitated, feeling that they were on shaky ground. 'My father never loved her,' she began slowly. 'Or so she told me.' As a girl she realised now how thoughtlessly she'd dismissed her mother's complaints, because she'd adored her father and could sympathise with why he'd lost patience with his sad and listless wife. But now she experienced a sharp pang of sympathy for her mother. To live without love was a terrible thing. To endure each day, knowing it promised no happiness, no hope. It made her insides quail with fear for the path she'd now chosen. What if Azim never came to care for her? What if she fell in love with him and ended up like her mother? It was, perhaps, more risk than she wanted to take and yet the alternative was awful. A cold, lonely existence of always guarding her heart, watching her step.

'And she'd loved him?' Azim's voice gave nothing away, but Johara could feel how his body had tensed against her.

'Yes, at least she said she did. But she also miscarried several times. The lack of children was a great disappointment to both of them, and especially not having a son.' She wrinkled her nose, tried for a little laugh, to lighten the mood. She knew Azim didn't like talking about love, and it made her a little uncomfortable too. 'I'm afraid I wasn't a great consolation prize.'

Azim's fingers brushed her cheek. 'You are a great prize to me.'

Johara's throat thickened with emotion. She didn't doubt Azim's sincerity, and her heart rejoiced at him saying even this much, for it was more than anything he'd said before, and yet…

She didn't want to be a prize. She wanted to be a partner. A lover, a soul mate, his heart's desire. The realisation bloomed and grew within her like the most fragrant and beautiful flower in any garden. She was, slowly and inexorably, falling in love with her husband—and she wanted, quite desperately, for him to love her back. The possibility that he might never do so was enough to freeze the smile on her face, everything in her aching with both hope—and fear.

CHAPTER THIRTEEN

'WE ARE TRAVELLING to Najabi.'

Azim stood in the doorway of her stillroom, looking alarmingly grave. Johara's heart tumbled in her chest, as it had a habit of doing every time she caught sight of her husband. They had been married for three weeks and, while it felt like no time at all, it also seemed as if things had been this way for ever.

They'd fallen into a sweet pattern that Johara treasured; she worked in her garden most mornings and she usually saw Azim in the afternoon, when he stopped by the women's quarters for a visit. They ate dinner together most nights and she'd spent every night in his bed.

It was more, far more, than she'd ever expected to have in this forced marriage, and yet in the quiet stillness of her own heart she knew she wanted still more. She wanted Azim's love, and she didn't have it yet. He was attentive, yes, and a most exciting and ingenious lover, if a little remote, often rolling off the bed and dressing the moment they'd finished.

They had developed a rapport of conversation, discussing ideas, politics, art, almost anything but themselves. At least, Azim did not discuss himself, and Johara had learned not to ask. The information he shared about himself and his past came in reluctant, tersely given snippets, and she treasured each precious new fact, few as they were.

The day after he'd visited her in her makeshift garden, Azim had sent a raft of new garden supplies and two able-bodied attendants to help her transform the garden's pruned perfection into the kind of wild and unruly sanctuary she'd had in France. He'd also arranged for one of the rooms of her quarters to be turned into a stillroom, complete with a deep, stone sink and a stove for preparing and distilling essential oils and making salves.

His thoughtfulness had both touched her and given her hope, and she'd spent many happy hours tending her garden and preparing her medicines. Word of her prowess had reached many of the occupants of the palace, and many days she was treating an attendant or official for some minor complaint or ailment. She'd gone to two state dinners, and had started to get to know Malik's fiancée Gracie before she'd returned to America to prepare for a final move to Alazar.

All of it gave her a sense of purpose and community, both of which she realised had been missing from her previous life.

'Najabi?' she asked now, her heart tripping at how solemn Azim looked. 'Where is that?'

'In the desert. I need to visit the desert tribes and assure them of my loyalty to both them and their traditions.'

'Which is where I come in,' Johara surmised. 'I need to play the dutiful bride?'

'You are a dutiful bride,' Azim replied with the flicker of a smile. 'But yes. It will reassure them to know that my bride is not corrupting me, and that I have her firmly under control.' He spoke lightly, almost joking, but Johara knew he was serious. And as excited as she would be for a trip with Azim, she wasn't looking forward to them playing these assumed roles. At least, she hoped they were assumed. She hoped they'd come a long way from the marriage of cold convenience they'd once had.

'When do we leave?'

'Tomorrow, for a few days. We will visit several different tribes. They are planning some celebrations for us. It will be hard travel, though,' he warned. 'The interior of Alazar is rugged, with few roads. Basima will help you pack appropriately.'

'And when we're there?' Johara asked with a touch of apprehension. 'What will I do? How am I supposed to be?'

'You can take your cue from me,' Azim said, which didn't help all that much. 'This is important, Johara,' he added, his tone grave. 'For us, and for Alazar.'

The next day they took a helicopter for the hundreds of miles into Alazar's interior, a barren, rock-strewn landscape of endless desert, the mountains of Alazar's impressive ranges piercing the horizon.

Johara spent most of the time gazing out of the window, marvelling at the stunning scenery and trying not to feel sick with nerves. Since they'd started this trip Azim had retreated into a tense silence that reminded her so much of the first days of their marriage, when they had been like strangers, and hostile ones at that.

She'd thought they had got past those early, awful days, but maybe they hadn't. The trouble was, she had no idea how strong their marriage really was, how real their bond. At times, when Azim was smiling at something she'd said or holding her in his arms, stroking her hair or moving inside her, she felt as if they were both on the cusp of everything. Of love.

But in a moment like this one she felt as if she was being ridiculous, reading emotion and feeling where there was none. She was being pathetic and needy, grasping at whatever Azim tossed her way, and she never wanted to be either again.

'Why aren't we taking a helicopter directly to where we're going?' she asked. Azim had already told her that they would land several hours away from the first tribe's encampment.

'Because as their leader it would be shaming to do so,' Azim explained. 'It would seem weak and unmanly.'

She shook her head slowly. 'And riding in an SUV doesn't?'

Azim gave her a ghost of a smile. 'We are not riding in an SUV.'

'But how are we getting there, then?'

'Horseback.'

'Horseback!' She stared at him, appalled. 'I've never been on a horse before in my life.'

'Something which will be remedied shortly.' Azim's expression remained unsmiling, not so much as a flicker of a smile to soften it. 'You will ride with me.'

He had never been into Alazar's arid heart before. His preparation for the Sultanate had been a life in Teruk and then the start of military school. Asad would have taken him into the desert eventually, Azim supposed, but he felt the absence of experience now.

He shielded his eyes with one hand from the relentless desert sun as Johara climbed out of the helicopter behind him. They were several hours' ride from the first encampment, in a bleak moonscape of undulating sand strewn with large, fearsome-looking rocks. A groom waited with their horses and supplies, brought from an outpost nearby.

Azim thanked him as he took the reins of his horse. He felt on edge, wound too tight, the first flickers of a headache pulsing through his brain. His conversation with his grandfather yesterday still ricocheted unpleasantly through him.

'She is making a fool of you.'

Azim had stared at the old man now confined to his bed, bitter and alone, and tried not to react. Asad struggled up to a sitting positon, his claw-like hands grasping the sheets, his breath coming in desperate wheezes. The doctor had given him a few months to live, if that, and when Azim had heard the news he'd felt nothing.

Once he'd felt something for the old man. He'd glowed under his tersely given praise, had sought to please him by working hard, by being tough. In the twenty years since his kidnapping he'd forgotten Asad completely, forgotten Alazar. But seeing his grandfather's face on the television had brought it all back, and the first emotion that had hit him in the face had been fury. A deep-seated rage at this man who had ridden him so hard, yielding no quarter or kindness. Now he eyed him coldly, refusing to rise to the obvious bait.

'I am travelling to Alazar's interior tomorrow.'

'Did you not hear what I said?'

'Yes, I simply chose not to respond to it.'

'People are talking. Whispers about how she spends every night in your bed.'

'I want an heir,' Azim stated flatly.

'And you go to the harem, almost every day.' Asad's voice was a hiss of disbelief. 'You are besotted with her paltry charms.' Azim said nothing, a muscle ticing in his jaw. 'What do you think the desert tribes will say?' Asad rasped. 'They will think you are controlled by a woman, and a European one at that.'

'Johara was the country's choice,' Azim returned. 'Her

blood is nearly as noble as ours. She has been destined for the throne as much as I am.'

'But she has not lived it,' Asad pointed out. 'Just as you haven't. Tucked away in France as she's been... People wonder, and you are making it worse.'

'Is that all?' Azim asked coldly. 'I have business to attend to.' He turned away without waiting for his grandfather's reply.

'People say you are like him, Azim,' Asad wheezed after him. 'Like your father.'

Azim slammed the door behind him.

Now he straddled the stallion that had been brought for him and tried to banish his grandfather's words from his mind. He was not like his father. He was not weak. Not any longer. He'd spent far too long being virtually helpless, at another's mercy, and he'd lived his life in a decidedly different fashion since. Yes, he enjoyed Johara's company—and her body. That wasn't wrong. It didn't have to be weakness. But he couldn't get his grandfather's words out of his head, and that irritated him.

'I didn't realise horses were so big.' Johara glanced up at him, swathed from head to foot in a linen robe both for modesty and protection from the desert heat and blowing sand.

'The groom will help you up.' Azim looked away, ignoring the flicker of hurt he'd seen pass across his bride's face. He'd been short with her since the conversation he'd had with his grandfather; he hadn't summoned her last night or spoken to her much on their travels here.

He felt a pang of guilt for hurting her, but he told himself it was necessary. Perhaps they both needed to be reminded of the parameters of their relationship. Perhaps he had been too indulgent, both of her and his own whims.

Then they would be able to move on in a way that was beneficial for them both.

The groom helped Johara up and with a muffled *oof* she sprawled across the horse, her breasts pressed against his thighs. She glanced up at him wryly, challenging him to see the humour in the situation, but Azim just took her arm and hauled her up to a sitting position, her back against his chest.

He wrapped one arm around her middle, under her breasts, and clicked to the horse. They started off, jolting across the sand, and Johara settled into him more closely. Azim tried not to react to the feel of her against him, the rightness of having her body pressed against his.

As the horse began to gallop, the wind streaming past them, he felt a sudden surge of primal, possessive power, an overwhelming sense that Johara was *his*—his to care for and to protect. To love. The word popped into his head and he quickly banished it. He couldn't think that way. Love was weakness. Trust was stupidity. He *knew* that. He'd seen it too many times—first with his father, and then with Caivano. Trusting someone meant giving them power. Loving them meant risking pain and betrayal.

His arm tightened around her middle and she looked up at him, a frown between her brows, a question in her eyes. Azim looked away from her gaze, at the stretch of sand in front of them, and rode on.

By the time they arrived at the Najabi oasis his body was aching from the hard ride, and he could only imagine how much Johara, who had never ridden before, felt. She had not complained once, though, and for that Azim felt more than a flicker of admiration. His wife was strong.

Now they approached the oasis, the leaders of the tribe assembled to welcome them. The moment felt taut with suppressed tension, suspicion and vague hostility. Johara had dropped behind him, her head modestly lowered, meeting no one's gaze just as she was meant to. What would have filled him with satisfaction and relief now he found irritated and even troubled him.

He didn't want Johara behind him like some lackey. He wanted her at his side, raising her face, smiling at everyone as he announced her as his bride. The urge to reach for her, to bring her forward, was almost overwhelming, and Azim didn't know whether to feel appalled or proud. Where had this feeling come from? The strength of it was surprising, disturbing. He nodded towards one of the leaders, who, after an endless moment, made his obeisance. And still he thought of Johara.

Johara could feel the suppressed male energy and hostility shimmering in the desert heat as several leaders bowed to Azim, their expressions stoic and grim. She'd kept her head lowered but she couldn't resist peeking up to see what was going on.

The silence stretched on, the only sound the wind starting to kick up. A horse nickered. Then, like a gunshot, a sudden eruption of chatter and laughter started. Johara raised her head, startled, and saw a bevy of women in brightly coloured hijabs and robes coming towards her, their faces wreathed in welcoming smiles.

The men, seeming to take their cue from the women, slapped Azim on the back and welcomed him into their fold. With relief she realised that the tense moment of uncertainty had passed.

The women enveloped her, pulling her along, and with one last startled look for Azim, Johara let herself be led away.

The women took her to a tent, chattering all the while, giving her nudges and winks as they remarked on what a handsome man the Sultan-to-be was, and then burst into uproarious laughter. Johara soon found herself caught up in the mood, laughing and chatting with them, even daring to make a few ribald jokes, which the women loved, although her heart still felt heavy.

Why was Azim being so cold? They'd spent hours riding together, and yet Johara felt as if she might as well have been a sack of potatoes he had to haul around. She didn't understand his withdrawal, or what prompted this sudden coolness. Was it simply a concern for the desert tribes—or something deeper and more alarming? Perhaps this was simply a reflection of his true feelings—or lack of them.

After plying her with glasses of cool *sharbat* and honey cakes, the women led her out to a sheltered spot in the oasis where they bathed, insisting Johara join in.

After several aching hours in the saddle, she was more than glad to wash off the sand and dust of travel, even if she felt a little shy stripping down. The women gave her a new robe to wear, of cream linen embroidered with purple and gold, fit for a princess.

Johara realised a meal was being prepared for her and Azim, a celebration for the Sultan-to-be and his bride. Her heart seemed to miss a beat as the women led her out to the circle of waiting men, who nodded in approval to see her so traditionally dressed. Johara peeked through the gauzy veil, looking for the only man whose opinion mattered. But when she finally caught sight of Azim, his face was expressionless, and when her eyes met his he looked away.

What was going on?

The evening passed in a miserable blur, although Johara tried to smile and laugh and chat for the women's benefit. She was confused and angry with Azim for being so remote, and cross with herself for caring. She had not followed her own directive at all, which was to stay calm and cool and in control, to be as remote as Azim was when it came to their relationship.

No, she'd done exactly what she hadn't wanted to do—been lured in by a few paltry presents and kindnesses, things that cost Azim nothing. And she'd built it up in her head, in her heart. She'd pretended it was enough, that it was something on the way to love.

After the celebrations Johara readied for bed in the tent provided for her and Azim. With the throw pillows and fresh, fragrant herbs scattered around, the flickering candlelight, it was the epitome of desert romance—and utterly wasted, as Azim was ensconced with the leaders of the tribe and did not look to be coming to bed any time soon.

It took her a long time to fall asleep, listening to the horses nickering softly, the wind rustling the sides of the tent. Eventually she dropped off, stirring only when Azim came into the tent. She rolled over, wanting to welcome him, but he simply took off his outer robe and lay a few feet apart from her, his back to her. With her heart like a stone, Johara fell asleep again.

She woke some time in the night, startling awake although she didn't know why—until she saw the empty expanse of sleeping mat next to her. Azim had gone.

Johara lay there for a few moments, undecided, before in one swift movement she rose from the mat, grabbing her robe and pulling it on over her nightgown. Then, having no idea where she was going, she slipped out of the tent in search of her husband.

The desert felt eerily silent and still as she moved through the camp like a shadow. Moonlight spilled on the sand like silver, illuminating the cluster of horses, the round, humped shapes of the tents. If Azim was in the camp, it wasn't obvious.

Guided more by instinct than anything else, Johara left

the tents for the oasis a short walk away, now glimmering like a smooth, silver plate under the moonlight. It was perfectly still and completely empty. She started to turn away when she heard the soft sound of splashing, and realised Azim had to be bathing in the sheltered spot of the oasis where she had been with the women earlier.

Tiptoeing now, her heart slamming in her chest, she crept around a stand of date palms to the small inlet where the women had bathed.

She saw his head first, then arms and a muscled torso cutting through the calm water like dark silk. He moved with sinuous grace and purpose, and Johara simply stood, admiring his perfect form, when Azim rose from the water like a selkie emerging from the waves, water sluicing from him and running in rivulets down his gleaming body.

A shaft of moonlight fell over him in a ribbon of silver, illuminating his muscled back—and Johara gasped out loud.

Azim stilled and then slowly turned. His expression, visible in the moonlit darkness, was one of terrible, ominous neutrality.

'What the hell are you doing here?'

CHAPTER FOURTEEN

SHE'D SEEN HIS SCARS. No one saw those, that shame. Azim had always made sure of it. He never changed in public, never presented his back to a lover, never gave anyone at all an opportunity to see those terrible marks of his servitude.

Since his marriage to Johara he'd made sure to keep his back away from her and dress as quickly as possible. It was the one thing above all the others that he'd wanted to keep secret. Judging from the horror and pity marking her face, Johara had just seen every wretched scar and knew what he'd allowed himself to be subjected to.

'How did it happen?' Johara asked in an appalled whisper.

Azim strode out of the water and grabbed his shirt, pulling it on roughly. Johara stretched out one hand.

'Azim...'

'I was beaten,' he said flatly. 'Like a dog. What else?'

'But who—?'

He shook his head, the movement abrupt, impatient. He was filled with a fury he didn't fully understand. Was he angry at Johara, for seeing something she shouldn't have, or himself, for letting it happen, for having the scars all? Or Caivano, whom he'd long ago destroyed, for what he'd done?

'Was it from the kidnapping?' Johara asked quietly. 'When they beat you?'

It would be so easy to lie and say yes, it was. Yes, his unknown kidnappers had marked his back as well as his face, had left him a bloody pulp in an alleyway in Naples. Wouldn't that be simple? Understandable, at least. But he couldn't make himself lie. Not about this.

'No.' The word was choked through a throat that suddenly felt like a vice.

'Then when? Not your grandfather?'

'No.' He let out a harsh laugh. 'My grandfather can be cruel, but he would never have marked me like that. Someone of royal blood shouldn't…' He stopped, because for some reason he could no longer squeeze the words out. *No real man allows himself to be beaten. Used.* As he had.

'Oh, Azim.'

'Don't pity me.' His word was the savage crack of a whip. 'I can stand just about anything but that.'

'I don't pity you,' Johara said quietly. 'But I am sorry for what you have endured. Why won't you tell me, though? I want to understand you, Azim. I want to know—'

'Fine, you want to know?' His voice was a harsh grating in his own ears. 'The man who rescued me from the hospital, who claimed he knew me, that he was a beloved uncle, the man who told me my name was Rafael Olivieri—he was lying. All of it utter lies. He saw a vulnerable boy, someone with no resources or friends. He saw a slave.'

Even now, twenty years later, the memory had the power to leave him breathless with shame and worse, hurt. He'd been so *grateful* to Caivano, had considered him like a father for the weeks he'd been in the hospital. Caivano had played along, bringing him presents, luring him in. And in response Azim, a lonely, hurting boy, had loved him. His captor.

'What happened…?' Johara asked, her eyes wide and round with the horror of it.

'He brought me back to his garage and forced me to work there without pay, like a slave. When I tried to escape, this happened.' He gestured to his back.

Johara's face was pale, her jaw slack. He'd shocked her. Horrified her. And Azim wished he hadn't told her, because how could she look at him the same again? She'd always see the scars, and remember how he'd got them. She'd see a victim rather than a man.

'How did you finally escape?' she asked in a whisper.

'It took a long time. Caivano was a Mafioso. He had friends in ugly places, which meant it was nearly impossible to get away. It was four years before I was able to figure out a plan.' He drew a breath, his chest hurting, the blood rushing in his ears. 'I got him drunk and found evidence of his crimes. I blackmailed him into giving me my freedom, and I used money I'd stolen from him to make my first property deal. And I always watched my back.'

'What happened to him? This man?' Johara asked.

'I ruined him.' He spoke flatly, without emotion. For ten years he'd slept with a knife under his pillow, one eye cracked open, always on alert. When he'd finally been able to ruin Caivano six years ago, the revenge had been ice-cold but still sweet, even if it had left him wanting more. Craving more validation for who he was, what he'd become.

'Ruined him? How?'

'I bought out his business and then destroyed it. It took me ten years but he had to declare bankruptcy, a broken man. My villa in Naples used to belong to him. I bought it for a song when he had nothing left.'

Johara's face twisted in a grimace Azim couldn't decipher. 'Did that make you feel better?'

'Yes, as a matter of fact, it did.' But not good enough. No matter who he destroyed, he still felt empty inside. Azim had no intention of saying any of that to his wife. 'I waited a long time for revenge.'

'I suppose I can understand that,' she said sadly. 'If it helped you to heal…'

'I didn't need to *heal*,' Azim said, his mouth twisting. 'I needed to right a wrong.' He pulled on his trousers and turned his back on her. 'Go back to the tent, Johara.' He waited a few seconds but she didn't move. The seconds ticked by, each one taut with pain and grief. 'Why are you still here?' he demanded.

'Why are you being so cold with me?' Johara threw back. 'Ever since you told me we were going to Najabi you have been more and more remote. We were getting along, Azim. At least I thought we were. But now I realise just how little you've told me. Shown me.'

His fists clenched. 'I've never shown anyone my scars.'

'But I am your *wife*. Were you going to keep your back from me for ever? I always wondered why you never let me hold you when we were making love. Why you dressed so quickly afterwards. But it couldn't have gone on for ever, surely? I would have seen some time. And then what would have happened?'

He didn't answer. What could he say? It sounded ridiculous, pathetic, to hide from his own wife, and yet all he knew was that he couldn't let someone see what he'd allowed to be done to him. He couldn't reveal that kind of weakness, see it in her eyes, feel the pity.

'I don't understand you,' she said in a soft, sad voice. 'I thought I was beginning to, I thought we were starting to…'

'I warned you, Johara.' His voice rang out in the stillness. 'I always warned you. This was never going to be the
fairy-tale romance you seemed intent on it being. There is
only one thing between us. This.'

Azim's hands came down hard on Johara's shoulders and
then he was pulling her towards him, his mouth crashing
down onto hers. What was meant to be a cruel reminder,
a punishment even, still had the power to spark her soul
and make heat pool in her belly. She wasn't going to let
him turn their lovemaking into something angry or venge-
ful. Not as everything else in his life seemed to have been.

Johara reached up and wrapped her arms around
Azim's neck, pressing her body into his, the damp linen
of his shirt wetting her robe, moulding them together. Her
mouth opened under his as she deepened and gentled the
kiss.

Azim let out a harsh cry, and Johara didn't know if she'd
made him angrier or she'd finally caused a crack in the iron
shell her husband had surrounded himself with for so long.

They stumbled backwards, mouths still locked in a
battle for punishment or tenderness, passion blazing with
darkness and fire. Still kissing, they fell onto the sand,
limbs tangling, hands reaching, everything urgent and
desperate.

Azim pulled at her robe, yanking it up to her waist, his
hands skimming her secret places, fingers probing, knowing exactly what made her melt and want.

Damp heat licked her insides as she opened herself to
him, accepted every angry caress and asked for more. He
would not win this battle. She would be triumphant in
seeming defeat.

With a harsh cry Azim drove into her and Johara accepted him, wrapping her legs around his waist, drawing

him in even more deeply, their bodies moving in urgent rhythm, searching for that desperate pleasure.

Johara slid her hands up under his shirt, holding on even as Azim tried to shrug her off, and she smoothed her palms across the deep ridges that criss-crossed his back, so many of them, and each one broke her heart. She could not imagine how Azim had endured such a thing, a young boy bent on his freedom, a near-man determined to be strong and proud. She touched each one with gentle, soothing fingertips, willing him to accept her caress, to feel the love that she was offering him freely with every touch, wanting to imbue him with the strength she felt.

Pleasure pierced her with its sharp sweetness as their bodies moved in sync, reaching for that shimmering apex. Then everything splintered into sensation-sated fragments and with a groan Azim relaxed on top of her, his body shuddering in the aftermath of their shared climax. Neither of them spoke.

Eventually he rolled off her, lying on his back, one arm thrown over his face. Johara blinked up at him, tears thickening her throat. She'd been shocked by the scars on his back, and hurt by the fury he'd shown, dismayed by the savage satisfaction she'd heard in his voice when he'd told her about ruining that man, and yet over all of it, stronger than ever, was a deep, aching love.

Watching him lie there now, she saw a man who had been pushed beyond all endurance, who had been broken and bound himself together again. A man who was incredibly strong. A man she loved.

'Azim…' she began, wanting to tell him something of what was in her heart, but Azim shook his head wordlessly. She rolled closer and saw, to her shock, a tear gleaming on one stubbled cheek. *'Azim.'* She reached for his hand. 'Don't shut me out now, please. Not because of this.'

He didn't speak for a long moment, his arm still covering his eyes. 'I can't stand the thought of you knowing. Thinking of me that way.'

'What way?' Johara cried. Azim didn't reply and realisation dawned slowly, a creeping mist. 'Azim, do you think I'd believe you to be *weak*, because of that? Because some evil, sick man beat you when you were young and vulnerable?'

'I wasn't that young,' he answered in a low voice. 'I was strong enough to have overpowered him if I'd wanted to.'

'Then why didn't you?' Johara challenged. 'If you could?'

He shook his head briefly, his eyes closed. 'Azim?' Johara pressed, sensing this was important. 'Why didn't you?'

'Because I was scared.' His voice was a barely audible whisper. 'As scared as a small, stupid child. Of Caivano and the power I knew he had. And also because…because there was a part of me…' He broke off, shaking his head again, and Johara waited, her breath held. 'I hated him,' Azim said slowly. 'I hated him so much. And yet he was the only person I knew. The only person who meant anything to me. I think I was afraid to let go of that, even as I dreamed of freedom. Yearned for it with every breath in my body.' He let out a shudder and tried to turn away from her, but Johara wouldn't let him.

'You are the strongest person I know, Azim,' she said steadily, wrapping her arms around him, refusing to let him go. 'For enduring so much and not just surviving, but triumphing. Look at the business you built up on your own. Look at the kingdom you are determined to rule, bound by your honour and duty. You're strong.' She held on and, after an endless moment, Azim put his arms around her.

They lay on the cool, damp sand, their arms around one another, neither of them speaking, for a long moment. And then Azim murmured two words, words Johara knew came from deep within him.

'Thank you.'

CHAPTER FIFTEEN

THEY SPENT THE next few days travelling from tribe to tribe, greeting, discussing, celebrating. At night Azim always reached for her, and Johara went joyfully. She had no idea what was going on behind her husband's inscrutable expression, but she felt they were going forward. She had to believe that. She longed to tell Azim she loved him, but somehow the moment was never right.

At night they barely spoke, communicating with their bodies, and during the day they were constantly surrounded by tribespeople, except when travelling, and galloping on a horse wasn't conducive to deep conversation.

When they got back to Teruk, Johara promised herself. Then she'd tell him what was in her heart…and perhaps he would as well.

Yet the moment the helicopter touched down Azim was striding away, leaving Johara to make her own way to the harem. She watched his retreating figure and tried to hold onto hope. He was a sultan in training, she reminded herself, and virtually running the country by himself since his grandfather was ill and bedridden. He was busy. He'd find her later, and then they'd talk.

But he didn't. Johara busied herself in her quarters, trying not to mind, not to panic. With each passing hour that Azim stayed away she felt her hopes flag and then plummet. A day passed, and then another, and Azim did not contact her at all.

Late in the afternoon two days after Johara had arrived back from the desert, she received an unexpected visitor—Gracie, Malik's fiancée. Johara had met her only briefly before she'd gone back to America, and seeing her again, looking so relaxed and friendly, clearly confident in Malik's love, made Johara feel both shy and envious.

'How are you settling in?' Gracie asked after Aisha had brought them almond and honey pastries and tea in the garden. 'It looks as if you've made this place your own. I remember these gardens as having far more shrubbery.'

'You stayed here?' Johara exclaimed in surprise.

'Briefly, when I first came here with Sam.' She made a face. 'I don't know how much you've heard…'

'I haven't heard anything.'

'I met Malik briefly a long time ago,' Gracie explained. 'And then had Sam, his son.' She grimaced again. 'I know what it sounds like, but…'

'Trust me, I do not judge.' Johara was just grateful *someone* was being candid and open with her.

'Anyway,' Gracie resumed with a grateful smile, 'we… reconnected a little while ago, and then we got engaged. It all happened fast—'

'Surely not as fast as my own marriage,' Johara interjected with a wry grimace. 'I met Azim only days before we wed.'

'It's hard, isn't it?' Gracie said softly, and Johara feared she saw too much in her face.

'It is hard,' she agreed slowly, trying not to reveal a tremor of uncertainty in her voice, 'but it doesn't always have to be, I hope.'

Gracie nodded slowly. 'Malik said you and Azim had been getting along well…?'

'I thought we were. But Azim…' Johara paused, not wanting to reveal any of Azim's secrets, knowing how precious they were. 'I don't think he expected us to have a real relationship,' she finally explained. 'A loving one.'

'Neither did Malik.' Gracie shook her head. 'These Bahjat men. They haven't had it easy, but they don't make it easy for us, either.'

Johara smiled at that, even though her heart still felt weighed down by sadness. 'No,' she agreed. 'They don't.'

It was two days since he'd seen Johara. Two endless days, and yet Azim still stayed away. After everything she'd seen, all that he'd shared, he was afraid to see her again. Talk properly, alone, and have their relationship deepen or be destroyed—he didn't know which. Did she pity him? Could he feel more for her, if he let himself? Did he even want to? They were all questions that tormented him and had no answers, and so he avoided her. Maybe it was a cowardly way out, but it felt like the only option now. He was too unsure, too damned raw, for anything else.

There was a state banquet that night to welcome European leaders, and he'd sent her a message to prepare for it. He found that, against all his apprehension, he was still looking forward to seeing her, maybe too much. And yet he also welcomed the leap of excitement he felt in his belly as he waited for her in one of the palace's private salons. He needed to touch her, to look into her face and see— what? What if he saw pity or worse? Azim swore under his breath, folding his arms and setting his jaw. He had to stop thinking this way.

The doors creaked open, and Azim turned, his heart tumbling in his chest at the sight of Johara. She wore an evening gown of deep cerise that cinched her waist and flared out in gauzy swirls about her slender legs. Her hair was piled on top of her head, and diamonds winked at her ears and throat. She looked magnificent.

The smile she gave him managed to be both tremulous and tart. 'Long time no see.'

He prickled, already on the defensive, still feeling far too exposed. 'I've been busy.'

'Of course.' She held her head high, her eyes glittering. 'Shall we?'

Azim hesitated, not wanting to start the evening with an argument. He understood why she was hurt, and yet he struggled to verbalise it. Half of him was insisting it was better this way, and the other half... 'I'm sorry,' he said abruptly. Johara arched an eyebrow.

'For what?'

'Not coming to see you.'

She shrugged her slender shoulders, her gaze sliding away. 'You said you were busy.'

She was hiding her hurt, a form of self-defence he understood all too well.

'Not that busy. The truth is...' Azim took a breath and blew it out. 'I haven't known what to say to you.'

Her wide, silvery gaze flew to his. 'What do you mean?'

'I feel like I told you too much.' He looked away, hating that he'd said even that.

'Azim...' Johara laid a hand on his arm, her touch gentle and yet still inflaming. An attendant knocked on the doors of the salon.

'We need to go.' Azim placed his hand over hers, his jaw set. He didn't want to talk about this now. He couldn't.

He saw resignation douse the hope in her eyes as she slowly nodded. 'All right.'

All evening long he was conscious of her on his arm, her friendly smile, the easy way she chatted with world leaders, treating everyone the same—as a potential friend.

She was lovely and warm and entirely genuine, and it made his heart both surge and contract. She made him feel, she woke him up, and the knowledge was terrifying. What was he going to do with it?

Towards the end of the evening Malik appeared by his elbow. 'There is something you need to see.'

Azim tensed at the urgent note of command in his brother's voice. 'Now?'

'Yes. Now.'

Azim made his excuses to the various dignitaries he'd been with and followed Malik to his office. 'This better be important.'

'It is.' Malik's face was grim as he took a paper from his breast pocket and handed it to Azim. 'One of our ambassadors sent me a scan of this just now. It hits the European tabloids tomorrow.'

Frowning, Azim glanced down at the paper—and then froze as he took in the headline. *Future Sultan of Alazar Once Held As A Slave and Beaten.* His jaw tight, his blood beating hard through his veins, he read the entire article, inwardly flinching at every terrible word that described his imprisonment with 'a nameless Mafioso', the beatings he'd endured, the failed escapes. The reporter knew everything. *Everything he'd told Johara...and no one else.*

'I'm so sorry, Azim.' Malik's voice was choked. 'I had no idea you'd endured so much.'

Azim tossed the paper aside. 'It doesn't matter.'

'It does—'

'No.' His voice came out like the crack of a gunshot. 'It doesn't.' He took a deep, steadying breath. Could Johara really have told a reporter about him? Sold his story—and for what? Money? Revenge?

He couldn't believe it, didn't want to, and yet...he'd been betrayed before, and by someone he'd wanted to love.

Someone he'd trusted, who had nursed him back to health, who had treated him like a father. He'd learned not to trust anyone, damn it, even the people he loved. Especially the people he loved.

'Do as much damage control as possible,' he instructed Malik. 'I do not want to be fodder for the tabloids. And if people ask, say nothing, give no details. The sooner this is forgotten, the better.'

Malik nodded, his gaze troubled. 'Are you sure...?'

'Yes,' Azim snapped. 'I'm sure.'

Azim didn't return to the banquet, and he didn't send for her that night. Johara went back to her quarters, the hope that had started as a frail and tender shoot in her soul earlier starting to wilt. What had happened? Where had he gone?

She tossed and turned all night, her mind in a ferment of worry and want. Finally, just after breakfast, an attendant summoned her, and Johara's heart lifted.

'Am I going to see Azim, ah, His Highness?' she asked as she followed the man down one of the palace's many corridors. The attendant didn't answer, making the butterflies fluttering in her stomach start to swarm up her throat.

She was let into a small, private room—a study, she realised—and Azim was standing by the window, his back to her. He didn't turn when she entered.

'Azim—'

'You will leave this morning,' he cut her off tonelessly. 'For France.'

Johara gaped. *'France?'*

'Yes. France.' He finally turned with a cold, empty smile. 'Where you wanted to spend most of your time, yes? Now you have your wish. We will have exactly the marriage you wanted to have when we first met.'

'But…' Her head was swimming and she felt dizzy. 'Azim, what has happened? Last night—'

'Last night I learned your true colours. And I realised how foolish I'd almost been again.' He shook his head. 'I will not make the same mistake.'

'What mistake? What's going on?'

He nodded towards his desk. 'That. But of course you already know.'

'That…' It took Johara a moment for her stunned gaze to focus on the paper on the desk—a printout of a newspaper's front page, one of Europe's trashier tabloids. She saw the headline and realisation slammed through her, leaving her breathless. 'You think…you think I have something to do with *that*?'

'You're the only person I told, Johara,' Azim answered coldly. 'The only person ever. So perhaps you should stop playing the aggrieved innocent. I find it rather distasteful.'

'Distasteful?' She drew herself up, fury warring with a deep and terrible pain. She chose fury. 'Do you know what I find distasteful, Azim? That you would think something this horrible of me. That you would make such an awful assumption without even asking me about it. I find that extremely *distasteful.*'

Azim's expression did not soften in the least. His eyes were as hard and dark as they'd been that first day, when he'd told her they would marry. 'Who else could it have been?' he demanded. 'No one else knew, Johara. No one.'

'I don't know,' she admitted. 'But it wasn't me.'

'A flimsy defence,' he scoffed and turned away. 'You can go.'

She stared at his broad back with the now-hidden scars she'd touched and caressed out of love for him. And she'd come so close to believing he might actually love her back—just as she'd once thought her father had loved her.

And just like her father's, Azim's so-called love was cheap and easy. Presents, a garden, sex. Nothing that cost him too much. When it came to the real and demanding price of love—trust and loyalty—he walked away, just as her father had. But this time at least she would have her say.

'Do you know what I think?' she demanded, her voice shaking. She ploughed on without waiting for Azim's dismissive response. 'I think you're a coward.' He turned around, anger sparking in his eyes. 'A big, cowardly *baby*,' she added for emphasis, and his nostrils flared, the skin around his mouth turning white. 'You've been so courageous for most of your life, Azim, and for that I admired you. I loved you. But right now you're being a coward— not about a beating or physical pain, but about the pain you can feel here.' She gestured to her heart. 'I think you know I had nothing to do with that article. How could I? Who did I call, do you think, to spill your story? And why would I do that? What on earth could I gain?'

'Money,' he said tightly, and she let out an incredulous laugh.

'Money? I'm the wife of one of the richest men on the continent. I want for nothing—'

'Your own money. Perhaps you wanted to run away again. Perhaps it was some kind of revenge for being forced to marry me.'

'And what about the last month? What about all the conversations we've had, all the times we've made love? Do you think all of it was an act for me?' She realised tears were streaming down her face and she didn't care. 'Maybe it was for you. Maybe that's what this is about. Or maybe,' she flung at him, swiping at her wet cheeks, 'you got too scared. You were starting to fall in love with me and this provided your convenient excuse to back away and stay safe. Because loving someone is hard, I know. It opens you up to all sorts of pain and grief, because when you love someone they have the power to hurt you. Devastate you.'

She drew a shuddering breath. 'Trust me, I get that. I've felt it. But I'm big enough to take it on. I'm sorry you're not.' A muscle ticced in his jaw but other than that his expression did not change. There was no emotion on his face, not even a flicker of regret or uncertainty. The fury that had been fuelling her sputtered to a stop. 'I'll go,' she said with as much dignity as she could muster. 'I don't want to stay anyway, if you're going to act like this.' With a shaking finger Johara pointed to the printout on the desk. 'But please, for your own dignity as well as mine, don't pretend I had anything to do with that.' Managing to keep her head high with superhuman effort, she stalked out of the room.

The slam of the door ricocheted through Azim's head, adding to the pulsing pain. He'd been fighting a migraine for hours, ever since he'd learned of Johara's betrayal. Her alleged betrayal, but what else could he believe? No one knew the kind of detail that had been in that article. No one but her.

Closing his eyes against a deeper pain than the one in his head, he fought both regret and doubt. What if he'd been wrong? What if he'd sent her away for no reason? Yet this was the kind of marriage they'd planned all along. One of convenience. And if she was in France rather than Alazar, who cared? He'd deal with the issue of an heir later. Maybe, God willing, Johara was pregnant already. That possibility brought another lightning strike of pain. *Johara with his child*...but he couldn't think about that yet. He couldn't think about anything. He'd just known he needed her away from him.

Blindly, the pain too great to ignore or suppress, Azim strode from the room.

Hours later, after a deep, dreamless sleep, the pain had finally receded, even as the pain in his heart increased, overwhelming him. Every pointed and hurt-filled accusation Johara had flung at him played on an endless loop in his mind, filling him with doubt. He wondered if he'd made an enormous mistake—and then wondered if he hadn't. He didn't know what or who to believe, and the last thing he was going to trust was the pointless yearning of his own heart.

A soft tap sounded at the door. 'Azim?'

Azim started to rise, and then fell back against the pillows. Let Malik see him like this. He'd been hiding so much for so long, and now it had all been exposed. What was the point of pretending he didn't get headaches, didn't feel pain?

'Come in.'

Malik came in, frowning when he saw Azim in bed. 'Are you ill—?'

'Migraine,' Azim answered shortly. 'I get them on occasion.'

'I'm sorry.'

He shrugged. 'Is there any news?'

'Yes, we've found the source of the article.' Everything in Azim tensed as he waited for the verdict. 'It's a man named Paolo Caivano.'

'Caivano?' Azim gaped at his brother.

'You know him?'

'Yes, he's…he was the nameless Mafioso of the article. The man who enslaved me.'

'Ah. That makes sense.'

'Does it?'

'I assume he wanted some sort of revenge. When he saw you were the heir to the Sultanate…'

'He thought he could discredit me, and probably got a

decent payment for his tell-all as well.' Azim shook his head. 'I should have guessed.'

'At least now we know. The other tabloids aren't picking it up, and Caivano's been arrested for questioning. Coming up with an article like that wasn't so clever on his part.'

'No.' Azim closed his eyes, realisation washing over him. Johara wasn't guilty. She hadn't betrayed him. And yet he'd tried and convicted her without a single question asked. He was ashamed, but more than that he was afraid. He might have lost the best thing that had ever happened to him, because he knew in that moment she'd been right in every point. He had been afraid…and he did love her.

CHAPTER SIXTEEN

FRANCE WASN'T THE SAME. The home she'd once missed, her beloved garden and stillroom, the friendship of Lucille and Thomas, even her cat Gavroche. None of it made up for the aching absence of Azim. Her husband and the man she loved.

The day after she'd arrived back at the villa Johara sat in the garden, Gavroche on her lap, her heart aching with a heaviness that made her feel weighed down and barely able to move. She'd spent the eight-hour flight from Alazar reliving all the wonderful moments of the last month, and then every agonising second of her final conversation with Azim. How could he have believed that of her? She felt flayed alive by both his accusation and judgment.

'Johara?'

Johara looked up in surprise to see her mother walking towards her. She couldn't remember the last time Naima had been out there.

'Maman…'

Naima smiled tiredly, her face pale as she sat next to Johara on the bench. 'I forgot how lovely it is out here. I should come out more.'

Johara simply stared, hardly knowing how to act with a woman who had absented herself years ago. Naima's smile turned knowing as she met her daughter's gaze. 'I'm sorry,' she said quietly. 'For many things.'

'You…you don't have to be, Maman.'

'But I am.' Naima sighed, the sound soft and sad. 'I have not dealt with life's sorrows as well as I should have.'

'I cannot blame you for that.' Not when she was suffering from her own sorrows.

'Still, I should have paid far more attention to you, and thanked God for the blessing I had rather than the blessing I didn't. It was only that I hoped for so much more from life. From your father especially.'

'I understand.' Johara's throat was thick. As much as she'd wished for her mother's attention and love, she could not begrudge its absence now, not when Naima was actually trying.

'You are very forgiving.' Naima's thoughtful gaze rested on her. 'And now I fear your own marriage might be in trouble.'

'Worse than that.' Johara swallowed hard. 'Azim has sent me away. He believed something terrible of me and now…' She shrugged. 'He wants me to live here.'

Naima's eyes were sad even as she managed a small smile. 'Well,' she said on a sigh, 'it is not such a bad place to live.'

'Were you angry that Father sent you away?' Johara asked. 'All those years ago?'

'Yes, at first. I was heartbroken. I wanted to be by his side, a true and loving wife and partner. But then I had so many miscarriages and each one disappointed your father terribly. I knew he didn't love me, and the losses made it all worse. I broke down, and that was something your father could neither endure nor accept.'

Just like with her, Johara supposed. Her father's 'love' extended only so far. 'I'm sorry, Maman.'

'I'm sorry, too. But perhaps now we can be happy together. Or perhaps your husband will come to his senses.'

'Perhaps,' Johara agreed doubtfully. She'd said a lot of hard words to Azim when she'd last seen him. She didn't know if he could ever forgive her, never mind about that awful newspaper article.

Two days passed with aching slowness. Johara tried to involve herself in her garden, and enjoyed her mother's occasional forays downstairs. They were rebuilding their relationship with painful slowness, but it gave her hope. Hope she sorely needed as the silence from Azim stretched on.

It was high summer and there was plenty to do in the garden, so Johara tried to keep herself busy. She was on her hands and knees, weeding a lavender bed, when she heard footsteps behind her.

'Lucille...?'

'No. Not Lucille.' The achingly familiar voice had her freezing where she knelt, hope warring with disbelief and a remnant of anger. Slowly she turned.

'You have the habit of surprising me in gardens.'

'You have the habit of being in gardens.' The smile Azim gave her was lopsided and wonderful. He looked tired, stubble glinting on his cheeks, his eyes shadowed with uncertainty. Johara sat back on her heels.

'Why are you here?'

'To grovel.'

A smile tugged at her mouth. 'That's a good start.'

'I'm so sorry, Johara. I made a huge mistake. One I can hardly bear to think about now.'

Relief was inflating inside her like a balloon, but still she remained wary. 'And when did you realise this?'

'When my brother told me that it was Caivano who gave the information for the article. He saw my picture in the newspaper and decided to attempt to discredit me, a desperate sort of revenge.'

'Ah.' Johara nodded slowly. 'So you realised you'd been wrong when you had absolute proof, in other words. No trust required.'

He grimaced. 'I admit, I jumped to terrible conclusions. I allowed one betrayal a long time ago to make me expect another.'

'You mean with Caivano.'

'When he rescued me in the hospital, I thought of him as my saviour. I… I loved him, like the father I'd never really had. He took care of me for weeks. He seemed so sincere, and I poured all my confusion and hope into him.' Azim shook his head slowly. 'Even now I wonder why he did it. Simply for free labour? Or was it more sadistic than that, some sort of quest for absolute power over another human being? I don't know.'

'Oh, Azim.' Guilt warred with regret as she took in the import of his words. 'I should have thought about that. I should have realised…'

'No, I should have realised,' Azim insisted starkly. 'You were right about everything. I was afraid.' His voice trembled and Johara knew how hard it was to admit it, and her heart expanded with love. 'Afraid of loving you,' he continued, 'of opening myself up to the kind of pain I gave you. I *am* a coward.' He shook his head in recrimination.

'No, you're not,' Johara said, a fierce note of determination entering her voice. 'I never should have said that.'

'But I'm glad you did, because it woke me up to different kinds of courage.' His eyes blazed as he looked at her. 'And you, my love, are the bravest of them all.'

Johara's heart tumbled in her chest as she took in his words. 'Yes,' Azim said seriously, reaching for her hand and pulling her up from the ground so she was standing in front of him, their hands clasped, sincerity emanating from every taut line of his body. 'I love you. I was fighting it, which was why I stayed away when we returned from the desert. And when the article came out…' He shook his head, regret etched in every line of his face. 'You were right, I did use it as an excuse. A way to justify to myself why I wasn't going to risk anything at all.'

'But I understand why you would have jumped to such conclusions,' Johara protested, 'when virtually the same thing happened to you before.'

'But I knew in my heart that you were different. I've always known you were different, from the moment I met you, and you showed me such spirit. I fell in love with you a little bit that day, Johara, and more and more ever since then.'

Her heart was full to overflowing as he slipped his arms around her waist and drew her closer to him, their hips nudging, her breasts brushing his chest. 'I fell in love with you a bit then, as well,' she admitted.

'Surely not,' Azim returned with a laugh. 'I was most certainly not at my best that day.'

'No,' Johara agreed, 'but you still fascinated me. And when you rescued me in Paris, as terrified as I was of you, I was also incredibly relieved. And thrilled,' she admitted. 'Something in you drew me to you even then.' And then, in case he didn't realise and also simply because she needed to say it, she drew back to look at him seriously. 'I love you, Azim. Never doubt it. I love you with my whole heart and I want a proper, loving marriage with you always.'

'As do I. When we were in the desert I didn't like how you walked behind me—'

'But that's what I was meant to do!' Johara protested.

'Yes, but I didn't like it. I wanted you by my side. I wanted you as my partner.'

She made a face even as a new hope bubbled inside her. 'What about the desert tribes?'

'They'd seen me, met me. And they've seen and met you. I need to live and rule as I believe is right, not to pacify one part of my people.' He brushed a kiss across her lips, his expression soft with love. 'So no more harem.'

'What?'

'You can keep your garden there if you like, or you can have an even bigger garden somewhere else. But you belong with me.'

'By your side or in your bed?' Johara reminded him with a small, teasing smile.

'Yes to both, and Sultana in your own right. I saw how you shone at the banquet, Johara, and everyone in the palace misses you. You've made a lot of fans, you know, in your short time in Alazar. And I'm your biggest one.'

'You're the only one I want, not as a fan, but a friend and lover and husband.'

'I intend to be all three.'

'Good.' She rested her head against his chest, her heart so full of happiness she felt as if she could float right up to the sky. Azim slid his arms around her, drawing her more firmly against him. All was right with the world at last.

'Let's go back to Alazar,' Johara said softly. 'Let's go home.'

* * * * *

MILLS & BOON®

MODERN™

POWER, PASSION AND IRRESISTIBLE TEMPTATION

A sneak peek at next month's titles...

In stores from 18th May 2017:

- **Sold for the Greek's Heir** – Lynne Graham
  and **The Secret Sanchez Heir** – Cathy Williams
- **The Prince's Captive Virgin** – Maisey Yates
  and **The Prince's Nine-Month Scandal** – Caitlin Cre

In stores from 1st June 2017:

- **Her Sinful Secret** – Jane Porter
  and **Xenakis's Convenient Bride** – Dani Collins
- **The Drakon Baby Bargain** – Tara Pammi
  and **The Greek's Pleasurable Revenge** – Andie Bro

Just can't wait?
Buy our books online before they hit the shops!
www.millsandboon.co.uk

Also available as eBooks.

MILLS & BOON®

EXCLUSIVE EXTRACT

Ruthless Prince Adam Katsaros offers Belle a deal –
he'll release her father if she becomes his mistress!
Adam's gaze awakens a heated desire in Belle.
Her innocent beauty might redeem his royal
reputation – but can she tame the beast inside…

Read on for a sneak preview of
THE PRINCE'S CAPTIVE VIRGIN

"You really are kind of a beast," Belle said, standing up.
Adam caught her wrist, stopped her from leaving.

"And what bothers you most about that? The fact that
you would like to reform me, that you would like for your
time here to mean something and you are beginning to see
that it won't? Or is it the fact that you don't want to reform
me at all, and that you rather like me this way. Or at least,
your body likes me this way."

"Bodies make stupid decisions all the time. My father
wanted my mother, and she was a terrible, unloving person
who didn't even want her own daughter. So, forgive me if
I find this argument rather uncompelling. It doesn't make
you a good person, just because I enjoy kissing you. And
it doesn't make this something worth exploring."

She broke free of him and began to walk away, striding
down the hall, back toward her room. He pushed away
from the table, letting his chair fall to the floor, not caring
enough to right it as he followed after Belle.

He caught up to her, pivoting so that he was in front of
her. She took a step backward, then to the side, butting up
against the wall. Then, he caged her between his arms,

staring down at her. Her blue eyes were glittering, her breasts rising and falling rapidly with each breath.

"This is the only thing worth exploring. Not what could be, but what you have. The fire that burns between you and another person. For all you know, in the days since you've been here the entire world has fallen away. And if we were all that was left… Would you not regret missing out on the chance to see how hot we could burn?"

She shook her head. "But the world hasn't fallen away," she said, her trembling lips pale now, a complete contrast to the rich color they had been only moments ago. "It's still there. And whatever happens in here will have consequences out there. I will help you, Adam, but I'm not going to give you my body. I'm not going to destroy that life that I have out there to play games with you in here. You're a stranger to me, and you're going to remain a stranger to me. I can pretend. I can give you whatever you need when it comes to making a statement for your country. But beyond that? I can't."

Then, she turned and walked away, and this time, he let her go.

Don't miss
THE PRINCE'S CAPTIVE VIRGIN
by Maisey Yates

The first part in her
ONCE UPON A SEDUCTION *trilogy*

Available June 2017
www.millsandboon.co.uk

MILLS & BOON®
are delighted to support
World Book Night